PRAISE FOR GENIE HIGBEE'S

THE VIOLIN THIEF, A Curious Tale of Lost & Found

RATING: 5 (!!) stars (out of 5)

"THE VIOLIN THIEF is a beautifully-written, distinct novel that blends an interesting plot, vivid characterization, and thought-provoking prose into a delightful story about a young boy and his love for music. Those who read THE VIOLIN THIEF will be transported into a world of intense feelings caused by love, loss, determination, and devotion. Douglas' journey—the book's plot—is complicated, and Higbee's deep understanding of human emotions and what motivates people to do what they do is commendable. The manner in which plot and character are intricately woven, combined with how internal and external conflict work together, make THE VIOLIN THIEF a remarkable story."

~INDIE READER

RECOMMENDED

"Higbee's prose evokes the works of Isabel Allende, Alice Hoffman, Gabriel Garcia Marques, Olga Tokarczuk, and Khaled Hosseini in a manner both adults and young adults can appreciate."

"The author's delightful, captivating, and unusual coming-of-age story set in the scenic Adirondacks in the violin's musically fertile era of the 1940s and 1950s more than fulfills her goal of realistically portraying nonfictional individuals. Her use of magic realism to do so shows enviable mastery. The planned sequels in the series will undoubtedly be eagerly anticipated."

~US REVIEW OF BOOKS

D0920822

The violin

A CURIOUS TALE OF LOST & FOUND

thief

GENIE HIGBEE

100 WINGS
HAYDEN, IDAHO

100 WINGS
Hayden, Idaho 83835
www.geniehigbee-art.com

ISBN 979-8-9863249-0-6 (paperback)
ISBN 979-8-9863249-1-3 (Ebook)
ISBN 979-8-9863249-2-0 (hardback)

The Violin Thief / Genie Higbee. -- 1st ed.

FICTION / Coming of Age / Magical Realism / Historical Fiction.
Family Relationships, Friendship, Romance, Music, Crime, Suspense,
Mid-20th Century, Small Town, USA.

Cover Design by Genie Higbee with Illustration from Adobe Stock
Book Design by Genie Higbee with Book Design Templates/Spark

Dedicated to Lloyd Eugene Frisbee
My beloved father, consummate source of inspiration

Music expresses that which cannot be said and on which it is impossible to be silent.

—VICTOR HUGO

HISTORICAL VS. FICTIONAL

To avoid spoilers, additional information about the historical elements can be found on the back pages of this book.

HISTORICAL

The 1720 "Red Mendelssohn," Violin by Antonio Stradivari, Cremona
The 1709 small "Mendelssohn," Violin by Antonio Stradivari, Cremona
Michael Rabin, 1936–1972
    George Rabin, father
    Jeanne Rabin, née Seidman, mother
    Jay Rabin, deceased brother
    Bertine Rabin, sister
Ivan Galamian, 1903–1981
Yehudi Menuhin, 1916–1999
Gregor Piatigorsky, "Grisha" 1903–1976
    Jacqueline Piatigorsky, née Rothschild, wife
    Jephta Piatigorsky, daughter
    Joram Piatigorsky, son
Paul Hindemith, 1895–1963
    Gertrud Hindemith, wife
Lilli Bohnke (née von Mendelsohn), 1897–1928
Robert Franz Carl von Mendelssohn, 1902–1996
Arthur Berger, 1912–2003
Rembert Wurlitzer, 1904–1963
Arthur Rodzinski, 1892–1958
Joseph Joachim, 1831–1907
Jean-Baptist Vuillame, 1798–1875
Luigi Tarisio, circa 1790–1854
Alessandro D'Espine, 1782–1855
Montagnana Cello, the "Sleeping Beauty," Venice, 1739
Elizabethtown, New York

Meadowmount School of Music/Milholland Lodge
Lilacs, a rental house
Windy Cliff, a Tudor castle

FICTIONAL

The Violin #253-1—An enigma, *called Magic Muriel*
Residents of the Smythe Home, Elizabethtown, New York
    Douglas Tryzyna, *later called Crowe*, American foundling, b. 1935
    Hester Smythe, *called Sister Elder*, American, b. 1900
    Tatiana Usolka, *called Sister Peace*, Russian, b. 1918
    Wing Wong, Chinese/American, b. 1913
    Astrid Wong, Wing's wife, Swedish/American, b. 1915
    MacAuley siblings, American (Hester Smythe is their great aunt)
        Mildred MacAuley, b. 1931
        James MacAuley, b. 1932
        John MacAuley, b. 1933
Residents of Conservatory for Violin & Piano, Elizabethtown, New York
    Peter Stoya, *called Professor Stoya*, German/Swiss, b. 1912
    Frieda Bachmeier Stoya, *called Mrs. Piano Teacher*, Swiss, b. 1912
    Wilhelm Stoya, *called Willi*, German/Swiss/American, b. 1935
    Siegfried Stoya, *called Siggi*, German/Swiss/American, b. 1937
    Narcisse Louise Boulez, *called LuLu*, French/Swiss, b. 1905
Hester Smythe's Sisters
    Evangeline Smythe, a widow, American, b. 1902
    Maurine Smythe MacAuley, a widow, American, b. 1904
Other Residents of Elizabethtown, New York
    Violette Dupont, American, b. 1935
    Ophelia Nolan, *called Oh-No*, American, b. 1935
    Lermontov, Russian/American, b. 1902
    A.J. Purvis, American, b. 1933
    Tattersall, school orchestra director
    Miss Brown, schoolteacher
    Vicar Hornsby

Butch, violin student
Resident of Lewis
   Ciazzo, musician, instructor
Luthiers in New York City
   Florian Roux, French, b. 1894
   Augustine Allard, French, b. 1901
Residents of Chodenzia, Ontario, Canada
   Gateau
   Bertok
   Noemi, wife of Bertok
   Oliver, son of Bertok and Noemi

✳✳✳

THE VIOLIN THIEF PLAYLIST (Listen on Spotify)

Basque music, Fiesta Bihotzean

Ilan Reichtman, Gypsy Nocturne

J. S. Bach, Prelude in C Major

Beethoven, *Fur Elise*

Bach, Prelude, Suite No. 1 in G

J. S. Bach, Minuet in G

Liszt, *En Rêve*

Franz Wohlfahrt, Etude

Clementi, Sonata in B flat Major

Handel, Sonata in A Major, No. 1

Weiniawski, Concerto in D Minor

Bizet, *L'Arlesienne Suite*

J. S. Bach, Partita in B Minor, Sarabande & Bourrée

Paganini, Caprices

Turkey In The Straw

Vaughan Williams, *Lark Ascending*

Borodin, String Quartet No. 2

Ravel, String Quartet in F major, 2nd Movement

Ravel, *Tzigane*

Castelnuovo-Tedesco, *Sea Murmurs*

L. Boccherini, Minuet

Seitz, Concerto No. 2, 3rd Movement

J. S. Bach, Violin Partita No. 1 BWV 1002

Hindemith, *Metamorphoses*

Hungarian Folk Songs

Dvorak, Slavonic Dance No. 2 in E Minor

Bela Bartók, Romanian Folk Dances Sz56

Ravel, Quartet

Liszt, Hungarian Rhapsodies, Czardas, Lullabies

Brahms, Sonatas

Kreisler,

    "Liebesfreud" ("Love's Joy")

    "Liebesleid" ("Love's Sorrow"),

    "Schön Rosmarin" ("Lovely Rosemary")

Chopin, Berceuse Opus 57 D Flat Major

Brahms, D Minor Sonata

J. S. Bach, Concerto for Two Violins

Bartók, Second Concerto

Richard Straus, *Salome*

Liszt, *Liebestraum*

Gluck, Melodie

Hanon, Virtuoso Pianist, Exercise No. 13

Bartok, Romanian Folk Dance

Brahms, Academic Festival Overture

The violin

A CURIOUS TALE OF LOST & FOUND

thief

I
EXPECTATION & BETRAYAL

[1]

September 1941

WELL PAST BEDTIME. A lullaby circles 'round and 'round, from the farm, across the river, up the hill, through the Smythe Home, and back to the musician—until the violin's voice issues a frightful squawk and plummets into silence! Douglas shimmies off the windowsill to follow Sister Peace as she limps into the yard. Her nightdress, tugged by the updraft, billows like a flag of truce. Boy and nanny join hands. Alert. Alarmed. The air quavers with an electrical charge.

The Milky Way trembles, a million trillion pinpoints of light gone jittery, blinking like scared children, all out of unison. The moon tilts leftward in readiness to fall just as a ghostly shroud diminishes its light.

Darkness. Douglas cringes. It's dark like hiding in the closet. Dark like wearing a blindfold. Dark like the minutes before Dr. Dankworth cuts out your tonsils.

And something flares across the river.

Fire. One bright streak through the forest becomes a fence of sharp orange tongues, and the orange-red-gold tongues lick their way forward. Quick-quick, flames making outlines of sheds across the river at the egg farm and the throat-sticking smell of a smoky fireplace is winging up the hill. Along with the cries of humans in distress.

* * *

EARLY MORNING. In the picturesque Hand-Hale district, with its broad lawns, tall trees, and historic buildings, Narcisse Louise is bewildered by the stench of smoke and haze that veils the surrounding Adirondack mountains. She's barefoot on the porch, Siggi beside her sucking on zwieback, when a horse-drawn cart turns the corner. The milkman comes a running, as he always does, glass and metal clanging like a tap dance.

"Fire," he says, handing Narcisse Louise the carrier of cream-topped quarts. "Fire. Middle of the night at the Ibarra place. Arson. Innocent folk forced to take off."

Peter Stoya, who's standing in the doorway, sneers, whaps Willi with the rolled newspaper, steers the boy by the shoulder, and both disappear into the stately stone residence that doubles as a music conservatory.

The milkman frowns. "Wife says the world at war is making beasts of us all."

* * *

LATE AFTERNOON. HESTER Smythe leans against the red Italianate rail of the Home's balcony, a veritable widow's watch, opera glasses lifted to her eyes. Deceptively calm, this afternoon, while the currents of prejudice and fear still roil. It's quiet. Too quiet. And he's late returning from school. Her other charges, three siblings, have already changed into play clothes, have already slurped graham crackers in milk, have already run off to play ball. The Guardian is left to wait, to worry. She scans the Ibarra farm situated across the meandering river below. The farm's south field is charred from last night's ravage while the north field remains earthy-ocher, saved by the unexpected fire break of a utility road. Just there, a crow soars. It catches her attention, a brushstroke of ink against gray clouds that float without intention. The bird circles, and when it dives she spots the child; how small Douglas looks. Eventually the wanderer appears on the Home's doorstep clutching a wooden object, biting his lip. A bicycle bell breaks the silence.

"What have we here?" Hester Smythe, called Sister Elder by the children, asks the boy, her eyes pinched at the sight of him hopping up the stairs, an object pressed to his breast. His knee pants exposing sturdy legs with one bruised shin. Slip-sliding socks and brand-new Buster Browns gray with ash. Hair sweaty from exertion. His face? A portrait of expectation. "Well. What have we here?" Her voice is rumbling, the voice she uses to make the older children settle down. Oh, the sight of him, his molasses eyes filled with trust. Sister Elder is not expecting an answer, however. Douglas may have turned six but does not yet use words.

[2]

DOUGLAS. MEET A child enamored with the immigrants who settled at the Ibarra farm this winter. A child who resists sleep to join these people around a bonfire, who moves his small body to the music as they do. Douglas has no words for the allure; he lives on the edge of words. Words slip into his mind, form like cirrus clouds, and escape as a sensation of thought, bypassing his mouth altogether. How might a child describe continuous explosions of fire, describe hypnotic rhythms that make feet stir up dust, make hands rattle and pound small jangly wheels? How could this boy explain his obedience to the invisible lady who calls him when a man pulls a stick across a shiny red box?

Night after night, spring through summer, Douglas leaves his bed and runs across Little Bridge to what is called the egg farm. Night after night, Wing, awakened by something intangible, heads out into the dark. Finds the boy in the settlers' midst. Night after night Douglas is forcefully dragged away, gently tucked into bed. The same sad song that comforts a settler's child puts Douglas to sleep, his window open to allow a view of the black-blue sky where a trillion jewels sparkle. Jewels that were glued by folk in the way long time ago when trees were that tall and men were that rich.

One day in the cemetery, Douglas sees that nice man with the shiny red box tucked under his chin, and that invisible lady's voice is wailing with unbearable grief. Everyone wears black, black frocks or black jackets, so many faces contorted, so many handkerchiefs. And as the voice sweetens, those who are crying wipe away their tears. Those who are cross soon forget quarrels and hug. Douglas' first conscious desire is born. He wants to make a lady sing from that box. He wants to make happiness come alive like that wonderful man does.

Mildred, worldly at "almost nine," responds to his obvious fascination. "Those people are scary. They steal little kids like you! They'll make you beg for money." Douglas disregards her warnings. He wants to be kidnapped and be one of them. He too will ask for coins in the market. Or use a box with a stick in the cemetery if they take him to live at the egg farm. If they go to a new place far away he too will ride in their caravan of strange trucks and cars.

It was late August when Wing, the cook, handyman, and cartoonist, baked him a birthday cake and gave his goodbyes. Sister Elder said that Wing was answering the Draft.

Astrid explains it better. Douglas looks up at her, this lady whose hair is pale as the moon, worn in braids wound behind her head, whose ears sparkle, each with a tiny blue jewel that matches her eyes in the morning. And she's saying that her husband, the Home's token father, has gone far away to be a sailor in the Navy and protect the country.

With Wing's absence, no adult in the Home is awake or aware of Douglas' continued escape at night. When the settlers' fire grows low, and the dancing slows, the child is led back to the Home by the violin-playing man himself. None the wiser.

[3]

"WHAT HAVE WE here?" his Guardian repeats. She tries to wrest the item from his grubby hands. He shrieks. "No words today, Douglas? Maybe you can say, *violin*?" Although Sister Elder encourages her charge to speak, she will admit to no concern. The youngest orphan in her guardianship seems tuned to a different world, his ability to mimic seemingly linked to his protruding but well-shaped ears. He's attentive to a world of listening all his own. Certainly not a mute.

The blue orbs of Sister Elder's eyes focus downward and away from him. Her eyelids close and she breathes in, for a long-long time; her square shoulders rise; her black dress keeps expanding above her white apron.

Douglas sucks in his breath, holding it until he hears her take a breath, sees her chest contract pulling the row of tiny buttons inward. Now he feels a stirring from her, radiating outward like ripples around a thrown stone. The ripples encircle him with trust. Sister Elder speaks. "I know what it is to desire something, my little man." He relaxes.

In that second Sister Elder snatches his precious possession.

* * *

HE WAS A CHILD who ignored rules when his own reason prevailed. Of course, Sister Elder warned him to come straight home from school. For no reason was he to explore the remains of last night's fire. But curiosity consumed him. He scuffed around the perimeter of the blackened boards, his eyes stinging while ash flew. The egg lady wasn't to be seen but her farmhouse looked sad. The chicken coop stood intact. The speckled hens softened the evidence of last night's inhumanity with soft, breathy clucks. The rooster stretched tall, thrust his head forward, out came a back-of-throat rasping as to say, "I'm alive, I'm alive."

As Douglas stirred up ashes, enjoying the wonderment, something more than charred rubble attracted him. Something glimmered just ahead. A metal object stuck in the earth, shaped like a cup. It proved to be a small brass bell, several inches of frayed red yarn tied through its circular opening. He shook the bell; a sweet jingling rang out. He rang it again and again, glad for a keepsake. He decided not to share it with James or John or Mildred. But over there just across the dirt road, there, past the remains of the workers' out-buildings was another something. A strange upright object in the dried stubble. Douglas wiped his eyes. Was that the egg lady's cat stalking a mouse? Or a wooden stick with a curled knob?

He was running, the tire ruts were catching his toes, he was stumbling. His heart flapped like laundry in the wind; he wanted to own that thing. Wanted to make it sing. *That man left it behind!* In seconds he's editing his assertion: *That man left it behind for me! Left it for me!* As naturally as one might pluck a pear from a branch, he gathered up the violin. A crow swooped over his head, cawing insults. A jet-black wingtip grazed his curls; he stumbled on a rock careful to keep a grip on the gift. Heart bucking like a creature stuck in quicksand, bewitching box clasped to his chest, with no one to hear his first word, Douglas spoke. "Mine."

[4]

MEAN OLD SISTER ELDER has sent him to bed for continuing to bawl. She has taken the dusty red box for herself. This is not the reality he's imagined. Sweet Sister Peace comes into the dorm. She gathers Douglas up in a consoling hug, causing him to cry anew. Crying first for the lost violin. And then crying because the strangers are gone. And latching onto the idea that the nice man is floating somewhere in make-believe just like his true mother, he sobs afresh.

Since Douglas will not straighten up, the family eats dinner without him. He can hear Mildred pleading. "Dougie is very sad about his violin, Sister Elder."

"We are well aware, Mildred. But thank you for informing us."

Later, after enforced bathing, Sister Elder brings him a frothy glass of eggnog sprinkled with nutmeg. "Even a naughty boy must have nourishment." She places the violin on the highboy, turns out the light, and standing in the doorway shadowed like a sorceress, she utters a final warning. "Let the violin sleep undisturbed, or there will be a price to pay."

After Sister Elder turns out the lights the bereft boy keeps his eyes open. *Will the lady in the box sing tonight?* The fingernail moon spies on him through the bark cloth curtains. Sees him pulling the stool to the chiffonier. The moon has no voice and can't tattle, can't tell on James and John who thrash about with pillows, nor on a *naughty boy* who sneaks into his bed the red box all dulled by ash.

After a bit, Douglas imagines the violin is whirring, a sensation like dragonfly wings on your cheek. Words there are none. And yet the box is communicating. He experiences the reverberations that flow through his small body as language, and he tries to grasp meaning. The fluttering continues. And halts, as if waiting for an answer.

Douglas throws off the cotton bed sheet and bounces on his knees. He claps his hands. "What?" Douglas laughs. "What did you say?"

The unvoiced box responds with a whir like the flutter of wings behind your back.

Douglas turns a somersault. "I'm Douglas. I like you too."

The voiced box responds quickly. {It comes clear| Douglas| you can understand this violin| |

"I can! And I know your name. It's Muriel. I see your picture with your name. In the drug store."

{Dear child| Such confusion| Can you count| |

"To one hundred."

{So| you will understand| My name is Two-fifty-three-dash-one| Myself| a violin| was named a number| for a reason| |

This time Douglas grasps the imagery as if a chalkboard had been written upon. "Your name is a *number*?"

{Yes| Although my number name is hidden| It is written in a dark place| where eyes may not see it with ease| |

"Hidden like the magic singing lady! So, I want to call you Magic Muriel."

{You may call me Magic Muriel| if you wish| You are yet a child| |

Douglas grasps this wordless language and ironically he is left wordless by the novelty.

{Only one human| before you Douglas| communicated with| 253-1| Myself| |

{His name Luigi Tarisio| His passion| his destiny| to recover forgotten violins from Cremona| |

"Luigi! Luigi? That's a funny name. Tell me a Luigi story."

{Ask perhaps another day| |

Silence between the two—a child claiming six years of life and a violin claiming an existence of one hundred ninety-two years—both overawed by the reality of their exchange.

Giggling can be heard from under bedsheets. James and John hear but one side of this exchange, and from Douglas? Their Douglas who has no words? "Be quiet Dougie-dummy," John commands.

The violin speaks to Douglas again. {Tis no mystery| *questo violino* has learned to reflect men's language| Many years with many owners account for this| but tis the blessing| 253-1 retains more than mankind's spoken words| all to be revealed in time| |

"I love you, beautiful Magic Muriel."

{Both of us feel desire for the other| And so it is| It is| |

Mutual desire; Douglas understands this concept immediately. "Yeah. Both. Desire."

"Who are you talking to, Dougie-dummy?" John asks.

Douglas jumps wildly on his bed. "My violin! Magic Muriel, dummy!" Seeing the instrument bouncing around he calms. Kneels. "Did the fire scare you very much?" he whispers, running his fingers along the violin's curves.

{Oh| shudder to speak of it| Last night| something flew into our place| It was no bird| but fiery heat| hiss| crackle| muted roaring| like a concerto of warning| |

"We were scared too."

{It broke the sweetness of our lullaby| for the tiny one who cooed| it stopped the *madre* who rang a bell| the air crackled| my human trembled| Of a sudden every whichaway he set to gathering| to clambering| to fleeing| In the rush *questo violino* slipping from his grip| bouncing on earth| thudding| rolling| coming to rest| |

"The man didn't come back for you."

{Indeed| He was not to return| Rumble of the caravan distancing| then gone| |

"I found you kind of hidden."

{Hidden| not touched by flame| Child| above all we *violini* fear fire| |

Hankering to extend the panorama of sensations he's experienced, Douglas fishes for something under his pillow, and holding it by the red yarn he shakes the tiny bell back and forth—his smile as gentle as the ting-a-ling.

The violin's cadence begins again changing from dreary to dramatic. {Courage have| Douglas| You are denied Myself for now| but in truth| suffer worse we may| before you acquire skills| and we are paired| So it may be| |

[5]

THIS SEPTEMBER EVENING, with smoke lingering from last night's fire, Sister Elder keeps losing her place in Agatha Christie's *Peril at End House*. She's too wound up to sleep. So is James. Just when she thought the children were settled, he appears in the parlor, his gray plaid pajama top unbuttoned. He rubs his eyes. He whines in a babyish treble voice, reminding Sister Elder of an earlier time. Of the year she acquired him. Acquired the three of them. A time when her heart opened like an oyster seeking a pearl that had not yet formed.

"I can't sleep," James whines again. He stands on one leg, scratching his other leg with his bare foot.

"Whatever can be the problem, child?"

He scratches his stomach. "It's too noisy in there."

"Don't be daft. You have a perfectly quiet dorm facing the river and the forest, you lucky boys."

Sister Peace soothes, as is her style. "James, what noise is it?" She's wrapped in a plaid bathrobe, looking more like eighteen than twenty-four, her Joan of Arc hair flattened and damp after a bath, her bare feet exposed with their high arches and knobby toes.

"Douglas keeps talking to the violin."

"What?" Two adult voices in unison.

"He's talking really loud," James repeats in his nasal whine.

Sister Peace with delight. "He's *talking*!"

Sister Elder with disbelief. "He's talking? To the...the *violin*?"

Sister Peace and Sister Elder face each other, jolted into silence.

Sister Peace, who arrived this summer, is not Sister Elder's relative. Nor are the women members of a religious order. Hester imposed the naming device for logical reasons. First, the title *sister* creates an illusion of family. And of teamwork, for which the uniform is a starched white apron. Second, Hester, being the *elder* and therefore the wiser, will assert headship over the children. Tatiana, who is a young, naïve, overly sympathetic nanny, must avoid contention. This submissive behavior is daily reinforced by her tag, *Peace*. No matter how much Tatiana disagrees, she must defer to Hester's strict parenting. Discord continues to arise despite their initial agreement. Nevertheless, on this atypical evening an amicable solution flies into the room like a dove.

"Listen, James dear, you may sleep in the guest room for tonight." Sister Elder's, a well-practiced voice of calm, hiding the electric charge coursing through her limbs.

"John can too?" he pleads.

"Yes, yes, quietly now," Sister Peace, all fluttery like a moth finding light.

The women embrace, but just for a very few seconds. They agree to avoid interrupting Douglas' interaction, crazy as it may seem. And so the night passes.

Astrid reports finding the stool beside the highboy and the forbidden object in Douglas' bed at dawn.

So much for one night gone well enough. But Sister Elder troubles over the situation. How to handle this boy and his attachment to a violin that isn't his.

[6]

THIS CHILD HAS been with her since October of 1935, found on the Home's stoop in a blanket-lined washtub. No clues to his identity, or so she tells the do-gooders and the buttinskies.

And there had been gossip. Gossip 'round and 'round Elizabethtown:

Could Hester be the mother?

She was in the City for months on "hotel business" preceding the infant's arrival, was she not?

Leaving Wing and Astrid to tend to the three orphaned toddlers, tut-tut.

A physique such as Hester's, short-waisted with ample bosom, could hide the early months of pregnancy and postpartum, couldn't it?

And listen to this, the businesswoman returns to the Home in September, and a month later the infant appears.

Enough said.

* * *

"PERHAPS THE NICE man will want his violin back," Sister Elder tells Douglas at breakfast. "Certainly, we can understand his loss. We must keep it safe until then."

Despite Douglas' continued pleas for ownership, Sister Elder wraps the violin in a black and white silk scarf and the contraband disappears. "Out of sight, out of mind," she tells Sister Peace. She keeps to her own counsel valiantly, hoping the situation might resolve post haste.

For five days Douglas misses school, stays abed, sick with fever. One afternoon he becomes engrossed with the thrum of raindrops. They plink in the birdbath outside the window. They drum in the drainpipes. *Where does the rain go after it leaves the pipes?* he wonders.

And the rain answers as if it hears his question. It answers with a thin tune. A tune without words, like a trickle over rocks and moss. Communication much like the beloved violin's. The distraction of listening to rain speak in this way backfires. Douglas' face burns. He shivers. He rings his brass bell, holding it tightly by the frayed red yarn. He calls out with great distress.

Sweet Sister Peace comes limping in to offer a small bitter pill. "Swallow. Not chew," she says, handing him a glass of water. She exchanges the warm cloth on his forehead for a cooler one. She combs her fingers through his damp corkscrew hair until he relaxes. The two begin to breathe with deep intakes of air until they find unison. When Douglas reaches out for a hug she bends over his chest and kisses his fingers, one by one, avoiding the embrace. She smells of spicy green, like smashed geraniums in the sunshine. "Beautiful your fingers," she says. The boy is too young to recognize his malaise as the soulful yearning for a lost love. Sister Peace, Tatiana, recognizes the symptoms; she returns with the forbidden 253-1. She unwraps it. Sets it on the bedside table where he might easily see it. "Better now?" she asks. She steps to the window and raises the sash.

Douglas runs a finger the length of each string, creating a sliver of a whisper. Trying again he strums across the strings and the violin's humming begins. The hum grows upon itself. Soon it stirs up energy that he feels moving through his fingers and throughout his body. His fingers, body, brain loop in an electrical charge with the nice man's instrument.

{Let your fingers caress my strings into tender voice||

Douglas plucks the strings. The resulting sound pongs, thuds, fails to satisfy the request. "I am not big enough to play you, not like the nice man."

{You may be small| isn't that right| But oh| you alone have a sensibility for my sentience| And who would expect it of a child||

"I can grow big very very fast."

{Growing takes time| so it is| All the while| *questo violino* has benevolence to offer| and you here| to spark it on my strings| Here's the pity| time is not promised us||

Perhaps the message is baffling for a child of six to whom every desire seems urgent. But the boy asks a thoughtful question. "How did you make your sounds come to my bedroom at night?"

{A violin's voice grows wings| See| And in the dark it flies across water| |

Douglas stokes the strings more deliberately, bringing them to a drone.

{A start we have on what lies ahead| Now you must learn the skills of fingers and bow| This may take years| Tis true| *questo violino* has spent decades in silence| Tis true| years have passed quickly| Yet having found you| Douglas| 253-1 grows impatient| Oh| may it be someone appears soon| to teach you technique| |

"When I grow really big will I get the hang of playing you?"

{Truth| child| you already possess the intangibles of spirit that cannot be taught| So it is| It is| |

Thunder rumbles.

Douglas turns to look at his nanny. She has been at the window bending from side to side with her arms over her head.

"Sister Peace, do you believe the violin?"

Tatiana sits on the bed with her head tilted like a quarter moon. She takes the child's face in her hands, and again the perfume of bruised flower petals, of violet petunias. "Douglas, I am not hearing the violin speaking. I hear you talking, you only. What does this violin say to you?"

A crack of lightning followed by thunder mutes the child.

The violin addresses Sister Peace. Perhaps this caring person can understand a violin's language.

{Tatiana| He approached| A mere child| a kindred spirit| My frequencies were his first language| men's words came later to him| For such a one *questo violino* has waited| a rare human in this world of beings| It was fire joined us| but it is mankind who would part us| 253-1 has known such conflict amongst men| So it is| Will you be our ally| |

A bolt of lightning. Tatiana's chopped hair stands on end. Instantaneous the answering peal of thunder. Without a word, kind Sister Peace rises to her feet and in one graceful motion performs a curtsey, a gesture of respect, a *grande reverence.*

[7]

AN ARGUMENT ENSUES after dinner. Raised voices—so rare in the Home where a sailor's lonely wife and a recuperating artiste allow the children's Guardian to dominate. "What have you done, Sister Peace, behind my back? Trouble, you're provoking trouble, or is that putting it too mildly?" Sister Elder's voice has dropped to the dark register. "Mark my words, Tatiana, misfortune will come knocking on young Douglas' door if he's allowed this rogue violin. And you will have yourself to blame."

Could a child-eating witch sound more threatening? Mildred hugs Douglas, who hugs Magic Muriel, a club sandwich of apprehension. "Don't listen, Dougie, she's just a grown-up. Grown-ups don't know anything."

Mildred's words are comforting. But Douglas can feel Sister Elder's energy swirl, again. Just like last week when Mildred asked Sister Peace *rude* questions. "Why do you walk so funny?" The answer, "Because my leg must heal." And Mildred didn't learn her lesson about being polite. The next day she asked, "Why is your hair all chopped off?" Sister Peace was calm when she answered. "To remind me what's important, Mildred." And after that Sister Elder's energy felt this same scary way; she got angry at Mildred, who had been running with the scissors. Or angry because Mildred had chopped off her own pretty hair and looks like a boy now. And boys get into more trouble.

* * *

"IS IT MY *true* mother's voice in the nice man's violin?" Douglas whispers when Sister Peace tucks him into bed that night. He's pathetic. More so, now that his treasure has been hidden away.

Asking this becomes his ritual over the next few weeks. Sometimes his nanny, whom he dutifully calls Sister Peace, responds casually. "Now, now, such imagination." These times she smiles, a sad wistful smile, as she leans over him. The ripples from her encircle him like a safety net and he curls up contentedly on his side.

Other times when he asks Sister Peace her answer slithers, and twists, and rattles a warning. "Now, now. Wild imagination can bring trouble. Pray the truth comes clear to us both very soon." These nights he lies awake with an awful sensation; the comfort he expects is replaced by an awareness of overwhelming compression.

[8]

IT WAS ONE of those days.

Douglas follows Sister Elder up and down the aisles, his head drooping like a late August sunflower. Her gambit, putting the violin out of sight out of mind, is a disaster. Accordingly, when Sister Elder, who's standing in line to pay for sundries at Castle Rock Drugs—boric acid, Epsom salts, milk of magnesia tablets, Curads, tooth powder, and Lydia Pinkham's Vegetable Compound—hears the morose boy speak up, she pays attention.

"I want that! You promised! You always say *another day*. She's so beautiful." The object he points to is a cigar box, its lid imprinted with an exotic woman. "She's the lady that sings in my violin!"

Sister Elder cringes as she watches the clerk key numbers on the cash register. "Muriel cigars, nasty and not for children." She checks the beggar's reaction. He's insistent. Douglas wheedles, pressing his hands together and whispering, "Buy for me, me, me, for me? Please."

"Can you imagine?" she murmurs to the clerk as she counts out her ration stamps, plunks down coins, and snaps closed her handbag. Despite her distaste, she yields. "That Muriel cigar box, please, if we may, empty of course."

Tears wiped away, a sullen boy transforms into a sweet, energetic saint. Douglas raises the prize to his nose. It reeks of cedar, brandy, and tobacco in a nasty, vulgar, and lovely way. He strokes the decorative edges, he picks at the torn blue stamp, lifts the lid and discovers another image of the lady. Magic Muriel with her Mona Lisa smile promises him something yet grander. In this moment his desire for the violin grows wings of determination; desire clutches him, and its claws become permanently entangled in his life.

"What will you put in there, son?"

"A tiny bell. Magic Muriel wants it."

The Hester hustles Douglas to the car. A willful disconsolate child can wear a parent down. It is one of those days.

[9]

FOLLOW RIVER STREET, south to Elizabethtown center, passing through the picturesque Hand-Hale district with its broad lawns, tall trees, and historic buildings. Find along Stoneleigh Way a building that resembles a castle. Out front a formal sign distinguishes this house from a mere home. Correctly so.

Inside a conversation takes place:

"The child hardly speaks. The girl Mildred talks for him. I heard her say, 'Dougie wants a turn. Dougie wants more cookies!' Hester, his Guardian, who calls herself Sister Elder, is not concerned. Do you know what she said? 'Where something is withheld, something otherwise increases."' Frieda plays an arpeggio up the keyboard and down. She scoffs, turns around on the piano bench to catch her husband's reaction.

"What does this Dougie look like?" Professor Peter Stoya asks. His fingers thrum along the crease on his trouser leg.

"Smaller than Willi though they're the same age. Scrawny. Strange, protruding ears."

"And of his disposition? He's a clever boy? Like our Wilhelm?"

"Oh, he's attentive to a world of listening all his own. Certainly not mute. Jah! He can laugh like our Willi. With a vocal range likely to shatter eardrums. He's only just begun to talk properly. Sister Elder made mention of strange whisperings to himself. Says he fancies mimicry of sounds—the ice cream truck, a dog barking, an engine stuttering, the percolator gurgling. I know it's so because the child performed rooster crowing for me. Such noises from a child's mouth! I never."

Peter steps to his music stand and flips absently through a book of etudes. "Curious," he says.

"Did I say he mimics horse hoof clop, bullfrog croak, and the wail of a violin?"

"Perhaps a case of perfect pitch," he says, turning to face her. "Frieda, so why did Hester invite you?"

"She wants to bring Douglas here with a request.

"Hoping we'd be prepared."

[10]

THE STOYAS ARE not prepared for the likes of Hester Smythe. She may be difficult to befriend. She won't accept your invitation for coffee, or chat with you after a town hall meeting. You won't be invited to the Smythe Home for Sunday supper, either. But she's fond of her wards.

Born Hester Smythe, Sister Elder lost her parents in a hotel fire, May of 1930. Ironically the Smythe couple was traveling in search of another hotel to purchase. Their demise left Hester with two self-centered sisters, five smoothly operating boutique hotels, and a sizeable income.

Hester settles in the touristy Adirondacks, choosing Elizabethtown—noted for Split Rock Falls, aptly dubbed Lover's Leap—where her newly inherited hotel could use some oversight. She lives simply, aided by business managers and a trusted advisor. When asked personal questions by the nosey citizens of Elizabethtown, she's forthright. She's single, not by choice but by circumstance. She's purchased real estate suitable for a European-style bed and breakfast in this quaint town, which attracts honeymooners and city dwellers, all escaping summer heat. She calls it *home*, much desired after too many nannies, tutors, boarding schools, and too many hotels erroneously termed *home*. She calls it *home*, what an endearing word, this shingle-style Queen Anne with double glass doors, wraparound porch, white with green trim, and a rock foundation. Walking distance from town, the site boasts a hillside location with the Boquet River bordering its west facing. She's hired a couple away from a Manhattan hotel, Wing and Astrid, whom she trusts implicitly. The two, along with a varying cast of sturdy locals in need of part-time work, assist her with daily practicalities.

She and her sisters may have inherited hotels, but during the Depression business has taken a hit. Quarterly checks diminish like everything else; sheets grow threadbare from washing and reuse, the soles of shoes wear thin, white oleo replaces yellow butter, wartime soup is watered down. The Home manages to endure with ration cards for three residents, Sister Elder's mastery of planning and budgeting, not to mention Wing's skill at fluting tasty dumplings filled with who-knows-which vegetables and scraps of meat.

And then overnight, well, four years have slipped by, the *pension* transforms into a children's home. Siblings—Mildred, James, John—poor kids, their parents die in a train derailment leaving them stranded. Their close relatives, possible guardians, beg off, making excuses. Hester steps up; how could she, their great aunt, turn the orphans away? She being sturdy and with plenty of room? Was this the beginning of a pattern? Was this how she ended up with a fourth? Douglas, arriving on her doorstep? Oh, she could raise children, she feels sure. She's educated, and she has a heart infinitely capable of love. Well, she used to. And so here she is raising other people's children.

[11]

LERMONTOV, THE CONFIDANTE Hester Smythe queried, was clear; only one man in town would be knowledgeable enough to offer advice regarding both a violin and a violin-loving child. Thirteen days thereafter, on a sunny October afternoon, spinster and foundling—having been formally invited—prepare to visit Professor Stoya and his wife, the local instructors of stringed instruments and piano.

Sister Peace irons a handkerchief. Tucks it into the boy's pocket. "Now stay clean," she whispers and leaves Douglas alone with Sister Elder.

"Am I going to Dr. Dankworth...for tonsils?"

"Your tonsils were removed, and I've told you what we're doing. Remember?"

"No."

"We'll talk to a man about taking good care of the violin."

"Why? I'm a careful boy."

"As I said, the expert will offer advice." Sister Elder carries a towel-lined box that holds the violin.

"Magic Muriel wants me. Just me! She said so."

"Stuff and nonsense! You'd best hold your tongue today." Sister Elder's voice floods the petitioner with apprehension.

Into the car's back seat then, a box with a violin, and a boy with a bellyache. Sister Elder's foot taps on the pedal. The engine commiserates; it bellyaches 'round and 'round until it bursts into a steady whine. "Remember, the nice man left it for me," Douglas wails.

Sister Elder puts the car in reverse, backs to the curb, and brakes to a full stop. Unmoving. A glimmer of hope heats Douglas' face. "We're not going?" The boy hears the woman's soft breathing, but her mouth is an upside-down smile. Gloom throws its arms around the moment and bear hugs all remaining joy to a pulp. They proceed.

Tires on the gravel, whistle from the angled wind-wing window, dogs barking, these sounds reflect a boy's joylessness as it circles a core of pain. Douglas has no idea what to expect.

Just a brief trip; they are parking. Sister Elder turns abruptly to address the captives in the back seat. "You may carry the violin to the house. Remember, we'll find the right thing to do." The 253-1 then, held like a serving platter by two sweaty hands; Douglas' face a masterpiece of adoration.

A hand-lettered sign: *Stoya Conservatory~Violin & Piano.* The plaque droops on the chain until Douglas disrupts its stasis with his elbow. The three-story stone house features a brick arch framing a first-floor window through which a concert grand piano looms as they approach. Up each step then, with pauses in between. One. Two. Three. Four. Five. Six. Advancing between the rock pillars of the front porch. "Here we are."

Apprehensive, two petitioners, in tandem but not in accord, as distorted reflections wiggle in the beveled glass of the tall wooden doors. When Sister Elder rings the doorbell, cathedral-worthy chimes appeal for residents' attention.

"How do you do?" Professor Stoya says. His mustache curls up like St. Nick's, but his eyes are not smiling. He drums his fingers up and down his trouser leg. He motions them in.

They're led along an antique hooked rug and pass by a potted philodendron before entering the salon. The interior smells of gingerbread. Pieces of an erector set, and picture books are scattered on the floor; *there must be kids here.* For just that minute Douglas forgets. Forgets to be cautious. He cuddles the violin like Sister Peace snuggles the baby next door, the Ludlows' newborn.

Sister Elder has no time for chitchat or pleasantries. She bends over the child. "Douglas, you must hand *It* to the Professor." And turning to the Professor, "This is Douglas, he's just turned six this August, I'm his Guardian. To the point, Douglas found *It* at the Ibarra farm after the fire in September."

"Pity about the fire. But better for us all those scalawags moved on. Not our kind. Curious how they passed through immigration, yeah?"

Sister Elder, publicly known as Hester Smythe, glowers. She follows her convictions. *No charity. Dignity.* For example, one of the immigrants was allowed to sharpen the Home's knives and scissors for which he received a dollar bill. Her answer to Professor Stoya, a rude retort. "Those you term *scalawag* are Basque, an admirable culture. They fled from war in Spain. They are relatives of the Ibarra family. They had legitimate work papers. Unlike you, they arrived without wealth, sir. I ask, from what county did you flee?"

Peter flinches. He had neither relatives nor legitimate work papers. His mentor had skillfully insinuated employment while conscientiously avoiding falsification. He will not answer this brash woman's question.

"Douglas, you must hand *It* to the Professor, now." Sister Elder's voice runs as thin and icy as an April rivulet.

With much trembling the boy holds fast to the treasure. His quivering face betrays a battle with tears.

Professor Stoya, a sturdy man whose creased slacks require red suspenders instead of a belt, agitates the child further with his strange accent and his booming voice. "Well, well, you little thief, what have you absconded with? May I?" He's grasping the instrument before Douglas can nod. Douglas notes the Professor's hands, how knobby like a giant's and hairy too. Larger than Wing's smooth hands.

"Hmmmmmm." The Professor's voice rises and drops like a song. "Hmmmmm," he repeats as he revolves Douglas' prize. He's observing the smooth curve of the violin's top and the handsome tiger-stripe flames in the grain of its back. He plucks a string. A pure silver tone sings out. Impulsively the Professor locates his bow, tucks the violin under his chin, and plays an impressive cadenza.

Douglas fidgets, rubs his impatient hands together.

Age can't disguise the predisposition of a musician; Peter Stoya recognizes an ardent soul. His firstborn, Willi, seems to lack this trait. "You like the singing of a violin, do you?"

Douglas nods while hopping from foot to foot.

"You want to make her sing all by yourself, do you?"

Douglas nods emphatically, jumping up and down.

Without explanation Stoya asks the child to hold out his arms. Using the yellow tape from Mrs. Stoya's sewing basket, the Professor takes a measurement. "Eighteen and three-quarter inches," he says. "Perfect size for a young violinist. Would you like to begin lessons?" Douglas beams, wordless hopping from foot to foot.

"The violin you carried off is too large for you to play, yeah?" The man holds the instrument up to the six-year-old's chin. Douglas sees the scroll of his beloved extend beyond the reach of his hands and he blinks wishing for a different truth. "It's a miracle it escaped the bonfire. And that you discovered her." Stoya places the violin next to his own. She needs a case; we'll see to that."

Failing to guide Sister Elder by the elbow, he instead leads her into the library. There beside the fireplace Professor Stoya offers to teach this eager student, at no charge—in exchange for the rogue fiddle. The conversation continues beyond Douglas' ears—and beyond those of Peter's wife, Frieda.

Professor Stoya directs Sister Elder back into the salon. He addresses Douglas. "Young man, here's the deal. I will find a small violin and I will teach you to play it. And for now, *this one* is mine."

The words scorch Douglas' brain. He rubs his eyes, but in vain; he cannot rub away the sting.

"You are paying me for lessons with *It*, jah? Then turning to Sister Elder, "Oh, now, don't be mistaken, this is in no way a good violin." Peter unbuttons his collar. He's perspiring.

Comes a child's inquiry. "But...but when will you give me my violin back?"

Peter stalls. Raps his bow on the metal music stand. *Clank, clank, clank.* "When? Presumptive young man, indeed! However, should you chance to become a virtuoso, ask me then."

Douglas sits on his knees, looks up from one towering adult to another. His world has gone topsy-turvy.

"Until then, you may *never touch a string* of this instrument. Nor dream of touching my Performance Violin. Mark my words, I will know if you do. And you will be a very, very sorry young man."

The words like flames leap out to sear. Douglas falls to his knees. He's been tricked. He crawls to the piano bench where the other red violin, the Performance Violin, lies side by side with *his*, the one Professor Stoya has just bamboozled.

The violin communicates. Her energy rushes through Douglas with the truth she accepts. She speaks inaudibly to him alone. {Here 253-1 finds her Red Sister| the Performance Violin| Here you find your teacher| So it was meant to be| So it is| |

The Professor's wife has sucked in her breath and her energy is suspended. She's unhappy about something.

Sister Elder smiles, a flickering, fickle smile. Her eyes narrow. She kneels so that she might speak directly to some very short boy.

He turns his head.

She adjusts the child's chin; looks again into his eyes. Holds his hand, holds it too tightly as if he might be headed somewhere dangerous.

He tugs away; he's not deceived. He can feel her writhing energy. *Something bad is happening.*

The clock's bird bursts free of its wooden confines. Ten *cuckoos*, from an informative fellow, as cheerful as he is annoying. The two molded pinecones, suspended by chain, remain deaf and dumb while the clock's pendulum, a carved maple leaf, clicks back and forth nervously. A prize has been given away. A promise has been formalized. Afterward one adult moves rapidly down stone stairs, one-two-three-four, five, six. Her black lace-up shoes clicking like a metronome set on *agitato.* The second party, a defenseless child, stomps his scuffed shoes, leaving the gray castle of a house to which he will return for years to come.

Once alone, two adults argue behind tall wooden doors. Professor Peter Stoya, founder of the Stoya Conservatory for Violin & Piano, has made a commitment and bypassed his wife's consent. She's furious! He's resolute.

Peter has been informed by Gregor Piatigorsky, famed cellist and local émigré, Elizabethtown may soon become a nest that fledges prominent violinists. Peter knows how to count cards. He needs an ace or three in his hand if he's to compete. This child's desire is priceless. It's infectious. By owning the violin, he owns the boy.

For the most part, this piece of history—that of two red sister violins from Cremona mysteriously joined after centuries of separation—yes, this story and its significance will disappear, like a pebble tossed into a green pool, to be washed smooth by time, and lost in the depths.

[12]

SISTER PEACE UNDERSTANDS Douglas' misery. "I'm taking the car after lunch. Kids need an outing, you need rest," she tells Sister Elder.

It's Douglas' turn for a window seat. The brothers wrestle over a position at their shared window. Mildred, in the front seat, stares into the side mirror; she has started using Sister Peace's crayon on her lips. Sister Peace drives through town, crosses a narrow bridge. *Astrid said I was a lucky boy today,* Douglas thinks. But the unlucky-lucky boy feels a dark pinch in his chest instead of excitement. He has just given away his violin. The reality repeats like one of Sister Peace's records, the black one with a green label where a storybook knight holds a sword.

The destination has picnic benches, swings, sharp smells, and a constant rushing noise. The boys are to stay with Mildred and *obey* her, their big sister.

"Douglas, take my hand," Sister Peace says.

Douglas kicks through piles of colored leaves, watching his freshly polished shoes disappear and appear. He tugs angrily at the puny adult who is somehow able to restrain him. Looking down, Sister Peace pins him with those eyes, hypnotizing eyes, outlined as usual with kohl. "Douglas, I want to show a thing. You can stay with me?"

This will be his first memory of the river, the two of them hand in hand climbing to a vista point where he's dwarfed by an enormous amount of water gushing past. What ferocious thundering! Water pounds, it roars, unceasing.

"This place, Castle Falls," she says, raising her voice. "Look, look there!" Dark water seems to drop at intervals and become white foam—stair steps of foam and streaming water, a repeating pattern going down, down, down, all of it rushing away. Rushing away. Douglas breaks into tears and sobs without even knowing why. She wipes his eyes with her shirt tail and then turns abruptly. He quiets, begins watching, listening, until he has no sense of anyone beside him.

After a bit Sister Peace says, "Come." He resists, he wails and tugs, not wanting to leave. She means for them to walk down the hill while staying alongside the river. He complies but keeps looking back over his shoulder so as not to lose that ferocious sight. His guide rights him even as she also stumbles on rocks underfoot. They come to a curve in the river with a matching curve in the footpath; they're able to continue walking alongside the spectacle. Yellow leaves swirl, spiral upward, some traveling in groups, some drifting alone. "Leaves do fly, Douglas, but after time must join earth."

A bit further along she stops. She turns him around to face up the hill from which they've come. "See now," she says. What a giddy sensation. The water roars with equal intensity as before. But now instead of pulsing away, away, away, the water comes dashing directly at them! The full energy of the river has seemingly reversed itself to make a dramatic approach! "You." She stabs his chest with a finger. "Me," she says, tapping her chest. "Your violin, too. You catch on? All going away yet coming back." Douglas blinks twice, shivers, not with an iota of comprehension but instead with a flash of altered consciousness—his first realizatioı paradox. Although he has no words for it. Douglas internalizes the moment, holding fast the intensity of their unified awe.

The passionate guide buttons two jackets against the breeze. Although she is lame, and the child unwilling, the pair tackles the hill, finding at last Mildred, the dutiful, pushing her brothers on the swings.

ONTARIO, CANADA

[13]

January 1954

"I BEGIN TO remember one morning," Douglas will say to Gateau. He will be eighteen but feeling as ancient as a fossilized tree. Sister Peace's spirit had entered him that morning like pure rushing water. But it's only all these years later when he is broken and adrift that he will understand what she had meant to show him.

ELIZABETHTOWN, NEW YORK

[14]

October 1941

WHEN HESTER SMYTHE introduced the troubled boy, the instructor responded to the child's magnetism. Douglas presented an enigma. Despite tears, reluctance to speak, and solemnity, the initial attraction was unavoidable. The boy's musical predilection glimmered, catching Stoya off guard. He had spontaneously offered to teach the child, at no charge, in return for the abandoned violin. This runt with his perfect pitch and inordinate desire would goad Willi out of his apathy. And inspire little brother Siggi. Dare a Professor hope all three might ultimately bring him recognition?

Somewhat later Frieda plays a scale in A minor. Then, looking up with a frown she grows bold. "You don't really want this rogue fiddle, do you, Peter?"

"The *boy* does. I think he's an asset. He'll elevate our Conservatory."

"Douglas seems bright enough but he's a little thief. Might be *your* violin he takes next."

"*Jetzt, Jetzt*! Now, now!" Peter says, irritated by his wife's stance in the face of his impulsive action. "May I remind you of our purpose? Growing our Conservatory."

"Years you're talking! He could up and quit, carrying off any valuable in the process."

"But no! I've brilliantly anchored this child in our tutelage. Tell me, what does he value above all? I'm holding it! Like a pawn broker awaiting payment."

Then Frieda softens. "I will say, Miss Smythe dresses him like a proper gentleman. She, however, that unlikeable woman, could do with a new frock. And a smile. In a word, she's drab."

Hester might defend herself. She prefers a modest appearance. Youthful flamboyance? Well, she had her day—although some may yet compare her looks to Sargent's *Portrait of Madame X*. That creamy complexion, aquiline nose, graceful neck. She styles her brown hair neatly tucked and rolled. Several high-waisted dresses, suiting her top-heavy build and enviably narrow hips, satisfy her everyday needs. Elegant gowns, dinner dresses, jewelry, capes, suits, and furs are tucked away. She sneers privately, comparing Frieda to a bird, a Bohemian waxwing to be exact. Denied outright beauty, the frau is intent on seeking elegance. That tailored gray dress, those black-rimmed glasses resting on rouged cheeks, that honey-toast fluff of hair. Best to be wary of a woman so concerned with appearances.

As if a woman could be judged by her attire.

[15]

PETER SETS ASIDE the Performance Violin and begins playing the newly acquired violin. Curiously, both violins have a carnelian-hued varnish. His heart beats with appreciation. "This fiddle is more suited to a Czardas than a Waltz. Listen to the depth of tone and volume."

"Glad you find enjoyment. We'll never see a penny for it."

The maligned instrument wonders if she might be understood by the man. It appears she is to reside in his presence and be under his direction. She transmits to him as she did to Douglas, in her gossamer way.

{My name is 253-1 | Albeit young| in the eternal stream of time | this much *questo violino* has learned| Our world is connected| by the simplest element| An element that surrounds| fills| links| caresses| For better or worse| it affects everything| To name it| Energy| |

{Energy affects *questo violino* too| See| this one is aware| Sensitive to| your desires| Your deceits| Your fears| See| human transmission| moves into| passes through| and alters my body| |

{All *violini* rely upon the touch of finger| drag of horsehair| to respond with voice| But 253-1 is unique| her voice is freed only by a player's quickening| by a flow of goodwill| To speak the magic of it| my wooden body converts goodness into music| Such sound re-calculates a listener's disposition| for a time| Men speak of this shift| with words| Release| Joy| Bliss| Exultation| Rapture| |

{If you require *questo violino* to sing| Professor Stoya| she asks but one thing| Quicken her with the positive energy of humanity| |

Peter Stoya taps his foot as the striped-red fiddle follows his request for a Czardas. His mind wanders; he's dancing with Frieda on *that* night of heated courtship. Oh, yes, he's affected by the violin's haunting voice, but he's deaf to her revelation.

[16]

PROFESSOR PETER STOYA never meant to ruffle his wife. Nevertheless, he has. He impulsively promised years of free instruction to a strange kid. What came over me? *Am I seeing myself in the boy?* Peter ponders the similarities. *Loss of father. Early fixated on playing violin.*

Peter Stoya's robust Papa had dissolved into a symbol rather than a memory. He'd become just a sepia image in a pewter frame. He'd become just the man forever gripping a basket of apples. Just the violinist to be spoken of fondly, whose violin then became sacrosanct. The Red Cross report had thrown Mama to her knees. Papa had perished during the French offensive in the so-called witches' cauldron of the Champagne district—on 26 September 1915. Peter had been only three.

That left Mama and his old maid Aunt Stoya to rear him, the sisters-in-law never withholding their display of contempt for one another. *Explains my bad temper,* Peter thinks. Or does the fault lie with an *alt kobold*, a demon with a pumpkin head and bandy legs who disciplined a stepson by locking him in the smokehouse, forcing him to endure windowless hours with the headless and the mute?

Obviously, Mama's hourglass figure charmed this Swiss haberdasher, who peddled wares to the Frankfurt shop where she clerked. He a widower, who swiftly wooed a widow with gifts, proposed marriage, swept the family of three off to Zurich. The man's adoption of Peter with all the paperwork and fees required might be deemed kindly. More likely, calculating. By bringing another child into his chalet, this father of four set one capable woman, Aunt Stoya, to tending five kids and kitchen. And her desirable sidekick, Mama, to tending conjugal fires.

I was given compensation. I just didn't realize the extent of it then, Peter thinks, grateful for his grandfather, Opa, who had rescued him from the cruel situation when he was ten. Back to Germany they'd gone. There to enroll young Peter in the Frankfurt Hoch Conservatorium as a music student. *Papa would have approved.*

Peter buries his face in a hot towel while he lingers in the past. Two events stand foremost. First, the marvel of Paul Hindemith as violist with the Amar String Quartet. In the heights of the gallery, Peter floated, intoxicated by the voice of a stringed instrument. Second, the phenomenon of Yehudi Menuhin's debut; Yehudi was only several years older than he! The result? Desire and Envy embedded themselves in Peter's constitution.

Contrivance aside for the moment, Peter Stoya feels magnanimous. *One needs a role model. I'll do what I can for Douglas.* "LuLu, I'm going out." He bundles against a stiff breeze and sets off on foot. Along River Street he walks where water flows as it always has. He crosses paths with a man soldiering against the wind, a gentleman looking comfortably warm in a Burberry jacket of gabardine wool; the man is Lermontov, whom Peter recognizes by sight but will not know by name for twelve more years. They nod, unaware they are both thinking of their youth in a distant homeland.

Peter hikes toward Milholland Lodge, puffing as he tackles the hill. He's reviewing the links in his chain of circumstances. Paul Hindemith prompted his move to Berlin and study at the Advanced School for Music. Here, Herr Hindemith drilled students unmercifully. Pitted them against each other until only the stalwart remained. If talented, a hardy soul might be rewarded with mentoring. Peter ranked as one of Herr Hindemith's chosen few.

Competition and Possibility had made excellent yokemates for an aspiring musician. *Would I have gotten to America without the opportunities Hindemith spurred? Or without my demon stepfather's Swiss citizenship, which saved my neck?*

BERLIN, GERMANY

[17]

1930-1941

AS A STRUGGLING student, Peter entertained in Berlin taverns and cinemas. Summers he played festivals in Swiss resorts—rain regularly caused his violin strings to snap, an expense that was hard to bear. The group? A cellist who made a hash of everything, a horn player who could not lip properly, a flirtatious-curvaceous-distracting zither player, and an organizer from whom payments, when forthcoming, were paltry. It was then that young Stoya met Frieda Bachmeier. Her musicality and her porcelain flesh, not to mention the way skirts wrapped around her legs as she walked, set Peter afire.

Time slowly changes relationships. Frieda and Peter exchanged love letters. Paul Hindemith and Stoya, despite their age difference, became collaborators and friends. Providence smiled on Peter; he was granted work as an Associate Professor for strings at the Stern Conservatory, propitiously located in the Berlin Philharmonic Concert Hall. It was then that young Stoya proposed to Frieda Bachmeier. She moved to Berlin and found work teaching elementary piano. Within months Frieda became not only his accompanist but also his wife, Frau Stoya. Soon thereafter, 1935, fortune smiled again upon the young couple. A son was born, Wilhelm, a pink-cheeked infant who suckled vigorously.

Opa took the occasion to gift his heir. "You've earned this." And so, armed with his father's prestigious violin—an 1860 Vuillame built in exacting replication of a Stradivari—Peter set his cap for acceptance in the Berlin Philharmonic. A sorry report can be made of that attempt. A subject, Frieda would warn, that is best left alone.

During this time Hindemith, having become an avant-garde composer, was denounced in Germany as a cultural Bolshevist and spiritual non-Aryan. He relocated to Switzerland and sought opportunity in the USA. He wrote to Stoya from New York advising Peter to seriously consider a move. One caveat, teaching was likely more lucrative than concertizing.

Frieda hadn't recovered from the birth of their second son; Stoya had heard his mother speak of this mysterious female hysteria. What to do? While considering Hindemith's urgent tone (and the man's lack of encouragement about concertizing), Peter's wound festered, sparking the humiliation of his unpardonable failure. He scowled at himself in the mirror, scratching a very pink scar on his face.

It so happened, a Swiss friend of Gertrud Hindemith's, an educated lady of French-Jewish descent, was seeking live-in security in return for domestic services. Adding this housekeeper-nursemaid to the Stoya household would ease two troubling situations.

Narcisse Louise Boulez accepted the nickname LuLu, preferred by the Stoya family—she, a grateful widow several years the Stoyas' senior. Hers, a long narrow nose, cupid bow lips in its shadow, diminutive chin. Voluptuous of bust and hip with a mane of brunette hair worn loosely gathered, Gibson girl style. Small ego, hers, not requiring commendation for tireless labor. Narcisse Louise cannot be comforted with this knowledge now, but she'll one day have an admirer who believes both she and her name are worthy of a Jean D'Albret perfume.

1939. Two more years have passed. For Herr Stoya, reasons to emigrate keep building. One July evening, the boys sweetly asleep, Peter pours two glasses of schnapps and broaches the subject with his mate. The idea of such drastic change jangles Frau Stoya. She relapses with nausea and a blinding headache. Peter and LuLu get her to bed.

Still, Frieda wakes, offering a flirtatious nuzzling of his ears, and when he reacts as expected she giggles, accepting him. Then, with an about-face, her good humor retreats as quickly as a kitchen roach. She weeps over muesli at breakfast, sobs in the afternoon, an arm flung over her eyes, music book opened to a favorite composition. Wilhelm, just four, entertains her in his clown-like fashion. Siegfried concentrates on his toys, often pushing his locomotive around her chair, giving her feet an exaggerated berth. Even so, the children are too much for her. Frieda exhorts LuLu to be more attentive.

Maybe the recent death of her father is to be blamed for her condition, Peter supposes. Nevertheless, he latches upon her respectable inheritance as defense for his goal. He sets her straight in a rather patronizing manner. Their emigration is financially feasible now. If they're smart, they can afford passage *and* a home in New York where European musicians are settling. Surely, he too can find work.

Nazification sweeps the country; intolerance pairs with domination and sets to business in full marching regalia. The Stern Conservatory is taken over by the Nazi Regime.

Stoya, as an Associate Professor, loses his position.

Hindemith issues a warning: "The time is now, don't wait." Indeed, the Nazis have recently issued a decree that all artists unemployed or not fully employed be directed to more *useful tasks.*

Paul Hindemith sails yet again to the USA; this time to stay indefinitely. Hindemith telegraphs Stoya. He's concerned for his wife, Gertrud, whom he's left behind. He had booked her springtime passage to NYC from Switzerland where she was biding time with family. Unexpectedly she'd lost her booking when Italian cruisers were recalled for military purposes. Lisbon seems to be the only friendly port, not only for Gertrud Hindemith but for the hundreds of hopefuls who are trekking to Portugal. He petitions that Narcisse Louise, also Swiss, be immediately allowed to join Gertrud. A plan is laid. Approximately ten hours after exchanging tearful farewells with the Stoya family, LuLu arrives at Zürich Stadelhofen. Two brave friends become traveling companions.

"Make plans. Leave while you can!" Hindemith warns again. "Your Swiss citizenship has become an asset." *Thanks to the alt kobold, how curiously life plays out.*

Peter applies for visas. Meanwhile he and Frieda nervously attend the women's progress, grasping for more than each telegram reports. Ensuing messages give only momentary reassurance that Gertrud and LuLu are steadily advancing to the coast.

17 July 1940. Departed Zurich with a brave Gertrud. N.L.B.

1 August 1940. Departing Geneva via Grenoble to Montpellier. Gertrud's kindness a boon. N.L.B.

5 August 1940. Depart Perpignan to Barcelona. Fortunate we two. Traveling by train. Omnibus. On foot too with masses fleeing Germany. N.L.B.

6 August 1940. Madrid to Lisbon. Hundreds of refugees all hoping to book passage to NYC. Joined by Basque. One plays violin and lifts our hearts. Please cable funds. N.L.B.

9 August 1940. Boarded SS Quanza with 317 refugees from Luxembourg. Netherlands. Belgium. Mostly Jewish. Basque peasants too. N.L.B.

The family rallies with news of LuLu's arrival in New York. She's been invited to stay with the Hindemiths until Stoyas arrive.

✳ ✳ ✳

FRIEDA'S CONDITION WORSENS as she imagines the uncertainties ahead. So many precious things and people must be left behind. Most pressing, how will she cope with the transatlantic passage? Pity, the luxury of a clipper ship is impossible for a simple man's family.

Peter observes his wife with condescension. She's weak, he tells himself, only to feel the pendulum of his heart reverse, and he's filled with lusty desire for this delicate-once-robust darling. Her doctor insists she have a curative regimen, preferably in Switzerland. A minimum of three months if she's expected to travel. Peter balks. *Spring? Impossible!* Hindemith's warnings cannot be ignored. Air raid sirens at night ramp up fear. Plus, the visas expire in mid-February.

Begrudgingly, the doctor writes Frieda a prescription. Librium 25 mg. as needed for anxiety and migraine. Cautions: may induce drowsiness, blurred vision, changes in libido.

Concern for Frieda may impact travel plans, but no more than Peter's self-indulgence. He's been invited to perform at a prestigious soirée to be held in the magnificent Mendelssohn Herrenhaus. Robert, a descendant of composer Felix Mendelssohn, owns a stunning stringed instrument collection, and once again Peter Stoya will have the honor of performing on the Red Stradivarius of 1720. The instrument was acquired by the family around 1928, quickly becoming the favorite of Felix's granddaughter, (the late) Lilli von Mendelssohn. This violin's more than two-hundred-year provenance is largely a mystery. But for all the unknown years there are unending and fascinating fantasies. What is true, however, is that the Red Stradivarius' angelic voice conforms to Peter Stoya's every whim as if it senses his heart's desires through his fingertips. He will not turn down the opportunity to have this rare creation responding to him in front of a prestigious audience. The festive celebration is planned for late December. With a breath of relief Stoya books passage out of Hamburg. Early January. He won't miss the moment.

Frieda sets to sorting possessions. Three steamer trunks dominate the tiny Appartement in anticipation of the final packing. Peter will offer his finesse at disguising the violin lest any sticky-fingered worker itches for an exposed asset. Furniture, china, the prized Hummel collection, the cuckoo clock carved of Black Forest linden, Frieda's heirloom linens—all this can be shipped once the family settles. Opa, aged seventy-four, still straight of back and broad of shoulder, accepts the task, understanding the young generations' need to flee.

Excepting an unfortunate mishap, the little family will pass by the famed Statue of Liberty, meet up with Narcisse Louise Boulez, and begin anew. Hopes hang on Hindemith's assurances of a better life in America.

Early 1941, the journey begins. Five bottles of Munstelander Schnapps Liquor offered discreetly in a doctor's valise successfully distract immigration officers. A thorough search of Frieda's trunk is omitted. However, before the pilot ship takes the lead in navigating to the North Sea, Peter is called into the Captain's cabin where he spies his name circled on the manifest. He's of an age to be conscripted; are they going to contest his adoptive citizenship? Did they search the trunk after all? Stoya's bowels nosily threaten disgrace during a session of questioning. After which the Captain releases him with a curt, *"Viel Glück."*

[18]

ONE MAY NEVER know how Peter Stoya's reaction to a dilemma that December of 1940 altered history. Perhaps you'd agree with his reasoning if he laid it out. His heart wobbles as the ship lurches and rolls across the Atlantic. If his secret were to be discovered, it would go badly for him. Nevertheless, he can, and he does, justify his intrepid choice. He'll find a way to make Frieda understand, he promises silently. Sometime later when she's herself again. It's enough to cherish her as his own Botticelli Venus—his own goddess of love. The other female, the alert one, the discerning one, from whom he must shelter his secret, is LuLu, akin to Bonnard's *Misia*, glamourous in a deceptive way.

NEW YORK, NEW YORK

[19]

January 1941

NEWLY ARRIVED AND exhausted, Peter Stoya hails a taxi. LuLu awaits them at a hotel close to the terminal; even so, the taxi fare is outrageous. Perhaps the lobby has all the gracious attributes of the Savoy; nevertheless, their room would not pass inspection in the light of morning. Even with its spiffy electric locks, instructions for guests taped under glass tables, a buzzer telephone, and fluffy pillows. The carpet is worn to the warp, and the bathroom needs help, more help than the help have provided to date. The wall clock opposite the bed has stopped at 2:53 a.m., an eerie coincidence that cannot be recognized at this juncture. The Stoyas, so travel-weary, they can neither complain nor distinguish the correct time. All four flop into the double bed without the promised cot and portable crib.

Stoya has chewed on his strategy for the entire voyage. He remembers that Hindemith recommended using the services of Rembert Wurlitzer, a renowned expert on matters of the violin. Maintenance had been the topic; Hindemith wasn't thinking of the other services his associate might require—appraisal and sale. At length Peter has fixed his hopes on a questionable fellow, one mentioned in an offhand warning by Hindemith. Easily found in the telephone directory. One over whom he dares to exert influence. With Lady Fortune on his side guiding him to the right accomplice, his deed will go undetected until time muddles clues.

Frieda's continued travel malaise facilitates his scheme; she's sleeping late this nippy morning as are the boys. He saunters to the hotel basement storage, key in hand, and opens Frieda's steamer trunk. He drops the heavy lid, stressing the hinges. *How to grasp reality?* Here he is, Peter Stoya, a German immigrant, an unsuspected savior. Or thief.

Whichever he may someday be judged, he is undeniably a bold player on the stage of world history. Lovingly he inspects his late father's prized violin, still ship-shape after an overseas adventure.

Fortified by a breakfast of *café leche with bollos con mermelada*, Stoya sets off whistling. He finds New York City larger than Berlin, bustling, and friendly. He adjusts the battered case slung over his shoulder and navigates the numbered streets on foot. He finds the luthier's shop on the third floor behind a door burdened with multiple locks and a peek-a-boo window. He waits patiently after ringing the buzzer. He taps his foot while wait-wait-wait-waiting. He listens for the sound of someone within while trying not to look suspicious. He fights the desire to ring the bell repeatedly. Perhaps he has the wrong address? No, the nameplate reads *Florian Roux, Sales & Repair*.

Stoya stalls. After all, he has his own violin for sale. The gift from his *grosvader*. The superior violin his father played before war snuffed out all the man's future cadenzas. Sentimentality, transparent and soft like egg white, washes over Peter as he rings the buzzer another time. To part with this family violin tears at his heart. Sentimentality transforms to a crisp glaze of determination when the peek-a-boo window opens.

A man peeps out as if passing judgment. Stoya resolves to stay calm, his palms sweat, he wipes them in his pockets. After metallic clink and rattle Florien Roux opens the door. He extends his sizable hand.

Stoya enters the cramped office fascinated by Florien's appearance. The luthier is taller than him by at least sixteen centimeters and is at least that many years his senior. Florien wears a white leather cap that serves to emphasize his massive skull—which in combination with his chiseled nose and well-formed ears conjures the cross between a giant and an elf. The luthier isn't prone to smiling, although his twinkling eyes speak volumes about his nature.

The minimal office serves as a foil for the locked room beyond. "I repair, consign, acquire, and sell stringed instruments," Florien says, reaching out. His broad hands span the neck of Stoya's case, his long fingers at the ready to undo the latches. "Shall we take a look?" His eyes stay neutral, offering no reveal.

He's intrigued, Stoya thinks. Will this Florien Roux know what he's looking at?

With a flourish the host offers his guest entrance to the secreted chamber. The smell of varnish overpowers Stoya at first, although tall windows with southern exposure are open and hung with gauze curtains, allowing airflow and light. So many violins, violas, cellos, all in various states of repair. Gleaming brown, orange, gold, or red, they occupy cubbies. They grace the ceiling strung by rope.

The luthier unexpectedly smiles, showing a row of perfectly square teeth. He's scrutinizing Stoya's most prized possession.

"An 1820 Vuillame. An inheritance from my late father. They say I also inherited his looks and his musicality."

"For sale, this violin, Monsieur? Or you seek appraisal? I have many collectors in my vest pocket for an authentic Vuillame."

[20]

PETER FANCIES THIS new life in Manhattan. By mid-January they are settled in a brownstone apartment. And look. An opportunity to perform with a quartet sprang up from casual conversation over vodka. Frieda pouts at allusions to living in the city permanently. *"Nein!"* It's expensive. It's no place to raise sons or even a daughter should God grant them one. Neither Frau Stoya nor Herr Stoya have a compromising bone in their body, an unfortunate pairing, because a balance between their assertive natures cannot be found when they differ on process and direction, as they now do.

LuLu adjusts just as slowly to the brownstone; she too misses the gardens of Berlin with their gentle slopes, large lakes, the abundance of shrubs and trees. "Back home I might take the boys for a stroll, let them play in the parks. This Lower Eastside is noisy and dirty."

Freda bemoans the absence of tulips. "Berlin has fresh air to breathe, and flowers everywhere, Peter."

"Take a stroll through Central Park," locals advise.

Others speak of small towns in upstate New York. They speak of rivers, lakes, spectacular waterfalls, hardwood trees, birch and aspen, country farms, stone houses, cottages for city folk to rent when they require escape from sticky heat. This locale appeals to Frieda.

Peter reasons with Frieda pointing out that life in the City has rewards and conveniences. Days later he cajoles. As last resort he uses male bluster. Still, Frieda won't give in. The husband wakes another, and yet another morning to his wife's chill. *Perhaps she's right,* he tells himself. The gleam of New York City wears off when tarnished by the toil of daily labors. And a bitter spouse.

Meanwhile his earnings from quartet gigs have been plentiful. Depression days of the past have yielded a celebratory environment for the Manhattan elite; invitations for musicians to perform are plentiful. After inquiry Peter resolves that Frieda's inheritance might easily purchase one of the abandoned houses for sale, at or below market prices, in upstate New York. As he must, Peter will accept the reality of moving north, the extreme winters, the lack of conveniences. Not to mention the commute. Two hours on the train? *Nothing-schmothing.* Teaching locally and performing in the City? *Okay for now.* He's young, not yet thirty, with a decent future ahead. The extra money from his hush-hush arrangement with Florien Roux will soon sweeten Frieda's disposition. *Patience.*

ELIZABETHTOWN, NEW YORK

[21]

THIS SUNNY AFTERNOON Peter allows Frieda an extended nap. It's hard on her, resettling again, adjusting to a tiny rental. "It's temporary, *Liebling,*" he reminds. He's off with the boys to sniff out a property the realtor has suggested.

His dream quickens like the first kicks of life in a womb. He can easily imagine possibilities for the Milholland Lodge. He can almost hear dozens of young musicians practicing their instruments—all at once. Pure Heaven right here. The bank owns this place. No price is listed; there's mention of an auction. It's to his financial advantage that people consider the abandoned Lodge haunted and have shied away for years. He doesn't believe in ghosts. He's not afraid of hard work.

Peter tromps around the snow-covered property sizing it up. Boarded windows offer no clues about the interior; never mind, he can envision it. Their year-round home and a summer Conservatory for serious students. This main building: create a large dining area and include a performance space. The cabins: fix them up as student quarters.

Positive thoughts continue. Willi and Siggi could eventually be taught right here, by the greatest; Hindemith could be persuasive in that regard. He and Frieda, of course, would give the boys a proper foundation. His legacy appears like the green swords of a spring bulb—Peter Stoya, father of two acclaimed violinists, founder of acclaimed Stoya Conservatory~Violin & Piano. He pulls a handkerchief from his pocket; wipes his nose. He calls to his sons who are hurling snowballs at each other.

Birch trees have been scrutinizing the three humans. With silent connectivity the grove senses future disturbance of serenity.

* * *

PETER OUTLINES HIS vision for the Milholland Lodge with Frieda. She's frightened at the prospect of owning such a place. He persists. "Jah, jah, sure, the place needs repair, after five years of being haunted-schmanted."

Frieda chews on her cheeks, thinking, thinking. The rental house they're squeezed into has northern exposure, modern plumbing, and antique mold. "Could be worse than *this*, us moving into that Lodge," she complains to LuLu. "Peter is so unrealistic. With perverse luck he'll win the damnable Lodge at the auction!"

"Unless you find something else first," LuLu says gently. Give LuLu credit—she bit her tongue for a day. She's not one to meddle.

Frau Stoya favors the upscale, established neighborhood just beyond Hand and Williams Streets. The realtor obliges, showing them an enormous three-story stone house with high ceilings, spacious rooms, five bedrooms, a charming salon featuring a bay window, and an extended back porch facing a private backyard. The kitchen, oh dear. LuLu has a few ideas for making it *akzeptabel*. This gem is also owned by the bank. And offered so reasonably. So affordably. So. The haunted Lodge or the spacious stone mansion? They can't have both.

[22]

THE STATELY HOUSE is enormous compared to their upstairs apartment in Berlin, the Manhattan brownstone, or the moldy rental. Peter brags about his purchase, note the large, thick-walled rooms, an acoustic asset for his dream Conservatory. He begins planning. Frieda tries not to gloat. LuLu relaxes.

Late winter offers sleet, sleet, and more sleet. Spring merely whispers its intentions like a capricious lover's promise. Frieda yearns for warm days with the kids playing outdoors. Never mind Siggi is four now and more self-sufficient. Willi, turning seven in June, attends school. Professor Stoya looks at his wife. *Lost in a daydream.* Two young boys underfoot seem to drain her, or is it the Librium? He'll have a serious chat with LuLu about taking on more responsibility.

Ah, Florien Roux comes through with a sale! Peter pencils out a plan computing possible expenses. His wife, the poor wilted flower, will brighten when she starts teaching again. "America is not as barbaric as I imagined," Peter Stoya acknowledges. "Mind you, this hamlet is no city. Still, I'm satisfied with our choice." His disclosure panders to his mate's contentment, if happiness is too much to ask. In this vein, a splendid piano arrives, a surprise for Frieda from a loving husband. "A Bosendorfer Grand, like new, made of Austrian spruce by Viennese craftsmen," he boasts, "to remind us of our European heritage. It just requires tuning."

Frieda pulls out her music books. She practices daily, to keep both skills and sanity. Peter relaxes. Willi and Siggi leave a trail of toys throughout the house without their mother's reprimand. LuLu can relax.

And then one morning as Peter bends to the mirror trimming his mustache, Frieda asks the question he knew was coming, eventually.

"How could we afford that piano?"

Frieda has no talent for sums. She leaves the finances to her husband. It's just that when Vicar Hornsby commented on the *impressive* concert grand Bosendorfer in their salon, Frieda got to wondering.

Peter, with a straight face and drooping mustache, collects himself. "You were still so distressed whilst we were in the hotel and even whilst in our rentals, my darling. I just carried out my business without worrying you, planning to share all with you when you were refreshed."

The wife accepts her husband's explanation, knowing what a drab partner she's been. "So how did you make it happen, *Liebling*?"

He explains it like a fabulous story. He'd located a luthier in the City, one who holds auctions.

"Located a what?" Frieda wrinkles her nose.

"Loo-thee-ur," Peter says, exaggerating the pronunciation. "You know, a violin maker. In olden days a lute maker." Well, to continue, he'd successfully auctioned his father's Vuillame. To replace it he'd bid on a violin with a spurious label reading Antonio Stradivari 1720. He'd won it. A real bargain; it couldn't possibly be a Strad nor of such an early vintage at the price. "You've heard me play it; you must agree it sounds almost as lovely as my Vuillame did. And to be practical, it's a perfectly acceptable instrument for a quartet player. More important, an excellent piano is *de rigueur* for a music conservatory, yeah?"

Frieda's face brightens. She knows she's been a pill. She slides out of her nightie just as Stoya nicks his cheek with the pointed tonsorial scissors, allowing a burst of crimson blood to splatter his undershirt. Peter chides himself for ruining the moment; he'd meant to be endearing, playing the valiant knight to her needy princess. Instead, she became a nurse, and he, the patient.

As much as it would ease Peter's conscience to be completely honest about his dealings, he simply can't, not yet. Inevitable how one deviation will spark off another. He wasn't in the habit of lying to Frieda; he won't make a habit of it in the future.

[23]

ACCORDING TO VICAR HORNSBY—he visits regularly to enjoy conversation, tea, and Narcisse Louise's pfeffernusse—Elizabethtown lacks musical instruction for its youth. The Conservatory will soon acquire students of piano and violin. Frieda agrees to teach piano; she'll accept just a few students until both boys are in school. After that Peter teasingly addresses his wife as "Mrs. Piano Teacher." "Professor Stoya," she says in return. They rather enjoy the formality. The titles stick.

In stagnant interludes Professor Stoya buoys their ambitions, reminding his wife, "Children of every locale have an instinct for music.

Certainly, this is so." To be noted, their son, Wilhelm, has yet to display this instinct, this affinity to music. The boy resists Frieda's introduction to using fingers on the keyboard. He prefers pounding with both fists. Or building with his erector set alongside the dampening pedal. Young Siggi's level of interest remains a question. Peter's frustration with his progeny grows. And he's not one to hide his pique.

Stoya's connections in New York City pay off. He's contracted to teach senior violin classes at Brooklyn Music School. When a diplomat inquires about commissioning a recital, Peter scoffs to Frieda, "I'll play, even though this fellow wouldn't know a Bach Partita from a Prokofiev March. Nor would he know one violin from another." *Knowing one violin from another...ah, there lies the mystery.*

[24]

SISTER ELDER BRINGS Douglas to his first piano lesson at the Stoya Conservatory armed with an agenda. Although Frieda Stoya gazes at the ceiling while Hester Smythe expounds, the spinster is hellbent on delivering her soliloquy with or without eye contact. She takes center stage.

Hester (dictatorial)

Let's be forthright, shall we? Most prudent if we first understand one another. I believe in individualism and self-reliance. I take a progressive stand on women's rights, reform, and education. I'm not favorable toward organized religion, social institutions, or encroaching industrialization. Action is better than contemplation. And I have faith that humans might transcend limits and reach astonishing heights, adding this caveat: such accomplishment occurs only if a child is taught self-discipline. I don't know what you believe in, or what you value. My point, now that you will have Douglas in your charge regularly, I pray you and the

Professor will limit your teaching to music and the disciplines thereof. And should matters of Douglas' behavior require a firm hand, simply inform me. Such taming will be at my hand, not yours.

It was a mouthful and Hester feels better afterward. Without invitation, she settles in the wingchair. She'll evaluate Frieda's skill as a piano teacher. Not too late to withdraw her charge, or is it? Surely the boy would raise an impossible never-ending tantrum if totally severed from the violin, which now lives in the Stoyas' salon. Her only recourse then, to be alert and wary.

Hester Smythe has refrained from favoritism as her four children have progressed from drooling to defiance. Love is painful. Her solution? Suppress one's gut reactions. All the same, during these six years of the youngest orphan's life, time keeps softening her hardened heart. Look: such bright eyes as he listens at story time. Grasp: his warm, strong hands, hands that obediently hold hers when crossing streets. Imagine: fingers that, despite her worries, she could envision flying up and down violin strings mastering harmonics and trills.

[25]

AT FIRST THE BLACK lines and circles on sheet music confuse Douglas. This is to be expected, Mrs. Piano Teacher guides him patiently. One day it clicks; his face lights up, and she beams acknowledging her reward. Dismissed, her fears of his thievery.

After several months of daily piano lessons Douglas exudes charismatic energy. He's lost his earlier restraint with a shift toward flamboyance; he plays his memorized pieces for anyone who will listen. Mrs. Piano Teacher encourages him to linger as she gives Violette's lesson, if in return he will keep tabs on little Siggi, almost five—LuLu takes her break at this hour of the afternoon. After guiding Siggi to a project with building blocks, Douglas can settle into the wingchair swinging his legs in time to whatever is being practiced by Frieda's prize student. Violette's lessons are paid for by the Elizabethtown Veteran Widows' Fund. Truth be told, Frieda would teach this talented one free of charge.

Douglas enjoys being at the Stoyas' house. With its music. With its distinct aromas: of furniture polish, of tobacco, of pumpernickel bread baking. *Pumpernickel*—the word has a nice sound to it. He and Violette repeat the syllables like a little song. Mrs. Piano Teacher allows them a freshly baked slice loaded with butter when she gives her boys a snack.

Sometimes Douglas entertains himself by watching the cuckoo clock pendulum. The lively bird is disabled after the noon hour, disallowing interruptions to lessons. Douglas wishes he could control time so easily; that way Violette's lesson wouldn't end. He enjoys the sound of Violette's fingers striking the keys. When Mrs. Piano notices his concentration, she tosses smiles his way. After Violette's lesson she bundles him up against darkening afternoons and he hugs this kind lady goodbye, so tightly, so warmly. She always says, "Why I could just faint, sweet child."

How could Frieda know that Douglas imagines he's hugging her prize student instead?

While Douglas develops charm, Willi becomes clever; he dreams up practical jokes to pull on his pal—a playmate who vies for both of his parents' attention. Over time this pranking becomes a daily occurrence. Mrs. Piano Teacher has recently taken on several beginning students. She more easily loses patience with Willi's behavior. *"Gehen wir!* Let's go!" she says after another devilish act, leading him by the ear to his room where he'll await a paddling from his father.

On these occasions Douglas pleads with Mrs. Piano Teacher, explaining away Willi's infractions, all to no avail. The orphan becomes downhearted and sits with his head buried in his hands until his pretend brother is allowed to rejoin him. Eventually, the piteousness becomes too much for Mrs. Piano Teacher; she sends Douglas home before the culprit receives punishment.

"*Nicht Gut.* What am I to do?" Frau Stoya asks the Professor.

"They are boys. They act as boys."

[26]

ABOVE THEM, ON an outcropping of rock, perches *Windy Cliff,* Piatigorsky's chateau-like castle. Behind it, meeting the sky, acres of wooded mountain where wild beasts roam, as the stories go. Peter inches his Torpedo Pontiac across the devil-may-care plank bridge, only to encounter a steep vertical climb, unpaved and narrowed by rock pillars. A normally insouciant Professor Stoya breaks into a sweat, never happier than when he is safely parked. Dabbing his forehead with a hankie he turns to the boys in the back seat. Just in time to see Willi pinch Douglas. "Behave today!" Pointing his finger at Douglas he adds, "I expect your very best, very best-schmest behavior!"

Jacqueline greets the trio. Stoya basks in her loveliness, her signature pearls, her smile. "Hello, Peter, and who have we here?" The boys declare their names, giggling, shy.

Willi runs toward a moose head mounted over the piano. He stands on the piano bench ogling the taxidermy. Douglas stops on the threshold. He stares into the room, attracted by a large wooden instrument. It gleams in the shadows of the corner.

"Grisha, our guests have arrived," Jacqueline calls.

So easy is Piatigorsky's long-legged stride, he reminds the Professor of a large cat. They've met a few times before, sharing a draught at the

Deer's Head Inn, performing together at Kiwanis meetings. Gregor seems preoccupied; he repeats what Stoya already knows. How fortunate he and his family were to flee France on the very last ship before Hitler's invasion. How horrific, current news of the Nazi regime. "I'm barely able to practice these days." He sighs.

"Hard times," Peter says, omitting detail of his own brush with Nazi powers. He swallows hard, recalling a specific daring act in Berlin. "What cello do you play?"

"It's a Montagnana. I am a fortunate man. It lay unused for over a century. At Berkeley Castle, owned by the Fitzharding family. 1935 they gave it to me. I name her the Sleeping Beauty.

Stoya examines the cello more closely and admires the golden-orange varnish. He consoles himself. *A fine instrument is meant to be appreciated by listeners. My decision was correct.* He relaxes again.

Gregor shows Stoya through the rambling levels of *Windy Cliff*. He procured this magnificent property at a very low price. He never imagined the issues they'd have setting the structure right after years of vacancy. Not to mention the raccoons who think they have ownership.

The men settle in the main room, rejoining a giant mirror, the cello, the moose head, and the piano. Gregor fumbles in his jacket pocket for his pipe and goes through all the necessary maneuvers to prepare it for a smoke. He begins discussion of the compositions he's been transcribing and arranging for cello—until the sound of piano playing interrupts.

They turn in unison to see Douglas. The child sits at the piano; the stool is too low for him, and yet he plunges into J. S. Bach's *Prelude in C Major*. Piatigorsky holds up his hand to prevent Stoya from interfering. The cellist listens attentively. He draws on his pipe and exhales aromatic smoke. Douglas plays from memory, each note distinct, tempo correct, and dynamics beautifully expressed. It's a simple piece and lasts only a couple of minutes. Grisha Piatigorsky nods his head in approval. Douglas hops off the stool; he again inches up to the lustrous cello. The instrument stands several inches taller than the almost-seven-year-old boy who admires it, the boy who looks as if he longs to hear it sing, the boy who has found a way to ask for music without using words.

Contradiction floods Professor Stoya's being. Initial pride surges, after which anger seeps in to pollute the moment. Why wasn't Willi the first to play as he had intended? And then to counter his anger a bolt of hope flashes, followed by a thunderous realization. Why should this moment be about Douglas only? No. Willi can perform just as well. *Salvage the moment. Impress Gregor Piatigorsky with our teaching expertise.*

Directed by his father, Willi takes his turn, playing Beethoven's *Fur Elise.* The piano is in tune and the simple repeated notes in the treble ring out beautifully. Willi moves maturely through the three-and-one-half minutes of playing. The father furrows his broad forehead, trying to conceal his pride, although his thumping heart must surely give him away.

Piatigorsky compliments both pianists. "A joy, enthusiastic students. I see plenty of depressed ones." And because he has understood Douglas' silent language, he makes an offer. "Shall I play for you then, on this cello of mine? Would you like that? Bach for you, Douglas. This is the *Prelude, Suite No. 1 in G.*"

Willi waggles his tongue in Douglas' direction.

Jephta skips to her father's feet where she sits. Douglas, oblivious to Willi's clowning, snuggles in beside her. The youngsters look up into the cellist's face expectantly. Jacqueline takes a seat, holding Joram on her knees—each showing reverence for this man's talent.

Willi crawls down the hallway. No one notices.

The sound of the cello flows in a mysterious way; a deep, shuddering resonance caresses the small group. Douglas imagines grasses swaying to the breeze of the music. He watches Gregor's face; it's just as expressive as the playing.

The trials of this Russian-born musician manifest through the passionate reverberations that flood the room. And as the tempo increases each listener feels his pulse quicken. Each remains in silence even after the powerful music has ceased. Jephta hugs her father's legs while looking up into his eyes—kind eyes glinting under their dark bushy brows. Douglas looks up too, with eyes equally bright.

When the men return to their discussion, Jacqueline takes the three children into the nursery where Willi already entertains himself with wooden puzzles.

"Your boys show maturity," Piatigorsky says.

"Frieda's been teaching them piano. I've bid on a small Italo-Argentine, quarter size—they are almost ready to begin."

"Yes, yes. Age seven, my first cello. Before that Father taught me on piano and violin."

Peter speaks boldly. "We're intent on establishing ourselves as a Music Conservatory in Elizabethtown.

Piatigorsky listens, his expression gentle, his eyes intense. And then, in his heavily accented way, he speaks of his mission: to show the beauty and nobility of the cello worldwide, to increase the repertoire for cello, to teach serious students.

Peter continues insistently. "*My* mission is to establish Stoya Conservatory for strings—right here, Grisha. I almost purchased the old Millholland Lodge, a perfect site. Been vacant for years. Do you know the place, just outside town? Frieda had cold feet. We chose instead to remodel a stone house with excellent acoustics."

Piatigorsky puffs on his pipe only to find it has gone out. "You know Galamian? Violinist, master teacher in New York? This man declares he'll be the finest instructor of stringed instruments in the USA! Some co-incidence, Stoya. This man's also looking to teach right here, here in Elizabethtown. Summer camp, you see." Piatigorsky then sows humilia-tion. "This Ivan Galamian, he might be needing your assistance."

"Really?" Stoya gulps, trying to be nonchalant. *Galamian trespass-ing on my territory?*

Gregor goes on to explain. "Ivan's given up the stage. Nerves and health, you see. And of course, fondness for teaching."

The descent from *Windy Cliff* offers Peter Stoya a spectacular view. There below, the Boquet River flows in multiple rivulets. Beyond, the river farmland hints at green. Spring's declaration of intent. Even so, the bu-colic scenery can't quiet the man's mind. This visit was meant to impress Piatigorsky. Now Peter's questioning his next tack. What the Devil? *Should I try to compete with Galamian or try to join him?*

Look at Frieda's body language—dozens of negative gestures. She listens as Peter's enthusiasm spends itself and dwindles. She dislikes his notion of collaborating with this Galamian. A man already famous; why would he be open to Peter's overtures anyway? No! What of their own plans for a conservatory? Remodeling the rooms along the hallway into practice rooms, purchasing a spinet or two. "The Stoya name must stand foremost and alone."

[27]

Late May 1942

PETER LIFTS THE golden violin from its case. "My winning bid stole this beauty—oh, not so high as to be stupid, Frieda. Willi and Douglas can take turns on it and inspire one another." His patronizing tone suggests he is rationalizing the expenditure. "It's a quarter-sized Italo-Argentine violin, built in 1919; not factory-made. His voice fairly lilts. "When they outgrow it, I'll trade for a half-sized one, and so on!"

Peter had shopped for yellow tulips before departing the City. Mrs. Piano Teacher had accepted the offering with a kiss. She hadn't argued about the extravagance of the small violin, then. While rinsing and chopping cabbage, however, she grouses to LuLu about the expense, thinking of the furniture they still lack. Empathetic female, Frieda's savior in this household of strong-willed males, gives her a hug.

[28]

AS PIATIGORSKY PREDICTED, Galamian decides to offer summer lessons to his students in Elizabethtown—serious students of Juilliard who typically regress during summer vacation. "Get them away from the city. They'll improve sevenfold in my intense seven-week course," he explains. He rents an apartment for his wife and himself and asks around for student lodging. Piatigorsky has a few cottages to rent at *Windy Cliff.* He suggests asking Peter Stoya, who has suitable lodging and practice space in his Conservatory.

Stoya, eager for any benefit, agrees to house the students, and to make himself available as Proctor while the teens practice their mandatory hours. When Galamian teaches, Stoya listens. Without comment he makes note of assignments. He overhears again and again two basic principles, these delivered in a heavy Russian accent. "More bow!" Galamian says. "Play so that the last person in the last row of the hall can hear you!"

Much to his dismay, Stoya finds that he reveres Ivan Galamian. The man. The teacher. He also imagines financial benefit. Galamian and Piatigorsky attract many musicians—a gregarious bunch who share parties and musical collaborations. Peter hopes to be included; perhaps his Berlin knack for politicking will garner invitations to participate in chamber music performances. Frieda privately takes credit for being in the right place. Westport/Elizabethtown.

After the first week of monitoring restless teenagers, Peter becomes irritable. Here he is assisting Galamian, just as Piatigorsky had suggested. The seeds of humiliation have sprouted. How to compete? No answer blossoms. A resolve is made. *Stay focused on the Stoya name while you take advantage of this organized expert's trust.*

Douglas is allowed to spend a week of overnights at the Conservatory. Willi had begged, knowing it was more fun to snoop with a buddy. Oh, these *glamorous* teenage musicians, Douglas thinks. Some students desert early and return late with tales of skinny-dipping in the river's pools and sunbathing at the falls. Intrigued by such stories Douglas and Willi prowl along the hall and sit outside rooms where couples giggle engagingly. If Frieda catches the young detectives, she shoos them away with a reprimand. At night the boys hang out the window, eager for sounds of whatever misbehavior is in progress.

Several times weekly Stoya and Ivan Galamian play chess—after the students have settled for evening practice. Out comes the vodka. "One glass is good," the teachers say as they raise their glasses. "Two is better; and three is not enough." His tongue loosened, Stoya reveals to Galamian that students have begun to disappear after breakfast, their instruments untouched during the required four hours. "Practice-schmactice, my friend. Flirting upstages industry."

Ivan strokes his dark curls, raises his expressive semicircle eyebrows. "Not to say summer music camp isn't a grand idea," he says slowly. "Hmm. One problem. Housing in town provides too many distractions. Isolation from such disturbances is vital."

[29]

ELIZABETHTOWN BURGEONS WITH the perfume of flowers. And grows dense with aspiration. The Professor's fervor for prestige mushrooms in the shade. Douglas' craving to play a certain violin overflows his capacity like water rushing over its boundaries.

The 253-1, quavers. {Have patience| see| Someone has appeared| He prepares to train you| Our time of fulfillment is approaching| So it is| It is| |

ONTARIO, CANADA

[30]

January 1954

THERE IN the unforeseeable future Gateau asks Douglas about significant moments in his youth. An inciting experience? He recalls the intermix of voices from Galamian's serious violinists who practiced late into the night. Oh, the rapture. Akin to absorbing harmonies that flew on invisible wings beneath the jeweled canopy of night, circling the strangers' enclave, crossing the river, and soaring into his childhood bedroom.

ELIZABETHTOWN, NEW YORK

[31]

September 1942

PETER BUBBLES with cheer. Galamian and his students have decamped, leaving behind zephyrs of inspiration. "You are old enough to begin violin lessons with me!" Professor Stoya announces to Willi and Douglas. He unwraps a small violin that glistens like buttered toast. "This is the only violin you are allowed to play. And only under my supervision! If you so much as touch either of my adult violins I will know. So much as one finger, I tell you, and you better believe all hell-schmell will burst loose on your scrawny butts."

Willi and Douglas have heard a variation of the deterrent regularly. This time the Professor's hoarse whisper threatens mercilessly. Yes, both larger violins are off limits. Only the Professor may handle either one. Douglas has been mature enough to obey since the first warning—the day he relinquished the abandoned violin into the tyrant's keeping. If Douglas even so much as fantasizes plucking 253-1's forbidden strings the unknown horror of Stoya's hell jolts him into submission.

And so it is that the two red violins lie within the boys' reach, yet untouchable, sometimes wrapped in green silk, sometimes exposed to daylight. More often, especially when other students occupy the music room, the stringed instruments nestle in the velvet of their closed and latched cases, out of sight.

Although the small Italo-Argentine violin is quite capable of resonant tones, screeches, scratches, and thin whines are heard in Conservatory. The boys practice in the library where the Professor reclines in his easy chair, coaching and deflecting sloppiness lest it become habit. First one boy performs and then the other. Scales and chords up and down until the little fingers fail from exhaustion.

One day Stoya drills the students. "You must learn to correctly speak of a violin's anatomy! None of these parts are you to monkey with!" The Professor is seated on the hassock holding the Italo-Argentine like a gift from the stork.

> Stoya (pointing as he speaks)
> The body—the back, and the belly with its F-holes.
> Ribs with their waist called C-bouts.
> Perfling, decorative yet functional strips of wood along all the edges.

Bottom button, tail piece, ebony fingerboard over which four strings float.

Two-footed bridge carrying the strings to the neck, nut, and the fine tuners.

Peg box and four tuning pegs.

The neck finishes here with the hand-carved scroll, the violin's head.

"The scroll is the flower part at the end, right?" Douglas asks. He presses his small body against the man's side; he can't get close enough to the instrument.

Willi sits cross-legged, his chin in his hands. Mrs. Piano Teacher thinks, *Willi's behaving!* LuLu observes, *Willi's bored.*

Stoya (continues)
What you can't easily see is Inside. The maker's label, the bass bar, and sound post.

"What is this violin's name?" asks Douglas.

"The Practice Violin. It's to be used *only under my supervision!*"

* * *

IN TIME THE students graduate to Bach's Minuet in G. "The tempo is marked Moderato," the Professor explains, pointing to a word above the lines. "That's for later. You will begin very, very slowly until you have mastered the notes and the timing." Precise execution of this short piece seems impossible to Douglas. His playing hurts his ears; Willi's does too.

One evening Douglas watches as Professor Stoya demonstrates a lesson on the 253-1. "Watch carefully how my fingers step along the finger board," he says. His fingers press strings along the narrow black surface as he draws the bow back and forth. "The touch of a finger will stop the strings' sound, do you see? Now the bow will make the violin strings vibrate and sing, again." Magic Muriel 253-1 cooperates, her voice lilting, lifting, and permeating the air.

The Professor's adult fingers climb like spiders, knowing exactly where to roam. His hands fairly burst from rolled-back cuffs of his starched shirt. Coarse hair sprouts there on the tops of his hands and on the sections of his fingers between the wrinkly bending places. Sister Elder says *knuckles* is the word for finger places that bend like knees. "Knees on legs," she says. "Knuckles on fingers." Douglas observes that Sister Elder and Sister Peace have no hair growing on the smoothness of their hands and long white fingers. Boys grow to be men. Not ladies. And he imagines with proud anticipation the time when hair will be sprouting from his own fingers, and nostrils, and upper lip. And the time when he will command the violin, *his* striped violin, like a man.

[32]

"TIME TO COME home. Blizzard soon!" Sister Peace hollers. She's instantly suffused by mist, just like the dairy horse, pre-dawn. She adjusts the collar worn over her woolen coat, silver fox fur, the color of today's sky. The nanny calls out again, insistent. The boys leave the hill, reluctant, dragging their sleds. Douglas follows the path of Tatiana's footprints. Here and there ice lies hidden by fresh snowfall, somehow powerless to upend an adult as nimble as she has become—a figure levitating over the lumps and bumps. In contrast he treads with caution, avoiding an accident. Yesterday he fell on a slippery place. He hurt his elbow, eliciting laughter from James and John. Memory of pain provokes him to catch up with Sister Peace; he wants to ask a rude question.

Huffing. "You don't walk *funny* anymore. What was wrong with you before?"

She. Matter of fact. "An accident. Broken bone in leg. Doctors say I never dance again."

He. Curious. "That's when you came to the Home?"

With affection. "Yes, here to heal. And make new family. You just having sixth birthday."

Excited. Cautiously taking each step. "Now you can jump and run and skip, just like me and other kids!"

Her next words are lost to a boy who is not keeping up. "Body can heal, Dougie. Maybe not heal up just like before. Still, can be okay."

"So, can you dance now?"

"I limber up on all days. Maybe I can dance again."

What to do with this information? Douglas turns his attention to movement ahead. Up there. On a hillock. The farmer's dog is circling a small deer. Are they *playing*? Sister Peace tries in vain to scurry the boys along, her energy pounding. James, John, Douglas stop. Three boys freeze in place, mesmerized by impending drama. The deer, foot-bound by heavy snow, can't kick in defense. Can't run. The dog, jumping, barking, circling, finds advantage, lunges for the throat. In seconds the fawn lies helpless, neck and legs at strange angles. And the dog? The dog, unsure of this result, cavorts around the fallen prey.

Later, Astrid is tugging off Douglas' hat and mittens, which are frozen stiff. "Boots off, boots off," she's telling the boys. "Mail for you, Tatiana."

Douglas feels Sister Peace's energy, a slow whir as she scurries through the mud-laundry room. He follows her, barefoot, past the icebox, past the butcher block table, past the breakfront with the candelabra and stubby ivory candles, into the parlor. Now she spies the entry table. She picks up a PAR AVION envelope—it's been positioned prominently in the polished tray—and she disappears into her room. Sister Peace can be heard crying in her room.

"Is Sister Peace crying because of her blue letter, Astrid?"

No answer. Her earrings spark like cool flame set against the coil of moonglow braids. Astrid begins rubbing his stiff-blue-white fingers. Very rapidly. "Your frozen violin fingers," she says.

"Then is it because of that cruel dog?"

"Animals are not usually cruel, Douglas. They behave on instinct. Humans have instinct too. Difference is we do have choice. We humans have kindness built into our hearts. We can choose to perform cruel acts instead of kind ones. When we are cruel, we wound others, and we wound ourselves too."

"Oh."

Astrid's energy sustains a fervent thrum as she tends his tingling fingers. "Another way to say it, Douglas. Feelings of tenderness come to us naturally. Like fear. Except if a person has been wounded too much, an act of natural kindness might be blocked. Then that person needs much kindness in order to be healed."

That night Douglas jolts awake. *A dream?* An animal had his leg in its teeth, sharp-sharp-sharp like an icepick. He was in pain, all alone, all alone and lost in a haunting gray landscape.

Outside the blizzard rages, hurls, lavishes snow, down-down-down upon Elizabethtown.

[33]

PROFESSOR STOYA STIFFENS with irritation. Oh, this prolonged session of coaching Douglas on a pizzicato technique. "Alternate between pluck-ing with your first and second fingers," he instructs, demonstrating on the Performance Violin.

Douglas switches from using one finger only of his right hand to attempting the motion with two. Again, and again he plucks, more dili-gently each time. Even with continued effort he fails to pick up speed. He grows sweaty and anxious because he's unable to demonstrate the skill. A quick look at Stoya's face, and a quick glance at the blisters forming on his fingers—a pause long enough to anger the demanding man.

"Blisters-schmlisters!" Stoya growls.

"I don't mind getting blisters, honest," Douglas says, searching the eyes of his instructor.

No signs of encouragement are given.

"Wilhelm, over here, son," the Professor says gruffly.

Willi laughs out loud as if not hearing his father's command. "Big fat robin. Tugging worms. Ye-uck. He eats them too!"

Despite his petulance Professor Stoya understands the futility of insisting on this May afternoon. Besides, he can't endure the failed attempt much longer.

Mrs. Piano Teacher, while reading Agatha Christie's *Death on the Nile*, has been listening to the threesome. "Peter, a kind word helps."

"I will not habituate a student to soliciting praise, that canker of insecurity."

"Perhaps the park instead of the pizzicato?" She's using a question as a suggestion, an annoying tactic of hers; today he accepts her lead. She, the handler, transforming a rabid dog into a powder-puff poodle.

Geduld, patience. Peter calms with thoughts of youthful summer days spent exploring the Black Forest of Germany with Opa. The enormity of the stand, the dark mystery, the ring of birdcall. This sylvan wonder lingers in his adult heart. If Willi and the Performance Violin are to thrill the world maybe Willi needs to experience awe. Douglas already on the *qui vive* must come along—this orphan, the flint.

They've driven to a site in the Adirondack Mountains where the clear waters cascade through groves of hemlock and aspen. Douglas breaks into a run, hearing the downfall ahead. It's a tricky climb even for the youngsters. Peter is out of breath, hands on his hips, when he finally reaches the top. White water, swollen with spring rainfall, comes rushing past and over the edge. Mist envelopes the expanse. Three viewers stand as unidentifiable as one tree trunk from another.

Willi whistles. "Geez, a giant faucet."

Listen. The almighty rush-hush of air and water as the falls plunge through a steep, rocky ravine. The torrential symphony overpowers Douglas; his ears require all other sounds to relinquish their hold. This spectacle, like no musical instrument, holds a continuous decibel unending. Douglas inches closer to the edge. He feels a bit woozy looking down; the falls form an intermediate pool and then drop into another cascade, forming a deep emerald-green pool far, far below.

Spray mists his face; Douglas sticks out his tongue to taste the drops. A hypnotic suggestion hovers like a whispering specter. *Join, join the water and wind. Be part of something far grander than yourself.*

Sister Elder calls this place Lover's Leap. He sees how certain urges could drive a person to take the leap. It could be glorious to exist in the violent down-rush of white water and sound. Douglas' euphoria builds.

Stoya regains his composure. He directs Willi downward. Only when he takes Douglas by the shoulder can he interrupt the mesmerizing effect. The three pick their way through rock and winter debris. Douglas hears the fall's music change as they descend. The rush is gradually being replaced by pure percussion as water strikes rock, pummeling the mid-level with such rapidity the boy is unable to count a meter.

At the base, the emerald pool they viewed from above stretches broadly, its surface bright with ripples. Douglas recognizes it. This is the swimming spot Sister Elder warns him of.

"'Teenager Missing.'" Last year she had read a headline aloud. "'Accident or suicide uncertain. No body found yet, only shoes.'" The article explained the danger of Split Rock Falls. Sister Elder had continued: "'The danger lies in the bounding ledges and dark hiding places where current clutches, where trout and unlucky divers alike hide in shadow."'

How can something so dangerous be so inviting? Douglas wonders, shaken by the reality.

[34]

TREE TRUNKS ARE blackened by rain, yellow green leaves twist turning upward, becoming silvery to match the sky. One robin alights on an empty nest wedged in the crotch of narrow branches. The breeze sifts and sighs as if school will never finish, nor summer arrive.

Violette's lesson is underway in the salon. Her striped umbrella sits in the entryway vase. Douglas' heart bounces like a marionette on strings as she plays Liszt's *En Rêve*. He lingers, listening to the rolling harmony. Mrs. Piano Teacher is clapping her hands, asking Violette for refinement of right-hand trills.

In the first practice room Willi halfheartedly runs through a Franz Wohlfahrt Etude; he's using the quarter-size Italo-Argentine. Douglas takes the second practice room. Soon he's polishing the same Etude. He uses a lesser instrument, one Professor Stoya has recently purchased and assigns to him.

A bit later, as is his habit, the Professor listens, unseen. His face gains color ripening like a cherry. He yanks open the door, charges into the first practice room. Look, Willi is flipping a page of *Superman*; the comic book dominates the music stand.

"You! Missing the half step. Again, and again! You practice mistakes, do you? Listen, I'll show you." The assertive teacher wads up the comic book.

"I know how, I know how."

"Ignoramus, you know already, then do!"

Willi fails to perform the passage as his father expects. The boy cowers, anticipating an outburst. Stoya does not disappoint in this regard. An outburst it is. "Douglas, come in here this moment!"

Douglas approaches hesitantly. Stoya hurries him along, drags him into Willi's practice room. The two boys are eye to eye. "This boy here, the boy in front of you, son, he uses his brain. While you get stupid!" Stoya raps Douglas' temple as he speaks. "*Danke*, Douglas, now show Wilhelm Stoya how to play these difficult-schmifficult measures." Then the father hisses under his breath, "Lord deliver me from such laziness."

Douglas obliges the Professor with the assigned measures, despite his discomfort. The Professor notes how this boy—who was once mute, for heaven's sake—can follow inarticulate guidance. While Willi is wide-mouthed, uncomprehending, fixed on the exterior habits of playing.

"Willi, my son, lazy-brain, burro, donkey-boy." And then in high pitched anger, "You read your comic books?! You pay better attention to your baseball?! You rather play ball, or you rather play music to impress the world? You cannot do both." Stoya grips the Italo-Argentine by the neck and shakes it at the boys. "This wood, this violin made of wood, can tell stories to stir men's souls. You prefer comics? You prefer *thud?*"

From blue to purple, the Professor's eyes grow darker like clouds before a hailstorm. Becoming blacker yet, and smaller. Douglas thinks this angry man's eyes resemble the buttons on Sister Elder's shoes; he keeps very, very quiet.

Mrs. Piano Teacher interrupts. "Ten minutes, Peter, until your next student, or I should take him?"

[35]

AND SUDDENLY A year has passed with only minor complaints to recall. Perhaps by braving these trivial woes one builds strength for misfortunes when they intrude.

As Willi steps forward older celebrated violinists are his competition. Even so, these stars will give way in time. Jascha Heifetz, Nathan Milstein, Isaac Stern, Zino Francescatti, Arthur Grumiaux, Yehudi Menuhin, each one will have his glory and then leave the endless grind of concertizing. It's an unforgiving world, that of the virtuoso violinist. Peter Stoya never got a foothold. But let's don't go there.

To compensate for what he lacked this father intensifies his firstborn's musical exposure. Willi is taken to concerts in New York City. Attends symphonies (first with Bruno Walter and then Leonard Bernstein conducting), listens to chamber music and soloists. The highlight of which this year is Yehudi Menuhin performing Bartok's commissioned Sonata for Solo Violin.

It's said that from every generation comes a prodigy. In Peter Stoya's generation it is Yehudi Menuhin, born in 1916. For those born in the 1930s it will not be Willi or even Douglas, rather a boy a year shy of their age named Michael Rabin. It's he who will win over audiences, appearing in double-breasted jacket with silk necktie. At age seven Michael had found a half-size violin and had fallen in love with it. Within months he had outgrown the tutelage of his father George, a performer with New York Philharmonic.

It's 1943. Stoya has yet to meet this larger-than-life talent.

[36]

STOYA GREETS SUMMER students in the rustic Milholland Lodge. They gather for the noon meal, hours of morning practice completed. He, Peter Stoya, had first conjured the dream for this site, *he* was the visionary. If you could see his aura today, you'd swear it was Red, Deep Red—no, perhaps Muddy Red. His vision? Well, he'd generously handed it over to Galamian. Remember when he'd brought Ivan with his wife on the picnic here? "The birch trees remind me of Russia," Ivan had said wistfully. "My motherland." *That had been the clincher.* Ivan had purchased the property. Ivan Galamian lives the dream. Stoya enjoys a bittersweet sense of personal achievement with not a little envy nibbling the corners off his pride.

So begins the Meadowmount School of Music— Galamian had learned his lesson about needing to maintain constant oversight. The old Lodge, instead of housing scary creaks and moans, is filled with the sounds of violinists, both the professional and the desirous who are housed on the grounds. One notable exception: the youngest student at Meadowmount, Michael Rabin. His family is sheltering him, renting *Lilacs* just a few blocks past the Stoya Conservatory. Peter Stoya mulls this over. *The kid's a neighbor*! Begging a question. Could this prodigy boost his son's mettle? Or quash it?

With pride Stoya tackles a position at Meadowmount, the job of assistant Proctor. He takes turns with Galamian; each walks along the connected cabins, mornings from eight to twelve, enforcer of the strict code. When the Proctor discovers a student goofing off, he growls: if he finds one struggling, he attends to the difficulties with patience.

Stoya wonders if the camp philosophy is beneficial. Seven weeks of total immersion in the study of string instruments—enforced practice, lunch, private lessons, group playing, dinner, exhaustion, sleep. Repeat. For every student aglow he sees one mired in misery, hears one cursing inadequacies. Wilhelm and Douglas, only nine, are too young to participate. Should he plan to place his son under Galamian's control in the future? Stoya reserves his judgment on the matter.

After closing Meadowmount in August, Galamian celebrates with Stoya and Piatigorsky. Three glasses of vodka are not too many given such a promising first season. A bit later Peter capitulates to hostility. Unfocused at first. Although focused today. Look at his Frau, Mrs. Piano Teacher, in concentration at the piano; she prepares next week's lessons.

She marks the music, her eyebrows drawn straight across her forehead in an almost single line—a line she often amends with rapid nips of her tweezers. She, the mother of his *average* sons. Siggi carries the Stoya traits in his physicality, broad shoulders, rounded forehead, sturdy ribcage. Oh, the love of music is nowhere to be found in his soul. Willi in contrast is slight and long-limbed like his mother. He has the hands of a violinist, long fingers with strength and agility. What would it take to stir his soul for anything beyond mischief?

Now that one, that Douglas, that one without creditable heritage, he was born with innate musicality.

Frieda remarks to LuLu, "These two violinists behave like brothers." Neither comments that Douglas has a sensitive nature as compared to Willi's callous disposition. Nor do they mention Herr Stoya's touchiness.

[37]

WING HAS ONLY just arrived. He drops his duffel and calls out. "Anybody home?"

Astrid shuts off the mangle, leaves a bed sheet half-in, half-out, half-pressed, half-rumpled, adjusts her housedress, unties her apron. Her hair zigzags down her back like crimped silk as she approaches her husband. "Buppy!" Wing draws her close without hesitation. Then holds her at arm's length. Gazes at her. "My beautiful Astrid," he whispers before he draws her into another embrace. They head upstairs without explanation.

It seems to Douglas as if half the day has passed before Wing reappears. He wants to snuggle with the man. Decides he's too old for it. He asks a question hoping it will buy some fellowship. "What is war, Wing?"

The returned soldier takes the boy by the hand and leads him to the porch swing where they settle. "You just six and quiet child when I leave. Now, just turning nine, and look at you asking me adult questions."

"Tell me about war, Wing."

"War? Hard to explain to boy, anyhow I try. War is when men are fighting for a purpose. These men over here believe their purpose is correct purpose." Wing pats the left side of the swing. "These men over here believe different." Wing thumps the right side. "Groups can't find way to agree and each be happy with result. 'Let's fight it out,' they say. The winner is group that makes other group give up. Understand?"

Douglas does. It sounds like fighting with Willi who gets his way by giving the worst Indian burns.

Wing continues. "War is ugly. War is not always the right way."

Douglas imagines tiny soldiers on either side of him just waiting to fight. "Were you scared or angry in war?" Douglas asks, his brown eyes glinting green.

"Be big lie if I say no. Listen, I believe in what we are fighting for, so I try to be good sailor."

Douglas muses, wanting to extend the conversation. "Wing, did you know my violin doesn't get angry or scared?"

Wing scratches his dimpled chin. "Tell me, does Professor Stoya still keep the lost violin at his house?"

Douglas nods, silent for a spell. Then in a hushed tone he's laying his heart bare. "Wing, can you keep a secret? Don't tell *her*, Sister Elder, she gets *extremely cross*, if I talk about *you know what*. Violette uses the word *extremely*. She says it means really-really."

"Wing *extremely* good at keeping secrets inside. Go ahead. Share."

Douglas flushes. He's wanted someone to validate his experience besides Sister Peace. "My violin talks. Just not out loud. Not in words."

The boy covers his face with both hands. Wing nudges his shoulder, a signal to continue. "My violin told me her name. She's 253-1. She lets me call her Magic Muriel." Wing whistles softly. "And she's waiting for me to grow up."

"Really, not just boy's imagination?"

"Yeah, for real, Wing. Sometimes the Professor plays her. Not us. We're *forbidden*. Kids can't touch her. Not even one string. Or the Professor will know. Somehow. And he'll punish us."

Douglas may not confide such things with Sister Elder. Never mind the concealment, she is aware of his fantasy, thank you, and it perturbs her. Who can say how the circumstances of his secreted birth and those first unsettled months have affected him? Some children imagine characters and will act. Some children imagine scenarios and will write. Some imagine tunes and will compose. Take a child who imagines language spoken by a wooden object, a language by all accounts both silent and unintelligible to others, what will become of that child?

[38]

DOWN THE ROWS Miss Brown goes, pointing her chalk-dusted finger, quizzing one child at a time. "What is your father's profession? Where does he work? What is your hobby?"

Violette stands as directed, her blouse now un-tucked from her plaid skirt. She flips her ponytail over her shoulder and brushes away wisps of hair that cling to her face. She's flushed from playing racehorse at recess. "My father was a National Guard. An extremely brave man. Leroy Jean Dupont. The army sent him to Tunisia—that's in Africa. And he lost his life. That was last February when I was in third grade. Mom and I moved into the Smythe Hotel. An author lives at the Hotel too. Everyone says he doesn't like children. I'm an exception, you see; he reads to me. We're halfway into *Kidnapped*. Want Mom's profession? Hesitating, Violette looks at Miss Brown. "She does bookkeeping for attorneys and doctors." Violette bites her lip. Douglas senses her slow release of self-restraint. She straightens her shoulders, standing taller. "My hobby? Exploring the dictionary and the thesaurus. Words bring gratification to my brain. And I study piano playing and music theory too, while to be accurate I wouldn't term musicianship a hobby."

Miss Brown smothers her amusement. Violette's answer is acknowledged with a request. "And will you share with your classmates a word you have learned, please?"

If your eyes were closed, you would think Violette was reading from a page in the thesaurus. Not the case. Look at her. Her eyes are focused on Douglas. And she manifests the nature of her chosen word. "*Benevolence*, noun. Synonyms—*kindness, tenderness, generosity, humanity.* Which recalls *felicity*. Want the antonyms?"

"That's quite enough for now. Thank you."

When called upon Willi turns to the class and spreads his arms like an evangelist. "My father is the great Professor Peter Stoya, famous violinist of the world. He teaches violin playing at our house, which he calls a Conservatory. And my hobby is baseball. Thank you very much." Willi bows. The boys guffaw. The girls glance around with silent smirks.

Douglas squirms like an upturned beetle; Miss Brown's finger is pointing at him. He speaks from his desk, too queasy to stand.

"Wing, he's my father." Classmates titter. "He mostly helps at the Home doing lots of things, except for Mondays he makes fortune cookies and dumplings at the Smythe Hotel."

"Now, Mr. Tryzyna. All spoofing must cease."

Violette attempts an explanation. Miss Brown shushes her.

"Well, he is the man who lives with us."

Miss Brown shakes her head. "No, Douglas."

"Okay, I'll say it's Professor Stoya."

Willi pipes up. "Yeah, Douglas and me, we're blood brothers. You can have Siggi."

"Enough! Your hobby, Mr. Tryzyna?"

Douglas feels all eyes upon him. Trapped like a linen gargoyle, looped and knotted into his desk with no escape. The prying interrogator stares insistently.

"I polish shoes. That's my hobby." It's a lie and he's aware of it. Fiery heat consumes him. He cautiously feels his nose, just in case it's growing.

Listen. The entire class is laughing as if he's a comedian. Douglas takes a mock bow just like Willi, much to the kids' continued delight.

* * *

"THEY LAUGHED AT me in class today," Douglas informs Sister Peace. She's on her knees weeding in the garden.

"Did they now, and do you know why?"

"Sure. I was being silly on purpose." His smile fades. "Tatiana, do I even have a father and a mother?"

Sister Peace drops her trowel; she's caught off guard. "Everybody does. Just how nature made it when male and female—"

"I know all that—don't tell me that! *Who* is my Mother?"

Sister Peace shoos a spider off her glove. "Not for me to say."

Douglas hurls a dirt clod across the yard. "Who can then?"

Sister Peace pulls off her gloves. She taps his head twice. "One day, plunk-plunk. Answer like fat raindrops, plunk-plunk into your brain."

"Next time it rains?" Douglas brightens at the thought.

"Mercy no, certainly whiskers will be growing on your face before answer sinks in."

The boy's frustration is patently evident. Instead of trying to soothe him Sister Peace stares into the distance. Cobble Hill stands unswerving in the clear October afternoon. *Who will be the one to break down and tell him?* she wonders.

That night a dream startles Douglas awake, or is it something he overheard? Is it true? Sister Elder and Sister Peace knew each other in the way long time ago, before he was born?

[39]

FRIEDA HAS DEMANDED it of Peter, and so Willi and Douglas' piano lessons continue. Not daily like violin lessons, instead twice monthly, always the two boys together, with practice and memorization required.

"Mrs. Piano Teacher, can we play this for you now? We've been practicing for an hour, already." Douglas is confident, eager to begin.

"We'll listen with the *piano's companion* keeping you honest. Willi, you go first. Douglas, set it to *Allegro* for him." Frieda's in her role of teacher, not mother right now.

As directed Douglas adjusts the weight on the metronome's pendulum; it swings back and forth with a repetitive click-clack. The small weight, shiny and gray, looks like a slug to Willi as it grips the ruler-like bar. The demanding teacher nods for him to begin Clementi Sonata in B flat Major. Willi has no choice except to cooperate.

The metronome continues steadily. Click-clack, click-clack, click-clack. It might as well be the Devil on Willi's left shoulder for all the rage it inspires in him. He loathes this wooden box shaped like an Egyptian pyramid. It's old, it came from Germany, and it's a torture machine. He'd like to hide the despicable key that winds up the contraption and allows its monotonous timekeeping. Back and forth the dingus goes, making it hard for him to concentrate. In the process of marking time, it accuses even the most conscientious student of ineptness. Such is the case with Willi's playing of the Sonata.

And then it is Douglas' turn. His attack is confident; his hands fly with passion along the keys. His body sways; he leans close to keys and away, enjoying the music's growing momentum. The bass notes pool like water. The staccatos are lively. His right-hand melody is dangerously close to being off the beat. Mrs. Piano Teacher discreetly stops the metronome; it makes no concession for Douglas' rubato. She listens with her eyes closed until the last chords resound.

Willi has fought for accuracy, and with no acknowledgment from his mother. In this situation a normal child would harbor antagonism toward his peer. In this moment Wilhelm's expression says it all. He has every reason to loathe Douglas. An upstart who has infiltrated his family. Has vied for his parents' attention. Attention, simple attention would be enough for Peter Stoya's firstborn.

As much as he might naysay, Willi does seek his father's approval, which is unconsciously given in physical gestures. Willi watches for these under a youthful guise of buffoonery and nonchalance.

Professor Stoya's nuances have significance when all three are offered in conjunction—chin jutted forward, eyelids aflutter, five fleshy fingertips pressed against five fleshy fingertips—gestures displayed at concerts, in the library, even last week while a disc spun 'round and 'round on the Victrola. "Nathan Milstein, listen and learn, son," his father had said. Painfully, this father paid such homage to that show-off Douglas.

[40]

PROFESSOR STOYA VISITS Florien Roux; trades in the small Italo-Argentine as he had planned; returns with an equally fine ½ size English instrument and a well-made bow. Jostling for practice time on the new English before and after dinner becomes the norm for Willi and Douglas.

These evenings the orphan sits at dinner with the Stoya family. He listens as the adults admonish childish rudeness—his own included. He develops a taste for cabbage. Red cabbage. Green cabbage. Cabbage prepared as sauerkraut or goulash. To be polite he chokes down Mrs. Piano Teacher's specialty, *Berlin-style liver,* shuddering with every bite despite the preparation's addition of mashed potatoes, fried onion, and baked apple. Willi gobbles his mother's concoction, while Siggi refuses it. Sharing family dynamics day after day eventually brings change. Douglas assumes he has parents and brothers without remembering otherwise.

* * *

IN TIME, BOTH ten-year-old students have become accustomed to the larger English violin. The fingerboard is just a bit longer although no heavier. One day while they wait for the Professor to begin their lesson, Willi whispers a secret to Douglas. "I played Pa's precious Performance Violin when he was on the pot yesterday! And he didn't even know it! He can't really tell!"

Douglas' eyes bug in astonishment.

"You're just joking me—"

"Am not, you little scaredy-cat!"

"Your Pa said if we ever—"

Willi cut him off. "If you tell on me, I'll say it was your idea and you did it first."

Little Siggi continues to race his metal cars in the adjacent library. He hears all. Current family dynamics direct him to a satisfying deed, a childish act with reverberating consequences.

"Siggi tattled," Mrs. Piano Teacher confides hesitantly as the Stoyas undress for bed. "He heard Willi boast to Douglas about touching your violin. Even so I'm afraid Douglas is not the guilty party in this...."

Professor Stoya's fury grows beyond even his wife's ability to conjure; his face flushed a frightening purplish red. Frieda, clutching her silk dressing robe, her chest heaving, watches her husband seethe, and pace, and pound. She's unable to utter so much as a pleading peep. She unwinds her chignon, hairpins clink into the crystal bowl. She's watching, waiting for the proper moment. She's unable to calm the beast in her husband this time.

The next day Professor Stoya stands the boys at attention and leans in. His bristly mustache threatening to scratch their soft cheeks, his in-your-face eyes ablaze. He pummels them with questions, observing that deepening his voice and slowing his speech raises ever higher anxiety in the delinquents.

"Pa, I would never do such a thing!" Willi's eyes widen with the acid burn of actual fear and feigned innocence.

Douglas denies the act boldly; he would *never-never-never* do such a thing. His piety confirms his guilt in Peter Stoya's mind.

Frieda holds Siggi close, her arms over his shoulders. Neither parent observes their younger son's smirk. However, his comment is heard by all. "Somebody's lying, somebody's nose will grow like Pinocchio's!"

A father chooses to ignore the smart aleck's assertion. And the offenders' denials. Professor Stoya brings forth his shaving strop; he intends no mere spanking with a paddle this time. He manhandles Douglas, clutching the back of his neck, shoving him aside. "You deserve this too, you sneak. You'll *both* learn to obey direct commands!" Every second torments Douglas. Willi wails, squalls, squeals, begs mercy. His father flogs and flogs the bared buttocks, unrelenting. Douglas cringing, grasping his belly, weeps, streams of saltiness running down his contorted face.

Seconds drag, they race, they multiply. The strop dangles, impotent. Willi falls to the floor, a puddle of dishonor, his vainglory in smithereens, unable to drag his pants over his angry striped flesh. He crawls away. Eyes and nose running.

LuLu tiptoes into the salon. She gasps at the scene; the soup tureen slips from her hands to the oak floor. Five sharp chunks of patterned china clatter, accenting the ordeal. "My Blue Willow," Frieda cries out, her concern split between the two extreme outcomes of tattling to Peter.

Stoya turns to the unpunished, the presumed offender, the strop in his hand set to whooshing, reinforcing the instructor's threat. "You'd better fly like the wind, Tryzyna, before I discredit my word to your Guardian and tan your hide too. You disobedient brat, you ungrateful liar. You thief. Go, go! Get out. You are not welcome here! Not anymore."

Professor Stoya winds the strop around his fist, angrier than when he had begun, and leaves each boy to sort out the misery. He falls into the wingback chair, his face as rosy as the welts on Willi's backside. His aura, if you observe such things, is certainly Black. In seconds LuLu reappears with a glass of water and half of a Lithium calming pill.

[41]

FOG MUTES THE sky; the sun has given up. Douglas runs, his boots crunching on the frosty earth. Behind him the birdbath holds only ice. In the bare garden there's no birdsong. All promise of joy withdrawn.

The cheated musician stumbles into the Home, incoherent and inconsolable. Nothing the adults can do will bring him to the dinner table. Not even Sister Peace can soothe his pain. Nothing Mildred can say will coax an explanation. After dinner James and John ignore him; he's just a kid with a pillow over his head. Such causal disregard is most skillfully displayed by older brothers; these battle through games of War, slapping cards on the table, gleefully vocal when an Ace overtakes a King.

The phone rings. Douglas hears Sister Elder's "Hello." Silence. More silence. And then the receiver bangs into the black, unsuspecting cradle. Within minutes footsteps proceed, polished button-up shoes click and thump toward the dorm. The door flies open. James and John turn to see an uncommon sight—their Guardian is perplexed. Her mouth a question mark. "Mrs. Piano Teacher on the phone just now. She says you are untrustworthy, and unwelcome, Douglas? She didn't explain. You come out from under that bedding, you sit up, collect yourself and join me on the sofa, and you will tell me what's going on...."

Sister Peace and Sister Elder question Douglas together. And separately. It's hard to understand the scenario he's describing. Douglas manages only a few words between sobs. "I'll never get to...never get to...never get her back."

Wing listens, upright as officer of the watch. Then without notice he surges through the parlor, ripping off his apron as he goes. Douglas has never seen the gentle man in such a rage; his round face contorts, his lips screw into a snarl. This kindly man who chuckles while he inks cartoon characters. Wing ignores Astrid, who blocks the front door, begging him to cool off. He pushes her aside. He flings the door open and leaves the Home with his hands balled into fists.

Douglas watches, shivering. Sister Peace holds onto him as if he too might dash away. He can feel the sharp comfort of her ribs and hip bones pressing into his back. He feels her shaking. Eyes filled with tears, he sees only Wing's gray trousers moving away, leg by leg.

Sister Elder turns him around. He looks up into her pale face. A single tear rolls down her cheek. He's never seen her cry. The fangs of some monster inside clutch his brain. And its jaws squeeze. He's upset everyone. Wails come unbidden from his mouth. The monster will not leave him alone.

After treating the accused with a calming bubble bath, the Sisters sense the enormity of the problem.

"Oh dear," they say privately to each other, clucking like the speckled hens at the egg farm. "Now what?"

Sister Elder cross-examines Douglas as she brusquely dries his hair. Perhaps he's fibbing to earn their sympathy—before an incriminating

story comes out. She's listened to excuses from many mischief-makers, li-
ars, and tattletales in her forty-five years. Douglas, obviously stricken by
an injustice, bears no resemblance to those rascals. She lifts his chin and
drills her eyes into his. "Can you hold your head up? Can you listen?"

He wipes his nose, he sniffles, his eyelashes glint rainbows.

"I believe that man has committed an egregious error. You. Just.
Wait. He'll be sorry before all is said and done!" Observe Hester Smythe,
bellicose.

Observe Sister Peace, naïve. She pats the violinist's cheeks while
searching his teary eyes. "Time will change all this—just takes little time.
You'll see."

If he believes the Sisters, his future still holds promise. What do
they know? His life, from here on, seems as gray as the cobweb strung
from light fixture to doorsill.

I'm untrustworthy, I'm untrustworthy, I'm untrustworthy, he thinks.
Sadly, one man's accusation influences a sensitive boy. He buries his explosive sobs under the blankets while the Sisters go about their business.
Tears eventually spent, Douglas stares at the shadow on the ceiling and
meditates on his doomed life. Eventually he determines the truth for himself. He is guilty. He's guilty, guilty, guilty. Hadn't he longed to touch the
untouchable? Not the forbidden Performance Violin, the other, his Magic
Muriel 253-1. An instrument equally forbidden to him. Hadn't he imagined setting her strings to quivering? Hadn't he pretended to drive his
bow across those strings and draw out her voice? Douglas continues to
ruminate on his punishment. Yes, he's just as guilty as Willi. Imagining a
forbidden act must count as a crime too. If this is true, then he must deserve the banishment.

Wing steps into the dorm, sits on the bed, shakes the boy's shoulder. He's calmer now. "Douglas? You hearing me?"

Douglas quiets his sobs. He rolls onto his back and looks up into the kind face.

"I think on this problem. Wisdom say, *When man angry he blow steam.* Professor hurting right now. We can't be blaming him, can we?"

Douglas wipes his nose on his sleeve. He's listening.

"Willi betrayed his trust. Right now, he wanting to believe that you the one who betray trust, not his own son. We can't change what happened. For me, my faith is you did not do wrong." He tugs the disconsolate child's ear. "Wisdom say, *Even upset Professor will be coming to senses.*"

⁜ ⁜ ⁜

DESPITE WHAT THE three adults think, when the Professor dismissed Douglas from violin lessons and contact with the 253-1, he plunged this longing boy into a void.

Magic Muriel 253-1 murmurs, repeatedly, albeit this comes across faintly at first. A dark soul may be difficult to reach. Patience may be required.

{For the joy of it| we may communicate as before| You must keep learning| keep learning| You will then become my *animatore*| in the fortuitous years that stretch before us| You following your path| and 253-1 fulfilling her purpose| As it is meant to be| |

"What's my path, what's your purpose? I don't understand."

{Douglas| in time you will grow to understand| and share| the purpose *of questo violino*| To speak it| sparking Compassion| Kindness| Joy| Thereby lifting hearts| especially those in Despair| |

[42]

FROST CLINGS TO the crab apple tree's branches and to each twisted young twig. It clings to porch rails, to shrubs, coating each upward irregular stem. Douglas thinks to tell Violette that Sister Elder calls the ice crystals rime and changes his mind. How can he face Violette? He helps Wing carry the fringed carpet, holds one end as Wing clips the other end to the clothesline. He's blinking back tears that freeze before they drip onto his cheeks. His boots crunch as he leaves the Home and trudges to school.

The crab apple tree's shadow spreads across the yard, simulating what is unseen, what lies buried underground. Similarly, Sister Elder's ire takes the form of outdoor housecleaning. She makes her way to the clothesline, her footprints creating a path of blue-gray indents. "This rug needs a beating," she tells Wing.

Within minutes she spies a car approaching. Stoya's Pontiac, all right, the only blue and tan four-door Torpedo in town. Sister Elder grips the rug beater like a weapon. "Harrumph, the audacity," she mutters. "Them? Here? With no warning, no invitation?" Hester wears a faded floral wrapper with a man's cardigan that almost hides her starched apron. Around her head, turban-style, a torn sheet. Nevertheless, she reacts to the imminent rendezvous with anger, not self-consciousness.

Professor Stoya parks the car. Mrs. Piano Teacher steps out, pulls herself into a regal posture. She minces along the slippery sidewalk, her black pocketbook swinging, her face a mask of self-righteousness.

Hester plants herself like a tree, possibly camouflaged by the patterned rug. Only then, when the unobservant, unwelcome guest waits on the porch does Douglas' Guardian call out. "If you're looking for me, Frieda, open your eyes."

Mrs. Piano Teacher pivots toward the voice, startled, composure lost for mere seconds. "I have something to say." Her face a fixed mask.

"Well, get right to the point, and then leave!"

Frieda collects herself. She pulls her camel cashmere coat more closely around her slight body. Tucks her pocketbook against her right side. Back down the steps she goes, halts on the sidewalk, not entering the gate nor crossing the grass toward Hester. "We have dismissed your orphan," she says. "I came here out of courtesy to tell you why."

"Courtesy has nothing to do with it." Sister Elder stands her ground, unconvinced that a single kind motive drives these musical thugs.

"I'm sorry to say Douglas disobeyed the rules the Professor so clearly laid out. Whatever Douglas may tell you, he regularly rummages through our possessions. He may be a thief in the making." Frieda's voice travels through the heavy air like a bullet. "We don't intend to wait out the full range of his bad inclinations." She elevates her chin as if the posturing adds insult. "This is the reason for his dismissal. Furthermore, Douglas is no longer welcome at the Conservatory."

Sister Elder flushes. Hormones, or outrage—who can tell with a woman of her age? Nevertheless, she negotiates like a lawyer. "We gave you the abandoned violin in good faith for years of lessons to come. Since you will not be upholding the agreement, we'll take back the instrument, today. Rest assured we'll pay something toward the four years you have so, so, *very* charitably given Douglas."

Mrs. Piano Teacher stares at this woman who dares to dispute the Stoya pronouncement. She shifts her pocketbook, holds it with both hands like a leather shield.

"Peter, Peter, come here!" She summons assistance without taking her eyes off Hester for one tiny second. Somehow her husband appears beside her before she can call his name a third time. Frieda sounds less the Queen than the Henchman as she asks Hester to repeat the counteroffer for her husband's benefit.

Hester shakes the carpet beater at Stoya. "We will pay toward your years of so-called teaching. And *you*, you, Professor Stoya, will return the violin to Douglas today. Don't pretend it's of any value."

Peter laughs. "You are the numbskull if you think I'll agree to that! Douglas broke-shmroke the generous agreement. So now you, you, Hester Smythe, have no say *whatsoever* about the arrangement. Get it?" He waits for a sign of weakness from her, a mother-figure called to the defense of her child. None will be forthcoming. Peter kicks the snow from his boot, eyes closed, thinking. And then as if required he adds an explanation. "The violin may be quite worthless. Nonetheless, other trustworthy students will be able use it. Yes, you see, for the elementary phases of instruction in my Conservatory."

Frieda croaks as if to alter her husband's decision; perhaps Sister Elder's offer of payment jingles enticingly. All the same Professor Peter Stoya is finished with the conversation. He tips his hat. Clutches at Mrs. Piano Teacher's elbow. They turn almost in unison toward the car.

Hester thwacks the Persian carpet, again and again and again. As temperatures increase one might mistake the sudden air currents for the Chinook itself. What just came over her? Her? Fighting for ownership of the rogue violin, and she the one, a handful of years ago, so hell-bent on getting it out of young Douglas' hands.

[43]

AS IF THE river halted its southern progress in mid-flow, ring upon ring of foam and debris are locked in place. One exact second in the river's life is frozen there for viewing. Sister Elder's voice plays in Douglas' mind, re-peating a rule. *Do not walk on the ice after Valentine's Day.* Well, rules aren't applying anymore. Not for him. He's followed Stoya's rules, hasn't he? And look at the result. He half hopes the ice will break and his tragic ending will make them all sorry. So very-very sorry afterward. He tiptoes to the frozen edge where tree trunks are encased, where bushes looking like upside-down brooms stand guard. The breeze freshens. An eerie groan escapes and continues, perhaps the combined warnings of ice, brush, trees. Douglas looks around. Death nudges him forward. He's near the hill where a dog killed a deer.

One step too far and the ice creaks. One more step, the ice groans, emits a sharp creak. Death encourages. Fear grabs hold. He tiptoes back to shore, flailing his arms like a frightened tightrope walker. Beneath the surface he can sense water coursing, snowmelt waiting to sweep him along. He shudders. What was he thinking? He's either a coward or a peabrain, or both. He's shivering, freezing. Once on shore he's pounding his hands on his thighs, which helps only a little. The truant adjusts his mitten, looks at his Mickey Mouse watch. School wouldn't be out yet, better wait, keep stomping around and try to keep warm before heading to the Home.

It's Willi who shows up. "You ditched again! I just knew where you'd go, stupid. You're in big trouble."

Douglas glares at this boy who was once his buddy. He removes his mittens and blows on his hands before he hurls out a question. "I suppose you ratted on me?"

"C'mon, I wouldn't rat you out."

"Bet you did! Us, blood-brothers? Nobody in class believed you."

"Wanna be blood-brothers? Like, make it really truly real?"

Experimentation follows. Self-inflicted wounds. Their secret vow.

Together they make their way beside the Boquet River, up the hill to the Home, Douglas limping along. Surely his feet have turned into grape popsicles.

Sister Elder regards Stoya's son, a preteen who looks innocent enough with his gangly arms and legs; he's removing his hat, revealing his stick-straight hair plastered to his forehead. She's frosty and unwelcoming, traits she has perfected. Hester Smythe jingles her keys like a jailkeeper. "Your uninvited presence here is most unexpected, Wilhelm. I suggest you run along now."

The truant flashes a compromised grin at Sister Elder, keeping his bloodied mitten in his pocket.

Willi protests, "Jeepers. Dougie and I were going to play."

"As if."

[44]

DOUGLAS CONTINUES TO ditch class after lunch, almost every day for five weeks. James and John make excuses for him. "He's sickly," they say to the teachers who inquire. Finally, the Principal calls Sister Elder and the confrontation begins. Douglas hangs his head. He won't talk about it. How can a boy of almost eleven describe his motivation?

He doesn't think to say that instead of pondering his science lesson he considers walking on the river half-hoping the spring ice won't hold. That instead of bullying him Willi loyally keeps his secret. That he feels a thrill challenging Sister Elder's dictates, and the school's rules. That the hum of the outdoors re-awakening brings him closer to the Magic Muriel 253-1. That instead of listening to a teacher he listens out here, free from walls and doors. That at the river's edge he hears wigglies slither as they navigate shallows to feed on mud. That water bubbles and curls around rock, emitting its own frothy music. That he attends to bird calls as shadows pass over, shadows of meadowlarks, hawks, or crows.

Sister Elder lays it out. "Disregard your responsibility and privileges will be withdrawn." Consequently, Douglas' privileges are withdrawn for a week. Each day becomes even drearier than the last without hope of regaining the violin, or freedom. And so, Sunday, the 24th of March dawns, Mildred's fourteenth birthday, the seventh tedious day for him with morning through afternoon spent alone. Five o'clock, playful sounds torture Douglas: laughing at dinner, opening of gifts, singing of songs, wishing on candles, delighting in chocolate cake, the making of taffy, the playing of games, the laughing, and more laughing. He's starved before Sister Peace brings him a tray of dinner—minus the chocolate cake and the laughter. Worse than dreary, this week. Grim.

Come bedtime, sleep evades Douglas, it scurries away like a mouse whose presence has been detected. James snores, a common occurrence; just why is it so annoying now? The prisoner kicks at his blankets, wrestles with his pillow. He can't stay in bed. The night clutches at him through the closed window. The darkness should warn him to stay indoors; instead it demands his presence outside.

Silent trespassing of stairs requires an acquired skill. Douglas is not as practiced as James claims to be. He tiptoes, slow-slow-slow, fearful each creak will awaken Sister Elder. Once in the yard he leaps like a fawn, one that could and should have escaped from a dog.

An unusual glow glimmers over Cobble Hill to the south. He's excited. *Cross the street, go to Little Bridge. A full moon will rise over Hurricane Mountain soon.* He waits, feeling jittery. The moon fails to appear, although the luminosity expands, reaching well above the mountaintops, filling the sky. He grips the bridge's rails in fascination, his bare feet gone numb despite the sharpness of its splintered planks. Beneath him the river sloshes noisily around rocks. If he looked down, he would see both foam and ripples reflecting a strange green-blue. He's looking up to see the colorful streak forming a coil, and he's disoriented. Dizzy, he's dizzy. The sky appears to be moving.

Sister Peace finds him there, still looking up, his face glowing green, as green as the sky where streamers of light fill the heavens.

Minutes later a ghostly glow sways left, then right. Back and forth it sways, undulating like a curtain in the wind.

Douglas feels as if to burst, here with Sister Peace, watching the sky while brilliant energy surges. Side by side, hand touching hand, they enter a rhapsodic space for unmeasured time.

Then darkness falls! Tentacles of fear sting as Douglas puzzles this spectacle. "Where did the lights go? Can't we bring them back?" Now his feet are cold, he feels the splinters, the river giggles, uncaring, running away as black as the newly inked sky.

"*Matushka!*" Sister Peace says, giggling as she twirls.

Douglas jumps up and down, wailing for a better explanation.

"Shh. No tears...no crying now."

Douglas sniffles as he looks up into her ecstatic face.

"Mother Nature, *Matushka*, gives us surprises. Surprise gifts, like the lights. We're feeling giddy. We're feeling newborn; this is called *awe*." Tatiana pauses; she's watching Douglas's reaction. He's thoughtful. Blinking back tears.

"*Matushka's* surprise gifts may quick-quick-disappear. But the feeling will stay inside. This is how our spirit grows to be strong for difficult times." Tatiana cups her hands, brings them close to her face, and blows, as if dispersing milkweed fluff. She breaks into a run and leaps, her arms extended skyward. "Come on," she calls, "come, come!" The two, so like in size, so instantly unfettered by troubles, bound across the field and the bridge toward home.

[45]

DOUGLAS ROLLS HIS shirtsleeves, baring winter-pale arms to sunshine. He pauses to observe fourth-graders playing hopscotch. He enjoys the metallic slither of chain, the rhythms of feet whether hesitant or decisive. He looks for Violette. These spring days she often gallops with her pals, their sashes untied and used like imaginary reins, white socks and polished boots defining them as racehorses. Today the girls pick clover, braiding the stems to form necklaces and wreaths. Ophelia Nolan, nicknamed Oh-No, holds a red clover under her chin. "Is there a rosy glow?" she asks. The others tilt their heads trying to catch a view of the coveted effect. Violette on hands and knees takes a closer view. "Yes, I can see it," she reports, "so Tommy *does* love you!" Each girl in turn continues with a red clover held just so under her chin. "What about me, what about me?"

Only girls practice this odd test of love, Douglas guesses, acting nonchalant.

"Somehow boys know when they're loved," Violette says.

Oh-No corrects her. "Mostly boys just know about ball games."

Violette's voice deepens. "Douglas knows I love him. And I know he mostly loves a violin."

Douglas absorbs Violette's oscillation, soft and steady as a kitten's purr; he flushes the same rosy hue a red clover offers on a spring day.

Willi runs past, followed by boys from Room 5. "Douglas, c'mon. Dodgeball!"

As the game progresses Douglas burns with new intentionality—he wants to be the last one left standing. He jumps sideways, skips, and side-steps, supremely confident.

And then it happens. The offending ball, forcefully thrown, blasts Douglas' shirt, arms, and neck. It passes as an accident. Willi drops back with a snarl. He knows the rules; if a ball is thrown and hits someone above the waist, the thrower must stop playing. Willi fumes. "Ah, shucks. Drat, just drat!"

Douglas' classmates know what's happened before he does. Willi besmirched the ball when it landed in the bushes; this insult was intentional. The gamers break position and chant. "Dog doo, dog doo, doogie-doogie dog doo, doogie-doogie. Doo doo Douglas!"

Willi doubles in a sidesplitting belly laugh. Violette, with flying hooves and reins, takes the inside track, and in overtaking Willi upends the bully face-first in a mud puddle.

Much later, no matter what the Nurse said to calm his ire, no matter how kindly Astrid undertook laundering the shameful shirt he handed over, all wadded in the brown paper bag boldly marked with his name, Douglas rages. How can something lovely coincide with something loathsome? Violette's proclamation of love has been diluted by Willi's hateful act of contempt.

Well, it wasn't the first prank. Nor is it to be the last. Wilhelm Stoya conspires to humiliate Douglas Tryzyna. "Doogie, Doogie, Doogie," Douglas' classmates taunt with distinct pleasure. The epithet sticks. For six more years, to be exact.

* * *

SLEEP BECOMES DIFFICULT for a boy who searches for music and loses his way, a boy who is sociable and attracts ridicule. One such night 253-1 communicates with Douglas in her private way.

{Free your mind and sleep| May our reality fill your dreams| Oh imagine it| someday we will set feet to dancing| we together as is our purpose| So it will be| |

"How can I imagine dancing?"

{You must feel your feet first| You must let them guide your body| Isn't that right| |

"I'm trying."

{Who would know it| so many| many forms of dance music| See| We might play each| Shall *questo violino* comfort you| with sensation of dance| |

"Yeah." This delivered by an irritated child.

In her wordless way 253-1 propels the rhythms of dance. {Cancan| Cakewalk| Cha-cha| Flamenco| Jig| Gigue| |

Her stirrings intrigue an impatient boy.

{Rumba| Allemande| Cakewalk| Macarena| Mambo| Quadrille| Tarantella| |

Motions soothe a yawning boy.

{Gavotte| Polonaise| Minuet| Bolero| Waltz| |

Vibrations cradle-rock a sleepy boy and so to slumber dreaming of loveliness while lullabies continue.

[46]

SOMETIMES DOUGLAS FINDS a tonic for his woes in the attic with Astrid and Wing. Wing opens a portfolio covered with paper—how deceiving, the print of bamboo stalk, a sepia image implying lyrical artwork within. Look inside. Giant lizards slither across skyscrapers. Darting tongues like snakes turn children into tiny, mechanized robbers. Birds with hooked beaks and lustrous plumage swoop up villains and drop them into pools of glue from whence they emerge like rubbery sculptures begging for help. Wing's imaginary characters are at once hilarious, enchanting, and disarming. Many evenings pass with Wing narrating their distracting adventures.

In contrast to Wing's fanciful distraction, Sister Elder takes a practical approach to set the boy right. Anyone could see that Douglas' indisposition requires a time-consuming distraction. "Douglas, maintaining my footwear is now your responsibility."

Douglas hangs his head, a normal reaction from a glum boy. A few years ago, Sister Elder insisted her wards have a work ethic. An authentic shoeshine kit served the purpose. The four kids polished their own boots. Now he has to polish hers?

Notice the kit. A painted box. Fitted out with compartments for storage, the top is surmounted with a cast iron star fixture. Long sides of the box, red. *Shine 5 Cents* in yellow lettering with green contour outlines. Profiles of a romantic couple painted in blue. A full moon gracing one side, a crescent moon on the other. Short sides painted green with white daisies in full bloom.

Follow the honored process: Remove debris. Apply shoe polish with a large brush; follow with a small round one for detail. Apply paste wax as a protective coat.

All of which allows time for Sister Elder to soliloquize filling the boy's mind with persuasions of her choosing. He may look tractable listening to her, knuckling down to the task. Never mind he fantasizes—he's captive in a cruel world where music is prohibited.

[47]

May Day Eve 1946

SISTER PEACE SCATTERS flowering boughs on the Home's doorstep, an honored ritual. "Witches are out and about on this night, Douglas," she explains. It's already too late, Douglas, thinks. Witches have already worked against me.

Last May Professor Stoya received a shock. And he wasn't alone. Piatigorsky telephoned to commiserate. Both men, naturalized U.S. citizens, had been drafted: Present yourself to the Board in seven days. The price of citizenship: protecting one's country in time of war. This obligation the immigrants had already accepted, albeit reluctantly, dreading the day they might face former countrymen and friends, weapon in hand. Mere days later news arrived bearing a reprieve for two adult musicians. Germany had surrendered to the Allies. (As the Russians invaded Berlin one significant piece of news did not reach Professor Stoya. And it's just as well.)

However, this May 1946, no reprieve appears for a miserable violin student minus music. *Reprieve*, one of Violette's favorite words.

II
TEMPTATION & INTENTION

"YOU WON'T LIKE her, Diva Evangeline, all highfalutin in her crepe silk."
Sister Elder leaves it at that as she and Wing prepare the guestroom. The
Murphy bed has been lowered. Sister Elder places a china cup with pencil,
fountain pen, and a bottle of Waterman's Violet ink on the desk. The low-
boy holds the blue lily Tiffany lamp from Sister Peace's room and a crystal
vase of fresh peonies.

Sister Elder has neither an ear for nor an interest in music, while
her blood-sister Evangeline Smythe Brody, now of Atlanta, lives and
breathes operatic overture. Their differences caused arguments when, as
young women, they parted ways in Europe, although both defied their father's directives. Years passed in mutual avoidance until an inheritance
left by the unexpected death of their parents forced communication.

Hester would say Evangeline was overly critical of her choices following the inheritance. The quips have been stored away in Hester's heart.
She can still hear the accusations.

> Evangeline (contralto roleplay as judge)
> Look at you. Thinking you could hostess a bed and breakfast
> without an ounce of sociability in your bones? Your first stupid
> decision! Now the second. Running an orphanage? You do real-
> ize you're wasting your inheritance and intelligence on four
> unappreciative brats.

Since Wing is gazing at her, his head tilted in anticipation, Sister
Elder equivocates. "To be fair, I haven't spent time with Evangeline for
years, not since her little stepson's tragedy. I offered comfort as one
would. Otherwise, we've kept it strictly business, she and I."

Wing listens expectantly. He arranges the matelassé spread.

"Evangeline's a widow, you know, Trenton a casualty of war. One hopes loss has enlightened her about family matters.

* * *

AN IMPOSING GUEST arrives at the Home on a Saturday, after attending to Opera Association business in the City and visiting with their sibling, Maureen.

Hester introduces the guest, Auntie Evangeline, who gathers the children, asking their names and ages as if they are auditioning for a party. Her persona seems to adore attention.

The sisters behave so differently, Douglas thinks. Sister Elder with her quiet, calm demeanor compared to this zestful lady. How strange, then, that they physically resemble each other—each with a long-legged, heavily bosomed stature and large head—like a queen, or an ice cream cone.

After Auntie Evangeline gets situated, she reappears, announcing with a great chuckle that she has loosened her corset to the last line of hooks and eyes. "Come, come, sit with me! Let's talk!"

Douglas sits as close to this sister's less-firmly bound body as she allows, comforted by her eloquent speech, her husky voice, and especially her deep-throated laugh. She seems to find the world endlessly amusing at a time when nothing can tease so much as a smile from him. Her dynamic energy slowly draws him out.

"I had a violin of my own," he volunteers.

Evangeline cocks her head like an alert owl.

Douglas stares at her, mesmerized by the crystals in her baroque earrings, which just then cast rainbow stripes across her chest and remind him of fairy dust. Once back in focus he begins his lament. "A nice man used to play that violin in the cemetery—you know, funerals. And in the market, mostly at the egg farm, though. One night there was a huge fire over there, over Little Bridge. I can show you where I found the violin. Want me to?"

"No, no. Off you go to fetch it instead. I must hear you perform!"

His voice drops to a whisper. "I can't have it anymore." He longs to expose his wounds to her kindness. He chokes; the explanation would be too painful. The rustle of fabric, the fragrance of roses, the proximity of her powdered face combine; he's embraced by this fleshy female creature who feels so unlike splinter-thin Sister Peace with her sharp edges.

Releasing him Evangeline fairly sings her words, *"I'll see to this."* And then dramatically, standing to straighten the wrinkles in her fuchsia dress, she adds, "Off with you now, Douglas. Pity for a child to linger indoors on such a *glorious* day."

With his departure an adult conversation begins. Auntie Evangeline, adamant. "Certainly, we can locate another instrument for the boy! And another teacher!"

Sister Elder, resolute. "This violin fetish simply does not serve him, don't you see?" And then she adds a dose of vinegar. "And what would you know of caring for children day after day, you with sixteen years of haughty disregard for my path?"

Evangeline isn't daunted by a peevish remark. She dilutes Hester's sourness with a rebuttal. "Perhaps you forget, I too cared for a child."

Douglas sits on the porch wishing the cheerful Auntie would come outside. He croons a song as he remembers it—a melody slicing evening air, crossing field and stream, music aimed like an arrow at his heart.

Evangeline and Hester suspend their dispute, halted by Douglas' sweet voice. Evangeline hatches an idea. Why not use Douglas' versatile musicality to draw his passion toward hers? To opera! Who better to teach the child than her? And how better to reframe a shaky relationship with Hester?

The plot evolves into a conspiracy between the Smythe sisters. Each has something to gain.

ATLANTA, GEORGIA

[2]

June 1946

IT WOULD BE difficult to dissuade Auntie Evangeline, who's rushing at him like a bucket brigade to a fire, overflowing with one intention: Given his focus, given his trained ear, given seven and one-half weeks, she'll save him by dousing one fire. And lighting another.

The Estate appears as they circle a gravel drive: rose gardens, weeping willows, camellia bushes, and flanked by guardian magnolia trees, the white antebellum with its wrap-around verandah—his home for the summer. All in contrast to Elizabethtown, all in service to Sister Elder's exhortation: "A boy-o with adversity shouldn't fritter away opportunity."

"Here is it then," Evangeline trills.

There to meet the car, a couple, husband and wife, each wearing a gray uniform. "Please meet Douglas Tryzyna," Evangeline says, holding the boy squarely by the shoulders. "How do," the duo says in unison.

"Meet Jeffers and Sunshine," says Auntie Evangeline. "Their families have lived on this land since the shameful time of slavery. They are my trusted employees. They take care of me, and they take care of my estate. Invaluable."

"Pleased to meet you," says Douglas, who has been coached on southern etiquette during the drive.

Jeffers takes Douglas' suitcase and heads indoors. Sunshine mentions the fresh refreshments she's placed on the verandah for them.

After the pleasure of shortbread cookies and fresh iced lemonade, leg stretching suits a traveler. "Off with you! Go explore the grounds. And

Douglas? Two restrictions I mean to enforce. One, don't go into the cemetery. Two, stay clear of the old well. Understood?" She drills his eyes with her own, eyes strangely enlarged by tiny round glasses. "And tomorrow we begin singing lessons. Six days a week, two times daily. Off with you!"

And so it begins, the crossfire of single-mindedness between a childless mother, young enough to encourage without impatience, and pressed to her bosom, a motherless child, old enough to nurse a desire without distraction. The setting, a magnificent drawing room with pastel pink walls, crown molding, crystal chandelier, Persian carpet, floor-to-ceiling windows open to the morning breeze—cool air inflating and shrinking sheer curtains. Auntie Evangeline plays the phrase her pupil must sing. The chestnut piano's intricate carving fascinates the boy. One might wonder why the teacher allows her student to lie on the floor. Does she know he's studying the rosettes and whorls framing the keyboard and turned legs? That the keys when struck by her fingers produce a rippling quality? Recalling Violette. After horizontal listening Douglas can vocalize the selection. His instructor praises him. "Perfect pitch," she says, "and you keep the meter too."

Douglas grows increasingly eager for Auntie's smile, her clucking, her husky laughter. In his free time he sings right out loud, not embarrassed, almost smug with the sounds he can make.

Although the violin's frequencies accompanied Douglas during his travel, they have slowed. Lately, 253-1 simply repeats her name. Soon Douglas squelches reception. Life is lovely here without chores. Or criticism. Or competition. Or memories. Douglas submerges Elizabethtown's injustices, trapping them in a pool of shadows.

* * *

"HASTE, HASTE, WE must, a month has passed," Auntie Evangeline says one morning. "Which reminds me, have you written a letter home? Hester will think me rude for overlooking your report."

Douglas unfolds a crumpled piece of Evangeline's monogrammed linen stationery. "Want to read it?"

> Dear Sister Elder,
>
> I like it here ok. I think your Sister is very nice because she talks to me after dinner and she lets me light her cigarette, also I'm doing good at her Opera lessons. I think her drowned boy is still in the well. I heard him for real once. And I couldn't find his stone in the graveyard. Say Howdy to Wing and Astrid and Mildred and James and John. Is Sister Peace being happy? I'll be ELEVEN years old soon. I'm sure to have birthday cake here. Sunshine bakes all the time. Anyhow. I wouldn't mind having another one when I get back home!!!
>
> From me, Douglas

While Auntie Evangeline reads, she's smiling and then she's frowning. "My-my-my." When she takes the boy by the shoulder, her nails dig. "Fair warning. You, young whippersnapper, stop poking around the well and the cemetery!"

No sooner has she withdrawn the painful clutch of fingernails and reprimand than she launches into pleasure. "Let's get started. I have a *fabulous* song in mind. Adapted to your vocal range." Into the drawing room he skips, assured of regaining her favor. What a novel experience, this comfort of being talented enough.

* * *

ONE STEAMY AFTERNOON, as Douglas savors his daily treat, Coca-Cola sipped through a straw from a perspiring blue-green bottle—lid expertly removed using the iron opener fastened on the wall beside the Frigid-aire—Auntie Evangeline begins conversation.

"To be perfectly honest," she's saying, stopping to sip her mint ju-lep through a narrow silver straw, "I had a very short career, and I was not actually a Diva."

Startled, Douglas drops the Coca-Cola bottle, then catches it be-tween his knees. She doesn't notice his near accident. "I performed in regional opera companies only—proudly, mind you. After those few years I began teaching. Not performing.

"You see, our passion for music can be fulfilled, perhaps not the way we imagine it at first. For instance, your passion began with violin. I'm saying your voice cannot be denied you...stolen like a violin. Your voice: once yours, always yours, if you care for it. Think about what I am offering you."

A stubborn pleasure flares. He won't tell her just yet how much he adores her attention. They sit side by side on the veranda in the wicker peacock-back chairs, breathing in the fragrance of camellias and magno-lias, listening to the buzz of honeybees.

A realization flowers. How self-centered he's been. "Auntie Evange-line, did you ever have children?"

Auntie's prolonged silence grows uncomfortable. Maybe she's go-ing to ignore his question. Douglas finishes his cola; he rocks from foot to foot tentatively.

"About children," Evangeline starts, placing a title on the chapter. "My late husband had a son. We lost Trenton Jr. many years ago. He met his untimely death in the rose garden. Straying from his nursemaid's care, going where he oughtn't. Fell into the well. Where you, Douglas, are not ever, ever to play again."

Douglas gives her a sidelong glance; her face is unbearably sad. Trenton's plight throws him into contemplation. *How deep was it, did he drown, how did they get him out? I shouldn't ask.* He drapes himself around the opera singer's neck, giving her the kindest hug he can manage. "How old was he?"

"Just a tyke, not even four years. My, oh my, he was keen, an observer of things we adults overlook."

Auntie Evangeline reaches into a slim silver box, its lid bearing a fancy engraved initial. She withdraws her *afternoon* cigarette and holds it elegantly between two fingers. She motions for assistance with her late husband's lighter. Douglas proceeds as she's demonstrated. Flame ignites paper and tobacco, not to mention his pride. Gradually the ash glows like a firefly, growing long, longer, breaking off, falling to the ledge of an opera singer's bosom.

She speaks softly. "Dear God, why is it always the dreamers?"

"Is it very, very hard to be a mother?" he asks, matching her tone.

"I should say. Mothers must balance, juggle to keep the household on an even keel. Mothers must be strong and unselfish. A mother will have her heart broken likely as not. Children are a treasure, though."

"Would I recognize my mother if I met her?"

"How am I to know? Do you think you would, Douglas?"

He closes his eyes as if conjuring an image. "Maybe."

* * *

CURTAINS BILLOWING, LIGHTS flickering. Crackle of light across the sky, compensating for the dark. And then, *Ka-boom!* Douglas and Auntie Evangeline experiencing the drama of a Georgia thunderstorm. She is sliding onto the piano bench. Attacking the keys, only the black keys. "Sing, Douglas, join the elements!" She is lifting her voice, deep throaty contralto. The electricity of her invitation sparkling as if she were 253-1's sister instead of Hester's. The sound of his voice joining hers. A duet of flooding elation with wind billowing, the sheers pulsating like ghosts. *Crash*. Brilliance. Darkness. Repeat.

Of a sudden, 253-1, communicating across miles, through atmosphere, directly into the boy's sensibility.

A soon-to-be eleven-year-old heart thumping like the milkman's cart with its broken wheel and a runaway nag in the lead. A word pelting him like hail. A heart-piercing word escaping his lips. "Muriel."

| Is *questo violino* to be abandoned | Is my voice not to be your choice | Will we not serve your kind together after all | |

[3]

WHILE DOUGLAS HAS happily been the center of attention the situation has been careening out of control. He wants to be alone now. How can he be alone? Auntie Evangeline has planned a birthday event in his honor. Here he is dressed in an itchy costume when he desperately wants to plunge into the pool below Split Rock Falls. "The show must go on, your Highness." That's what Auntie Evangeline said when he complained of a stomachache. The event just steamrolls over his protests. Guests arrive. Adult students perform. He's stuck.

"Seraphina will sing *a cappella* for our finale," the teacher announces, wresting Douglas from his torment. He straightens to attention. Auntie Evangeline plunks down beside him and folds her hands.

Seraphina opens her mouth and sound flows like a lullaby, like night music over a stream. The beauty creates liquid pain. He will not drink the potent elixir; to do so would be to feel the loss of the violin all over again. Seraphina's voice, a moan, a call, plaintive, her lips curled back over teeth, her body swaying, her knees slightly bouncing, her chest rising and falling. He won't feel. He won't let it in. It's too beautiful. It invites him into the lush world of opera even as it sends him into the void of his lost love.

The birthday boy looks over at Auntie Evangeline. She embodies the music, her breathing in unison with Seraphina's, her hands grasping each other, veins like blue-green worms under the skin.

Douglas shudders. The voice is sending a dagger right beneath his ribs. Seraphina releases a musical tangent so pure and honest it makes a straight path from her soul to his eardrums. His eardrums pound, his throat closes, he forgets to breathe. *I won't let it in. I won't let it in.* Even in the moment of denial his heart vibrates with reverence.

Auntie Evangeline is patting his back. "Douglas? Douglas?" Fingers holding his chin, pulling it up. Their noses touching. Quietly then, "Calm down, calm down."

Douglas hears, "Come drown, come drown," as if it were a small boy's voice muted by the deep-deep well. He stares blankly at Evangeline.

"Tell Seraphina and the others how much their singing moved you. And then we'll consume your birthday cake, eleven layers, one for each year—Sunshine outdid herself! And Jeffers churned peach ice cream. Up with you. And smile!"

* * *

"THIS AUGUST HEAT prohibits the expenditure of our energy," Auntie Evangeline says, meaning he should take it easy. After a sandwich, cola, and chips, Douglas disregards the instruction to rest. He idles along the stream where a weeping willow offers shade and curious reflections. The mystery of Trenton Jr. at the forbidden well intrigues him. *Morbid fascination,* Violette would call it.

He peeks down the splintering cracks between boards that form the door. If only he could open it. First to release the hasp. After many attempts the hasp gives way. Starting on his knees—the wood heavy, he too short—he struggles to raise the covering to a vertical position. Then rising to his toes, he unsteadily allows the door to fall onto the pebbles, exposing the gaping hole. Observed: spongy moss, mosquitoes flittering away, stink rising. Is there some water below? A plum would do the job; he drops one, listens for a splash; an unsatisfying soft thud from below yields no information. He lies on the pebbles, peers down. Rays of light slide along the walls to expose a rope ladder, frayed and dingy like a sad flag. *Climb down*, a child's voice seems to instruct. Fear grips Douglas.

Four minutes later, Douglas slouches in a peacock chair, his throbbing thumb in his mouth. Would he have obeyed the ghostly child's command to climb down if he hadn't heard footsteps? A moth lands on the cap rail in front of him and crawls along, unhurried, wings tucked flat. Moments later it slides into the dark join of the rail and column. Douglas tiptoes to the spot and kneels. The insect must be there, though somehow it remains as still as the wood itself. *How strange*, he thinks. *To exist, yet to be unseen, unheard.*

At this moment the sensation of 253-1 breaks through, repeating her question. {Is *questo violino* to be abandoned| Is my voice not to be your choice| Will we not benefit mankind after all| |

Auntie Evangeline's mansion seems to hide and silence the *real* Douglas like a small insect. Losing violin lessons has hollowed him into a lady's empty corset. He's dark and bottomless, like the well.

The *well*. The word probes his heart like a garden spade gouging red Georgia clay. He's been disobedient just like Willi; worse, he's felt proud of it. This realization frightens him. Another possibility is even more unnerving. He'll be turned into an Opera Man if he complies with Auntie Evangeline's rules. Tears spring to his eyes. Violette's words jump into action. How could he be so *truculent* as to disregard the kindness of this queen-lady, whose *fervor* matches his own? It's just that he doesn't want to trade being a violinist for being an opera singer. He doesn't know how to tell her.

* * *

FIREFLIES ARE WEAVING overlapping arcs of light against the dark mass of trees. Evening air clings to flesh like damp garments. Douglas wishes Auntie Evangeline would say something. Unawares, his companion quietly sips a Confederate Highball while he harbors guilty thoughts, ones he dares not reveal. They listen unspeaking to the occasional clink of what she curiously calls *rocks* in her drink. Her easygoing face has been replaced with a worried one.

An owl screeches; another displays a high-pitched tremolo moving from one location to another. Douglas slides off his chair and peers into the expanse, although it's obscured by foliage.

"Thank you for my *exquisite* birthday party," he says, using one of Violette's favorite words to please Auntie Evangeline, while not looking in her direction. She may see into his devious heart. May see his lack of appreciation, his selfish desire for something she is not offering.

"Why you little gentleman, you. You did enjoy it then? I wondered." She pauses and he turns to see if she's smiling yet. "How about a light, sir, for this lady's cigarette?"

"Yes, ma'am." His struggle to strike the lighter's flint with his wounded thumb brings a frown to her face. Her crayoned lips turn sharply downward and she purses them just as Sister Elder often does. That look, so familiar on Sister Elder's face, and usually trivialized, stirs anxiety.

"Up, up, let me see the problem with your finger."

Douglas hangs his head, quickly hides his hand behind his back. She inhabits so many interconnected beings in his heart. Sister Elder's sister, his splendid teacher, his entrée to only-child privilege and delicious crème d'menthe diluted with oodles and oodles of cream.

When she takes hold of his arm, pulls it forward, and inspects his well-developed hand, the twice-wounded thumb, with both round scar and raw abrasion, becomes obvious. "If I had to speculate, I'd say either an alligator's been biting you...or you've been playing where you ought not...and I don't think there's an alligator hereabouts. So? Out with it!"

Silence. Douglas looks at her pleadingly. *Don't make me tell you,* he's wishing as fervently as any eleven-year-old could. With the back of his good hand Douglas swipes at hot tears.

Auntie Evangeline commands him, her voice changing pitch, deepening like the contralto *profundo* she had declared herself to be. "Speak up, speak up! Let's be adults here, shall we?"

Maybe she can understand his secrets. He searches her eyes, intently looking for a scrap of evidence. She blinks quickly, perhaps a sign. He begins hesitantly. Soon he lets loose the whole of it, describing his intrigue at the forbidden well, the ghostly child's voice calling him down, and the accident with the heavy plank and hasp.

"I'm going to disregard your disobedience and address the underlying issue. You still fancy playing the violin, losing your dream hurts, really bad, and you need to act like a brat to let me know. Yes?"

Again, one owl trills and the other answers, almost cat-like, providing a distraction; Douglas hopes his silence will be overlooked.

"You can't stay sad forever, my man. *You can't stay sad forever.*"

One owl trills into the painful truth. "Do you understand what I'm offering you?"

Sniffling.

"Sister Elder and I have engaged a suitable voice teacher. You'll begin lessons with him in September. I'll coach you myself when I visit the Home. Next summer you'll come back for our private lessons. Maybe audition for the Children's Theatre!"

She sounds so convincing. And really, what is he going back to? No violin. No lessons. He looks up into her rouged face and blinks his eyes. With effort he offers a wan smile.

"So, we've made our agreement, young Douglas?"

"Yes but...." Her generous offer quickly turns into a disenchanting variation of itself. *Yes, but. To choose opera singing would mean not choosing violin playing.* He can't give up dreams of his 253-1. He can't! Douglas slides to the floor, his back against the peacock chair, head in his knees, rubbing fists at hot tears. *I can't, won't, give up the violin! But...I'll disappoint Auntie Evangeline.*

"Out with it. You have something to tell me."

Douglas shrugs.

Again, Auntie Evangeline clinks the rocks in her beverage. "Another day then, perhaps?"

It's a pathetic excuse for another smile that Douglas gives; off the hook...for how long?

[4]

HIS SUITCASE IS packed. Jeffers will drive him to the terminal after lunch on the verandah. There is only this last hour to make Auntie Evangeline accept his rejection of her operatic tutelage. He understands her message—there is more than one way to fulfill a dream in music. *Not for me. Not for me.* He gathers his courage. "The violin says she is waiting for me."

Her face reveals amusement, indulgence even, as if he's told a make-believe story.

Douglas chews thoughtfully. The bologna and cheese sandwich has lost its taste. Even the most perceptive adult can be disappointing.

"What else does it say?" Auntie Evangeline asks, looking around for her silver monogrammed case, lighting her *morning* cigarette, turning back to face the boy who feels her energy fluctuating like the wings of a bird trying to land on an unsupportive bough.

"The violin says I could never understand what it felt like to be a tree even if she could speak in human words."

"So, the violin talks to you? Hmm. And yet, not in words?"

"Yes. See, it starts when I feel a buzzing right here." Douglas thumps his chest. "Then it whooshes through all of me! It changes into meanings. He uses his napkin, hoping to rid his face of mayonnaise. Maintaining an adult presence is all-important.

"Auntie Evangeline looks skeptical. "Would you indulge me with an example?" She sips her tea; the ice offers an encouraging clink.

Douglas pats the white bread, flattening it on the bologna and cheese and lettuce layers. "Her name is 253-1. She's been owned by priests and noblemen and sailors. Not just the Basque strangers. A man named Luigi found her because he went looking for the old violins made in Cremona. He could understand her. Like I do."

Auntie Evangeline flicks ash from her cigarette. "For a mid-sized boy, you certainly have a large-sized imagination. Pray, *just when* does your violin speak to you?"

Douglas rolls his eyes in unconscious mimicry of her incredulity. "I can feel her from the Conservatory when I'm at the Home. And at the Conservatory when I'm at the Home. Sometimes I feel her here too."

Auntie Evangeline takes a drag of her thin brown cigarette. She stares at the boy, the disarray of his copper hair, the emerging freckles, and the ancestry in his burnt sienna eyes. A boy who at this moment has the countenance of a poet, a visionary, or a simpleton.

"You think I'm Looney Tunes, don't you?"

Auntie Evangeline laughs out loud; his sincerity is disarming. "No, no, I don't think you're crazy! I understand you now—to a point."

"Promise, cross your heart you won't tell Sister Elder all this?"

* * *

SOON THEREAFTER IN communication with Hester, Auntie Evangeline reports the northbound itinerary. Although she planned to be tight-lipped, she's overcome with the urge to conclude with an observation. "Douglas finds it difficult to draw a line between the imaginary and the genuine, an immaturity not unlike yours, once upon a time. In Panicale, Umbria, if memory serves."

Later Evangeline heads into the rose garden with clippers; hasn't the heart to cut a bloom; has herself a long cry. That night she pens a confession in her journal.

> *These days, Hester,*
> *I'm less inclined to judge you for clandestine affairs of the heart.*
> *Love springs so randomly into our lives.*

ELIZABETHTOWN, NEW YORK

[5]

IN THE STOYA Conservatory Douglas' absence creates a void in the summer soundscape, although there is little silence. The Professor suffers as Mrs. Piano Teacher's students begin lessons with the playing of scales, sloppy, and arpeggios, raspy. After which the girls click up and down the keyboard with rebelliously long fingernails. The boys plink out their exercises with careless fingers, dutiful, though distracted. For every earnest student five others labor in the piano salon—either bored, obstreperous, lugubrious, featherbrained, or bribed into acquiescence. On languid afternoons the Professor feels his heart lurch as he listens to sweet Frieda coaching; he imagines that each uninspired student in their conservatoire exposes his own ineptness.

Eventually, lassitude sidles into each room of the stone house, threatening to stifle Frieda's energy, and the self-same summer lethargy slowly enervates Peter. He's remembering the keyboard a-twinkle with artistry that German children achieved, remembering Frieda's shy pride as she followed her students' recital at the Mendelssohn Herrenhaus. His wife is an excellent teacher and a sensitive accompanist. Even a dimwit could see the incredible progress her student Violette has been making. The solution? He scouts for another exceptional piano student, seizing upon Ophelia Nolan. She'll pair well with Violette; the two can be schooled as accompanists.

So much for Frieda. What to do about my equally exasperating violin students? He won't ask for advice. Not from Galamian. His unnerving competitor says things are picking up at Meadowmount. Two years ago, Peter encouraged Ivan and Judith to lease the Milholland Lodge despite its condition—the property had no electricity and the roof leaked. Judith hired two teenage girls for dishwashing and odd jobs. She herself cooked and served the thirty-odd campers, and the staff, from a kitchen equipped with only an icebox and a wood-burning stove. Both summers Peter proctored at Meadowmount, three days a week. He's seen the progress firsthand. Today the roof is intact. The Lodge has been wired with electricity. The kitchen boasts a commercial stove and double ovens. Galamian reports the number of pupils has swelled to fifty.

Galamian's Meadowmount has become a magnet for impressive guest instructors, too. Piatigorsky. The revered violinist, Isaac Stern. Joseph Szigeti, the Hungarian who has commissioned concertos by Béla Bartók and Ernest Bloch.

Just remember, I'm the one with foresight, thank you. Jah, say it, I conceded. I lost a battle with Ivan Galamian. Hang on.

Peter sets a new goal. The Stoya Conservatory will become an equally impressive entity by developing *young* pupils. Ideally these up-coming students will be standout quality by the time they reach Meadowmount, excelling in competition, showing brilliance on stage. This is an honorable goal.

Peter ignites like a correctly gapped sparkplug. He and Frieda attend a concert in the City, holding hands, swaying gently to the rhythm, just as they had when courting in Berlin. Freed from resentment he turns to a more personal challenge. Doesn't he have the God-given abilities to bring at least one virtuoso into the world? And this luminary will be? Wilhelm Stoya, of course.

All that's lacking in Willi's case is a competitive companion; the peer-rival tactic was working before. Go ahead, call it a mistake to dismiss Douglas. He can find another gifted violin student, one to fire up Willi's genius. He vows to Frieda, "I'll whip our lazy, schmazy Wilhelm into shape for the Spring Ratings if it kills me."

What the ambitious music teacher can't ignore is a slinking, sharp-toothed fear. Fear that Willi lacks elemental love for music and its natural byproduct, motivation—this son whose byword seems to be *fun.* And as he admits this to himself a fissure separates today from tomorrow. This void filling with fear could almost vacuum his hope for Willi's future clean away. And the lack of hope could settle like a tramp squatting outside a bank, begging, cup in hand.

[6]

A LANKY KID ARRIVES at the Stoya Conservatory looking serious in his spectacles and seersucker jacket. Nevertheless, his slouch, his rolled socks, and his pompadour, both aromatic and winsome, speak of a casual nature. "AJ. Purvis at your service," he says, extending a bony hand. He happens to be an intermediate student, two years older than Willi, whose affluent family recently moved to Elizabethtown. Professor Stoya listens intently as the boy plays his selected Grieg from memory. AJ.'s long fingers manage chords and trills easily; he demonstrates raw energy as he saws his way through the lyrical pieces.

"Ach," Peter tells Frieda later, "his bowing technique is subpar." Frieda smiles. "*Goot*," she says with a knowing air.

Hmm, the Purvis kid may be a godsend, Stoya decides. So, what if he needs improvement? It could be beneficial to let Willi feel superior. To a point. Craving superiority was never his own youthful motivation, if anyone is asking.

Oh, it's not fair to compare Willi's nature with his own. Oh, how can he not? Where he had a musical ally in Opa, Wilhelm has suffered with *him*, a mishmash of father/disciplinarian/instructor. Sadly, although understandably, he's not played a very encouraging role with Willi.

The question lurks, unanswered. Is the musical drive inborn, or can it be acquired?

By the age of six he'd become an eager piano student. In contrast Willi had hidden to escape such lessons. By age twelve his grandfather was taking him to hear chamber music. He remembers being impassioned by the combined voices of violin and viola. In contrast Willi fidgeted while Piatigorsky displayed brilliance on his cello just a few months ago. Peter kicks himself as thoughts of Douglas shoulder into his memories. *AJ. must become the positive example Willi needs. Sooner than later.* He'll throw all energy into the rich kid's bowing skills. His son will naturally step it up and compete.

* * *

"BOWING TECHNIQUES SET a great player apart from mere fiddlers," Stoya explains to A.J. and Willi. He demonstrates *detache*. He keeps the bow moving through a range of volume, soft to loud: *piano, mezzo, forte, fortissimo*. Both students struggle to achieve this dynamic. *How can it be so difficult?* Peter paces, his fingers thumping on his pant leg. "Try again, again, again!"

He demonstrates *sul tasto*. The boys practice keeping the bow over the fingerboard, trying to produce a soft-thin tone. *Why does Willi's bow defy this instruction?* "Listen to your playing, gentlemen—you call your tone soft-schmoft?" They practice *sul ponticello*. "Keep the bow near the bridge! You should hear higher harmonics if you are in the right position." *Why does A.J.'s bow slide down the fingerboard when directed otherwise?* "Try again! You should produce a lovely ghostly sound."

Willi hovers his bow dramatically above the strings. "Woo-woo, woo-woo," he sings in falsetto. A.J. chuckles into his sleeve, knowing better, knowing he will be cuffed by a frustrated instructor, and not caring. Sadly, A.J. proves to be fashioned of the same cloth as Willi. The boys continue to distract each other with much guffawing at their ineptitude.

Peter is no idiot. A new tactic must be employed. Galamian's austerity is not working for him. He resolves to comport himself *playfully* and thus garner their attention. To no effect. LuLu hints he isn't carrying off the *good humor act* very convincingly.

Professor Stoya's impatience with Willi bulges and finally wrestles the man's best intentions to the mat. He snaps. He fumes. He beats his baton on the music stand. If Willi disliked his violin lessons before Douglas' departure, could one wonder why he despises lessons now? The equation for progress lacks what it seems only Douglas could offer, once upon a time.

Mrs. Piano Teacher observes all. She often enters the stressful space, clucks, runs a hand through her frizzy mushroom-blond curls, makes a benign albeit lengthy comment. Her teasing eyes, for Peter only, hold a flirtatious promise; Frieda's way of quieting things. Her way of creating a bypass for some, if not all, the anger flowing through the stone house, as if she alone might open invisible passageways and release the intensifying toxins. When she spies Sister Peace at Saturday market and makes a point of smiling, perhaps offering a compliment, does her husband need to know? Perhaps even Sister Elder can forget the exchange of harsh words—or be willing to forgive.

GEORGIA TO NEW YORK

[7]

DOUGLAS' ENERGY QUAVERS in that dimension between leaving and arriving, that space between detaching and joining. He experiences the transformation of self that perpetuates the narcotic of travel in others. As unknown regions stream endlessly outside his coach—Tennessee, North Carolina, Virginia, Maryland—a realization dilates. How enormous the world beyond his awareness? Questions he never thought to ask impose upon his consciousness. How many people unknown to him there must be living their secret lives, waiting at the crossings, in terminals, in trucks, on horseback or bicycles? How many millions more unseen, laboring, playing, laughing, crying, in offices, schools, churches, homes, hospitals? How many, just like him, practicing music? What does he know of others' joys and sorrows? He's been so wrapped up in his own—the brute force of Professor Stoya, the fickle friendship of Willi. He frowns, catching his reflection in the window. Ah, his desire for spunky, sweet Violette wallops his consciousness. His smile flashes, evidence of elation even though there is not one passenger who witnesses.

As steel wheels roll along steel track in New Jersey, he grasps his state of being as if he were contained within the bellows of an accordion. Bellows compressed, which until now had kept him folded in a narrow hallway of existence. Bellows that expanded within Auntie Evangeline's red clay kingdom, of white-, brown-, and black-skinned people who share a slow-twangy dialect, who taught him, entertained him, treated him as an adult. He's returning, no longer the crybaby. He's outgrown all that by finding a larger breadth of existence.

Amidst the view of Pennsylvania's forestation, Douglas grows pensive. In the process of realizing personal triumph, he's been disappointing Auntie Evangeline. Possibly Sister Elder will accept his rejection of operatic study, though she may call it *failure*. While he'll welcome the brotherly squeezebox of the boys' dorm, he can't allow motherly compression from her, Hester Smythe. Or from other bossy adults who try to squash his desire for the 253-1.

After eighteen hours, having covered almost nine hundred miles, he both dreads and desires Home. "New York City, Penn Station," the conductor calls. And then a few hours later, here is Wing greeting him in Elizabethtown. It strikes Douglas like a dark musical chord; he's returning to the emptiness of no music teacher at all.

Sister Elder, Sister Peace, and Astrid encircle Douglas each noting the *overnight* changes of a young man who's grown so tall. Here's Mildred, James, and John urging him to blow out eleven candles, begging for large slices of chocolate cake and three scoops of homemade strawberry ice cream. Perhaps Home can be tolerated.

He feels optimistic until the next afternoon when Willi and classmates cycle by, hollering overly familiar insults. James and John say he should go canoeing with them and forget everything else until school starts. Mildred says, "Skedaddle!" And then she advises, "You should choose Orchestra for an elective, so at least you'll have a violin to play."

ELIZABETHTOWN, NEW YORK

[8]

THE HORRID FIRST day of school. He carries his apprehension like a hot baked potato, juggling its position so as not to get burnt again. Just listen. The same taunts, disgusting and derogatory, humiliate Douglas as he climbs the steps. And now what? Willi and Violette side by side in the hall? Douglas' anger winds round and round, one coil upon the other, anger with its eyes hooded, its tongue darting, its raised head ready to strike; anger ready to poison.

Violette brightens as he comes alongside. "Hi, where did you go all summer?" she asks. Oh, he has stories, and now someone to tell. Willi gives him a shoulder shove. Violette inclines her head away from Willi and gives Douglas a questioning smile. She wears a look of amusement as if each moment offers intrigue.

Willi tugs on her hair bow; the untied black ribbon streams down her straight back, releasing her braids. "Oh, Willi!" She slaps at him. He flat-foots it away backward, laughing as he watches the pair so awkwardly reconnected. And as Violette turns her full attention to Douglas, Willi places his thumb on his nose and wiggles his fingers. Douglas has never seen this gesture. Never mind that the five-finger salute cannot be mistaken for anything except disrespect. Douglas laughs out loud—what else can he do but laugh? All those desires to hurt Willi, his first friend, weaken. He rubs a round purple scar on his thumb. Violette hugs him, giggling. "Douglas, I learned to type this summer!" She smells of green, of freshly broken birch bough.

School means having few choices. No choice except to be seated directly behind his rival, to have the roll call—Stoya, "here;" Tryzyna, "here." Daily, their names linked despite broken and dishonored bonds. Regardless, when Willi cracks a joke for the class's benefit Douglas laughs loudly; he has no choice but to feel unconstrained appreciation for the comic. When assigned as math team captain, he chooses Willi first. No choice but to utilize the kid's sharp mind.

Try as he might during these classroom moments together, Douglas, aching with curiosity, can't bring up the subject of Professor Stoya or violin lessons. Fear overrides choice. Is Willi still playing violin? He finds out soon enough. From Violette. The answer is *yes*, her lessons with Mrs. Piano Teacher overlap with Willi's lessons. Sometimes Professor Stoya even has them play simple pieces together.

It hurts. This simple truth. That those two are paired like horses pulling a hay wagon. Has Violette fallen for Willi after a summer together while he's been out of the way?

[9]

DURING AFTERNOONS FOLLOWING compulsory subjects Douglas goes to his elective, Orchestra—it's the only place where he has the privilege of playing a violin. Willi strolls by the Music Room on his way to Shop, peers in the glass, and thumbs his nose at the captives. At Douglas in particular. It's as if Willi gloats, knowing Orchestra with Tattersall is worse than a lesson with his father, the intimidating Professor Peter Stoya.

Tattersall arrives with the class bell; he ignores the unruly behavior of his students who climb on chairs, who flourish rulers like batons, who pound on drums, who hide while others seek. Once perched on the riser, shielded by the music stand, the slight man claps his hands. "Shall we?" he asks the rowdy bunch as if they were ladies and gentlemen. Fearless, intriguing, and very much mimicked, Tattersall manages to take charge.

This strange man, his face as round and white as a china saucer, his oiled hair as black as licorice, begins energetically—eyes blinking, head waggling, conductor's baton shearing space. He's dressed in saffron silk and herringbone wool, an Orthopteran of a man seemingly hell-bent on debunking the fable's claim of grasshoppers' procrastination or laziness.

Twenty-seven would-be musicians follow his lead. Thirteen violins, one cello, one double bass, one flute, three clarinets, one horn, two coronets, two trombones, two drums, one xylophone.

No student ever falls asleep with the stimuli Tattersall provides. Especially since Tattersall exaggerates. *Crescendo* means loud—now! Douglas plays more loudly so he can hear himself. *Diminuendo* means soft—now! Douglas plays so quietly he can't hear himself above the others. *Allegro* means fast—hustle. Douglas speeds up, all the while despising the futility of music-making in this situation where nuance is unknown.

Each week Douglas hopes the intimate group lesson might offer criticism, compliment, or even correction; none is forthcoming. Tattersall plays along with the thirteen kids. Note for note. Douglas suffers; he can't hear his own intonation. Or the crispness of a *spicatto.* Detached strokes become *legato* and vice versa. Forgotten is dynamic shading. Douglas, like each of Tattersall's students, becomes absorbed in the mere playing of notes, one note strung after another.

Little by little Douglas distances himself. Who needs the social club of musicians and his disappointing instructor? He walks home alone unless Violette inserts her presence, skipping along and chatting. All the same, a snowmelt of vehemence continues carving into the boy's heart, like the spring river he is hurtling along, restless and insensitive.

"I'm quitting Tattersall's stupid class," he tells Sister Elder. "Here's what I'm going to say to him. April fools, I'm not your Bozo anymore!"

Sister Elder reacts to the message with unexpected sternness. One wonders if she thinks the practice of music will humanize the hungry devil in Douglas' soul. Or is she teaching him a life lesson? "You, boy-o, will not shirk your commitments. You demanded to take this elective even though I disapproved. You will stick with that class however ludicrous until you begin high school."

Douglas seeks Sister Peace, looking for sympathy. He tries to explain his dissatisfaction: "And Tattersall kicks his right foot on the music stand when we play. Bang, bang, bang!"

"Always his right leg, hmm?" She pronounces each word carefully. "His left leg must suffer shame of unequal development. The man never notices his left leg is growing small?" Douglas and Tatiana guffaw like siblings until their bellies ache.

[10]

SPRING TREES MELT together like pastel finger paint; their colors join with the sky and the fish scale clouds. Douglas spends his free time running. Running through the meadow, along the river, past the egg farm, up the hill to the great outcropping of rock. He stops, catches his breath, and then with all the lung power Auntie Evangeline trained him to use, he screams. The glassy falls stilled by ice deflect his rage and hurl the scream back. How he despises the non-music of the Tattersall's fake *orchestra*. How he is wasting his time.

[11]

SLEEP BECOMES DIFFICULT for a boy who craves music and produces only noise under Tattersall's direction. One such night 253-1 communicates with Douglas in her private way.

{Free your mind and sleep| Oh to dream of possibility| Someday we will achieve a myriad of sounds together| |

"What's myriad?"

{Oh to say it| myriad is many| many| more than many| Shall *questo violino* comfort you with an alphabet of sounds| |

"Yeah."

{So to start| Airy| Breathy| Bright| Clear| Dreamy| Five beautiful distinctions to help you sleep| Humans all need sleep| is that not so| is it not the way of things| |

To another kid such words may be heard as simple syllables. Not so for Douglas. Not when the 253-1 utters them. From each a specific dreamscape blossoms like a rhapsody.

Finally sleep overtakes a calmed soul. The next night Douglas repeats the request. "More!"

{To set dreams in motion| seven nuances selected from many| Crisp| Dark| Delicate| Deep| Edgy| Full| Gentle| So now to sleep| is it not the way of things| |

And yet another miserable night 253-1 soothes Douglas.

{Let us begin again| eleven qualities to entice sleep| Mellow| Punchy| Rich| Round| Smooth| Spacious| Steely| Sweet| Transparent| Veiled| Warm| So now to dreams| is it not the way of things| |

In time Douglas' unconscious being is saturated with a multitude of tonal possibilities.

[12]

PROFESSOR STOYA FIDGETS. Alone with his curiosity, except for the companionship of notebook and pen, the pair quite willing to accommodate his opinions. He's joined an audience where children make their presence known: squeals from small siblings being teased by larger; *shh*-ings from serious-minded teens; yelps from victims of spit wads hitting their targets. Parents of these young musicians exhale the frosty air of envy, all nod politely to others who must experience similar unease, all hold smiles longer than required, all avoid eye contact.

Peter studies the program. *A Boy and His Violin.* Deceptive title. For one thing the violin is not owned by the boy. Rembert Wurlitzer loaned Michael Rabin an Amati just days before the performance, according to Galamian. It would surely be a test of any musician to feel comfortable on a new violin so quickly. *How will the boy fare?* He's thinking. Thinking of eleven-year-old Willi in this situation. Thinking of Douglas—not thinking of Douglas—trying not to think of Douglas.

Frieda agreed to stay home with their sons; a trip to Providence, Rhode Island, on a Wednesday didn't seem prudent. Besides, the spectacle of a prodigy in concert, ten years of age, for Heaven's sake, might be more of a curse than a blessing for his three beloved family members who, frankly, were lacking oomph these days.

It was Piatigorsky who had encouraged Stoya to attend. Promised he wouldn't be disappointed. "Bring the lads; this wunderkind will give them a spark. Willi. And the boy, Douglas."

"Grisha, Douglas is no longer under my tutelage," Stoya had said rather too quickly.

"Pity, showed promise, zest, intuition, a real affinity."

"He failed to respect rules in my school. Outright disobedience. An orphan of no count. I turned him out."

Piatigorsky had been taken aback. "How old was the lad when he erred?"

Peter had postured in defiance, arms akimbo. "Last year, he was almost eleven, old enough to know better."

"Harsh perhaps, you think? A loss to our talented fold. Were we not ourselves boys once?"

Stoya finds that he has stopped breathing as young Rabin performs. First, Handel's Sonata in A Major, No. 1, followed by the Weiniawski Concerto in D Minor. By intermission Peter is speechless. He overhears parents as they pass in the aisle.

"That's his mother Jeanne accompanying; they're unbelievable."

"How does she get him to practice, to that degree?"

"They say she's a relentless backstage mother."

Although Stoya has been astonished by the first half of the program he is wholly unprepared for the second. Paganini? Sarasate? *Really?* Rabin's boldness, sheer technique, warmth, and brilliance? *How is it possible?* This program would challenge a seasoned virtuoso and yet Galamian says the child has been studying for three years. *Only three years, since the age of seven!* If Peter hadn't been there to see and hear for himself, he would not have believed such a thing possible.

✳ ✳ ✳

PETER UNFOLDS THE newspaper. "Here's what the Providence Review, dated April 24, 1947, has to say, Frieda. Proof I'm not exaggerating. He reads aloud:

"'Very rarely is it possible to acclaim genius with reservation and predictions are not in our line. This time it seems safe to state that this was a genius in action, and it seems safe to predict that Master Rabin is due for prominence in the near future.'"

[13]

THE ESSEX COUNTY High School Band marches down Main Street, trombones blaring and heroic, flutes shrill and silvery, drums boom-booming. The drum major swivels his head around as if to say, "Steady-steady now." When the musicians reach Oak Street, the sounds dwindle to a gravelly rat-tat-tat signaling the parade's end. It's a spring tradition, a finale for the school year's end, this parade to the park and a celebration of the arts.

Professor Stoya takes Mrs. Piano Teacher's always-cool hand into his own always-warm hand and squeezes. They share a look for which no words of translation are necessary. Today's group of teens strides with an unmistakable jauntiness sporting gold and blue uniforms, led by a color guard of their peers. An unvoiced comparison is launched in two minds. How unlike youngsters marching through Berlin wearing brown and black uniforms led by a plucky adult. Willi was just a *kleinkind* the year they emigrated from Germany; he's twelve now. He walks alongside his parents unburdened by that past, seemingly on the lookout for his pals.

Some townsfolk relax under the cherry trees where rings of pink blossoms have formed. Other folk purchase hot dogs, potato salad, cookies, and lemonade from expectant vendors. Conversations between parents take a quizzical vein—whose children have passed, whose will attend summer school, whose are likely to get into mischief? The students, insensitive to their parents' concerns, clown on the playground equipment noisily relishing imminent vacation. Eager boys push the merry-go-round and watch girls' skirts billow. The wheel spins faster and faster, the girls laugh more gaily, the boys' sturdy shoes dig an ever-deeper rut in the sand. All the while, cherry blossoms scent the humid air.

Mrs. Piano Teacher strolls as Peter purchases lunch, her blond hair tending to green in the shade. She gazes at children's paintings, clothespinned along yards of twine. The artwork flutters in the breeze, threatening to fly away, as do many precious things in life. She waits for a crowd to clear so she can better view an attention-grabbing panorama, the image of Split Rock Falls— rendered in tempera paint—featuring angels, a rainbow, and doves. She can hear snips of narrative from a self-designated docent: "Awe-inspiring, yes. Our Split Rock Falls transports seekers to

rapture. Devastating, yes. Our Split Rock Falls lures teenagers to suicide."
Hearing this, parents lean together. Girlfriends hold hands. Hankies are
withdrawn and used on tearing eyes. A suicide punctures the weave of
generations, altering the warp and weft of life and death.

The Mayor appears on the bandshell stage outfitted in a linen suit
with a wide-brimmed Panama hat. He rings a handbell. Young children
gather on the grass at the stage's edge. Adults perch on slowly sinking,
slowly tipping, white chairs. Teens sit in the back rows, aloof.

Frieda, whose dress matches the cherry blossoms, stands, smiles,
nods as local music teachers are acknowledged. "Our own eminent Musicians and Instructors, Professor Peter Stoya and his wife, Frieda."

Also introduced, "Miss Edwina Coolidge, piano, and Sir Herbert
Johnson, violin." Herbert, curiously attired in a frayed baseball cap and
orange bow tie, claps for himself. The Stoyas nudge one another. "Edwina's a crabapple," Frieda whispers. "Herbert's a charlatan," Peter
answers with a sneer.

Douglas folds the Spring Concert program into a cootie catcher,
pinching and releasing imaginary victims from his knee as tap dancers tap
and poets recite rhyme. When the Junior High Orchestra is announced,
Tattersall, regal in a saffron silk tie and white dress shirt, raises his baton.
At attention his twenty-seven would-be musicians: one cello, one double
bass, one flute, three clarinets, one horn, two coronets, two trombones,
two drums, one xylophone. Thirteen violins, Douglas one of the unlucky
string group.

It is with absorption and horror that Stoya listens. He can distinguish Douglas' playing, especially in the waltz. *What has happened to the
boy? This lack of musicality? This rushed nonchalance?* Frieda simpers in the
silent, sarcastic language they share. Oh, she can hear the boy's playing
too. Stoya feels regret; it rises like acid to his throat. Has he betrayed this

unusual child by dismissing him? Frieda's expression would say she thinks so.

Later Professor Stoya and Mrs. Piano Teacher bask in the attention of Orchestra members' parents who are frankly dismayed; the duo heads homeward, encouraged about the prospect of new students. The Professor slows. "Look, Frieda." Ahead of them something flutters on a twig. It looks like a newly emerged butterfly drying its wings in preparation for flight. "Butterfly?" Frieda asks. The breeze quiets as they step closer; the object is revealed as two tender leaves merged visually as one. "Ah, too early, or too late for butterflies?" she asks. And all the while cherry blossoms scent the humid air.

[14]

SISTER ELDER ALLOWS Douglas to quit Tattersall's Orchestra after hearing the Spring Concert. Just like that. And then, "I've hired you a new teacher," she says, just like that. And now Wing is dropping him off in Lewis for his first lesson with the new guy.

Douglas climbs the interior stairs. The building smells musty. Studio 210, the door is ajar; should he wait for the man at the piano to acknowledge him? His quandary allows him a minute to scan the space. The walls are hung with autographed photos of baseball players. Music books cover the floor, some open, some closed; sheet music decorates table tops.

This teacher seems to have some physical disorder causing him to blow his hawklike nose and wipe it repeatedly. He replaces the hankie in his shirt pocket, and once again his fingers roam the piano keys searching out a jazzy melody.

"My four o'clock?" the pale man eventually inquires, giving Douglas a quick once over. "Douglas Tree-zinn-ia, is it?" He accents the second syllable almost distastefully.

"Not like a tree or a flower, just Tryzyna," Douglas says, blood rushing to his ears.

Ignoring the correction, the interrogator continues. "My students call me *Sir*." Sir Herbert Johnson opens a cardboard case and withdraws a dark brown violin. "Missus Smith and I have selected this nice instrument especially for you."

"How old are you?"

"Almost twelve," Douglas says promptly.

The new instrument finds its way into his hands. He holds it to his chin. He worries with it. It feels large. Much larger than the lovely Italo-Argentine. And larger than the English he'd been getting used to at Stoya's before his banishment. Larger than the school loaner, *that* pitiful thing he'd rather forget.

"This violin seems kind of big."

Sir Johnson proceeds in his overly accentuated fashion. "From age ten onward a child should play a full-size violin. This way you will learn the correct intervals. Some fools argue that an overly large violin will stiffen a child's muscles. Rubbish! We shall see progress. That is, *if* you are the serious student Missus Smith suggests being the case.

Douglas rankles at the man's inability to get their names right. And then twenty-seven minutes have passed, and Douglas has not yet drawn a bow across the violin. The man lectures as he paces the room, jingling the change in his right trouser pocket. The prisoner's mind drifts to sounds of Magic Muriel's strings responding to Professor Stoya's hairy fingers and long bow.

Still pacing and jingling, Sir Johnson asks, "Do you know to play a C major scale?"

Douglas scoffs. He begins with confidence, which turns to discomfort as he stretches his way up the elongated fingerboard.

"Just try harder, Mr. Zinnia." The instructor titters. Blows his nose. *Huh-Honkkk!* "Let's hear you find scales in all keys, *if* you please."

Douglas plays scales, arpeggios, and chords in every key. He pauses each time the teacher raises his hand, retrieves his hankie, and blows. *Huh-Honkkk!*

Sir Johnson completes the lesson with a warning. "I teach Fun-da-men-tals, Mr. Tarzana, not "Fun." The man titters again.

Douglas feels like someone on trial. Which outcome would be just? To be accepted by this teacher? Or to be released?

Sir Johnson becomes judge and jury. "We'll begin serious lessons, two per month."

Douglas sighs. Lessons with this man fail to excite him. There is one small compensation, however; he now owns a violin of sorts. And a music book. Not a book of compositions by Bach or Mozart or Wohlfahrt. Etudes composed by Sir Herbert Johnson, Instructor of Merit.

[15]

DOUGLAS REMAINS IGNORANT of what Sister Elder chooses not to communicate. That Sir Johnson approached her in the park after the Spring Concert. At first with compliments for the young musician. Next, with inquiries regarding plans for Douglas' *Advanced Training.* "Indeed, the child deserves and requires more than he could possibly gain from an overworked orchestra leader." Finally, a proposal for lessons complete with a suitable violin for sale. "Excellent value," he assured her.

[16]

AT FIRST DOUGLAS experiments. Such freedom. So many sounds he can make with the violin and bow. He repeats his discoveries. He plays them for the family. He plays them for Violette. Violette makes a title for each little masterpiece and reads aloud with appropriate reverence:

"Screech of Crows"

"Slosh of Creek over Rock"

"Spill of Hail"

"Plunk of Coins in Piggy Bank"

"Scratch of Chickens"

"Rustle of Auntie Evangeline's Dress"

"Glide of Shadows Across Tall Grass"

For safekeeping Douglas places the typewritten list under the Muriel cigar box.

* * *

OVER TIME DOUGLAS has learned to hear a distinction between violins. The Performance Violin rings with a bell-like purity. The small Italo-Argentine he and Willi played produced brighter tones. Magic Muriel 253-1 sings with a full round voice that vibrates his innards. Each of the three instruments delights him in its own fashion.

The factory violin can make noises; this much he gleefully discovered in his first week of ownership. Though when it comes to playing music on this thing? How disappointing. He tries to act grateful so that Sister Elder will not be upset.

Sister Elder addresses Douglas' melancholy, seeing beyond his polite excuses. "This violin is your own—you can practice on it here. Anytime, just as you choose. You're no longer dependent upon the Professor's whims. It's time, Douglas; you must accept reality. The other violin is not yours! Besides, the Basque may return for it." Sister Elder observes the child's uncompromising attitude. "Don't give me those hangdog eyes."

Sweet Sister Peace offers Sister Elder a confusing gesture, both of her hands aflutter. Wordlessly she marches Douglas out the kitchen door. She strides across the meadow to the river. Viewed from a distance her hair flashes iridescence ranging from emerald to bronze, like a starling's or a common grackle's feathers, altogether giving the impression she could fly away.

He, of the hangdog eyes, hurries to catch up with her; they stand side by side on Little Bridge attuned to the gurgling rush of green current becoming foam as it rises over hidden rock. "Listen, water talks to you. You hearing? It's saying, 'Make what music you can, now. With gift.'" A blunt reminder, the factory violin is after all a generous gift from Sister Elder. As are the lessons with Sir Herbert Johnson.

There on the bridge, heeding encouragement, glancing back to Sister Peace's sympathetic face, Douglas resigns himself. One question only needs to be asked. What if he had never learned to make music spill from a box of wood? Life would be unbearable. Someday he will play the 253-1 again, he vows, even if enduring the grating squeaking is what it takes.

Summer freedom, a private instructor, and a violin to call his own, a new resolve begins to drive Douglas. He reasons the instrument must be a young creation and the process will take patience. After all, it took years for his own speech to be developed.

[17]

AN ENVELOPE FOR Douglas in the silver tray! Return address Atlanta, Georgia, sealed with an embossed red wax circle.

> *June 8, 1947*
> *My Dear Douglas,*
> *In lieu of an Atlanta trip this year, I thought you could use a racy bicycle. Let's have Hester take you to the bicycle shop where you can select your heart's delight, my early birthday gift to you.*
> *Lovingly,*
> *Auntie Evangeline*

Douglas waxes the Monarch Deluxe on Saturdays while Mr. Ludlow, the next-door neighbor, washes his car. Douglas tucks playing cards in the spokes of the wheels like Violette showed him. James and John call it a sissy thing to do. So what? He likes hearing paper rustle against wire. Winding through the neighborhood avenues, paralleling the river, upstream and down, turning east, he saves the Stoya block for last, his ears alert. He circles the neighborhood, slowing as he passes the Conservatory. Again and again he circles. Sometimes he hears the screech and whine of violin, sometimes piano clamor—students laboring in the chambers forbidden to him.

Douglas repeats this bike ride daily, always a tune and a rhythm playing in his mind. As if musical selections were lined up like records in the jukebox of his brain awaiting the coins of his desire. The waltz Violette played at a Saturday recital, were it a record, would be well worn.

[18]

IT'S CRUEL CIRCUMSTANCE that continues to send a talented boy to Sir Johnson for violin instruction. A pathetic excuse for instruction at that. Listen to the lesson in progress. Douglas plays one of the man's Etudes; the teacher studies baseball stats, his face buried in the newspaper. He sneezes, *hu-honk*, blows his storybook-sultan's nose, and wipes. The radio hums with a game and Sir Johnson breaks into cheering with each home run. Upset by these outbursts Douglas sets his bow aside and waits. Johnson, eventually noticing, simply waves him on. "Again, Mr. Zinnia."

Lesson after lesson Sir Johnson shrugs off Douglas' diligence. Johnson's disregard goes unmentioned. Douglas leaves his lessons, shouldering a pretense of optimism. Evenings he continues to practice, although the factory violin will not respond; the G string sounds tubby; the A string sounds tinny. "Arrgh!" he screams after an hour of torture.

Such a travesty. Perhaps this is what happens when expediency overcomes parental judgment.

[19]

DOUGLAS' BIKE IS his salvation. Ah, to control something. Even if it is just pedaling and leaving places behind. He feels new power in his legs as he ascends Fiddler Hill, approaching Meadowmount day after day. Students of stringed instruments have returned. It seems so long ago that Galamian housed young musicians at Stoya's Conservatory. Musicians he spied on—and envied. Musicians he still envies. Now they practice in rustic cabins for hours at a time with a Proctor in charge. According to the Professor's tales they're not so free to ditch these days.

He daydreams as he pedals: If I was studying under Galamian at Meadowmount, I'd never miss a minute of practice. If only I'd been left on the steps of Windy Cliff when I was a baby, Jacqueline would be like a mom. By now I'd be performing on a swell violin as passionately as Piatigorsky on his cello.

Douglas pedals past the converted Milholland Lodge, leaving behind the cabins and the cacophony. While descending the hill he's refreshed by air rising from the rivers and lakes—zephyrs. Violette especially likes the word *zephyrs*. He spreads his arms exalting in the speed. Sister Elder would say he's riding *like a maniac*. Sister Peace, however, approves. "Wheels take you fast away from troubled mind."

One day, just around the block from Stoya's house, a terrifying terrier —with incisors sharp as an icepick—draws blood from his ankle.

As he tends his wound, sounds alert him. *What is that?*

Limping around the corner he finds a painted sign and stops again. *Lilacs* marks the two-story white wooden house, a summer rental. The music he's just heard comes from a low side window here! A violinist inside repeats a passage—running through a sequence of notes time after

time after time. Douglas begins to count the repetitions. Twenty-one....
Thirty-five...forty-two.... A screen door slams, interrupting his concentration, and within seconds someone is tapping his shoulder. He turns. "Hi,"
he manages to squeak.

"That's my brother you hear. He has to do one hundred times—
Mother said so. Because he was out of tune." This girl is pretty, round-
faced with curly hair like images of baby angels in Sister Elder's *Art History*
book. She's wearing a blue sundress with ruffles over the shoulders and
looks to be about his age. "He can't stop his practice until Jeanne comes
back from shopping. He's much better at music than me. I play piano. Actually our whole family is musicians. My dad, his name is George, he
plays for the New York Philharmonic, and my mother, her name is Jeanne
like I said, she accompanies my brother when he performs for an audience. We've been staying here for the past three summers so my brother
can go to Meadowmount where he studies with the famous Ivan Galamian. See, we live in the City. We used to go to Professional Children's
School—not anymore, no more playing marbles in the street, no more
stopping at the candy store, no more time with aunts and uncles along
the way home, no more time for friends. See, my brother has tutors because he has to practice his violin so much, he's almost famous. He has
free time at three o'clock most days if you want to come back. Have you
heard of him? His name is Michael Rabin. I'm Bertine."

Douglas feels peculiar. This stranger has divulged more to him in
two minutes than anybody he has ever met. Is it because she's a girl?

"You'd better scrambola!" Bertine gives a sweet smile and a hurried
little wave as she disappears behind the screen door. In a few seconds
sounds from two musicians at practice float along with Douglas as he
pedals away, charmed.

Several days later Douglas rides through the upscale neighborhood of Hand and Williams Streets, past the Stoya Conservatory, a block further—avoiding the threatening terrier—and on to *Lilacs* where he finds Bertine and a boy sitting on the porch. They certainly look like siblings with their round cheeks, fair skin, and dark curls. Douglas stops, his heart beating quickly. He's about to meet the violinist he keeps hearing. He mumbles a greeting.

"This is my brother, Michael," Bertine says proudly. "He's eleven, his birthday was May second, how old are you?"

Douglas leans his bike on the fence. He shoves his hands in his pockets. "Almost twelve. My birthday's in August," he says.

Michael pipes up. "Do you play baseball? You know what my mother says?" Without waiting for an answer Michael's voice breaks into falsetto. "'No baseball for you. Your precious hands, keep your hands safe.'"

Michael's mimicry of a witchy voice is hilarious. Even so, Douglas holds back from laughing—it might be rude. "No baseball. For me either," Douglas offers. "I play violin too—a little, sometimes."

A camaraderie strikes up. They've so much in common. "Want to play a composers quiz? I'll quiz you, and you quiz me. See, you name a composer and I'll give you his dates. Birth, and death. Then I'll name one and then you give dates."

Douglas kicks the sidewalk; *this is Michael's idea of fun?* "Johann Sebastian Bach," he says trying to be a good sport.

Michael rattles off, "Bach, Johann Sebastian, March 21, 1685 to July 28, 1750. Now mine for you. Lalo, Édouard-Victoire-Antoine."

Douglas shakes his head. "I don't know."

"Lalo, Édouard-Victoire-Antoine. January 27, 1823 to April 22, 1892, silly. Who are your favorite composers anyway?"

Douglas shrugs.

Bertine interrupts. "Michael's favorites are Paganini, Lalo, Bach, Saint Saëns, Fritz Kreisler, right, Mike? And he can beat everybody at this game so it's not fair, we have marbles, want to play? I'll get them and draw the circle, right back."

She returns with chalk and a bag of Agates; they argue over shooters. It seems no time has passed before Michael's mother hollers for her children. Her voice bawls through the screen door and disrupts Douglas' well-aimed shot at Michael's favorite aggie.

Michael dutifully heads indoors while Bertine gathers the marbles, taking her sweet time. Once finished she gives Douglas' bicep a jab with her very pointed knuckles. "Will you be his friend?" she asks. Her question sounds like a command. Douglas grins without hesitation.

Michael must be the luckiest boy in the world, Douglas thinks as he rides away. The luckiest boy in the world. He goes to fiddler camp. He has a famous violin teacher. He's getting trained. How will I ever earn the 253-1 if I'm stuck with Sir Johnson?

[20]

FUNDS ALLOW DOUGLAS only two lessons per month; Wing, always a welcome ally, drives him to the neighboring town. After his four-syllable pep talk—"You can do boy"—Wing cuffs him on the ear and sends him upstairs to endure the ordeal.

"Like batting practice," Sir Johnson explains. "Repetition, repetition, repetition. And please, forget the emotion, not for beginners. Some players try to slide into base with that *grease*. Here's the truth. No worthy home run is made without the solid *crack* of a bat against a ball."

Douglas jumps as the word *crack* is spit in his direction. Sir Johnson's baseball metaphors fail to convince him. He longs for affirmation of his disbelief; dares not seek it from Sister Elder. Returning home from yet another discouraging lesson, he addresses his ally. "Wing, Sir Johnson says emotion is useless in music. He says it's like a fancy uniform in baseball when your team is losing. Do you believe that?"

"This Sir Johnson, he shows you how to play without, without emotion?"

Wing has touched on a truth. May to July, five lessons given. Has Johnson ever shown him *anything*? No. This teacher has yet to pick up his own violin to demonstrate a passage. Has yet to play a recording to elevate Douglas' understanding. Has yet to speak of a violinist he admires.

[21]

AUGUST 1947. IT comes so quickly. Douglas waves a sad goodbye to Michael and Bertine Rabin as thistle fluff floats, as grasses turn ochre. Meadowmount strings are silenced. Goodbye, goodbye...all the inspiring musicians are gone. Nothing except crickets fiddling away. He's left with Willi, who still calls him Doogie, who still wants to fight. And with Violette, who joins him to race twig and leaf boats under Little Bridge.

Now even Sister Peace abhors hearing Douglas practice the annoying Etudes. Music should offer, at the very least, a pleasant distraction for both player and listener. Now and again, James sings nasally as he mimics the violin's voice. Mildred goes to the library of an evening, even though she is not an avid reader.

Although Sister Elder takes no stock in predications or omens—unlike Sister Peace—she fears Douglas' fixation on the heathen violin is an unrelenting curse. Nothing worthwhile has come of it. The child suffered mistreatment with Stoyas. His skills declined with the Orchestra. She's sent good money after bad paying Sir Johnson for naught. And if you will, just look at the resulting impact on the household. Mildred is even more temperamental than usual for a fifteen-year-old female. James uses profanity like Mr. Ludlow. John sasses. Who can stand it? Rue the day she allowed that accursed fiddle into her household.

[22]

ORANGE LEAVES DRIFT and gray geese fly. Douglas is left to ruminate. He's quit the Orchestra only to be squashed by the disrespectful hands of Sir Johnson. His attempts at practice cease entirely. Nothing except crickets fiddling away.

The school secretary calls to set up a conference with the Principal. *Now what hijinks is Douglas accused of?* Sister Elder cringes. She's remembering the school's complaints against Mildred, James, and John these past few years. James taped the photo of a naked woman in a bathroom stall. John threw a rock at the cafeteria window and denied doing so— even though he was seen in the act. Mildred wrote a note with swear words and passed it during class. These troublemakers of hers!

"Attitude, Miss Smythe," the Principal explains. "*Attitude* is the problem. Douglas is borderline rude and in non-compliance with our expectations of demeanor. Monday he was punished with the writing of *I will not ignore my Teachers*, one hundred times on the blackboard. Still, we see no improvement. Our next step is suspension for three days. You may take him home now, please."

Violette comes to the Home wanting to comfort Douglas; he refuses to see her. Violette, in tears, begs Sister Elder, "Please do something."

* * *

IT'S QUIET HOUR in the Home. The incorrigible kid has finally returned to school. Wing and Astrid have gone shopping. Sister Elder knocks on the bedroom door. "Tatiana, may I have a word?"

The phonograph is turned off. The door is opened to reveal Sister Peace in what is termed her *limbering up* costume.

Sister Elder closes the door quietly and leans back upon it. "Can't we just talk? I'm only asking for some suggestions here."

A previous conversation is being re-opened. Sister Peace gives no sign of cooperation, her arms crossed over her thin torso, her feet planted heel to heel, her hair bundled like an outcropping of obsidian.

Sister Elder stares. She so rarely sees this young woman's shape; it's usually camouflaged by men's attire and starched apron. Regaining composure, Hester restates her issue. "Young Douglas' runaway imagination is a growing problem. He believes that the rogue violin communicates with him across time and space. Evangeline recognizes the problem too. A boy his age, almost a teen for heaven's sake, must give up fantasy and finally be grounded. Surely you agree?"

Sister Peace doesn't offer a reaction. She maintains her obstinate stance.

"Do you understand the consequences of, what shall I call it, his destructive tendency?" Sister Elder waits. She stares unblinkingly at the young woman. She unties and reties her apron strings with a few brisk maneuvers. "All I ask of you is help in arresting the boy's detrimental predilection. You could offer some suggestions, perhaps?"

Tatiana spins around, no longer facing Sister Elder. She walks across the room, sets the needle on the record, and as the music begins takes fifth position at the bamboo pole. "If you don't mind—"

Sister Elder is not to be ignored. "Sister Peace, remember our agreement: *Peace, Sister Peace.* Each year Douglas detaches further, and you, my dear, seem to encourage him like some fanciful faerie."

"I do not see him as you do, Hester. Douglas thinks the way of artist. Do not ask me to meddle there."

Hester wears her patience like a laurel wreath and so she keeps her aggravation with this *fanciful faerie* in check. Never fear, she will remember Tatiana's stiff-necked lack of cooperation as a transgression. And forgiveness from Sister Elder is hard-won.

[23]

TO BE FAIR, Sister Elder might have let Douglas off the hook with Sir Johnson if she'd been made aware of his unprofessionalism. So much for teaching kids stiff-upper-lipped stoicism. *Finishing What You Start, and all that jazz.* Ten lessons later, his very own violin in its cardboard case, the book of Etudes in his satchel, Douglas rides to Studio 210, Wing attempting cheer at the wheel. Even Wing, this creative cook, this imaginative cartoonist, this optimist, holds out little hope for salvation.

* * *

AFTER THE ELEVENTH violin lesson, after a bath, Douglas examines the clustering freckles on his cheeks, the fuzz appearing on his upper lip; adulthood looms dismally ahead. Like the shuffle of a distant deck of cards, 253-1 is speaking to him.

{This one also endured what was not of her choosing| *Violini* can bear neglect for time upon time| Silence is but small enemy| Oh not so with abuse| not so with misuse| Not for long can a *violino* bear ill treatment| Structure may sag| crack| loosen| strings droop| voice growl like a beast's| bleat like the hurdy-gurdy man's| useless except for displeasuring| Humans too suffer from neglect| suffer too from abuse| |

"Yeah."

{*Violini* are built of wood and may not alter their treatment| Oh for the sadness of it| humans are not as easily repaired as *violini*| 253-1 speaks with wisdom of years when she says| Remember you are human| made of flesh, not wood| while you are alive you have choice| |

"Doesn't feel like it." Douglas examines John's razor.

253-1 offers encouragement. {Hold steady while you seek release| It is said| ask and you shall receive| |

Douglas briskly shaves off the fuzz. His passion takes the form of fervent prayer: *Please an instructor like Michael's Ivan Galamian.* He pleads to his reflection, although it's 253-1 he's addressing. "How else am I going to find Stoya's favor and earn you back?"

[24]

ONE BLUSTERY EVENING, next door neighbor Ludlow invites Douglas to join him in his garage. "Wanna learn about a crystal radio set kid?" Maybe Ludlow is intrigued by the development of this musical boy who didn't speak for six years. Or perhaps the man's found someone to split his kindling. Or let's say he's simply taking pity on a mistreated kid. You see, many factory violins in cardboard cases are sheltering with dust bunnies under children's beds. Gossip about Sir Herbert Johnson does go 'round and 'round Elizabethtown; dispirited parents do complain.

Nevertheless, after multiple sessions of splitting wood and listening to Mr. Ludlow's crystal radio set Douglas can't comprehend how the contraption works. Ludlow twists the knobs, a stogie stuck under his long upper lip—a lip that turns under in its grasp of the wrapped stick, a stick that grows shorter while the ashy end grows longer. The man seems more interested in listening to unseen broadcasters than in speaking to a boy hovering over his shoulder. When Ludlow tries to explain the wire-wrapped cylinder's function the technical jargon escapes the fifth grader's understanding. Besides, the sight of Ludlow speaking with the cigar in his mouth offers the kid plenty of distraction.

While troubling over a class assignment Douglas has a brainstorm; what if he could report on a radio's mysterious function? He finds a book shelved as *Science* numbered 537.534. "An excellent choice," the librarian says while stamping the date card. Her eyes look like slits under heavy brows, and Douglas wonders if this deformity is caused by reading too many books.

By page 22 of the library book Douglas no longer thinks of lunch or recess. *I'm like a receiver with a specially tuned antenna. That's how I understand my violin.* Fortified by the example, Douglas examines his introverted ways. Since Stoya's dismissal he's been inhabiting a private realm where the companionship of Magic Muriel 253-1 has compensated for his withdrawal from friends and family. To the exclusion of sociability.

He'd long ago stopped sharing the violin's tales with Sister Elder. "You have a commendable imagination," she'd once said. "Better keep this particular goofiness to yourself." Sister Elder's skeptical advice had jangled in Douglas' head like a string of tin cans behind some newlyweds' Oldsmobile.

Better not tell Astrid, he's learned. She chides Wing when he encourages Douglas to repeat the violin's tales to them. "You cannot let the boy say such things—people will think he's gone bananas."

Wing simply accepts him as he is. Although Wing doesn't really believe either. He explains Douglas' behavior to Astrid. "No problem if Wing say lizards large as Empire State Building? So. No problem if boy say violin speak like friend. My wife not understanding imagination?"

Wing continues to be kind even if he doesn't get it. "Boy who dream when awake is poet," he tells Douglas. Encouraged, Douglas shares with Wing. Mostly when he cannot control his excitement. Mostly when Astrid is not around. His new insight can't be contained. "I'm like a receiver with a specially tuned antenna. That's how I understand waves of energy that the cells of a violin broadcast."

Wing chuckles. He tapes a blank tarot card to his drawing board. Within minutes he's inked a cartoon, an alien boy with antennae projecting from his head. "My next character! Antenna Boy."

Douglas reaches for the black and white image. "Hey, that's me! Oh, Wing, can I have it, please?" Into the cigar box of treasure it goes, safe from James and John's teasing ways.

It's only Sister Peace, his Tatiana, who gets it. Who doesn't wrinkle her forehead or sermonize. A luminosity shoots through her eyes as if the aurora borealis were reflecting there. "You can tell me what your violin says, when just we two are together!"

They bound across Little Bridge and skirt the egg farm, leaving boot prints in the frosty grass alongside the slushy stream, all the while Douglas shaping Magic Muriel's stories, the parts that he can translate into words. Only Sister Peace truly believes.

Enlightened by science, Douglas wonders: Why should I keep to myself? And he concludes: I'm not a freak. Not a weirdo because I can communicate with a violin. I'm simply more sensitive.

Accordingly, his behavior changes. If they expect him to find a separate table at lunch, they are in for a surprise. Douglas sits shoulder to shoulder with classmates. The Norwegian-inspired healthy Oslo lunch, recently introduced to his school, consists of a salad sandwich made on whole meal bread, a bottle of milk, and a piece of fresh fruit. As usual, Willi approaches. Snickering comrades know the gig; young Stoya has taunted Douglas since last February. "Give up your apple, sucker!" Willi says this softly enough to escape the Cafeteria Monitor's ears. "Give it up, Doogie, doo-doo. Give it up, Doogie, doo-doo," the loyal chorus goes. Today Willi's powerplay fizzles. Douglas takes five enormous bites of apple and hands over a slippery core, not the rosy treat he habitually surrenders. He grins at his would-be-tormentors with a surge of renewed self-respect.

[25]

"MY REPORT IS titled *Radio Waves*," Douglas announces to the class. Willi's throaty scoff bypasses the teacher's awareness. Violette gives Douglas a supportive nod. Her five nimble fingers interlock, index fingers forming a reverential steeple.

> Douglas (like a reporter full of confidence)
>
> We have electromagnetic radio waves flying through the air hitting everything. Including you! These radio waves can travel at the speed of light, 186,000 miles per second. A sound wave is different. It travels only 766 miles an hour. That's called the speed of sound. Think about it like this. If you record a violinist in the Social Center of Elizabethtown and transmit it over the radio, the radio wave can reach Atlanta, Georgia, in an instant. It gets there before the violin's sound wave reaches the very last row of seats at our Social Center.
>
> Sound waves need particles to pass through from one place to another. Guess what? Radio waves are energy waves like light and don't need a medium to help them travel.
>
> Did you know that astronomical objects give off radio waves too? I think people give off electromagnetic radio waves of some sort. Everything does, I think.

Douglas beams. His energy is captivating; this is no shrinking Doogie-doo in front of the class.

> Douglas (holding up a poster board with diagrams)
>
> These silent electromagnetic radio waves have different frequencies, amplitudes, phases, or pulse widths. We describe this as FM or AM. Some waves are sharp, narrow, and tall; some are round and wide. Some waves stay the same as they travel; some repeat

patterns. A receiver's antenna can be tuned to respond to preferred signals and to reject ones it doesn't want. The receiver then converts the signal to a usable form. And that's communication. THE END.

Douglas has been commanding the class's attention. The sixth graders sense that a personal mystery has been divulged and yet none can seem to apply it.

[26]

I'M OLDER NOW. I'm going to stop acting like a brat. I'll make Sister Elder understand by talking like an adult. It worked with Auntie Evangeline. Her words repeat in his mind. "You see, our passion for music can be fulfilled, maybe not just the way we imagine it at first."

The air smells of earth, damp dark earth accepting Saturday morning's gentle rain after a night of pinging hail. He finds Sister Elder on the porch, sipping coffee from a gold-rimmed cup. She's reading.

He senses her quiet energy and takes it as a positive sign. "What are you reading?" he asks.

"Astrid chose this for me." She holds up the Agatha Christie. She wears a hand-knit sweater; just now she buttons it. Seven wooden buttons sliding into their assigned places while Douglas watches and waits.

"Sister Elder, can we just talk?"

She marks her place, rests the book on her lap as if prepared. Still, she remains passive, the two of them on the swing, feet pushing in unison with the creak of chain and wood as accompaniment. She, looking unaffected as if she does not also feel the damp breeze crossing the fields and the river, as if she does not remember the Basque and the call of his violin, as if nothing affects her.

In the face of her self-assured calm Douglas' insides boil, molecules of anger speed up, and his rage flies apart and evaporates into a presence not entirely invisible to Sister Elder. *She's not going to listen to me!* He holds back his scream. *Can't she see how upset I am?*

She remains silent. Silence, she knows, asks the difficult questions by opening a void in the space.

As he gathers control, he feels her pulse, her receptive pulse, a pulse she so rarely exhibits. And now he's obliged to trust her. It seems only she has the power to change his fate, once again. As if one's life was continuously being molded by the one who had changed your diapers.

"Anyway, I want to talk about music," he begins, speaking so rapidly that his words engage before his brain can catch up. "When I used to play the violin it was like something coming alive, like all of this is coming alive!" He gestures with his arms as Sister Peace might. Douglas stops and gulps a breath of air, his heart beating *allegro appassionato*. He looks sideways at her, afraid to catch her eye, a child as vulnerable as a stinkbug crawling under the icebox.

Sister Elder gazes at the boy's face as if trying to detect chicken pox, or mumps, or adulthood infecting this foundling, this child, her responsibility. She speaks quietly. "Auntie Evangeline and I have been in conversation. About you. Did you know that?" The boy is holding his breath. "She's discerning if nothing else when it comes to you."

Douglas fidgets as they swing—he doesn't know what to say next. His boot unexpectedly catches in a plank of the porch, stopping their glide. He's jolted out of silence. "I heard a boy, this summer, we're friends now, he really-really-honestly-truly plays violin, because he's getting seriously taught, at home in New York, at Meadowmount too all summer. He practices even when his mom doesn't make him. His sister is so cute—she plays piano. Her talent isn't as great as his—she even said so." Douglas pauses, revving up.

"Hester! Listen to me. It's time to find me a real true teacher, because I know the difference and I am serious and I will not go back to Sir Johnson, cross my heart and hope to die."

Douglas smiles to himself. He called Sister Elder by her first name just like an adult, and he sounded an awful lot like Bertine. Relief washes over his face.

Sister Elder sees his sweetness reappear after this declaration. She will not succumb to a reaction. She'd lived with a father whose temper burst temporarily out of control; she'd learned restraint. *Whoever these Rabin children are, they've accelerated Douglas' desires. Now what?* To keep herself calm Sister Elder reflects on patterns in lacemaking, flowers, spirals, birds of paradise, and scallops. How they repeat. She reflects on the patterns in people's lives. How they repeat. She resists or finds confusion when trying to define her own life patterns. She used to say *people are naturally good. Everyone's potential is limitless.* Hester lets out a sigh, realizing she doesn't believe this anymore. Look at Douglas, so vulnerable, so wounded. Has his potential been diminished? She's furious with Stoya for damaging this child. Where is the good in the Professor? Or in Mrs. Piano Teacher? Cowering woman, who should have challenged her blustering husband's behavior.

Why then, when Sister Elder speaks, do harsh words rush from her mouth? "Where is your gratitude, boy-o? Auntie Evangeline gifted you with a summer of singing lessons, and when that didn't suit, I purchased you a violin. Found you an instructor, paid for months of lessons. What do you do? Complain. You tire me. Be off."

And then Sister Elder is back to the confusion of self. Is this her new pattern, an inability to forgive? She's angry with her sister Evangeline for leading the boy on, letting him believe he could become a professional musician. Sister Elder swats away moths circling. They've gathered as if light glows from her head. In that instant she envisions herself; she's like beautiful tulle, except there's an error in the lacemaking of her soul— twisted, knotted, looped—like a bird of paradise with a botched wing. When she looks up, there he is, right there. Douglas is waiting. His face demanding a different response from this unforgiving, this uncharitable woman. "We'll sort it out, Douglas, I promise." Sister Elder chucks the petitioner under the chin, a most unusual gesture from her. "Let's rustle up the others for some pumpkin pie."

Sister Elder, who prides herself on imperturbability, is driven to a humbling act. With a heavy heart the Guardian decides she will acquiesce to Evangeline's counsel, whatever it may be. She writes a nine-page letter revealing the progress of the problem. Suffering qualms, she stamps it with her black wax seal, mails it at the Postal Office in Denton's Grocery, and with trepidation awaits a response from her ever-meddling sister, the much-favored Auntie.

The full history of Douglas' decline while studying with incompetent teachers is exposed in that letter. Auntie Evangeline acts before responding to Hester; she will not tolerate this loss while she still breathes. Not while she can still command respect in the world of music.

III
ADVANCE & RETREAT

[1]

CIAZZO SLOGS THROUGH Evangeline's tedious letter. In his estimation the twelve-year-old has most probably lost crucial formative time, incentive, perhaps even trust. Ciazzo's respect for Evangeline, not a desire to claim victory over a lost cause, determines his reply. Four months is his commitment, January through May; teaching Douglas Tryzyna beyond this depends solely on the boy's progress. *Progress, really? Unimaginable.*

On the other hand, Ciazzo remembers the name Peter Stoya, an accredited German musician known in New York circles. Rumor has it the man arrived in early 1941 with two violins—one of them classified as Fine and Rare. The value of that one supposedly skyrocketed in a clandestine bidding war. *Well, if this was the boy's first teacher? Five years of solid technique with Stoya,* Ciazzo conjectures, *might possibly have been providential, despite the current digression.*

[2]

THE BUS HAS grown steamy. So many people in damp clothing breathing cool air in, breathing warm air out. Douglas swipes a window with his sleeve, clearing a transparent circle, daring to hope for deliverance from what Violette terms torpor. Of a sudden, rainstorm promising hail strikes the window. White staccatos of light hit the asphalt like stabs of anticipation, quick-quick-quick, a million whisperings, like mankind's simultaneous prayers to a god. How can a single prayer be distinguished, or one teenager's prayer in particular?

Clutching his violin case Douglas watches for landmarks and signage as they enter Westport. Main Street seems a confusion of pedestrians crisscrossing through traffic, their faces hidden under black umbrellas. He unfolds the lined paper and reads the directions yet again. Ciazzo's studio is to be found:

1. after the stone cathedral with its mismatched spires

2. beyond the iron and glass overhead walkway

3. just past the billboard for Beverwyk Beer

Yes, he sees it! The Beverwyk Beer billboard dominates the side of a tall building. Douglas disembarks, opens his umbrella, dashes through the downpour, dodges a streetcar, enters the flatiron building, and breathlessly rides the cage of an elevator to the seventh floor. An *honest-to-God musician* here might be his teacher! Sister Elder wasn't too encouraging, though. She suggested the improbability of his being accepted. Her message: Ciazzo teaches emerging professionals, *and very occasionally the exceptionally talented youth.*

Douglas finds the studio door open and offering the smell of an apple orchard, of oiled leather, and of rum-soaked tobacco. With these comforts, a flash of newfound courage ripples through his gut. Across the room on the window ledge sits a gentleman smoking a cigarillo. The fellow appears to be gazing at the rainclouds. Douglas shifts from one foot to another waiting to be noticed. It's a sepia photo in hammered silver frame that attracts him; pictured is a young boy dressed in a cutaway jacket. Given the broad notched lapels, covered buttons, and frilly neckline the garment looks old-fashioned. When Douglas glances up the gentleman is heading his way with an outstretched hand—a milky brown hand. Douglas returns the gentleman's grasp while watching the large hand encompass his smaller, paler one.

Douglas stares. Wow, this is the Ciazzo whom Auntie Evangeline wrote about. Ciazzo is impressively tall. His black hair bristles upward from a widow's peak outlining perfect triangles of forehead. Even a thirteen-year-old boy cannot ignore the man's full, well-shaped lips, lips a Miss would envy, or wish to kiss, or mistake for sneering.

Before Douglas can speak Ciazzo points to a scroll bearing medieval ornamentation and calligraphy. "What does it say, this?" he asks. Douglas struggles to decipher the six elegant characters.

"Does it say, *Listen*?" the boy asks timidly.

"*Sí*, that is correct. Now settle your umbrella—just there, please."

Ciazzo leads his student to the window, to a view of gray-blue sky and an irregular horizon of buildings. "Close your eyes. And listen." Douglas immediately feels a magnetic pulse. Ciazzo's energy.

Minutes pass, holding Douglas spellbound. He listens to a coarse symphony from above and below. He listens as sound travels around and around: sounds of rain, engines, brakes, crows, garbled voices. As these noises recede, softer sounds intensify. Pigeons coo; Ciazzo breathes; his own heart thuds.

"*Hasta que está escuchando*. A violinist should not begin practice until he is listening." With that dictum Ciazzo asks Douglas to play a favorite memorized piece.

Hesitant, embarrassed, Douglas opens his cardboard case, sets aside the green silk. What to play for this precise man with his third-rate violin and bow? Not even the pieces he once enjoyed performing appeal to him now. He chooses a composition by Leopold Auer; he's rushing the tempo; the faster he races through the piece the more vividly he recognizes his inadequacies. A tone that wails. A left hand that lacks agility. "I haven't been practicing much," he says in self-defense, stopping short of the final passage. He sets the troublesome violin into the case.

Ciazzo signals for Douglas to hold out his sweaty hands. "Every hand is different. Some fingers are too fat, some bend when firmness is asked, some are too short for even the first position. Your hands and fingers, Douglas, by my observation, are enviable. However, it is said there are just three classes of players. First, those who cannot play at all.

Second, those who play badly. Third, those who play well. You have advanced to the second class."

"I know. I play badly," Douglas says.

Next the instructor picks up the boy's violin. He raps the back, the belly, the fingerboard, draws the bow across the strings. "You despise this violin, do you not?"

Douglas hangs his head while his downcast eyes tell the story.

"You hear the difference between such and so. Excellent! And you know what? If you can make this poor box sing you will have an audience in tears when you play a quality instrument. ¿Lo entiendes?"

Ciazzo hurriedly closes the window—the wind has changed direction. Douglas wonders what comes next; anticipation pings again like the stabbing rain. Here it comes! "We will start now at the beginning. Scales. I ask for unremitting watchfulness while you are at work. Attend each note. Mental labor is the true source of all progress."

Douglas plays his scales. Ciazzo watches on, circling, circling, circling, analyzing the musician's alignment. Douglas expects a barrage of words. Ciazzo uses none. He molds the student into proper position. He gives an upward nudge to the elbow, lifts the thumb ever so gently, watches to see that the thumb remains loosely held. Ciazzo nudges downward on the boy's wrist, little by little repositioning the left arm, wrist, and hand. In eloquent silence like a sculptor finalizing his masterpiece this man has communicated proper alignment. "Hold this position in memory. Now I will demonstrate how it looks."

Taking up his own violin Ciazzo plays several scales in succession. The elegance of this instructor's line is immediately apparent. He holds the violin at a steep upward angle, his left arm at a right angle to his torso. Douglas comprehends Ciazzo's gentle grasp of the violin's neck, comprehends the fingers poised almost vertical to the strings as they maneuver with graceful motion up and down.

Ciazzo keeps his own violin at the ready and asks Douglas to again hold his violin correctly. This position feels strange and difficult; if Stoya taught him this he has forgotten it. Douglas attempts. Ciazzo stops the boy, demonstrating again and again correctness. "This is how you must hold it when you play."

After a bit the patient teacher puts the physical lesson into words. "Keep your eyes fixed on the head of the violin, let your fingers fall perpendicular, keep your left arm forward under the violin. Do not rest it on your shoulder. Now try."

The tone from his violin will not cooperate. Douglas withholds his usual foot stomping. He stifles the raging tantrum; he must make the violin sing. He rearranges his shirt.

"Let me see!" Ciazzo is almost laughing. He inspects the red item under Douglas' instrument. "Forget this silly thing—you are losing one third of the tone! Can you see, it acts as a mute?"

Douglas flinches; mortification displays itself. He tosses away the silk cushion Astrid made for him. Ciazzo says kindly, "I'll select the proper chin rest for you. A violinist must be comfortable to do well. And now, again, show me what you have learned."

Fifty minutes of practice later, Ciazzo says, "Now you require ten minutes of rest. Let's talk." What of his past lessons? What are his goals? Does he have dreams?

Douglas communicates with a shrug. Words to describe his ragged history? Those words are unbearable to speak aloud. Of a teacher who played right on top of his student's playing, of a teacher who attended baseball when pretending to teach. Worse, of a Professor who banished a boy from lessons and then unfairly kept claim to a boy's special violin.

Ciazzo has an endearing way of raising his bold eyebrows while he listens to what is not spoken—eyebrows that try to join across the bridge of his nose, failing only slightly. He watches the boy struggle with dark and hurtful memories.

Ciazzo knows a thing or two about this boy, about his forestalled aptitude and his aberrations. Evangeline's letter spared nothing. Nevertheless, a crucial component of the boy's spirit hangs in the balance. The man once again takes up his Giuseppe Tarasconi, 1899. In his hands the violin expresses a voice of crystalline beauty. As Douglas listens, the lyrical passage from Bizet's *L'Arlesienne Suite* as performed by Ciazzo charges him with undeniable passion; tears form. This man's energy seduces him, a mystery, like geese finding flight, how they're running on water's surface, how they're stretching forward, how the extended wings are flapping. One knows these are just feathers, sinew, and bone, and yet a goose is capable of agitating air currents with an instinctive rhythm until it propels itself skyward. An awe-inspiring implausibility to witness, both on the river and here with a flesh and blood human who not only attains but inhabits a rarefied atmosphere.

Douglas lingers in the spell. When the power of speech returns, he wants to know what the music is about. Ciazzo explains it is a tragic story about unrequited love in which the beloved never appears.

The beloved never appears? Douglas' knees buckle, he sits down hard, almost missing the piano stool. Violette, his beloved, what if she's stolen by Willi? What if the 253-1 is never returned. Such thoughts are hard to bear.

The two, a Spaniard and an orphan, resume having found unspoken commonality. Concluding, Ciazzo makes an offer. "If you are serious about lessons with me, go home. Practice your scales daily. Practice the

Auer composition until you know it backward and forward. Come again next week and show me what you're made of."

Douglas returns the factory violin to its cardboard case, carefully wrapping her ordinary body in green silk, which of course makes it seem no lovelier to his eyes.

"You have a violin. Accept it. Use it to advance your skills." Ciazzo's expressive eyes drill into Douglas' conscience. It comes clear; *I'm an ungrateful kid.*

[3]

VIOLETTE PASSES DOUGLAS a typewritten note. Her word? *Forbearance.* Using it she attempts a phrase of encouragement, not knowing how else to help her musical friend. He's lost lessons with Stoya. He's quit Orchestra. He's quit Sir Johnson. In response Sister Elder and Auntie Evangeline have hired Ciazzo. Gee whiz, how can Douglas possibly please Ciazzo with such a bad attitude?

Of a sudden 253-1 vocalizes. Hers, a forcible assault, as if a hundred bells toll, seventy violins screech, fifty drums drive a rhythm of impending doom. It occurs for Douglas while watching Wing use a wispy old brush to render a guitar-playing dragon.

{My kind| survivors of indignity| recipients of honor| harbor a million elasticized cells| in the fibers of backs| of bellies| of sounding posts| Is that not so| In truth| the sound of a *violino*| comes from wood| string| horsehair| Still| wordless magic of music requires the vibration of a player's usage| |

The message sends shivers up and down Douglas' spine.

{253-1 longs for your sensitivity| for the vibrancy of your maturity| You asked| You were granted| When you disdain your practice| you abandon Me| Myself| It is so| |

Douglas reverses, he comes to terms with the factory violin. She serves me in her own way. She doesn't have a heritage to express. No secrets to reveal. No history of masters, or even of crummy players. She can't help it if she's insensitive. She's simply a tool. Every tool has a function. I'll stop comparing her to the 253-1. I'll respect her.

"Age and use may make a good violin better; sadly, age won't make a bad fiddle good." Ciazzo stated the reality. With this acceptance Douglas experiences a lightness, as if a knight's helmet has been lifted from his head. He's no longer at battle.

Douglas practices at the Home remembering Ciazzo's advice: "Begin with slow strokes, ten to twelve seconds for down and up strokes. Stop as soon as fatigue is felt. Play scales through two octaves using finger pressure only for now. A student who is not observing and criticizing the whole tones and half tones is merely perfecting his faults."

Next week. It's Douglas returning to the Westport studio, once again engulfed by the smell of apples, of oiled leather, and of rum-soaked tobacco. It's Douglas shifting from one foot to another, pleading to the boy in a sepia photo who can't really do a thing for him. It's Douglas gaining his own steam and playing the Auer with conviction.

In response it's Ciazzo posing a question. "What will it take for you to become a virtuoso?"

Doulas grabs into the edges of the piano stool. The woven upholstery slithers and hisses under his sensitive fingertips. *This is a dangerous question, a trick question.*

"Will it take artistic instinct? Certainly. And I see the instinct in you, Douglas. Pues, *no es suficiente*. Well, that alone is not enough. The process will take struggle. Years of it. Patience. Like you can't imagine. I ask for nothing less from my students. Even then I can't promise you success. Who can promise an undeserved spark of genius?"

Douglas twirls on the piano stool, inferring unworthiness in this man's presence.

"You may return each week until May if you are prepared to engage in such a quest."

[4]

AS LESSONS CONTINUE into February the student and teacher tackle another basic. The bow. How to hold it. There is no science, Ciazzo suggests, so first try to hold lightly, and lower the wrist. "Gently as if holding a baby bird. However, each player must listen and use the bow to make his instrument sing. Or else, who could *bear* hearing our violin's voice?"

Douglas laughs for the first time in months. His family at the Home has surely found his playing *unbearable*!

Under Ciazzo's guidance Douglas takes pride in each bit of progress. This teacher reminds him of an industrious woodpecker, steady-steady-steady at his task, taking unexpected pauses before briskly hopping on to the next point of attack. Sometimes Ciazzo accompanies his student on the piano, an upright Steinway, having a luster as rich as its owner's eyes. Sometimes they listen to a recording, appreciating a great player's interpretation. Occasionally Ciazzo guides Douglas through sight-reading. Sometimes Douglas cannot do anything other than stare in awe at this discerning man, whose ears are defined by sharp angles, not curves, and set well back, whose square jaw ripples with anticipation.

[5]

HERE IS SISTER PEACE placing flowers on the doorstep, her superstitious May Day Eve ritual. And here is Ciazzo reminding Douglas that his promised months of lessons have been completed. "Regular practice by yourself is what I advise next," he says. "Come September we'll decide if we're to continue together." This teaching wizard offers his *goodbye*; he departs for his tour.

Summer vacation. Yes, Ciazzo is gone. A man who listens. A man who teaches by example. A man excited by the voice of a violin. Douglas writes himself a memo. He folds it in quarters and places it in the Muriel cigar box alongside the bell and Violette's notes.

> I will not hate Willi even when he calls me names
>
> I will not be angry with Sister Elder anymore
>
> I will not let the poor violin discourage me ever again
>
> I will show Ciazzo
>
> I will get what I want

[6]

STOYA HOLDS HIMSELF in control. Galamian can be the most annoying man. Wasn't attending the man's select students in concert enough? Hadn't he and Frieda traveled into the City explicitly to sit through the entire event at Town Hall? Hadn't they kept a lid on their stew of envy while hearing Michael Rabin play? Thank you very much, he prefers not to hear Galamian gloat about his eleven, or by now, his twelve-year-old Boy Wonder.

No matter. Ivan's reading aloud a review in the *Montreal Gazette*, October 31, 1947; here *he* is being polite. *Admit it, I'm curious. What the hell is this teacher doing right?*

Galamian continues reading about Michael; pride surges through every facet of his being. "'He plays cleanly, accurately, with authority...best of all, with a beautiful sense of musical values...

"'From the Sarabande and the Bourrée of Bach's Partita in B Minor he was able to draw an astonishing amount of grandeur and profundity inherent in them...

"'But it was with the Paganini Caprices that he awakened most of the audience to a sense of what he is worth. Never faltered...sturdy, modest boy, with a cherubic sensitive face.... He executed each caprice with a minimum of fuss and a maximum of energy, with absolute accuracy and a truly magnificent sense of phrasing.'"

"Some student you have there!" Stoya offers. Negative thoughts jackhammer his head, his stomach, his chest. He hopes Galamian is too caught up in glorying to observe his spite.

"Michael will be at Meadowmount again this summer." Ivan Galamian glows. You must come listen to him in our recital events."

"Well, my dear Ivan, I hope you and Judith will have dinner at the Conservatory and hear my Willi. I'd be honored to have your insight. I'll just say, he's advancing nicely."

Galamian responds positively. He adds an unexpected comment. "I hear Douglas is studying with Ciazzo now. That youngster certainly impressed Piatigorsky. At his tender age with such innate musicality. I'm surprised you let him go."

"Sir, it boiled down to a matter of integrity, a lack of character." Stoya speaks with a conviction he doesn't necessarily feel.

Galamian lifts his eyebrows expressively as he shares some insight. "A wunderkind ought not be handled like the normal child, Peter. Circumstances affect them oddly."

Professor Stoya fights outrage as he drives home. Is Galamian comparing Douglas' inborn ability to Michael Rabin's? After only such brief encounters? And the news that Douglas is with Ciazzo? Is this true? He stops on a bluff overlooking Elizabethtown. Rubs the curved scar on his cheekbone. Frieda will ask him what's wrong; somehow his face gives him away. He rolls down the window, shivers in the chill breeze; the June sky is pearly gray and hints of rain. The honking of geese intrigues him before he can see them. And then they come into view, returning to the Adirondacks. Three separate strands form a vee and proceed noisily. One bird trails. Peter watches as the loner falls increasingly behind, encountering more air resistance than those in the group.

I gave Douglas a chance back then, he thinks. *I gave him a solid foundation.* Peter puts the car into gear and drives home, fingering the scar on his cheek.

[7]

SCHOOL IS OUT. With freedom from a routine. Douglas bikes up to Fiddler Hill where he notes the caretaker's preparations. Speeds past the Stoya Conservatory. Yes, he's an invisible alien with antennae. Unless Violette is finishing her lesson, in which case he's a very human boyfriend who waits for her around the corner. She rides his handlebars, offering news about each music student's progress. After which the musicians afflicted with puppy love wade barefoot in the shallows. There the water flows fairy-green as it passes over thousands of round moss-frosted stones. There wild spiraea blossoming along the shore reflect as pink as carnival cotton candy.

If Violette does not appear, he pedals around an extra block, avoiding the terrier, and so to *Lilacs* where he stops. June 5th, the curtains are closed at the rental house with no sign of occupants. June 10th, the lawn has been mowed. A few days later Douglas brakes hard. Listen! Sounds of scales being practiced on a piano. Sounds of something difficult being played on a violin. *They've returned!* He stops at the gate where he rests his bike. Should he knock? A sign warns against disturbing the household. A Pekinese peering out the neighbor's window yips at him; bees buzz menacingly. He sits on the sidewalk beside his bicycle, riffling the cards tucked in the spokes. Time passes. He entertains himself matching card clicks with the steady beat of the Minuet.

The ice cream truck's familiar tinkling of *Turkey in the Straw* brings Bertine to the porch. "Michael, come on," she hollers. Douglas waves to the driver, pulls out his coins. "Three cherry popsicles, please," he whispers to the driver. What fun it will be to see his friends' surprise.

Bertine skips toward him and the vendor. "Michael, c'mon out, Douglas is here, and guess what, he bought us popsicles!"

The kids sit on the shady porch lapping their icy treats, wiping drips off their chins with the backs of their hands. A small plane drones, the truck's repetitious tune fades, chickadees chatter, chirrup, and trill, a gentle breeze silently stirs shadows. Douglas records this squishy sensation; he's melting with pleasure.

"Where's your mom?" Douglas asks, wary of the bossy lady they call Jeanne.

"Shopping for dinner stuff cuz Dad's gonna be here tonight and she's cooking for a bunch of people from people from Meadowmount. Anyway, where's your mom?"

"Dunno. She left me at Sister Elder's when I was a tiny baby. Maybe she's dead now."

"That's awful. Just awful." Bertine pats Douglas' sticky cheek, offering a frown as she continues talking. "We had a brother, he played piano like, like, well, like he was a prodigy..."

"A *wunderkind*," Michael corrects.

Bertine again. "See, he's dead now, too."

"That's awful, just awful," Douglas says, wondering if he should pat Bertine.

After a period of silence Michael changes the subject. "I've got to keep on with the Paganini."

"Paganini is like candy to my brother, and Mr. Mozart is his nemesis." Bertine offers this nugget as an aside to Douglas, who pretends not to hear the critique.

"How does it feel to be famous?" Douglas asks, halfway holding his breath. He really wants to hear the answer.

"Dunno," Michael answers. "How does it feel *not* to be famous?"

Bertine laughs first, and then the boys join in. It seems so hilarious.

"So, bye." Michael hops up the stairs, not all like a kid who hates practicing. He turns around. "Hey, if you come back at three o'clock, I have a Brownie camera. I can take your picture if you like, and you can see my stamp collection, or we can play ping-pong. Are you any good? because I am."

Bertine taps Douglas on the chest. "Let's play marbles you and me, now, pretty please, I won't practice until Jeanne comes back and makes me unless you'd rather play War, we have cards."

"Hey." Michael opens the screen door. "Nobody uses my marbles!"

"I know, I know! Don't need to tell me, you creep." Bertine rolls her eyes.

"Bertine, your brother, the one who died, what was his name?"

"Jay. Jay Rabin. I wasn't even born yet, I don't remember him of course, we keep a portrait where he's sitting at the piano all dressed up and he's so sweet, I wish we had him now, it was sad, he got a bad fever and just died, it almost killed Jeanne, that's our mother, just so you know I would never give up my baby like your mother did, especially not if it was you, and I don't care if Michael is a dork, he's my best friend."

"I don't have a best friend anymore," Douglas says, wishing Michael and Bertine lived in Elizabethtown year-round.

Michael reappears at the screen door. "Mr. Galamian is my best friend. He's arranging a recital for me just before we leave. Wurlitzer loaned me an Amati for my first concerts." Michael frowns. "My style of playing, it's too big for Amati instruments."

Bertine clarifies. "Amatis have really restrained tonal characteristics, right, Mike?"

"Yes, Bert. So Galamian got me the loan of a 1703 Joseph Guarnerius for now. You want to come to a recital?"

"Elizabethtown Social Center," Bertine says. "Please come, it's just for Meadowmount families and friends."

[8]

TURNS OUT, SUMMER vacation extends only hypothetical freedom. Wing regularly needs help around the Home. Sister Elder insists Douglas read daily after polishing her shoes. Mr. Ludlow next door pays him a trifle to weed the garden. Douglas has his own agenda too; he *just has to* improve his playing and impress Ciazzo next fall. Or the unthinkable; he'll lose the privilege of lessons.

Douglas thinks about Michael's practice technique. If it works for this talented boy, he'll try it. So simple and yet so difficult. The elements: a bowl, five marbles, a selected page of music. To proceed, if the selection is played perfectly, one marble may be dropped into the bowl. How lovely the first tiny thud of glass on bamboo. The goal is to have a triumphant swirl of five aggies, glass contours clicking. The catch is this: every time a mistake is made all earned marbles must be removed and set aside! Then the challenge begins anew.

Douglas begins Michael's routine in earnest. *What a super-duper way to practice!* Taking the music phrase by phrase and polishing each like parts of a bicycle. Even Ciazzo has not taught him a technique for being *this* thorough.

He concentrates on one recording Ciazzo spun for him, Vaughan Williams's *Lark Ascending*, with the Boyd Neel String Orchestra. "Have you ever seen a lark taking wing?" Ciazzo had asked. "This music paints that common miracle."

"Yes!" He and Sister Peace had watched the circling, the ever-circling that conveyed a small bird heavenward.

✳ ✳ ✳

MILDRED SPENDS TIME at the library too, reading romances and waiting for a studious fellow who shelves books. After his shift this heartthrob accompanies her, arm in arm, to the drugstore; they share an ice cream soda with two straws, allowing their lips to meet.

"You look stupid kissing him," Douglas informs her.

"Don't you dare tell Sister Elder!" Mildred warns. She repeats the directive with a threat. "If you do, I'll tell her you snoop around Professor Stoya's, every day. She'll believe me instead of you and you'll get grounded for the entire summer!"

If her threat were to be made good? *Arrgh, Mildred has a cold heart.* Her scenario would surely play out if Sister Elder thought he was in contact with the Stoyas. Then he'd die. *No more Michael? No more Bertine? No time energized by the sounds from Meadowmount cabins?* He imagines it like being stuck under a ledge at Split Rock Falls. Smothering. Drowning. Never being saved. Death-dealing deprivation.

[9]

{DEPRIVATION| LISTEN PLEASE| I know of Deprivation| |

{*Questo violino* finds her Red Sister| the Performance Violin| in the Professor's Conservatory| Myself delighting| As kin| Sister will be eager to commune| |

"What do you mean?"

{See| In proximity| stringed cousins waken playfully| to engage in a scherzo of silent vibrations| Otherwise they sleep until bid by finger or bow| |

"But you don't sleep."

{By some miracle| 253-1 was granted consciousness| and memory| |

"You really are amazing."

{Red Sister wakens when sensing my presence| yet to my dismay| she refuses to engage| |

Douglas ponders this reality. "Why?"

{My arrival awakened in her| our birth challenge| We two *violini* have been embedded with rivalry| See| Our makers joined in a challenge of ego| Their ultimate battle for preeminence lives in us| Fate has pulled us together| The Performance Violin| my Red Sister| distances like an enemy| in preparation for the duel| |

"A duel? Which of you will win?"

{Win| Which of us| indeed| We both have gifts| Sister has been given the gift of Obedience| Here's the pity| while she can produce what beauty a player might command| she cannot summon grandeur from her history| |

"What's your gift?"

{My gift is enduring Awareness| and being such| 253-1 may elicit as needed| Healing| Forgiveness| Joy| |

"I understand! When the nice man played you in the cemetery sad people stopped crying. Angry people stopped arguing and they hugged."

{And to speak of deprivation again| Douglas| *questo violino* senses worse deprivation looming ahead| |

"What are you are talking about?"

{A time of envious deeds| For the tragedy of it| Such deeds 253-1 has seen before| Outcomes of such deeds cannot be undone| *Questo violino* shudders with the oncoming| though it be years away| And yet| a wooden instrument cannot foretell the future||

[10]

DESPITE HIS NATTY attire Professor Stoya appears to have aged a decade in the last hour. After Michael Rabin's appearance at Elizabethtown Social Center there is no more self-assurance. Stoya's eyes see no one. He's turned inward, tortured by the significance of this whiz kid's performance. "Must I keep bowing to lord-schlord Galamian?" he mumbles as he strokes his mustache.

Frieda strides along in practiced affectation. Using her charming Mrs. Piano Teacher persona, she greets locals cordially, always on the ready for a new student. She chooses to ignore Meadowmount attendees and instructors. "It's simply a matter of repertoire," Frieda whispers to Peter.

"Galamian didn't exaggerate! Rabin's advance is outrageous—one year younger than Wilhelm, for heaven's sake."

Willi runs ahead of his parents; surely, he wants to escape the comparison he overhears. *Never good enough. Never good enough.* Frieda watches him join teens who dance on the bandstand. "He envies them, he must," she says to Peter. "We monitor him so closely."

Her husband is not listening. It was bound to happen sometime. Now Willi has heard young Rabin play circles around him.

Mrs. Piano Teacher touches Professor Stoya's arm. "If Willi and AJ. were to play these same *lesser* compositions, having been instructed by you of course, they *too* would impress."

"*Verdammt*, he's given nine recitals this year, Frieda," he quips. Peter unbuttons his collar; he should be home enjoying a beer.

"No Beethoven. No Brahms, Peter."

Frieda has a point. Peter latches onto it. "To think of it, Frieda, Menuhin had already performed a Beethoven violin concert with the NY Philharmonic by the age of eleven."

"And Rabin is twelve. With no Beethoven under his belt," Frieda says, abetting her husband's snark.

The differentiation offers both Stoyas an iota of disdain for Galamian and his pet. Frieda squeezes her husband's hand, quieting the fidgeting fingers. "The life of a prodigy is trouble," she warns. "Don't wish for it." Her head pounds; she's queasy. "Get me home, Peter, now."

* * *

UNOBSERVED BY THE Stoyas, Douglas has stayed in the auditorium. He's making his way through the crowd to the stage. Michael, surrounded by admirers, sees Douglas and pulls him into the center of attention. "This is my pal, Douglas. He likes to memorize composer-lifetime-dates as much as I do!" Douglas reacts with a self-conscious giggle. He's being introduced to the accomplished Meadowmount teenagers who've held him awestruck. He's the little kid who could only listen to them through the walls of Willi's bedroom.

Bertine pats his shoulder. She's wearing a soft yellow dress with tiers of ruffles over her smooth shoulders. She cups her hand and whispers into his ear. "Can you come over Monday for games or something like that, we're heading back to the City in a few days and Michael has a gift for you, and maybe we can go swimming or something like that."

Later as he bicycles homeward Douglas feels as if he'll lift off, lift off like a kite being tugged into the vast forever of sky. *Michael likes me. We're really friends. Now I feel sorry for Willi. He doesn't even know Michael Rabin. Or Bertine.* A series of sequential thoughts expand his thinking. Thoughts of possibility. Thoughts of exquisite music, and he is the musician. Thoughts of listeners, joyous listeners, of soft yellow dresses, and ivory skin, and smiles. Thoughts of his Magic Muriel singing as he wields a bow. Hasn't he been practicing with marbles like Michael, working for perfection? The thoughts tie one to another like the tail of a kite that is catching an updraft.

[11]

August 1948

THIS DAY, HIS thirteenth birthday, Violette wears her hair pulled back in two fat braids showing off her ears, appendages tilted like an elfin fairy's in an illustrated book. Her hair shines like burnished copper, the colors of maple leaves in fall. A good sign this, Douglas thinks, their having almost the same color hair; it gives him claim to her somehow.

She carries a red pocketbook, crocodile skin, with a rusted brass latch, and a zippered pocket from which she selects two tokens and pays both trolley fares. Taking the trolley has been her idea. She, newly sophisticated, offering an invitation, using a purse, having money, a different Violette than the one at her piano lessons.

Town becomes surreal as it slips by. The same air that brushes her cheek brushes his in succession. How close they sit, shoulder to shoulder, swaying with the trolley's jerky rhythm. Experiencing her energy is like playing pizzicato on the violin where one plucks the strings for sound. Douglas plans to ask her for a kiss. Though the reality of kissing is stuck like a dumpling at the bottom of Wing's pan.

At the butcher shop Violette changes her mind. She can afford two dill pickles; it's an ice cream she wants instead. They stand outside the ice cream parlor; she counts her coins again. "Only enough for one. Will you share?" she asks. "Chocolate okay?" Douglas has never felt more agreeable.

She runs away carrying the purchase. "Only if you can catch me, Douglas Tryzyna!" Her footsteps strike the pavement in $^4/_4$ time as she skips. The tempo changes to ¾ as she runs backwards to taunt him with the cone, slowing now and again to lick the melting treat. Douglas hangs back, clutched with fear of kissing. And kissing Violette is what he desperately wants to do.

As they near the bandstand, Douglas envisions the Basque man there playing his violin, his impassioned music accelerating, the accordion girl smiling, swaying her hips. The illusion tangles into a mix of brilliant color, and the sound ends with an explosive chord. He approaches Violette slowly, step by step, as if she might bolt should he hurry. Chocolate is melting down her arm and dripping off her elbow. As she holds out the cone the soggy remains slip out of the tissue and fall into a puddle. Violette does a little jig. She laughs and laughs, her hands held over her mouth. The happiest sound Douglas has ever heard drenches him with the same glee. She holds out her sticky fingers. "You can lick if you want. Are you brave enough, Douglas Tryzyna?"

A blur of copper, rose, white, Violette with thin arms stretched toward him. The fingers of her right hand curve like the ribs of a small animal. These same curved fingers used on the piano keys are this instant touching him. Her smooth, delicate fingers in his mouth as he tastes the chocolate there, knuckles like little ridges, like chicken bones. Sensations flood him, those of Sister Peace, the egg farm, and finally the beautiful striped violin.

"I will buy one for each of us next week," Douglas says, entranced. Money seems irrelevant. Keeping Violette matters. So much else has slipped away from him.

She withdraws her hands. She wipes them on her dress. Struggles with the clasp on her pocketbook. Pulls from it a fresh hankie. Laughingly she wipes the boy's sticky lips. "Is that a promise?" she asks.

"Here's a promise," the suitor says, trying to sound like Cary Grant. "Hold out your left hand and close your eyes." He takes a small object from his pocket and slides it on her ring finger. It's a gold embossed cigar band he requested from Mr. Ludlow. It's too large for her fourth finger.

Violette remedies the situation; the paper ring almost fits her thumb. "I'll wear this forever and ever," she says. "Except when my mother is around. Or when I'm practicing piano. Or taking a lesson. Or having a bath!" Violette blushes. She closes her eyes, dramatizing the length of her thick black lashes.

[12]

BEFORE HE KNOWS it, Douglas is waving a sad goodbye. The Rabin family is driving away. He's left with gifts from Michael. A piece of sticky yellow rosin wrapped in waxed paper. "For your bow," the prodigy had explained. "You can have this too if you want." Michael had held out a photo. In it two summertime pals are posing awkwardly by the *Lilacs* sign. Bertine had taken the snapshot with Michael's Brownie camera. Douglas places both gifts in the Muriel cigar box. For safekeeping.

[13]

TELL ME ABOUT your summer," Ciazzo requests. He's returned from his tour as promised. He sits on the Home's porch swing with Douglas, whose fingers are secretly crossed in his pants pocket. Ciazzo hasn't brought up the subject of lessons nor has he asked the boy to play.

Douglas answers eagerly, fears aside. "The most exciting thing, I'm friends with Michael Rabin and his sister Bertine. He's a kid who performs for adults. They rent *Lilacs* because he goes to Meadowmount. He practices violin all day, really all day."

"Oh then, you've met. Yes, he's certainly a prodigy. So, what about you? Have you been practicing?"

Douglas hesitates. He's proud of his efforts—until compared to Michael's industry. He manages a quiet, "Yeah."

Ciazzo smiles; his eyes sparkle like Sister Elder's cut crystal decanter filled with brandy.

I don't have to prove myself by playing? Douglas wonders. He feels his body soften like the just-melted chocolate he sees in Ciazzo's eyes. Only chocolate comes to mind in this delicious moment. He's been so afraid that Ciazzo will dismiss him.

Surprise. An invitation is offered, an opportunity to hear Ciazzo perform with his string quartet at Lake Placid. Sister Elder tenses when she hears of the offer. "It's a test," she tells Sister Peace. "He's testing the boy and the Home. Evangeline says he's extremely particular. I can't bear to be a part of his decision."

Sister Peace drives, windows down, her hair held in place by a net—she calls it a snood. Douglas laughs; such a silly word, *snood.* On her feet high-heeled pumps, not the usual boots, and she wears a dress, not dungarees. Douglas stares; she resembles a flower, her body as slender as a green stem, her rouged face and lips as soft as peony petals. White gloves, borrowed from Sister Elder, complete the transformation. The drive takes them northwest, along winding roads, beside waterways, the Adirondack Mountains always beckoning. How celebratory it seems, the two of them on an adventure, the anticipation of a concert, and the anticipation of lessons to come.

"Have you ever seen a quartet in performance?" Ciazzo asks as he greets the pair. Douglas answers with a silent, wide-eyed gaze. "We're just four normal-looking persons sitting in a semicircle, two violinists, one viola player, and a cellist. You've heard me play my violin alone. This is different. A quartet requires four instrumentalists to cooperate. Listen and you'll hear each instrument's distinct voice."

Douglas sits forward on the red cushioned aisle seat. "Dazzling!" he whispers to Sister Peace, using one of Violette's favorite words. Indeed, the polished violins, the viola, and the cello capture brilliance under stage lights. Ciazzo steps forward. He introduces the group members and the first selection, Borodin's String Quartet No. 2.

The players sit in a semicircle looking serious at first, nodding to one another. Their eyelids flutter. They begin. Ciazzo sits quietly while the others play. Soon the teacher/performer joins in, his violin ringing out a poignant tune. Douglas recognizes only the third movement, the Nocturne. A sad, yearning theme, like someone uttering a prayer twelve times twelve. The other players hold soft undertones as the supplication continues. Then a burst of change, a lively-rippling-happy melody. Each of the four sways this way and that; each leans while handling a bow, with fingers busy on strings. It seems to Douglas the second violinist is in pain; her face contorts and flexes with every nuance of the sound. Ciazzo's eyes capture the same range of expression as he draws out the tone. The cellist tips his head as if listening, listening, and then bends over his large instrument like a giant hovering over a child. At first Douglas seizes primarily on the visual: four instruments attended to by four persons, each lost in the unity of concentration. At some point he lapses into a trance, attentive as a voyeur to a forbidden conversation. How many selections the quartet plays, he's unaware.

The reverberation hovers, filling the humid air long after the musicians lay aside their bows. It is not until the tone completely fades that the audience begins to applaud. Applaud and applaud and applaud. They will not stop clapping until the quartet acquiesces with an encore. "Ravel's String Quartet in F major, 2nd Movement," Ciazzo announces. "An early composition by Ravel; despite his youth, only twenty-eight, he managed to capture an exhaustive array of shimmering textures and colors. Please enjoy."

The instruments take turns carrying the melody or percussing as rhythm. The four voices melt together as they become water rippling, birds fluttering, bumblebees buzzing, fairies all astir, the pluck-pluck-plucking of petals, patter, splatter of rain. The outpouring of each performer's soul carries Douglas away, beyond the crimson chair, the stuffy room, the sultry afternoon, away from Sister Peace's gloved hand holding his sweaty one. On and on Ravel's composition goes as it liquefies words, clutches breath. Until it concludes, sprightly yet fading like stone skipping across water.

How rosy his cheeks as Douglas describes the performance to Sister Elder. "Some people say there isn't true music until many instruments join in. And that's exactly what I want to do!" Douglas says. "Someday I will, really!"

Sister Peace beams. She stretches both arms above her head, her arms like slender green leaves reaching for sun. "You have found your way! I now may also, my child."

[14]

ONE WEEK LATER, Douglas politely surveys the fragrant Studio while waiting for Ciazzo to return. Nothing has changed. The wall directly ahead is lined with bookshelves floor to ceiling, housing alphabetically ordered music. Shelves on the right of the piano continue to hold hundreds of 78 records in cases. So lost is Douglas in examining the collection that he's startled by Ciazzo's question.

"What did you think of the quartet's music making?" Ciazzo asks. He's seated on the piano stool; the upright Steinway awaits Douglas' answer with a satin sheen matching its owner's eyes.

"This sensation came into me. I don't know how to say it...tiny maybe, like a bubble popping, or giant also like at the waterfall, like it enters your body and not your ears."

Ciazzo's full-lipped mouth opens with a radiant smile exposing more than his perfect white teeth, had anyone else been witness. Sister Peace would have seen that Douglas has passed a test; Sister Elder would have foreseen that trials lay ahead. Douglas fixes on the framed sepia photo of young Ciazzo. His stomach twists like a party clown's balloon. What if his answer was childish?

"Seven months we spent correcting your bad habits and testing your desire for this difficult journey," Ciazzo explains without referring to Douglas' answer. "You, no doubt have friends who are preparing to play for regional ratings in May. You, however, aren't yet ready to be heard in that situation."

"I know," Douglas says, his hands folded. Having heard Michael Rabin practice and perform, having heard Ciazzo in concert, Douglas knows what's possible.

"We are about *perfecting* your technique this term."

Fidgeting.

"I'll teach you the revered Ivan Galamian method. The very same practice required of Michael Rabin and students at Meadowmount. You'll find it exhausting, I promise you. Exhausting. We begin with practice on one string, and one string only. Then on to the next string as we work through technique. Scales, octaves, arpeggios, all variations of length, groupings, rhythms, and complex bowings. What's it going to take, *mijo*?"

"Patience."

"Yes, and endurance. Listening, always listening."

Douglas explores Ciazzo's inscrutable face.

"When you are finally heard in public, *niño, te sorprenderás.* You will amaze! My promise—*only* if you practice as I teach you. If you do not, *adios, adios.* I do not waste my time."

This Ciazzo, Douglas realizes, is at once stern, kind, generous, passionate. And yes, brutal. The thirteen-year-old straightens up like an adult keeping his boyish hands folded. He resembles a wooden statue. Curiously he feels as droopy as a dishrag.

Ciazzo cuts into his student's apprehension. "And, *mijo,* above all maintain good spirits, no long face. Smile! You *do* have what it takes. The expert, Mr. Leopold Auer, might describe this joyous fusion of head and heart, *'l'esprit de son métier.'*"

[15]

MALE CRICKETS WITH their violin legs serenade, *amore, amore, amore.* Sister Peace tells the boys that female crickets are silent as they search for partners. Perhaps love is both noisy and quiet for humans too, she says— there's the flirting in public and then there's the private tryst. Douglas wonders about love. Could his violin playing, eventually, make Violette fall totally and completely in love with him?

Green apples drop onto the Home's yard. Leaves float on the breeze and carpet Elizabethtown with gold and rust. The first hard frost in the Adirondacks comes overnight in October. Crickets are suddenly as quiet as the honeybees on Sister Elder's embroidery. The boys pull flannel pajamas from dresser drawers and woolens out of the mothball-filled trunk only to find the garments have seemingly shrunk.

The librarian teaches Douglas the Dewey Decimal system and allows him to enter the stacks where he lingers. *I am as smart as Michael— just wait and see who wins marbles.* He reads about composers and memorizes their dates in preparation for next summer's competition.

Ah, here's a book on Ravel, one of Michael's favorites, Douglas thinks. He finds a 1937 recording of Heifetz playing *Tzigane* by this composer. *Stoya called Heifetz first-rate,* he remembers. Over and over Douglas plays the Ravel 78 until the librarian's assistant, the one with dark braids looped around her ears, tells him, "Time is up." Another afternoon Douglas takes his violin along and the librarian with square spectacles confronts him. "You may check out a record. And please be advised, our new policy forbids practice here."

Sister Peace, equally as offended as the boy, allows Douglas to use her Victrola turntable. Just one portion of the borrowed black disc compels him. The outside band of grooves. Here the music is slow and lyrical; it seems within his grasp to decipher. He smiles as eagerly as the dog that listens so intently, the one pictured on the red label. As the record circles, Douglas memorizes as much as he can each day. Before long he is playing along in the privacy of Sister Peace's room. *Ciazzo will be astonished,* he thinks—*astonished, one of Violette's favorite words.*

Just before Thanksgiving Douglas feels prepared.

Ciazzo is not astonished, however. "Yes, you listened to an artist—this is of benefit. Next is to analyze for yourself. Your style will come from here." Taking Douglas' right hand, he presses it to the young man's breast. "From your heart. Let your music-making flow free. Do you understand?"

A student's eyes glaze. A vision of free-flowing music takes him away. The Basque man is playing by the fire. He's casting a silvery trawl of tones over the field and across the river until the net of sound circles him, sweeps him up in its long, sinewy arms and takes away his breath.

[16]

VIOLETTE MINES A thesaurus. The thick coral book is her own, a gift from Lermontov. Study hall allows her time to excavate the categorized pages for words. One expects she's gathering the brightest, most reflective words, those crystalline of sound and meaning, after which she'll type them in combinations. Perhaps Violette intends to encircle her chosen reader's heart with a halo or a caress. Who would expect she also aims to impale a bully?

Look at her diligence today, her triangular face a flip-book of expressions: cheeks sucked in, eyes squinched, brows lifted, forehead scrunched, a pout, a sly side-look at Willi, a grin. The silent mimicry of meaning is broken by an infectious giggle. She heads to the typewriters and proceeds to compose with a steady click, clickety, clack, clack—ding.

Later, Violette tags Douglas at his locker. She thrusts an object into his hand and skips off with Oh-No. The object elicits a smile. Today's typed present is folded into a cootie catcher. Opened, it reveals a curious array of words chosen precisely for his benefit.

> Title: Willi
>
> Ignoble, inglorious, idler, illaudable, irritant, irascible, icky, illogical, inept, infantile, infectious, immature, incriminator.

Douglas laughs. Obviously, Violette's infatuation today is the initial letter "i." Even so, the words are secondary. Oh, he appreciates each choice. However, her words strutting, marching, screaming so loyally across the page are, by definition, one thing entirely. Could only be one thing. A love letter to him. Douglas shivers, remembering their shared dill pickle and the sticky touch of their lips one hot afternoon.

[17]

OVERNIGHT A WINDSTORM raged. The neighborhood is littered with leaves. Fall trees show bare limbs. The river flashes with a freshened current. Winter is announcing herself. Summer reels like an old movie, where Michael Rabin was the star.

Michael has his choice of fine old violins, Douglas thinks. The only violin Douglas wants, whether it's fine or not, is the 253-1. Does he remember correctly that it was promised to him when he was six? He's been banking on that promise for a long time. Now he's obsessed again. When he questions Sister Peace, she shrugs. "Here is a difficult man." She pauses and then changes the subject. How are your lessons with Ciazzo?"

"Good. Really good." Back into his funk. He neglects, rejects, dismisses the good fortune of Ciazzo.

Tatiana looks distracted as if she hasn't heard his answer. She reaches for a photo album and gets lost in the black and white images.

Douglas takes this as a signal to leave her alone. He brushes dry leaves off the peeling paint and plunks onto the porch swing. He pushes himself back and forth, back and forth, faster and faster, making the chains creak, making the chains groan. Higher and higher he flies on the swing, kicking and pumping vigorously.

And then come the questions of a different category. Troublesome realities in his thirteen-year-old existence. Why is Elizabethtown full of sadness? With things that kids wish weren't true, with things that adults won't talk about. Why do people set fire to poor immigrants' stuff? Why do men steal violins from little kids? Why do mothers yell at industrious sons? Why do girls abandon innocent babies? Why do ladies allow photos to steal them away?"

He keeps pushing himself back and forth, back and forth, faster and faster on the old swing. The chains creak, the chains groan.

Violette continues to type notes during study hour. Her offering one day, having neither title nor preface, expresses sympathy and hope.

Abhorrent. Exonerate. Bliss. Crescendo. Euphoria.

[18]

December 1948

CHRISTMAS comes and goes, bringing little satisfaction to a frustrated teenager. Douglas wakes early, takes the hot chocolate Wing offers, and sits on the porch wrapped in an oversized tartan plaid robe, a gift from Astrid. He stares and thinks. Stares and thinks. Snow clings tenaciously to trees. Each delicate branch of the yard's maple tree carries a coat of frosting yet manages to stay perky. Evergreen boughs droop like sullen children, diminished in girth, their color muted, each unwavering like some anomalous marble statue. On these mornings the sky meets horizon like a gray wall; distant hills and even neighboring houses cease to exist. No breeze nor gust alters this tableau.

January 1949. One morning, the wall of sky splits into horizontal slits; the sky resembles blinds slightly open running across window of sky. The sun beams her warm hues of dawn and shadows appear. *A sign,* Douglas thinks, *a good sign.* Even so, just as Wing serves the youngsters breakfast and Sister Elder begins to sip her coffee, light and shadow recede. The gray wall encloses Elizabethtown again.

February. The heavens display a flotilla of clouds—there in the sky preparing for war, tankers, battleships, pocket battleships, cruisers, destroyers, aircraft carriers, tankers. Atmospheric guns are brought to bear.

March. The sky at 6:00 a.m., the softest powder blue. Douglas is unable to distinguish sky from clouds as the mix of blues and whites confound his analytical mind. Simply puzzle pieces without a hint of pink. Violette's typed words offer counsel on attitude. *Tenacious. Intrepid. Sanguine. Staunch.* At least *she* believes there will be resolve in his sorry situation.

April. After six days of cloud and constant rain Douglas senses a collision in slow motion. Several elements tangle.

The sunlight: it misdirects attention. Because of it Wing gets distracted by the yellow markings of pine siskin at the feeder. He measures coffee hurriedly into the percolator; he leaves the cast iron skillet on a high flame for too long.

Frustration: it swaps places with Sister Elder's patience. "Leftover pork fried rice crisped to a fare-thee-well, and weak-kneed coffee, Wing?" She picks up the newspaper and unfolds it with a shake.

Wing's upturned smile reverses to a frown. He wipes his hands on his apron and disappears into the kitchen.

The *Elizabethtown Gazette*: it negates the pleasure of today's sunshine with something in print. The newspaper responds to Sister Elder's trembling grasp with a rustle as she reads a headline—and then the paragraphs below.

Throat being cleared: it always precedes one of Sister Elder's announcements. Around the mahogany table—with its starched white linens, its polished silver bridal baskets awaiting summer fruit, its plates of picked-at-breakfast—Mildred, James, and John cease their chatter. Sister Elder faces the teens. Their faces as ivory as the nubs of wax in the candelabra, they sit motionless like a frieze of respect. What has she just read to disturb her so? Her shoulders square as she releases a pulsation, which agitates Douglas. He shivers with the heebie-jeebies. Hester Smythe clears her throat again.

A warning: it stirs the air as Sister Elder reads from page three.

> *YOUTH PLUMMETS TO HER DEATH*
> *Tragedy at Split Rock Falls, Elizabethtown, New York.*
> According to one observer, a teenage girl lost her footing while climbing a treacherous trail above the falls. She fell into the turbulent water and did not surface. A witness stood by waiting for her body to appear. He stated, "I just kept watching, you know;

she never came up. It was horrible." Hours later the girl's body was discovered downstream. The victim, Susanna Tibbits, 16, resident of Elizabethtown, was familiar with the falls, her parents said. Like others, she misjudged nature's strength, especially after a week of rain. Many people have died here over the years, according to New York State Trooper Captain Paul *Heinke. The funeral for Miss Tibbits will be held on Monday at St. Luke's Presbyterian.*

Mildred wails. "No. No. No. It can't be true. Susanna? Oh god."

Imagination: it projects Douglas into the onrush of water, the tumbling, the grasping, the swallowing, choking, the collision with Susanna there. Mildred's sobs bring him back to the table, to the newspaper rustling, to the bitter smell of burnt rice and pork.

Interrogation: Mildred surely invites it as she croaks, "Susanna wasn't careless!" Sister Elder removes her glasses. "You knew of this?" She takes Mildred's smooth hands into her own wrinkled hands—hands with veins meandering under freckled skin. "Talk to me."

Sister Elder re-anchors the rolled curl of hair at her nape. Lips pursed, forehead furrowed.

Silence: if kept long enough it has a way of extricating that which one hesitates to say, so finally after withholding, Mildred speaks. "She threatened to..."

Sister Elder. "My poor dear, I'm so dreadfully sorry."

Mildred casts a glance at the three boys, who look distressed as well. Her eyes seem to project anger at each one of them. She stirs her pork and rice. The small scraping sound of fork against porcelain seems to stretch the length of her silence. 'Round and 'round the fork goes, gathering clumps—tan, brown, black. "It wasn't an accident."

Mildred breaks down in sobs; her shoulders shake. She crosses her arms across her belly and rocks.

"Had her virtue been compromised?"

Mildred covers her mouth with her napkin.

Hester studies Mildred for a few minutes. Her eyes brim. She seems to understand what has *not* been said. Hester and Tatiana exchange a soul-searching stare. Had Douglas been older, or suspicious, or better informed, he might have grasped meaning in the women's silent exchange. As it is, he senses earsplitting harmonics; he shivers. A boy reacting to the tragic news and not to the secretive relationship of his two mother-figures.

Pushing away from her chair. Upright like a caryatid bearing a weighty entablature. Sister Elder stands at the head of the table, her apron tied neatly under her full bust. Wisps of graying hair catch a halo of light. Not one of the three teenage boys can ignore Hester Symthe, their Guardian, mother de facto, as she addresses an issue each will likely face soon.

"I have tried to teach you self-discipline, adherence to a few key rules. Granting all this, a crucial factor to include is this: Some things cannot be undone. Further, forgiveness isn't automatic, even if deserved."

"Unless you are Catholic," Mildred whispers. "Susanna was not."

"And we are not, either!" Sister Elder ends the conversation.

Forgiveness: It's easier to expect than to give, Douglas fears.

All the while Sister Peace has remained silent. She's folded and re-folded her starched napkin so many times it's a crisscross of lines.

[19]

PROFESSOR STOYA HAS just read aloud today's troubling article in the *Elizabethtown Gazette*. Willi gasps. "I...I know her. We have Algebra together." He and Siggi excuse themselves, looking numb. The adults stare at each other without focus. Such sadness, the death of a young person at their town's landmark. Death *again* at the falls? Death circled their lives too frequently in Germany; why did they imagine it could be avoided here in another country?

Frieda whispers, "Do you think, if disappointed, our Willi could, would ever...?"

"Don't speak it! Don't *dare* speak it!" Narcisse Louise Boulez hisses her warning. She's wearing her go-to-town maroon dress. The Stoyas turn to see her framed by the kitchen's white double doors. They acknowledge her right to speak. Narcisse Louise, their LuLu, as always, is attentive to a shift in the household's emotional barometer.

The mother does not finish the question about her son.

The father counters what his wife meant to imply. "He's got a good head on his shoulders, LuLu. He's showing moments of greatness, you know. The fellows had only commendable things to say after he played for them in the City last week."

Stoya kicks back his chair and enters the salon, where he lifts the Basque man's violin from its case, not the Performance Violin he prefers. He tunes up with aggressive strokes. Death. Yes, they have seen death. He. Frieda. Narcisse Louise. And he suspects this fiddle has seen more than her share—however old she may be.

There is no joy to be found. If Peter's face reflects his heartache, so does the music he plays. Melancholy pours into his playing, and the 253-1 releases it without hesitation. He plays a wistful tune, a descending scale that steps up and down in stately progression as the music searches for resolve. Frieda sits at the piano and accompanies the hymnal with just a single note. Repeated, repeated. Then a single chord. Repeated, repeated.

There is no joy to be found. The plaintive hymn arises from memory of Peter's father. His father, an honorable man. His father, a man who grew roses, played violin, and built model airplanes. His father, whom he'd lost as a toddler. He never really knew the man. A sepia wedding photo of a soldier and his mother must serve. The longing persists.

Peter plays for his mother and for his old maid aunt, the women who did their best to rear him. Both have succumbed to flu. He plays for his cousin who fancied lads and died at his own hand. The 253-1 continues even without direction expressing what needs to be heard. Her voice reveals a yearning both sweet and dark as it spreads lush shadows of tone in a minor key. The mournful music comforts just as it pierces; it asks a question, it gives no answer, and finally slows to a sustained lament.

There is no joy to be found. Frieda leaves the piano looking dazed. She winds the cuckoo clock as is her daily habit. Touches the little bird before shutting the door, strokes the pinecone pendulum. Peter stays put with the 253-1 under his chin, pressed to his breast. His right arm dangles, in his hand; the bow is loosely grasped.

Narcisse Louise walks toward the Smythe Hotel seeking comfort. Now and then she wipes her eyes with a freshly ironed hankie.

[20]

APRIL. DOUGLAS SENSES a new oscillation from Sister Peace this gray chilly spring. In her he feels an irregular spin like a beanie propeller on a gusty day. This troubles him. Oh, she's been distracted before; this is different. Her change began when the mailman first delivered a thin blue envelope addressed bearing a strange stamp. Sister Elder had positioned it upright in the silver tray on the hallway phone desk.

Yes, it's as if she's started waiting for something better than the here and now. She gathers up the mail, flipping aside the bills in search of another blue envelope. When the telephone rings, she's first to answer. Why is she speaking in that strange language? She sounds like a badly tuned radio full of unnecessary hisses and crackles. Douglas tries to decipher her conversation. Impossible! Unlike pig Latin with a clever pattern, this is surely a foreign language being spoken backwards.

Today, she again answers the phone, and after some silence on her part, Sister Peace giggles. Her laughter, a trill of gaiety repeating as naturally as birdsong. Today's giggle, however, fills Douglas with foreboding. A loud girlish giggle as if she were being tickled and liked it. Thereafter Sister Peace's every action becomes suspect.

Many Friday afternoons to come, Sister Peace leaves with extra hugs for Douglas. Minus the quotidian apron and key belt, outfitted in her perky hat and fur-collared coat, she looks like a movie star to Douglas. He's aware because girls his age trade cards with black and white images of actresses; Violette has shown him her collection, a whole shoebox full, rubber-banded into fat stacks. The actresses look alike mostly because their skin glows, their narrow eyebrows arch in perfect curves, and their eyelids, lined with black, are hooded. Neither Sister Elder, nor Astrid, nor Mrs. Piano Teacher compare. He wonders if Sister Peace, his Tatiana, might secretly be a movie star. When she returns on a Sunday, he's too angry to inquire.

[21]

"HEY DOOGIE, YOU'RE invited to my house!" Oh-No leans forward to whisper, "It's going to be a kissing party." She plays peekaboo using her locker door as a foil. Douglas is captive. "A.J. had one when his parents were out. My parents think a party at home will be innocent. Oh, don't worry, they won't check on us."

Douglas' jaw drops, his eyes widen. "Who's invited?"

"Willi, Violette, and A.J. For sure. My cousins will be visiting. They're both real cute. And another guy from my block. We need an even number of boys and girls. Please come. Willi and Violette had to kiss last time. He acts like he owns her because of music practice together."

Oh-No's invitational enlightenment excites Douglas as much it nettles him.

Sister Elder's "No" means *no*. Pleading is useless.

No kissing party for Douglas. He spends Friday night practicing bowing techniques in a distracted state. His imagination rushes like Split Rock Falls in spring—out of control. Maybe Willi's passion is like an uncontrolled fiery horse, just as described in the Personal Hygiene film. After his cajoling, Mildred tries to explain kissing party games.

A vivid imagination is a curse. Douglas' mind bristles with images of Violette wearing her soft blue sweater, the one that clings to her chest—more correctly, to her breasts, pointed breasts, now that she wears a bra like Mildred. Also, a skirt with pleats that ripple when she walks and outlines her hips, thighs, and all the mystery of her lower body. Every thought of Willi and Violette necking sends cockroaches scurrying through Douglas' veins. Maybe Willi can talk Violette into doing more. Maybe Violette will get a baby in her lady parts. Maybe she'll commit suicide like Susanna.

Mildred escalates this worry as she continues. "Susanna was so sorry. That ratfink talked her into it, really didn't love her. She would've had to give up her baby, not even get one itty-bitty peek before they took it away. She was so sorry afterward."

Douglas shudders. So sorry afterward? So sorry afterward? Am I somebody's so sorry afterward?

In the next note, Violette's typed words bewilder him.

Relentless. Chagrin. Demise. Bushido.

Is she writing clues to personal scandal? Or is this reassurance of her loyalty?

Magic Muriel is aware of Douglas' conflict.

{See| we *violini* have no imagination| while you humans| have volumes| Oh for the rapture of imagination| when it brings forth delight| Though 253-1 begs you| take heed| when imagination| like floodwater| gushes unchecked into dark chasms| Then imagination may drown the good| So it is| It is| Take courage from Violette's words| |

Perhaps in time of wretchedness to come, Violette will type a letter. It may find its way to him, a penitent who was once her sweetheart. One hopes her meaning then will no longer be confounding.

[22]

HE'S LOST A companion. Sister Peace didn't go with him to find streams gurgling with snowmelt. They didn't trek to see thousands of green leaves emerging on the forest floor. Didn't see trout lily, the first wildflowers of spring, make their appearance. She didn't return to see the yellow blooms or exclaim over the abundance of snow-white-stinky trillium. He reasons on it. Trying to make sense. Her eyes must see thrilling things he cannot see. Her eyes must no longer be thrilled with what they do see together. She's preoccupied. Who talks on the phone with her, anyway? Who does she see on weekends? That person, that rival for her attention, he already dislikes that guy—one he has yet to meet.

Come May Day Eve, Sister Peace forgets to scatter flowering boughs on the Home's doorstep, an honored ritual. "Witches are out and about on this night, Douglas," she used to say.

At school they sing like they always do. *Round the Maypole / trit-trit-trot / See what a Maypole we have got / Fine and gay / Trip away / Happy is our new May Day.* Douglas finds this song as lame-brained as it used to be lighthearted. He slams his locker door after lunch, frightening Oh-No.

Sister Peace was right about the witches and their spells. He's been overtaken by an evil heart. Where is the lamb's heart filled with cotton candy? It's been replaced by a python's heart coiled around black tar. He can't look Sister Peace in the eye anymore. He stiffens with her hug and kiss goodnight. Nonetheless he feels her energy pulse through his young body, her uniqueness like a river cascading over rocks. And then she's gone. Gone from his life.

Just a handwritten letter. That's all he has left of her, of this woman whose passion has opened the mystifying universe in ways Sister Elder's pragmatism could not. Just a stupid letter saying how grown up he is. Saying how she is inspired to find her path again, now that he's on his path with Ciazzo. Adding some mush about their hearts being joined. And lies about finding each other another time. He reads the stupid good-bye letter again, and again, and again, hungering for more.

Douglas wants a piano. Wants to strike the keys with a ferocity unknown to Mrs. Piano Teacher whose fingers are tamed. Wants to force the pedal down while he pounds black keys in D Minor diminished. He needs the dark sounds, the loud sounds, the music of rage. *Sister Peace gone. No goodbye.* He hates her. He hates arms that could squeeze his Sister Peace so tightly that she became invisible and poof, just disappeared. Just disappeared. Just a stupid letter, that's all he has left of her.

[23]

THE WEEK THAT Sister Peace left, birds abandoned their nests, raccoons devoured the chickens and their eggs, dogs barked and howled through the night. The day that Sister Peace left bees swarmed, left the hives they'd filled with wax, honey, and pollen. Left to find another home.

Sometimes his playmate, sometimes his nurse, sometimes his teacher, Sister Peace was always his Aqua Fairy. With her came the times closest to bliss. *Bliss,* a word Violette adores. *Bliss,* a word Violette typed on a slip of paper for him. Douglas had learned to relate the word *bliss* to time with Sister Peace. Come on now, if he's honest he remembers how, without warning, she could turn away as if her eyes and ears tuned into a different place, far away. At those times she was neither companion, nor comforter, nor giver of wisdom. He could feel the change, when her lilting rhythm, which sometimes could be joined, became a wall. Like now. She was gone. Someone's Tatiana. Not his Sister Peace. Out of range.

Douglas conjures on life. Violin lessons with Stoya, a delight, then forbidden. A violin that speaks to him, denied. A sky of wondrous light, unplugged. He's Pinocchio, deserted by his fairy. His truth? When a boy's experience draws dangerously close to bliss, disappointment soon follows. What is the secret joy Sister Peace reveled in?

IV
GAIN & LOSS

[1]

TIME STOPS FOR Douglas Tryzyna, and no one seems to notice. The moon forgets to cycle, twenty-eight days of waxing gibbous, and it seems no one is paying attention.

The NOA May Rating Event comes and goes, granting Stoya encouragement. Nevertheless, the Professor will not compliment Willi or A.J.'s *above-average* marks; instead, he pressures his prize students to strengthen skills noted as *average*.

Ciazzo is somewhere in the wild blue yonder. He left with an exhortation. "Keep practicing. And, Douglas, always include something you're passionate about."

The violin is not deserting her chosen one; she's urging him onward. {Sad songs| 253-1 carries in her cells| sounds of men mourning those who expire| Though 'tis a mystery where mankind's vibrations go| If you ask| *questo violino* could croon bitter| melancholy tunes for you| Truth to tell| in years to come| you may beg for the comfort of my songs| See| for most humans a time of Great Woe arrives| Arrive it may for you| It may| |

"What am I supposed to do?"

{Fill your soul with joyful music| learn it well| All this in preparation for the days ahead| |

How wise that advice would seem if anyone could find a pinnacle from which to view the future.

[2]

FIND EGGS. SUGAR. Cornstarch. Vegetable oil. All we need." It's Sunday morning and Wing directs Douglas in the Hotel kitchen. "Measure each ingredient into small bowl."

"What are we making, Wing?"

"You'll see. First you beat eggs, little bit, gentle." Douglas finds no pleasure in the task. Round and 'round with a whisk, watching bright yolks merge with translucent goo and become pale yellow. "Now you add sugar, beat with intention to make smooth as pudding." While Douglas stirs the egg and sugar mixture Wing takes a small amount of egg batter to mix with water and cornstarch. This goes back into the glossy mixture.

"It doesn't smell like much," Douglas says, an imposter wearing kitchen whites.

"Toss a drop of water on the griddle," Wing says. "See sizzle? We are ready. I show first, then you." Wing drops a spoonful of the batter onto the griddle. Immediately he spreads this into a circle, three inches and not too thick. In seconds Wing turns the circle over to brown the other side. "Bring box of small papers over here, choose one, and read message out loud."

"Your road to glory will be rocky." Ah, the project becomes clear. "Wing, we're making fortune cookies!"

With one swift move Wing is folding the cookie over the paper and pinching the warm edges closed. He presses the stick into the arc of cookie. "Making butterfly shape."

The two bakers work side by side, carefully browning cookies, adding fortunes, folding, and crimping. The repetitive task is not unpleasant for Douglas. It's obvious, though, Wing is trying to distract him from his woes. Just maybe it's useless, maybe he's cursed to disappointment.

"Now you make cookie for yourself," Wing says. "Go ahead, you write the fortune you want on one of the blank papers."

He's embarrassed. He handles the paper so Wing can't read the bold words he's writing.

They're leaving the Hotel. Douglas scuffs along, head down. "You wonder why I teach you to bake the fortune cookie today?" Wing doesn't wait for a reply. "Today you need lesson. Wisdom say, *Life like fortune cookie.* Get it? You thinking Chinaman put note with fortune in your life every day. You read it, you say, 'Oh, no, I no like.'"

Douglas gives Wing a glance to show he's listening.

"Challenge. You no like what those words say about your future? You remember, each day is like fortune cookie. You no like what today is saying? You make change today."

[3]

RAZZING CONTINUES EVEN after school lets out. Willi and his pals race by the Smythe Home on their bicycles. Chortling. Taunting. Jeering. Hurling the nasty moniker.

Sister Elder says, "Ignore them."

Feeling grumpy he complains to 253-1. At least she will listen. "I'm a dummy. I can't remember anything about getting born. Or about my really, truly, mother. And nobody will be honest with me."

{It is natural to be curious about one's beginning| Albeit the time of beginning is unconsciousness| |

"Yeah."

{Men speak of my beginning| The Duration of Cold| bitter cold in Croatia| My beginning| breathing| growing in a cluster of my kind| knit above and below earth| slowly| slowly| in The Duration| building size and strength| each icy sun shift| sap ring upon sap ring circling a core| Some men may spy a *violino*| inside such as 253-1 was then| |

"You were a tree, of course."

{Indeed| Just look what Myself has become| |

"You're so awesome."

{See| You may be an abandoned boy| Rather think on the man you may become| |

[4]

"THIS SUMMER YOU polish shoes at the Hotel," Sister Elder says. "No school. No music lessons. You're not going to mope around. I want you to head over there today and meet my friend Lermontov. He'll give you his requirements."

Years ago, Sister Elder insisted her wards learn to polish shoes—and establish the habit. Back then payment was a token nickel or two. John cut circles out of brown paper. He authenticated the paper coins with pencil drawings. On one side, the Indian's profile complete with braids and feathers. On the flip side the buffalo. How precious to receive these nickels. Douglas knew they weren't real, couldn't be used as spending money; nevertheless, they had value since time and talent had been invested in their creation.

During his twelfth summer Douglas polished Mr. Ludlow's shoes for authentic nickels, ones with the imprint of President Jefferson. Mr. Ludlow used to position his foot on the cast iron *star* fixture, read a newspaper, and smoke a cigar, allowing Douglas time for contemplation. *A scenario with Lermontov will be similar*, Douglas presumes. *Not too exciting. Oh well.*

Little does he expect Lermontov's generosity. One dime per pair. Little can the youngster anticipate the two will entertain each other by telling stories, this summer and beyond.

"Lermontov leases the Penthouse," Sister Elder explains.

At Smythe Hotel Reception Douglas is told, "Go on up, you're expected." The soon-to-be-fourteen-year-old takes the elevator, lugging along the shoeshine kit, a loyal friend. Decorating it, the painted man and woman ever youthful, the crescent moon waxing yet, flowers faded though perky; time has stood still on the box's colorful exterior. Meanwhile, *he's* been changing both inside and out.

What do we know of this Lermontov, so respected by Sister Elder? This Lermontov Douglas is about to meet? The author lingers over coffee and toast in the Hotel dining room while perusing *A London Review of Books* and the *New York Post*. Without notice he takes the train to Penn Station and overnights in another of the Symthe sisters' New York City hotels, ear to the ground, nose to the air, sniffing out scenarios. He sometimes weekends in Montreal; his French is impeccable, his eavesdropping discreet. He claims to despise children, with the exception of one precocious companion.

Douglas is welcomed with a brisk pat on the back, after which he finds himself staring. To be noted, the man needs a shave. Also, the ears, large and slightly flaring. The well-shaped nose with a slight bump on the bridge. Jawline bulging a trifle given the expansive, oversized jaw of teeth it conceals. Deep-set eyes guarded by squared forehead and expressive dark eyebrows, quite heavy. Those eyes feast on the sight of Douglas. Full circle of the iris blue, with flecks of gold like a starry night. A Russian novelist finding fuel in the presence of another passionate being.

Douglas realizes he's seen Lermontov out and around town. This novelist regularly goes on a walkabout through Elizabethtown, or New Russia, in even the harshest weather. Macintosh rubberized raincoat on days of downpour. A Burberry jacket of gabardine wool, vents under armpits and across the back, worn on days of drizzle or wind. Returns to the Hotel, having forgotten to don his Wellingtons, shoes caked with mud, scuffed on rocks, discolored by puddle and stream, laces crusty and stiff. This man requires a patient shoeshine boy. A boy who will tend a man's shoes as carefully as he tends the sounds he makes on a violin.

Spotting the antique kit, Lermontov gives his shoeshine boy one of those looks, glasses down over the bump on the bridge of his nose. "No, I won't be posturing on that silly thing!" He laughs so easily. His round eyes, growing rounder, bluer yet while studying Douglas' response. The gentleman is intrigued, which seems his natural state. He's silly, he's suave, he's shrewd. Accused of having military airs with the Hotel staff, yet he's positively fraternal with a kid of almost fourteen.

This Lermontov. A widower of simple tastes. Seems older than Professor Stoya or Wing. Maybe fifty? So spirited, who can tell? Thick ash-blond hair slicked back today with Brilliantine, Douglas recognizes the jasmine and chrysanthemum scent.

He's pointing to more than a dozen shoes tossed upon a canvas tarp. "Start first on the brogues, will you?" Lermontov takes a seat at a glass-top table in front of his Triumph, a German-made typewriter. He faces a view of Cobble Hill, verdant this June afternoon. He lapses into thought. His left hand, holding a freshly sharpened pencil.

"What do you write?" Douglas asks after he has tackled the muddy brogues, seeing that Lermontov hasn't moved all the while. "I write fiction." Lermontov swivels to face Douglas. "Nice job there. The brogues." And continuing without a breath, "I simply take fragments from lives of human beings. Each starts from gossip, you see. And my imagination takes over." Lermontov swivels back around in his chair. As if freshly inspired he positions a sheet of paper in the typewriter, slides the carriage to the right, and begins to type furiously.

Douglas picks up a black loafer with a dime, not a penny, in the slot. He attacks caked mud along the shoe's sole. Continues with the right loafer working until the pair is buffed to perfection.

Lermontov swivels back around in his chair. "Do you want to hear something?" Without waiting he begins to recite an essay:

> *Why cannot joy stand alone? Always to be accompanied by sadness, loss, grief, regret, pain? Like Siamese twins with two heads. Feed one chocolate cake and excite the brain with delight, inspiration.*

Feed the self-same chocolate cake to the other head and scramble the brain with mal delusion.

"Isn't that hilarious?" The novelist again laughs without restraint.

Douglas' face puckers into a quizzical scowl.

"Lighten up, Yevgeny! We ought to laugh at our own duplicity. Lovers and sinners that we are."

Is Lermontov reading my mind? Douglas wonders. He has so often contemplated delight and misery, inseparable pairs.

In answer Lermontov recites another line:

Oh, a broken heart will heal, discounting the burr that threatens to snag every silken moment.

[5]

IT SO HAPPENS that Douglas soon trusts the novelist. One afternoon he bares the anger of being a stray with no sense of his parentage. "Auntie Evangeline probably doesn't know. Sister Elder thinks a blurry photo is an answer. Sister Peace ditched before ever giving me a real answer."

Lermontov is a perceptive listener. "Shall I make up a story for you? Will that make things easier? Having a rope to climb from your dark cave, sad underground spirit? Will you then find the light and spread your wings once again? As if you were shoes, I might scrape away the debris of your wanderings. Apply the polish. Bring your soul back to its original dazzle. At least that is my intent in telling you a story, fiction though it may be, fabricated from an acorn of gossip as is my style. Hold the tale gently like a freshly gathered egg; it might break if you don't.

Lermontov begins using a classic storytelling style:

We have a woman, in her thirties, unmarried, not unattractive, owner of several hotels. Her Manhattan hotel's policy of offering discount rates to artistes attracted stimulating guests. Let's just call her Hattie. You see, Hattie savored these fleeting associations so reminiscent of youthful days abroad.

Of an evening these guests mingled with businessmen and visitors at the lobby bar. You'd see musicians quenching their thirst, gentlemen these, lighting cigarettes, bow ties hanging loose, capricious after a successful performance. Especially so when a dance company was in town, when giggly corps de ballet ingénues floated in. Exotic creatures, features exaggerated by stage makeup, capes over slip dresses, bringing with them an aroma both salty and sweet, of sweat and perfume mingled with smoke. Some of these dancers casually played musical bedrooms with musicians several evenings in a row. And then off to the next city.

Hattie, her time abroad seemingly eons ago, found European flair more and more appealing as years went by. She began to dress elegantly for these evenings in the lobby bar, to style her hair, wind pearls around her throat. She's only thirty-five for all that.

And then of a sudden, one rarely expects to lose peers in an accident, she acquired three orphans, siblings, all under the age of four. They soon wearied our blind-sighted guardian. Hattie began spending more time away on monthly Hotel visits. The domestic couple in her hire rose to the challenge at the bed-and-breakfast-turned-orphanage, and happily so, unable to have children of their own. Her initial absences of a few days grew to a week or more.

It was during this time Hattie became friendly with an exotic viola player, an alternate for the Ballet Russe de Monte Carlo. He had passed through several times a year on tour with one ballet company or another. Energy oozed from every stroke of his bow. His musical expressions thrilled her such that she booked a seat in the front row for many ballet performances, hoping each included him. His unrestrained attentions finally swept this cultured lady of a certain age, hotel owner, off-balance, never mind her penchant for discretion. Giddy days of youth had passed and yet...and yet her unmet desires, her lust, her trembling flesh were barely disguised under layers of constricting fabric.

One November, a ballerina, raven-haired, thin-chested, clinging satin dress exposing her assets, immodestly flirted with the same viola player. One evening he bought her a Drambuie; they danced, close as peas in a shell. How can I compete? worried the older woman. One evening while she pretended not to care, the Viennese flirt singled her out. You can imagine the rush she felt. After the lobby bar cleared the two met in her room. Not something she planned, and without a plan, a sensible "No" became a sensual "Yes." Break of dawn, Hattie, looking prim in a plaid robe, embraced the Lothario goodbye, farewell. He backed out the door, gallantly pausing to blow her a kiss. Neither realized that three ballerinas lodged on the same floor were right then in the hallway headed to barre class. It was the same ingénue, the one who shared a Drambuie, a girl with ink-black hair knotted at the nape of her neck—she couldn't be more than sixteen, could she?—who shot daggers at her competition as she passed by. This will-o'-the-wisp of a girl, the one swallowed by a man's fur-collared overcoat, linked arms with the same enigmatic violist leaving the theatre that very evening.

By the time Hattie suspected her condition, some two months hence, she felt pure panic. She extended her Hotel visits to weeks, and then to a month, and to another month, feigning a contagious illness and the existence of a City doctor whose remedy required regular treatments. "No travel allowed, you see." The pair of domestics back home worried. Worried and conjectured. All the while, tending three siblings without questioning their employer and friend.

One morning a gentleman leaving his suite in the Manhattan hotel heard unholy wails nearby. Locating the suite, its door ajar, he discovered Hattie paralyzed by pain and fear. A miscarriage in progress. Kind soul that he was stayed with the mother-not-to-be, remained bedside at the hospital, offered her encouragement. So began a friendship.

The next spring it was the same foreign dancer with flinty eyes who chanced upon our lady in the lobby bar. Recognizing Hattie, the ballerina left her group. Vivid makeup couldn't hide the worry on her face. She approached accusingly.

Lermontov mimics dialogue quite convincingly. He continues:

The two women exchanged words: Anna wailed. "You two together. Last November. That morning he was leaving your room. I see this." Hattie sucked in her breath. She knew exactly who this girl referred to. The Viennese violist, really; who else had she been intimate with? She didn't want to hear the answer; she asked the question anyway. "You and he were...?"

"Man like that does not belong to anyone. This girl a sucker to think so. You know where is, this man?"

"No, no, I do not. He was returning to Europe, I do believe."

"I have child, his, in belly."

"His child, are you sure?"

"Very sure, yes, very, yes."

"Can you inform him?"

"Not know where to find. Thinking he with you."

Soon the young thing, having chugged her champagne, was sobbing, arms wrapped around her belly. Together to Hester's room. She had a Russian name, which she abbreviated to Anna. She jumbled words in a humorous way, given to abrupt sentences. Graceful port de bras gestures compensated for her lack of English.

Over mouthfuls of Welsh Rarebit and sips of tea the dancer reeled out her story. Anna had left her mother and five younger siblings when she was ten, food was scarce, and the family was penniless. She made her way to Leningrad hoping to study with the Mariinski Ballet. Chance allowed her to audition for René Blum, ballet director at the Monte Carlo Opera. In no time at all she became pet of Tamara Toumanova, the Ballet Russe de Monte Carlo's principal dancer, and toured with the company, in the corps de ballet.

Here Lermontov segued into the history of Russian Ballet. At length he concluded with:

This was following the romantic era of Nijinsky and Pavlova, which had inspired Anna. Gregor Piatigorsky, resident here in Elizabethtown, played cello for the Bolshoi Theatre in his youth around about this time.

Lermontov's tone changes. "Back to our story:"

You see, now Anna had troubles. That's why she confronted Hattie— she was looking for the seductive violist. He'd been her lover; not that they'd made promises before he left. And Anna was almost too far pregnant to hide her expanding belly. The ballet mistress would notice, would suspend her any day. With no job, alone in a foreign country, what is she to do?

Both women realized what they had in common—an intimate relationship with the same disarming musician who had probably returned to Europe and become a soldier. Both females had been reckless, had been unwise, both had been caught up in passion. Hattie had suffered. She knew Anna would too.

Anna learned that she might rejoin the company—without the baby. And only if she kept up her skills. Hattie arranged for Anna to board at the Hotel until after the birth. The child would be given up for adoption.

A bond manifested between the two women. Before the infant arrived, Hattie's heart melted; blood as warm and as sweet as maple syrup flowed through her veins. I'm already beset with three little kids. What's one more? Anna mustn't give away our lover's child. Hattie dreamed she would dote on the baby and raise this one herself. What a comfort in old age, someone to dote on her in return.

Hattie further promised to be security for Anna. If ever she needed a home or help.

And what could a touring ballerina do for Hattie? The dancer inquired. Hattie fretted for a few weeks before deciding on an answer—an answer that was to have a meteoric impact.

"If you were to in some way lose your dance opportunity, you might come to help raise the child." However, there was one promise Anna must make. "You must never, ever, reveal to anyone, that you are the child's mother." Anna agreed.

Hattie suffered second thoughts. From a dark crevice in her heart delusion seeped, as bitter as the appetite-inducing medicine Dr. Dankworth once prescribed. Hattie needed to claim, and, yes, guard the child's loyalty. Was it wise to let Anna entertain thoughts of returning? How unfair if Anna were to waltz in after many years and lay claim to the child's heart.

Nevertheless, Hattie and Anna's plan seemed foolproof enough for the time being. Hattie's widowed sister, Martine, over in Jersey, would tend the infant for the first six weeks. Then the child would be dropped on the Home's doorstep anonymously. Hattie would raise it with the three siblings—like a beloved waif. She knew she couldn't have faced the world's judgment as an unwed mother, not at her age, not with her status. Her miscarriage had been a blessing in disguise.

Hattie hid the birth certificate. She feigned ignorance of the child's parentage beyond a surname. To assure diversion she'd taken a shadowy photo of Anna. The ballerina had signed it anonymously, with love, to be saved for the day the child would inquire.

There lurked a tiny problem. Anna was the one person in the world who could blow the lid off Hattie's secret. The End.

Douglas blinks. He takes a deep breath. Exhales noisily. Seems both Wing and Lermontov are hell-bent on glossing over his heartache. "Dubious!" he says, using one of Violette's words. "It's a stupid story. I know you're trying to cheer me up. Sorry, it didn't work."

Lermontov sounds a drumroll using his pencil on the glass tabletop. "Might seem that way. Might seem that way, today."

Douglas has nothing to say.

[6]

OH, THE JOY of free time. Sister Elder is reading the latest novel, Orwell's *1984.* A warning against totalitarianism, she says. She and Wing are debating Truman's failure to stop communism in mainland China. Mildred, owner of Sister Peace's Victrola, is listening to Monroe's recording, "Ghost Riders in the Sky"—over and over. James and John are playing softball.

Douglas, after two hours of violin practice, and the polishing of shoes, is riding his bike and relishing the return of his musical pals.

And then it's hot. Middle-of-July hot. Rosy-breasted finch gather at *Lilacs*. Today three birdbaths tempt pine siskin; they drink or bathe with much splattering. The flock flutters off as Bertine pours a fresh supply of water into each basin. She calls them back, mimicking their sharp twittering cheeps. "Sure is hot today," she says, reporting the obvious to Douglas and Michael, who compete at "composer dates" and marbles on a shady stretch of sidewalk.

Douglas has three of Michael's aggies in his possession; his trick has been to choose composers who have created for instruments other than the violin! Once the librarian taught him the Dewey Decimal System, he was in business. *I can memorize as well as Michael.* Win or lose, Michael's good humor appears inexhaustible. Perhaps it's simply the guilty pleasure of frivolous time with a pal he savors.

Of a sudden Willi rides by. He hollers as he rears up on the bike's back wheel. "Doogie! Hey Doogie doo doo, doo doo, whatcha doin'?"

Bertine hollers back at the cyclist as he speeds away, "Hey, that's mean!" Bertine turns to Douglas. "Do you know him?"

"Yeah. We're sorta friends, kinda brothers, I guess."

"What's his name?"

"Willi, Wilhelm Stoya."

Willi circles back like a hawk zoning in on a rodent. "Hey Doogie doo doo! Doo doo, whatcha doin'?" He skids his bike to a stop. He surveys the trio, his nose twitching in a sneer. Turning to Michael he offers advice. "Better watch out, this nincompoop's a real stinker."

Bertine puts her hands on her hips and stomps toward the offender. How surprisingly aggressive, this angelic girl in her blue summer dress, in her bright red sandals. "How's about we call you Willi Wee-wee, huh? How'd you like that, Willi Wee-wee?"

Douglas gazes at Bertine with fresh admiration. And Wee Willi? He's powerless against her comeback. Off he rides. Bertine wipes her hands back and forth as if officially dispensing of the offender. "There, that got rid of him, he isn't your friend, Douglas, I can tell you that, sure is hot today, where's the ice cream man when you need him, sure could use a popsicle or something like that."

Mike shares his latest. "I've been practicing the Wieniawski Concerto in F-sharp Minor all day. I have two recitals in November, Jeanne accompanies me, so I never get away from her. Wish I had my bike here. Same kind as yours, Douglas, 'cept mine has reflectors, headlight, and speedometer; I can cruise over thirty miles per hour!"

Brotherhood surges in Douglas. "You can take my bike for a spin right now if you like."

No hesitation! The young violinist hops on the bicycle and pedals around the corner.

Bertine fills the silence. "Did you know that Mike won the Stillman-Kelly Scholarship Competition? He got prize money and Galamian says he won't have to enter competitions anymore 'cause he's getting so famous, only trouble is he's gone so much, just me and Dad at home, we send him telegrams sometimes."

Douglas beams with adoration for these siblings; he's in awe of their lifestyle. Michael of wit, of knowledge, of talent. Who cares if he brags a little? Bertine, of charm and loyalty. "Maybe we can go swimming when Mike gets back?" This ploy for more time might just succeed.

Bertine brightens at the suggestion. "Swimming, how fun, let's go to Lincoln Pond, we went there before, I'll ask Jeanne right now!"

* * *

BY SUMMER'S END Douglas prizes his small collection of aggies won in contest with Michael Rabin. Five marbles fit nicely in the bamboo bowl from Astrid. Five marbles are enough for practicing correctly. Along with new hormones, a much-needed rush of inspiration flows throughout his maturing body thanks to the raconteur, Lermontov.

I'd better make Ciazzo proud this fall. Or else. Douglas writes a note to Auntie Evangeline, who demands to be kept informed. Brief his communication, even so he hits the highlights. Of the novelist. Of the Rabin kids. Of Ciazzo's return.

[7]

September 1949

CIAZZO picks up his violin, white hankie under his chin. He pulls the bow across the strings—*naaaaaaaaaa na-na*; the sound flows. It seems effortless for the Spaniard to charm his audience in this way. Douglas senses Ciazzo's energy, like the pull of a magnet drawing him close and safe. The demonstration ends in less than two minutes.

"I want to learn that music!"

Ciazzo's chocolate eyes sparkle. "I thought you'd like it! It's titled "Sea Murmurs." By Castelnuovo-Tedesco, an Italian-born composer.

"How do you make sounds like water...like, so sparkly and then so smooth?"

"Let's just say a worthy violin in the hands of a skilled player can offer subtle colors of mood just like a painting: the lyric, dramatic, heroic, passionate, gay, carefree.

"Really, how can I do that with this factory violin?"

"You can use tempo. Accents. Energetic stresses. Tender delicate touches." Ciazzo tilts his head from side to side, his neck making tiny cracking sounds. As he straightens, he meets Douglas eye to eye. He drums his index finger on Douglas' violin. "If you can learn to find subtlety with this lowly creation, imagine what you could do with a decent one!" He waits for a response. Getting none, he pulls a record from its sleeve and places it on the Victrola. "This is Heifetz playing the same piece I just played. "Sea Murmurs." Listen and then tell me what you think."

They listen as Ciazzo plays the track five times. Five times more.

Douglas hesitates. "Well, you play it slower, more brightly."

"Top-notch observation. I interpret what I think the composer intended. Each player interprets when he feels the music—as you will too. For the time being I want you to finish your practice sessions with this piece. And as you play it you must ask yourself, 'What is the effect being produced on my audience?' Wing and Astrid are your listeners, right?"

Ciazzo rummages through his shelves until he finds the sheet music. "We'll start learning it right now! By next summer perhaps you will have mastered it."

"*Next* summer? It'll take so long?"

"Longer yet, *mijo, if* you aren't diligent."

[8]

CIAZZO EXPLAINS THE National Orchestral Association Rating Event to Douglas, whose heart chug-chugs at the very idea. "You'll play three compositions from the NOA's pre-selected list. Don't scowl. It's fair. The committee has chosen pieces appropriate for an entrant's year of study. I'm suggesting these for you. "Minuet," by L. Boccherini, unaccompanied; this lively tune will get the judges' heads bobbing and toes tapping. Next, the Concerto No. 2, 3rd Movement, by Seitz, a German Romantic Era composer; the song has a lot of variety and will allow you to show several different skills. Last and most difficult will be the Violin Partita No. 1 BWV 1002, by Johann Sebastian Bach."

Ciazzo rolls up his sleeves. Douglas feels the man's inaudible persuasiveness. Ciazzo plays through each selection for a student who listens with respect, if not dread. The student's fingers twitch with unselfconscious mimicry, his body following the varying rhythms.

"I believe you're ready." Ciazzo sets aside his violin and bow.

"Jeepers, I'm not! You just don't know! How can I play like you? I flub up in front of people.

"I'm not surprised you flub up, as you say. Listen to me. We can overcome the problem."

"You think so?"

"*Claro que si.* Of course. First, don't fret about interpretation. I guarantee you what comes from your violin and bow will not sound like Heifetz, not like Rabin, not like Ciazzo. It will be of you. You."

Douglas nods while concern crumples his face. He's a small airborne vessel, victim to the pitch and yaw of a turbulent sky.

"Remember, if you rouse your audience, if you convince us you are unveiling beauty's soul, well then, your interpretation is justified. El *señor* Virtuosity will come with experience."

Douglas takes a deep breath. A sudden tailwind seems to steady his celestial navigation.

"My admonition. Keep on practicing relentlessly. Just like your pal, Michael. Who knows what is possible!

[9]

ASTRID AND NARCISSE LOUISE acknowledge one another in the Elizabethtown Library. It seems they choose the same day and hour to scour the Mystery aisle. If it's insight about authors they discuss, who can say? The library is, after all, a place for whispering. And if their voices should be heard by the librarian's assistant, the one with dark braids looped around her ears, she tells them to shush. After a typical session, Astrid, or

Narcisse Louise, one or the other, surveys Nonfiction while the other seeks the librarian, the one with square spectacles, date stamp in hand. On these afternoons two errand runners are reminded of what they share. Interest in a certain boy's progress toward maturity, for better or for worse.

[10]

January 1950

THE STOYA CONSERVATORY schools more than three dozen impressive students. Weekday afternoons the sounds of scales, arpeggios, Czerny, Hanon, Clementi, repeated phrases, repetition, repetition, Professor tap-tapping his conductor's baton, Mrs. Piano Teacher clap-clapping.

The indefatigable metronome tick-tocking the tempo. The cuckoo cloistered for the duration. Tall front doors opening and closing just before and after each hour. The coat rack strung with sweaters, jackets, scarves, and hats, many of which are left behind for weeks at a time.

Narcisse Louise, in the kitchen, listens to the Stoya boys banter as they make their way through an after-school snack, their favorite: bologna/pickle/cream cheese sandwiches. The brothers harangue each other about division of chores or complain to compassionate LuLu about unfair tons of homework.

Willi's violin lesson begins promptly at 7 p.m. every Tuesday and Thursday. Mrs. Piano Teacher watches on. After which LuLu rounds up Siggi—who is always constructing something or other, indoors, or out—and serves dessert to the family. A sulk can be adjusted with sweets, she and Frieda agree; the offering—be it pudding, cake, or custard—can set right the snappish, sullen, exasperated, testy male members of the Stoya household.

Boys upstairs, LuLu off-duty, Professor and Mrs. Piano Teacher analyze their situation while sipping brandy. Her giggly eight-year-old memorizes without effort. Her shy nine-year-old displays enthusiasm. His four pre-teens show new promise. The weekly group lesson, which includes Willi and A.J., proves to be effective.

Frieda dreams up strategy. "Come summer we'll invite the Galamians and Piatigorskys to another recital. We'll say, 'Look at the future we're preparing for Meadowmount.' Jacqueline is quite involved at Meadowmount, I understand."

Stoya agrees. He goes on to imagine Frieda's oratory at this imaginary recital. She'll be waxing poetic with metaphors of seeds germinating, or of buds becoming blooms.

[11]

NIGHT AFTER NIGHT the 253-1 woos Douglas with her confidences. Her tone has become more serious.

{Douglas| Is it not true| Men will do evil things| Indeed they will| For Power| Also for paper and coin called Money| And men will do evil things for the strongest hunger| desire for another's caress| When men discover my heritage| such desire will overcome them| At the right time| 253-1 must reveal the secrets of her *raritas* to you| For only you| can protect *questo violino*| |

Douglas wishes he could ask Rembert Wurlitzer for advice. His only recourse is to concentrate on the immediate. "253-1, how are you doing in the Stoya Conservatory without me?"

[12]

ACCORDING TO DOUGLAS one color dominates this April morning. The tree-covered hills are bathed in such a glaze one would swear all the trees were blue. Not green. The clouds resemble floating fish skeletons on an enormous blue platter. Oh-No hangs her new blue raincoat in the locker next to his. And when Tattersall approaches—the man has been promoted to High School Orchestra—Douglas avoids eye contact; looking down, he notes the fellow's blue cardigan. Ugh. Blue reminds him of the thin music book he's come to despise—just open the faded blue cover and there you'll find the dreadful Bach Violin Partita No. 1 BWV 1002. He hasn't memorized it yet. Time's running out.

It keeps approaching, steadily, steadily, closer. The Rating Event. He will be heard, and he will be judged. Ciazzo says he *should* be ready. If he keeps up his practice. The way Ciazzo emphasizes the word *should* makes Douglas even more nervous. Violette reports Willi and A.J. have just begun Shirmer's Intermediate Book of Classics, and Professor Stoya has prepared them for the Rating Event, too. Douglas wonders, have his skills kept up with Willi's? An old competitive hunger gnaws at Douglas' insides. He imagines a small rat with a voracious appetite and never-brushed-yellow incisors chewing him alive. Oh, he'd be furious if Willi got to play his 253-1 for the Rating Event and then outscored him!

[13]

STOYA QUICKLY SELECTS his seat on the left aisle, Row 7. He's eager to review the *teachers' only* list of participants in the National Orchestral Association Rating Event; he wonders why in the world he's on edge. Releasing his miniature fountain pen from the lanyard around his neck, he withdraws the marbled celluloid cap, tests the flow of ink, and carefully circles the names: A.J. Purvis, Wilhelm Stoya, and, yes, Douglas Tryzyna, #32. *Well, well, the lad's finally appearing at a Rating Event. Been almost three years since he studied with me.* Stoya scoffs. *Lessons with Tattersall in the so-called orchestra, and then with that snake oil salesman, Johnson, certainly derailed the boy. Threw him off the competitive track, one that I had adeptly laid during formative years.*

Despite this pompous internal dialog, the great Peter Stoya can't pinpoint which outcome he desires. More gratifying if Douglas' debut is inspiring? Or if it's tedious? Which will reflect favorably on me?

The stage is set with a grand piano for the designated accompanist. A temporary screen blocks all views of an entrant from both audience and judges. Five judges representing the NOA, clipboards in hand, take front row seats.

The students shuffle backstage to be sorted by age and alphabet. They appear one by one; everyone can sense their quaking. One judge prompts and encourages. She stands to do so. She wears a red felt hat with a polka dot feather. Her exaggerated elocution commands obedience from even the most fearful. Peter attends to each entrant's playing, notebook and pen at the ready. He has no qualms about poaching a promising student from another teacher.

At noon, Stoya unwraps and devours his sandwich, liverwurst on pumpernickel garnished with robust mustard and pickles. He washes it down with ginger beer from his thermos. LuLu packs exactly what he likes. Eating quickly leaves ample time for his twofold agenda—persuade and probe.

First, he'll detain the parents of the participants he's targeted. *Most parents melt upon hearing a few words of praise for their child; they always do.* Once captive they listen to his vision for their currently under-served prodigy, during which they recognize a true professional and succumb. He's unwavering in his mission to be a premier teacher. *I'm magnetic,* he tells himself. *Look at the three youngsters I recruited last year.*

After this he'll shake hands with his peers on the judging panel. He'll make polite inquiries with a keen ear for idiosyncrasies and bias.

"Number 18," the bald judge calls. *It's A.J.* Excellent playing of scales followed by uneven tempo on arpeggios. A.J. breezes through the selected passages of three selections. *I've taught him well,* Stoya reminds himself. *He'll get no praise from me, however. No coddling-shmodling.*

"Number 27." Stoya tenses as he hears the judge calling the most important number. Wilhelm Stoya is on the stage, though hidden behind the screen. The father visualizes his son raising the violin and positioning the bow. The father's heart pounds. "Come on, you jackanapes," he whispers. "Listen to yourself playing, jah?"

Willi begins with good volume. The scales and arpeggios go well. *Ouch,* with the Bach Partita Willi is flat; the judges stop him immediately. With the Beethoven he falters at first, *nein, nein.* Improves before he's halted. *Ah,* the Schubert, the judges will let him continue. At last Willi gains confidence; he finds loveliness in the melody as his playing accurately demonstrates the skills he's acquired.

Peter pounds his fists on his thighs, unable to remain quiet. "Yes, jah, jah, good schmood! Practice—this monkey is going to practice his Bach Partita like a jackass. Teach him to let his gooseflesh take control!" As if his son displayed an amalgam of animal traits to address.

And in a blur, before the father calms, four youngsters have taken the stage, played their selections, and departed. Notice the shift in posture—his attention is caught when the judge calls for a particular entrant. "Number 32, please." #32 on the list, *Douglas Tryzyna,* begins tuning up. Normal everyday tuning up. Followed by silence. Continued silence. Continued silence. "Shall we begin?" The judge, the feather in her hat responding to some private draft, makes the polite inquiry. "Shall we begin, then?" The sound of footsteps from behind the screen answers; a boy on the run. "Make note, Number 32 has withdrawn."

"He's choked, he's choked! Dear God," Stoya whispers. His heart lurches as a wave of nausea hits. An old memory like something fetid dredged from the river bottom overwhelms his composure. He remembers walking toward his own exam in Berlin. Violin bow well rosined, strings tuned to a quiver and resembling his every neuron.

Passing the Academy's exam would have opened the doors of opportunity. Would have clinched Frieda's acceptance. Would have earned a chair in the Berlin Philharmonic's string section. Why couldn't he overcome stage fright? He'd left before playing a single note. Just like Douglas Tryzyna. Stoya feels liverwurst come up into his throat. He'd failed. Hadn't overcome his own damned stage fright. He hadn't deserved Frieda. She remained loyal. Not counting the interlude when a hurled boot hit its mark. He rubs the scar on his cheek. *Frieda has a temper rivaling mine.*

After his failure, after her thrown boot, the two of them began with a new intensity, Frieda continuing as his accompanist. Every composition attacked phrase by phrase. Repeat, repeat, repeat, until perfection was reached. And then repeat again. It had taken him another year to permanently join a quartet; the Philharmonic remained out of his reach. Those years of love and constant togetherness with Frieda bloom even now, causing his heart to beat erratically, and his scar to itch. As he scratches, his mind returns to the present Rating Event.

After ever so many entrants have faced their fears, exposed their egos, fought for excellence, pushed through challenges, annoyed listeners, tested patience, lifted hearts, surprised, or disappointed even themselves, Stoya sighs. He gathers his belongings. Rolled paper bag, empty thermos, black leather gilt-edged pocket notebook with its red ribbon marking a page titled 10th May 1949, *Wilhelm's Second Rating Event.* He hooks the lanyard to the metal ball on the miniature fountain pen's cap.

"Don't forget your hat, sir."

"Yes, hat and coat," he says, noticing for the first time the bespectacled gent two seats over who has probably heard his every impassioned whisper.

He can report to Frieda before the official scores arrive in the mail. Wilhelm Stoya did not impress, not until the Schubert. Nevertheless, technical prowess can't be denied. He'll challenge the rating if Willi doesn't *Pass with Merit*. And A.J., undeniably, must *Pass with Distinction*.

Cluck, cluck. Tryzyna, poor wretch, taking a non-score. Stoya, momentarily forgetting his own youthful debacle in Berlin, sees Douglas in the far corner with Ciazzo. What is a teacher to say in this circumstance? He can't remember an instructor encouraging him, the esteemed Professor Peter Stoya-to-be, at his lowest. He'd just kept on. Sheer will. Muscle. A disregard for snubs. He'd bounced back. "Keep on!" That's what he would tell Douglas if the poor devil were his student.

If he were my student. The words give Professor Stoya pause. He reflects on the day he banished ten-year-old Douglas Tryzyna from further lessons. And for what? Supposedly touching a violin. *Supposedly.* According to LuLu the child was innocent. Regret and compassion brew as he follows his flickering shadow to the car. *Poor kid. Did I make a big mistake kicking him out back then?*

In seconds rationalization makes mincemeat of all that caught-up-in-the-moment weakness. *Well, from here it doesn't look like you made much of a mistake, Peter Stoya.*

As Willi skips toward the Exit, he spies Douglas, his fraternal enemy, in the corner with Ciazzo. "All ham-fisted today, Doogie?" he hollers.

Ciazzo ignores the taunt as he heads outside with Douglas. "El *señor* Experience came teaching today. Learn from him."

Sunlight blinds the flummoxed entrant. He's unable to take courage from kind advice. His brain rattles like a dried gourd.

Ciazzo continues. "Douglas, my touring season begins next week. I'll be away for the summer. Practice "Sea Murmurs;" you're almost there,

so have it truly perfected by my return. And don't neglect the other assignments marked in your books."

[14]

DESPITE THE COACHING Douglas fails to practice after Ciazzo leaves. It's
painful. Pointless. He's pathetic. Be that as it may, he joins Wing and
Astrid after dinner. He sprawls on the floor as he did so many nights in
the past, watching incense smoke curl and roam. The book of exercises for
bowing technique remains unopened.

Evening after evening Wing shares cartoons featuring Antenna Boy,
whose dramatics are calculated to make the miserable young man laugh.
Wing's hero defies the limitations of earth. Normally Douglas would light
up. How can he be cheery when humiliation reigns? Silent as ever Astrid
sews, witness to all. Under the presser foot of her machine something
lined with red satin flows. Something embroidered with gold floss.

Wing sets aside his cartoons. His tone is matter of fact; however,
one would suspect he's exasperated by the teenager's continued gloom.
"Wisdom say, *Boy who no practice no improve.*"

Astrid speaks up. "Boy who *no* practice? Correct English, please.
Boy who *does not practice...does not improve.*" She's caught Wing by surprise. He gives her a mischievous smile.

"Wisdom say, *Wife no correct husband when boy in room.*"

Wing and Astrid chuckle agreeably. Astrid returns to her embroidery. Her amused husband, still shaking his head, picks up his ink pen.

Douglas grins at their friendly crossfire. Though only momentarily.

And then one evening Wing questions Douglas. Such an atypical
thing, a man like Wing prying. "Where does your heart sing, boy?"

Douglas, jolted as he is, answers without thinking. "At the falls."

"I already know this," Wing says with a smile. He flicks his pen and
watches black droplets splatter across a sheet of blank paper. "Wing just

ask to see if *you* remember." He laughs so easily, this short man in his square-cut clothes, obviously tickled by his own clarity. "You must go there with violin. To falls. You must play there in morning quiet time."

"And you must wear this, every time," Astrid says. She holds out a vest, black linen lined with red satin; the garment she has been making these past evenings. She radiates, her energy like breeze from a fan, swift, gentle, refreshing. Douglas feels himself in the center. As she extends the gift her wedding ring catches his attention, a gold band graced with two stones, blue ovals smooth as robins' eggs. The ring makes him aware; Astrid and Wing have joined together to help him, like parents. Tears well in his eyes and he blinks as he tries to hold them back. Astrid opens the vest. "See here, hidden on the inside, I've embroidered a dragon holding a pearl. You wear this next to your heart, for power. He's called Loong; he rules water. This Dragon brings good fortune for you, Douglas."

[15]

USELESS. IDLE. DOUGLAS, surrendering to transparent mist, warm air, mossy rocks. Fallen trees where beetles bustle, worms slither, spiders crawl, he observes each little life at work. He ponders the industry of creatures; he's merely one of them, he decides. He too must toil. *Practice is my work.* This, a fruitless resolution. He's overcome by the dread of trying, and of failing, again.

Perhaps it's the mail waiting for him one afternoon that precipitates his recovery. A postcard arrives from Cuba. Pictured on the front is the Havana Racetrack. Written on the back:

> Dear Douglas,
> Having a very good time. Sorry you couldn't be here too. Everything is very exciting—the bus drivers go very fast blowing their horns and missing cars and people by inches! It's crazy lazy too with afternoon siestas and motor boating.

Haven't seen any racehorses yet, if I do, I will try to photo-
graph any for you. See you this summer.
Your pal,
Michael

Douglas glows, reading it again and again. Energy surges through his being. Remember Michael's public acceptance of him at the Social Center? And look at this tangible proof of friendship.

Douglas rises at dawn with Wing, eats breakfast, packs wontons, pedals to the falls, his violin in its case slung across his back. Long before tourists and teens arrive, he finds the privacy he seeks. Only an occasional hiker intrudes on his practice sessions.

Wing's idea to play at the Split Rock Falls proves to be genius. The setting—wildly contained. Here the canopy of trees is his shelter, rocks are the walls of his auditorium, nature his orchestra. Here he joins with something majestic and enduring where stage fright is irrelevant. Accompanied by the percussion of water, the rustle of trees, the randomness of bird call, his pulse quickens.

He might as well be the Basque man, beside fire, under the dome of stars for all the abandon he feels while playing. Here, collaborating with nature, Douglas' passion exceeds the strength of his self-doubt. The floodgates of musicality open fully. "This is who I am, this is who I am," he repeats aloud for the benefit of every life form. He dismisses Lermontov's fantasy of his parentage although it daily rumbles through his brain like a locomotive satisfying a timetable. *That was made-up nonsense.*

Each day he returns to the Home taking the long way, past Fiddler Hill—and one day the purr, hum, and whine of stringed instruments greets him. The Meadowmount season has begun. This June he's no longer an outsider or a quitter. He can't wait to see if Michael and Bertine have returned.

Dear Auntie Evangeline,

Guess what! I can really make a lady sing from a box with strings!

Maybe because Wing and Astrid are so kind. When I go to the falls

it happens. Yes. Even with my factory violin. Nobody could believe

it, I'm sure. Except Michael Rabin. I'm going to bring him hiking up

there.

From me, Douglas

[16]

MICHAEL AND BERTINE chatter as they make their way past the Split Rock Falls marker and follow the trail Douglas has traversed daily these past weeks. He points out a gray and blue snake coiled in the leaves. "Watch out!" Bertine tilts her head like she's listening for snakes in the underbrush.

Jeanne says she'll relax on a bench under the trees. They have an hour, one hour only. She's brought a music score to study and a thermos of iced tea.

The trio passes through an opening in the feathery green trees. Bertine giggles. "Hey, you guys, look!" Straight ahead water rushes between the granite walls of a mountain ravine. Heavy rain last night increased the waterfall's flow; it turned the downpour to froth. This afternoon waves bounce through the pools and bounce off rocks. Bertine claps her hands. "This place reminds me of Cubism, or something like that—you know, Picasso and Braque."

Douglas isn't sure what Cubism is. "Yup," he says very softly, wondering if Cubism has anything to do with Cuba. He clambers down to the largest pool and chooses a large flat rock where they spread their towels.

"I brought us each a Sugar Daddy, 'cept we should wait a while. Is there a shallow wading place, Douglas?" Bertine steps out of her shorts and yanks her shirt over her head. Douglas has never seen her in a bathing suit. It's two-piece, red, with pleating and bows. It reveals her trim legs. Her narrow ribcage. And ivory flesh overflowing the crisscrossed top.

Bertine comes back from wading. She's slipped and fallen; she's dripping wet. Douglas thinks her flesh shines as if it's painted. He tries not to stare at the geography of her body as she stretches out next to him, wiping her nose with a corner of her striped towel.

"Tell me more about Cuba, Michael," he says, turning away from the intrigue of Bertine.

"We visited Uncle Arthur Rodzinski at his home in Havana, a big old Spanish-style house. There's so much grass and flowers there. He's the conductor I played with. We first met in New York, you see, and now he lives over there. I took a lot of photos I can show you. Wish we'd gone to the horse races." Michael tears opens the wrapper on his Sugar Daddy and sucks on the sweet hard caramel.

"We're saving them 'til later, Mike."

Michael ignores Bertine. "I flew in an airplane for the first time and I'm going to keep a log of all my travel," he says. "And can you guess? Because of how important this trip was, I got a better violin to play, a loaner. A del Gesú, from Rembert!"

"How do you know violin names?"

"Some violins are named after an important owner. Most have their maker's names only. A long time ago families specialized in work. Like, some made leather stuff, some made cheese, some made wine, some raised sheep, you know."

"Like our family is all musicians," Bertine says.

Michael ignores his sister and continues. "The Amati family made violins in Italy, 1500s, 1600s. Nicolo Amati had learned from his grand-dad, his uncle, and his father. And his skills were advanced. Nicolo Amati's violin set the standard for years. I had one made by him on loan for a while. Because you can't perform in public on an ordinary violin."

"Well, you shouldn't," Bertine says, sounding like an authority.

"I know how bad my factory violin sounds compared to Stoya's and Ciazzo's," Douglas says. "I'd never play it in public."

"I have lots of concerts scheduled with American orchestras this year, and, well, I've been loaned an Amati. Her tone is sweet. Awfully thin for my playing in a big auditorium, though. Ivan G. thinks so too. He told Rembert it wasn't suitable."

"Who's Rembert?"

"Mr. Rembert Wurlitzer. He deals in string instruments, the totally premier guy for knowing about these things."

"What kind do you really want?" Douglas asks, while making a mental note to meet Mr. Wurlitzer someday.

"A Stradivarius, silly!" Bertine says before Michael can get the words out.

"True," Mike says thoughtfully, adding in a most adult fashion, "I dream of owning a violin by the maker Antonio Stradivari, from Cremona, Italy, 1656–1737. He's the most famous in the whole world!"

"How could anybody know if they saw or heard a Stradivarius?"

"Well, for one thing it says so inside. There's a maker's label inside a violin you can see with a tiny flashlight through the F-hole."

Years ago, Douglas heard the Professor speak of this. He wonders if the 253-1 even has a label.

"A Stradivarius sings like an angel even if you play a little badly," Bertine says dreamily.

Mike frowns at her. "The thing I like is that an Antonio Strad almost plays itself with the gentlest bowing. I got to try one at Rembert's."

Douglas feels ignorant in the company of Michael and Bertine.

Michael continues. "After the Amati, Rembert loaned me a 1703 Joseph Guarnerius." Michael's tone reveals that he wasn't thrilled. "This Joseph Guarnerius just didn't respond to me. 'If I'm going to have a Guarnerius,' I told Ivan, 'I want one by Joseph's son, Giuseppe Guarneri del Gesú.' He's probably as famous as Antonio Stradivari. They were like friends and rivals in Cremona back then."

Douglas tries again. "Well, *my* current violin...it's either a Strad," he pauses, "or a factory violin. And it's not a Strad."

Bertine laughs out loud. "You're funny, Douglas!"

"If you listened to me practice on the thing, you'd hate it!"

Mike rubs suntan lotion on his face. He nods sympathetically.

"You look like that sad opera clown, Pagliacci, with white stuff all over your face." Bertine is pointing at Mike and giggling. The giggle becomes an uncontrolled belly laugh.

Mike gives his sister a jab in the arm. He talks louder since she can't stop laughing. "So like I said, I'll play a Guarnerius, the Count Doria del Gesú on the *Bell Telephone Hour*, next week. And I get to use it again for my Carnegie Hall recital. It's valued at $35,000! It might be better than a Strad, I don't know."

Douglas speaks boldly. "I used to own a fine violin—I really did. It's at Professor Stoya's house right now. It might be better than a Strad too."

Bertine stops laughing. She and Michael look at each other with raised eyebrows. Bertine politely changes the subject.

Before long, Jeanne appears at the edge of the trail, waving something red. She blows her whistle like a lifeguard. "Time's up," she hollers.

Once they've joined her Michael asks if they can't have a little more time, hike to the top of the falls maybe. Jeanne thinks it's dangerous to do such a thing. She's read of suicides. Perhaps there's a compulsion that height brings on. She snaps her fingers. "We're on a schedule anyway. Back to the Paganini the instant we get home, young man."

[17]

FRIEDA STOPS WHERE the trail reaches a glade with mature aspen flickering shadow. "Let's picnic here," she says. After Peter spreads the blanket, she continues their argument. "Don't you see? The danger is in overdoing. I'm not criticizing, Peter. Still, do you recall Rabin's Carnegie Hall appearance? And remember what Isaac Stern overheard Arthur Berger saying about Michael? That he'll burn out, poor child. To quote, 'Such a Herculean work ethic is robbing him of his youth.'" Frieda hands Peter a sandwich, his favorite, liverwurst and pickles on pumpernickel. "I mean, I hope we're grooming Willi for a career *and* a full life."

Peter responds casually, sounding self-assured. "Agreed. The next three years are going to be crucial. A cutthroat cycle of musical competitions tempts us. Trust me. I'll manage wisely."

Frieda takes a sip of the ginger beer. Reclines on an elbow, listening to this man she's vowed to love and respect. "Yes, yes I know," she answers. Adding then, more gently, "And do you get the point, Peter? Sometimes you're a jackhammer. You need to relax. For the boys. And for your health."

Peter pretends to ignore her. Poor Frieda's blind. Our son needs the laziness driven from him. And he requires the use of a fine instrument. Thanks to me, he'll be using one of the finest for his public debut! And A.J.'s family? If they're committed to advancing their son's career, they need to make a serious investment, soon.

[18]

DOUGLAS TAKES THE bus to his September 1950 lesson with Ciazzo. After a summer of diligent practice at the falls he's confident. He's practiced scales and arpeggios in every key. He's perfected "Sea Murmurs" until he imagines he could play it at Carnegie Hall without a twinge of stage fright. He tackles it for Ciazzo, who listens, the Spaniard's face as chiseled and unmoving as a bronze work of art. Douglas finishes. The room is thick with apprehension as he awaits the solemn man's reaction.

Ciazzo remains silent, cigarillo smoke curling toward the open window. "I'm encouraged," he says softly. "The bowing exercises have been of benefit." Ciazzo continues his observations. He uses words like *maturity, sensitivity, finesse*, words strung together with enough explanation that Douglas' mind leapfrogs from one glorious pearl to the next.

Following this Ciazzo has a proposal. "Let's prepare for performance." He outlines a plan for the months ahead. Douglas will participate in a series of intimate recitals for students of the quartet members. He'll join seven teens, advanced students of violin, viola, and cello. He'll be accompanied by piano. He'll be paired for duets. If all goes well, next year he'll join a quartet.

Douglas lights up. The initial thought energizes him. Within seconds reality pierces. *How, with my factory violin?* Before he can dwell on the dismal reality of his violin's voice Ciazzo throws another hurdle. "You're going to hear about your weaknesses and your failed attempts. You'll be expected to acknowledge by applying the advice. There's no space for excuses. No time for pouting or being stubborn."

Ciazzo drums his finger on his violin's belly, waiting for a response. Douglas manages a mere blink. Thoughts of Professor Stoya's degrading critiques freeze both his gut and his voice.

"Need I say, students who resort to negative behaviors are dismissed from our circle?"

Dismissed. The word exudes an alarming reverberation.

Ciazzo continues. "You are a serious student; you'll be playing with other serious students. It's only right that you should be using a worthy instrument. With a quality bow."

Douglas' deepest longing for *one* very fine violin to call his own boomerangs, hitting his most tender spot; his knees wobble as his stomach flip-flops. His teacher speaks as if all possibility exists.

By the time Douglas leaves Ciazzo's studio it's freezing outside. Whitened trees line the streets, looking like powdered ladies with many brown-gloved hands. Once home he broods. James and John grumble; afterschool softball practice has come to an end for the season. Mildred complains about her ratty winter coat. Well, she hasn't outgrown it; perhaps she's pining for the one in the window of Stein Bros. Sister Elder says she should manage her money better; after all she has a job at the Hotel now. Sister Elder won't offer Douglas money either, especially not for a decent violin. He knows this without asking. His earnings from shining Lermontov's shoes will amount to a laughable bankroll even in a year's time.

No problem for Michael Rabin, who has Galamian and Mr. Wurlitzer eager to bestow excellent loaners. How in the world will *he* come up with an acceptable violin and bow? How in this unfair world? Douglas questions the universe ruefully. To a nobody, life has presented an impossibility, just when he dared to believe things were going well.

[19]

DOUGLAS ARRIVES AT Ciazzo's studio a bit early this December afternoon. Ciazzo walks an older student to the door with the manner of an affectionate uncle. "Learn to attribute every sound to a movement with a specific part of your body. This is how you will gain more control. Next week then."

"She already plays so well!" Douglas says. He's intimidated by the girl's enviable skill. "Last week with her Bach, remember that?"

Ciazzo frowns. He pulls a thin box from his starched shirt pocket, withdraws a cigarillo, and lights it. "She takes el *señor* Criticism to heart. That's why she plays as well as she does."

Douglas kicks his toe at the floor. "I didn't want to flub up last week in front of the group. I didn't freeze, but anyway I'm sure I sounded awful."

"Yes, good observation." Ciazzo closes his eyes as he exhales a spiral of smoke.

"I couldn't help it."

"Certain things happen when we're performing for an audience. We may hurry our playing. Or we may drag the tempo as if it's too hard to go on. If we're smart, we anticipate these tendencies. The goal is to play a piece just as we have practiced."

Douglas nods as he plucks the violin strings. The twang barely resembles the violin's singing voice. "All summer I hiked to the falls. I wore my lucky vest with the dragon next to my heart. The forest felt like a cocoon. With people around—"

"Hmm. ¿El *señor* Stage Fright is your Achilles heel, *sí?*" The man has a Roman nose with flaring nostrils. He might wrongly be accused of sneering. And yet his eyes sparkle with kindness. "The more you know, the more you know how high the bar is. As you progress you should have more stage fright, not less."

Dismay throws an uppercut to the crumb of remaining confidence. *This scaredy-cat stuff isn't going away?*

Ciazzo stubs out his cigarillo. "We musicians learn to evade. We bob and weave by using our own rituals."

Together they scheme, step by step, planning private rituals Douglas will follow before a performance. Ciazzo cautions. "Be mindful of each step. Let it be meditative; it can clear your mind. Finally, take a deep breath, smile, you're ready begin." Ciazzo taps Douglas on the shoulder with his bow. "*Escucha.* In time this habit will make the difference between paralysis and a solid performance. Do you believe, *mijo?*"

Douglas practices his preparation routine religiously for the next two weeks and he tests it before the December group recital. He realizes with some comfort that the other players he practices with are initially just as terrified as he is. Each one persists by following Ciazzo's advice.

[20]

"NOT LONG UNTIL our recital for family and friends," Ciazzo says. "Right now, let's imagine we are there, and your turn comes next. You take the stage, violin and bow in hand. First your sequence, calming yourself; always. Then you begin with confidence. Play for me now the Bach we're perfecting." Ciazzo's eyes, darkened by his heavy brows, cast a ruthless spell of expectation. The cigarillo ash grows as he waits for Douglas to settle himself.

Douglas takes a deep breath. He feels all jittery. He hesitates. The smoke's aroma seems comforting, though, woodsy, familiar, and gaining courage he begins without looking at his music.

"I see that you've memorized the Bach in its entirety since last week." The observation is as close to a compliment as can be expected. Ciazzo takes another drag from his cigarillo.

Douglas concentrates on making his fingers climb up the length of his bow and back down. *Is there a negative jab coming?* He keeps listening despite his fear.

"El *señor* Depression often piggybacks our pursuit for excellence. The remedy? Find the delight, the joy, all along the way—this is the answer." Ciazzo begins tapping his foot, picks up his violin and extracts a vibrant melody. Perhaps his face looks sorrowful with a wooden box pressed under his cleft chin. Listen, the music reveals his exuberance.

"That was wonderful!"

"Here, try this violin and bow yourself." Ciazzo thrusts both items into Douglas' hands.

Douglas hesitates. Touching an instructor's instrument gives him pause even after all these years. Stoya's rules have embedded psychological shrapnel. Douglas stares at the object he holds. "Hey, wait, wait, this, this isn't your Tarasconi!"

"No, just the same it is *my* violin, a D'Espine, the one I first used as a soloist. I will loan it to you as my student. Now the bow, that's another story. The bow is yours to keep and it is first-class."

Douglas clasps the D'Espine with reverence. "She's so beautiful."

"Indeed. She's classified as both Fine and Rare. Starting in January you'll practice on her twice weekly, here, before your lessons. It's time."

Douglas may never know if a certain Auntie arranged for him to compete with this violin and gifted him this excellent bow. Well, he has a good idea. Adults try to keep so many secrets.

> *Dear Auntie Evangeline,*
>
> *Thank you for arranging lessons with Ciazzo because of you doing this I now have a killer-diller violin to practice on and it sounds so lovely by itself or in a duet. The new bow (a mystery gift) handles just great you can't guess how much difference it makes. I hope you will be in town for our big Recital this spring. From me, Douglas*

[21]

CHRISTMAS MORNING TIPTOES onto the stage, pulling back the iridescent drapes of dawn, exposing the rotunda of blue. Christmas morning
whistles for attention. It seems to taunt, "Hey, look what's missing." Missing so obviously, the gift of Sister Peace's playful spirit. Glass baubles
strung on silver cord circle the tree, serving as poignant reminder of who
used to decorate, of who is gone. *I should have seen Sister Peace getting
ready to leave. I should have seen it coming.*

There have been no postcards, no letters in blue *PAR AVION* envelopes, no phone calls. Nothing from Sister Peace since that ruinous May
day. Nothing, even now, Christmastime. Sister Elder declines to comment,
doesn't seem to notice. Astrid says, "Once she's gotten her feet on the
ground, we'll hear from her." What did that mean, *her feet on the ground?*
Had Sister Peace been pretending to care?

In contrast, gifts are plentiful. A box of wrapped fancies mailed by
Auntie Evangeline—oranges, chocolate-covered fruits, pralines as large as
frogs, recordings of favored musicians. Each resident unwraps a book
from Sister Elder. Each teen is gifted with flannel pajamas from Astrid.
Each receives a personalized drawing from Wing—Antenna Boy with a flying violin for Douglas.

Christmas noon, the arrival of a welcome guest. Violette. She
knocks at the Home's bedecked door, shivering, stomping her feet, looking less than joyous. "Come in, child, come in," Sister Elder says. Violette
hands her a package and proceeds to tug off boots. "And how are you this
Merry Christmas afternoon, Miss Violette?" She takes a minute to admire
the square gift wrapped in white tissue paper with green yarn while Violette hangs up her coat and hat in the entry.

Violette crosses her arms and hugs herself. "Missing my father,
mostly, Sister Elder."

Sister Elder, finding it difficult to respond appropriately, crosses her arms too.

"Well anyway. Brought a present for all of you to share. Poetry. I've written the entirety. Perhaps it's too eclectic for your taste. Well anyway. Is Douglas here?"

Douglas waltzes in carrying the D'Espine; he's eager to show it off. "Can you believe? She's such a beaut, a loaner from Ciazzo for practice and performance—I got to bring it home for a week. And look, my very own bow!" Violette beams, her radiance so befitting the holiday, and taking nary a self-conscious second, the girl hugs Douglas with an intensity that loosens a knot in each heart—foundling, couple, and stoic spinster.

"And we've a gift for you Violette," Douglas says, his face flushed.

"*Tender Buttons* by Gertrude Stein," Sister Elder explains as Violette sets aside the nativity-blue wrapping. "May it suit your unorthodox heart to a *T*."

Time flies while Douglas performs on the D'Espine; he's basking in Violette's undivided attention.

Sister Elder appreciates the distraction this girl brings to the Home. "Surely, you'll honor us and stay for dinner, dear?"

"Thank you kindly, but no. Mother and I are having dinner at the Hotel with our little group—Lermontov calls us the Allies and Orphans." She gives Douglas a pinched smile, indicating her disappointment.

Wing offers to drive Violette when she's ready; seems he needs to pop into the Hotel kitchen for a minute.

After that Christmas afternoon plods along. Until dinnertime with customary guests—the Ludlows and their giggly daughter. With customary dessert—Mrs. Ludlow's famous mincemeat pie. Regarding which, Sister Elder demands the eating of as a display of good manners. Of which Douglas eats only the flaky crust; the spicy-gooey-lumpy-brown filling finds its way into a napkin. Douglas would prefer Sister Peace's fudge, preferably eaten with Sister Peace at the table.

Christmas evening lingers, during which Astrid serves each resident a cup or two of hot buttered rum. Nevertheless, one resident is no longer a resident here, and only one resident isn't very sad about that.

Just before bedtime, Christmas cannot resist wringing Douglas' heart inside out. Perhaps it's Sister Elder's traditional, oh-so-dramatic reading of *A Child's Christmas in Wales*. Just that one lingering sentence perhaps. "It snowed last year too: I made a snowman and my brother knocked it down and I knocked my brother down and then we had tea." Dylan Thomas knew a thing or two about the complexity of family.

Off to bed. The Home, released from Christmas expectations for another year, grows silent. Except for the odd creaking of old rafters. And James's intermittent snoring. And someone's quiet sobs. John reads by flashlight, something more adventurous than that weird Christmas story. Douglas fluffs his pillow, curls into a ball, and pulls the quilt over his head, unable to sleep.

Later he fingertip-knocks on Mildred's door, hoping she's awake. He plops on her bed. He's overheard things, before Sister Peace left, of course. Things no one ever explained. Gathering courage, he asks Mildred his troubling question. "Why did Sister Peace want to leave?"

"I thought you knew, dingaling," Mildred answers in her sarcastic-affectionate fashion. "Sister Elder and Sister Peace were having arguments. About you. Too many for Tatiana's comfort. Oh, kiddo, it isn't your fault. She was probably going back to her old flame sometime soon, anyway."

"I don't understand."

"Remember when she came here? You were almost six. She had just broken her leg. Well, she and her beau had just broken up, too. She came here to heal, and to nanny us kids. Sadly, she and Sister Elder always disagreed about raising you."

Douglas hangs his head. He chews the circular scar on his thumb.

"Remember all the airmail letters? The fella was still carrying a torch for her. You've grown up, Douglas. She felt free, seeing you'd found your way with Ciazzo. C'mon, you have a girlfriend. Tatiana's flesh and blood, too. And, just like you're passionate about violin, she's passionate about dance. Naturally it was time for her to go back to Cuba, to him, to her career."

[22]

January 1951

THIS VIOLIN. THE very one Ciazzo used as a young soloist. Imagine, here *he* is practicing on it two times weekly. At first with trepidation, handling it like a newborn kitten.

What of the bow he owns? Ciazzo won't say. Perhaps a certain opera teacher coached a mezzo-soprano to stardom; yes, perhaps the student's father gave a certain opera teacher this well-crafted German-made bow in appreciation. It may be that this opera teacher asks Ciazzo not to tell Douglas. Her reasoning? "I don't want the boy to feel beholden, nor do I want him to think of me as a perpetual Santa. Nothing to sully or diminish the natural ambition."

Douglas falters for words. It's juvenile to say *thank you*, yet again. Ciazzo waves his agile hand as if brushing away a gnat. "Let's just say, Michael Rabin has his Galamian; you have Ciazzo, minus a stage mother...plus, you have Señora Benefactor in the wings."

Some things haven't changed for Douglas. Willi and cohorts regularly chant vulgarities as they run past his locker. Tattersall confronts him during lunch, soliciting a violinist's much-needed participation in the High School Orchestra.

Alternately, Douglas has changed. He carries a warm glow in his gut. Self-respect. He's improving as a musician. He's able to ignore the bullies. And oh, it's easier to say "No thank you" to Tattersall without resentment. After all he was just a kid when he used to feel so angry.

[23]

WHY DOES THE D'Espine violin sound so much nicer than my own? Douglas wants to know. Ciazzo thinks that's a worthy question and places the factory violin on a draped tabletop for viewing. They take turns looking through the F-holes. "If a violin's label has the words *hand-made*, that's almost a guarantee that it's not. We've both heard your instrument's uneven volume across strings. Look." Ciazzo points to a scuff. "Painted purfling, a bad sign. Plastic coated pegs, these are not ebony. The bridge is too thick and a bit high. I fear she's missing corner blocks inside. As if this isn't enough, the poor creature is much too heavy."

"What is she worth in dollars?"

"A violin is only worth what a given chap will pay for it at the time! Now yours here, I'd guess $25 wouldn't be high."

"I'd like to know more about violins!"

"Oh, one can spend a lifetime learning about violins and recognizing the superior ones. Most musicians know only the basics, *mi hijo.*"

The D'Espine is generous, willing, sensitive to Douglas' command in practice and in monthly performance with duet partners. Ciazzo seems to approve of his progress. The D'Espine sings with a quality all her own, unlike the Practice violin, the Performance Violin, or Ciazzo's Tarasconi. Even as Douglas finds his skills accelerating—at a rate he'd never experienced—the voice of the violin from Turin grows lovelier. Created for a royal Italian audience, hers is a regal tonality befitting a queen, or first wife in a harem.

In contrast Douglas thinks Magic Muriel's tonality speaks to common people, to wild spaces. This quality that resonated with him as a child hasn't lost its allure. He's convinced, only through the striped, red, the beloved 235-1, will his spirit be heard.

[24]

Spring 1951

TWO TEENS, BOUND by a fickle friendship, taught with divergent approaches, advance in skill. Surely Douglas benefits from playing on the D'Espine under Ciazzo's watchful eye. Willi, no doubt, responds to newfound favor shown by his father. *Thank God, tomfoolery with A.J. is a thing of the past,* Stoya thinks as he listens to his son, never making the connection between his own good spirits and the boy's conduct. "Just listen to him, Frieda! How he relates to German-born Brahms as I myself do."

"Even Galamian will be impressed!"

"Good-schmood, my angel," Stoya says, tweaking the corners of his overgrown mustache, noting the need for a visit to the barber. He takes her strong, long-fingered hand in his virtual paw. "How I love your piano hands. Headache gone this evening?" He kisses the backs of her hands and then her palms. In his next breath he calls out to Willi, who has set his violin aside. "Try it again! And this time concentrate. Mind the tempo—you've gone ragged-schmagged!"

Weeks later Stoya overhears Willi improvising. One lively tune with an intricate 4/7 count especially impresses him. "I must reach out to Hindemith," Stoya whispers to Frieda, his ultramarine eyes alight. "Willi should definitely attend Tanglewood Academy this summer. And next."

Frieda huffs, puts a leather placemark in her Agatha Christy mystery. "Why send him to Boston when Meadowmount is in our own backyard?" One can't mistake her fault-finding tone. She folds her hands, placing them under her chin. She closes her eyes. One would think she was at prayer.

Stoya inches to her ear and hisses. "My dear, because Hindemith teaches composition, not just technique. We must give Willi every possible advantage."

[25]

"DINNER TIME, SIGGI," the Professor calls. Before the boy answers the man is arrested by a spring-time spectacle; the western sky is impossibly bright, in front of which tiny, winged insects swarm. Feasting on these gnats, agile birds dart with split-tailed urgency after which they tuck into the eaves and disappear. The sight holds Peter spellbound and he enters an altered consciousness.

There in the half-light his son's silhouette rattles a memory. He flashes on the sight of Siggi bashing pumpkins, face crimped like a gleeful troll—a twilight aggression witnessed in October—a sight he categorizes as *not the son I was expecting.* Tonight's sight is different; it startles him. Siggi lifts a log into place on a sophisticated structure. This son's construction? Has the boy hauled fallen logs by himself? How often has he busied himself sawing and chopping lengths to suit? An architect's instinct, the father thinks. Developing muscles too; the Stoya physique. Blessedly not the Bachmeier. He's remembering Frieda's uncle, a tall, gangly man. Willi takes after the fellow. Peter shakes his head. He files the disappointment along with a string of others.

"Come along then, Siggi, your brother's birthday cake awaits."

With such reverence Frieda displays LuLu's creation. German chocolate of course, Willi's choice. "Happy birthday, especially for you, my deserving son," she says. "Sixteen! Can you believe?"

Just now Peter's deep-set eyes, caught by the low sun, sparkle like two hard-won aggies. Pride, newfound pride, enlivens his face. *Ah, the*

National Federation of Musical Clubs Award. Willi beat out twenty-eight competitors, took second place and $125. No small feat. He wonders how young Tryzyna would have fared—dismisses the thought.

Peter Stoya forces eye contact with Willi as he basks in his son's achievement. His son's playing elicited a judge's handwritten compliment. Peter has memorized that compliment on the Rating Card along with each high mark. All week he's rolled the achievement around in con- sciousness fascinated by its sweetness, its smoothness. An atypical smile bursts, shadowed by his waxed mustache. He stares at Willi as the teen helps himself to a second slice of chocolate cake. *If the heavens above grant me a favor-schmavor the young man is going to have a career,* he thinks. Willi licks buttery frosting from his fork; Professor Stoya relaxes like a pa- tient hearing good news for a change.

* * *

AS IF TWO men were in psychic communion a letter arrives the next week from Hindemith. The man rarely uses a salutation; instead he jumps right into the subject.

> *New Haven, 12 April 1951*
> *I've received an appointment to teach at Zurich University and to alternate on a yearly basis with Yale. Gertrud would bawl me out good and proper if I were to decline. We'll go to Glattfelden and begin in August.*
> *Meanwhile I'm working on the score for Balanchine's ballet Meta- morphoses, basing it on themes by Carl Maria von Weber. Forgive me, I must again complain about performances of my compositions. Musicians these days play everything in the Wagner-Strauss man- ner, which means of course what should be light, and elegant, and flowing, becomes heavy and ponderous despite an unholy number of rehearsals.*

In my spare time little springs of composition are flowing fast. In front of me Suite of Violin Sonatas which I've scored with symphonia as accompaniment. My students have proven its playability. If not immodest to say, this composer has pinned down on paper the sweetest kisses of Frau Musica. Unlike passé standards, this Suite enlivens, thrills, the audience. I've dedicated this pièce de resistance for a violin soloist's debut to your firstborn, Wilhelm Stoya. The score will arrive with my permission to have it performed when you see fit.

I look forward to silly parties with you all again. Gertrud sends her greetings to Frieda and Narcisse Louise.

As ever yours,

Paul

[26]

CIAZZO'S SQUARE JAW ripples as he surveys the faces in front of him. How these seven students perform at the publicized Recital tomorrow will reflect squarely on the four professionals who teach them. "Practice at home tonight as if your life depends upon it!" The teenagers leave solemnly, instruments in hand. Ciazzo holds Douglas back.

Yikes. Maybe my rehearsal wasn't up to par. Douglas panics.

Ciazzo's kind eyes pierce the boy's concern. He speaks. "Take the D'Espine home again, just for tonight, practice as you usually do. I suspect you and she will find an even deeper bond."

Douglas is all aquiver. If Michael were in town he'd head right over to *Lilacs* and share this windfall. He'd brag. Not only does he have a great loaner; he also gets to practice it at home one more time!

Westport to Elizabethtown usually requires fifteen minutes travel by truck; today it takes longer. Wing drives with special care, dodging winter's potholes. Douglas clutches the D'Espine like something fragile although it's sheltered in both its leather and canvas travel cases. He can hardly believe it. Bringing the D'Espine to the Home again! He hums through the three compositions he'll be playing, his head full of dreams.

Auntie Evangeline quietly observes the different violin he carries; it's housed in tan canvas in lieu of black cardboard. She greets Douglas explaining she's in town for Hotel Association business; by chance it coincides with the Recital weekend. For someone way off in Georgia, this opera teacher surely continues to be involved in his life. After picking at his dinner Douglas excuses himself for a practice session. He especially doesn't want to disappoint Auntie Evangeline. She follows him to the stairs. "Up you go." She beams. "You've earned this reward."

"A reward, and also a serious responsibility," he says soberly. If Sister Peace, his Tatiana, were here she would muffle his qualms with a hug; her scent of green—grass, pine needles, clover—energizing him. Pity, she isn't here to do so.

Once upstairs Douglas reviews the instructions from Ciazzo. He should always carry a length or two of stretched tested *firsts* (A-strings) in his pocket before he goes on stage because perspiration rags the strings. He shouldn't slacken the strings each time he puts the D'Espine away because this makes the violin nervous; it's accustomed to normal strain. He should keep it clean, removing dirt and rosin from under the strings. He's never to mess with the varnish; loss of varnish can age the violin. Ciazzo's last requirement rings in his ears. "Never, never, let the violin get damp." When Ciazzo had said this, words had flown out of Douglas' mouth. "Oh, I know that; the 253-1 tells me she is afraid of water." Douglas had glanced up, had caught his teacher's expression guarded in rectangles of shadow. If Ciazzo had found the comment curious he chose not to address it. Who knows what stories must be allowed to thrive in the imagination of a creative individual?

Wing lights incense, allowing airborne fragrance to welcome their guest. After sharing tea, the hosts settle into projects. Wearing his vest, Loong facing inward, Douglas follows his established ritual. It's become a habit, especially useful tonight with the impending event. Following the formula, he breathes deeply, a calming routine, then plays the selections he's memorized for the Recital. The couple attempts to stay occupied; what is different? It's impossible to ignore his music tonight. Astrid stares at Wing as if to say, *Listen, listen to this!* Wing tilts his head to one side, his pen poised, inactive.

"As usual I must finish with something I really like," Douglas says to his audience of two. "Apologies, I'm choosing Hungarian folk songs. As usual." Wing and Astrid offer inconsequential nods. As usual. The performer cradles the D'Espine and slides his new bow across her strings. Sir Johnson's nagging-debilitating rule flits into his consciousness. *Rule #3, We pass on passion. We use our heads.* "Forget that!" he whispers. Nothing is as usual now. Passion unfurls!

Douglas' newfound freedom permeates the D'Espine, transforming into melody, transforming into tonal percussion. Remembering songs once heard at the egg farm, he fiddles with wild abandon, much like the Basque who sparked his childhood fantasies. The factory violin's tone had always fallen flat, no matter how carefully he had tuned. Now, now with a superior instrument and new confidence Douglas commands radiant sound. The D'Espine isn't as prissy as he thought. She's expressing his longings, a common boy's longings.

{If you can excel with the royal D'Espine| imagine the results with your 253-1| The time of mastery is upon you| as it is meant to be| Meant to be| |

Streams of enchantment sift like flour through the wooden rafters and ceilings into the rooms below. A youngster's practice, routinely as annoying as common dust, instead glimmers like flecks of gold floating effortlessly, filling drab spaces.

Sister Elder smiles; her brow releases a decade of maternal worry. Listen. Each note a gift. A suspense. And the murmuration of notes that in their gathering acquire the majesty of an uncountable many.

"How is he doing this? When did he learn?" Sister Elder rises to her feet, unable to sit still, infused with joy. She twirls tentatively at first. Auntie Evangeline smiles at her sister. "Why Hester," she says, "I do believe you're enjoying the boy's music!" Auntie Evangeline leaps up. She advances like a fawn navigating a forest in spring. Academics of Parisian dance class forgotten, adrift in movement, across the parlor she jumps, almost nimble, almost airborne. The Smythe sisters are not to dance alone. In spirit, Sister Peace twirls down the hallway, her arms held out as if to embrace the air through which she spins. Her movements as light as a milkweed, as quiet as a dandelion puff, her white apron as if a propeller and she in preparation for liftoff.

Surrounded by the joyous sounds, Astrid sets down her mending. She walks to Wing, who listens, pen poised midair. She kneels and reaches to stroke his cheek. He gazes at her expectantly. A gaze leads to an embrace which leads to a kiss, one that doesn't cease even when Douglas notices their ardor.

A sense of liberation rushes through Douglas. And as he thrills, the Home's nightly discord is filled instead with a resplendent hum. The hum sets up a trembling that reverberates, that passes through each ceiling, each wall, each floorboard. Wood responds to wood, carrying music throughout the Home in waves of unfamiliar celebration. Even the smallest nail oscillates, emanating a metallic tremolo.

Perhaps the gargoyles on Sister Elder's embroidered tulle loosen their floss boundaries and soar. Who knows for sure what transpires throughout the Home? That morning Astrid finds disarray in the hallway closet; eight coats cluster with their sixteen sleeves entwined.

Douglas awakens at sunrise with optimism. Kneeling by his bed at sunrise, he prays like a neophyte. He prays that some almighty power might allow him to pull a bow across the strings of the instrument that he longs to own. The instrument that in reality owns him.

And then he summons 253-1. "I'm sure Ciazzo's violin was helping me last night. What is the D'Espine's gift?"

{Have you not guessed| The *violino* from Turin offers listeners and players release from personal confines| Freedom| |

[27]

CURIOSITY TAKES STOYA to Westport for the publicized *Seven Students in Recital*, offered by Ciazzo and the Quartet. He's remembering how Douglas choked at the Rating Event just last spring. "Here's the test-schmest. We'll see if another year with that conceited teacher has changed anything," Stoya whispers to Frieda. He opens the black leather, gilt-edged pocket notebook, flipping the red ribbon to a page where he pens with midnight blue ink, *1st May 1951—Douglas Tryzyna in Recital.*

Yes, the audience is waiting. Waiting while Douglas hesitates. Hesitates before beginning the cello duet. Waiting the few extra seconds for the teen to settle himself—nevertheless, Douglas Tryzyna calms.

Anyone would agree that Douglas has *almost* mastered Dvorak's *Slavonic Dance No. 2 in E Minor*, while everyone would agree he's *absolutely* mastered his stage fright. Stoya catches sight of Ciazzo, who affirms the duo's success, clapping as enthusiastically as the audience.

Stoya's mind whirls; he isn't paying attention as all the players take their turns in varying ensembles. Frieda elbow-jabs Peter. Young Tryzyna is taking the stage by himself now. A quick glance at the program informs him that Douglas' solo is to be the final performance with a Bela Bartók composition.

Douglas smiles at the audience, looking composed. The D'Espine placed into position, a few tuning strokes, a nod to the pianist who plays the introductory chords, and they're off! *Romanian Folk Dances Sz56*. The audience responds.

You, you there in the audience, you understand the steps these voices command. As the music continues, pianist's steady chords climbing against the voice of the violin, directing so many feet in motion, you too must dance. You step, you twirl, you frolic to wild fireside playing in a minor key.

Only Professor Peter Stoya resists the compelling draw. He listens. He misses nothing: the power in the crescendo; the nuanced melody; the ornamentation; the pizzicato. The discipline of every bowing exercise being brought to bear. Douglas plays with all the fortitude and energy demanded, while attending the delicacy in each refrain. The last impassioned section sends chills down the length of Professor Peter Stoya's legs.

There are some things that can't be taught. The young man on the stage has displayed them. He's being called for an encore! "'Sea Murmurs,'" he announces, "'Sea Murmurs' by Mario Castelnuovo-Tedesco." Haunting tones arise. Douglas' eyes are closed; it's as if he's lost in a private reverie. Just now the music threatens Peter's heart, the music coils and strikes, it poisons him with longing. The lovely phrasing, trills, repeated phrasing, harmonics; all elements in collusion quaver their way into him. Minutes beyond the violin's final ghost-like whisperings the instructor forgets to classify the sound as *sul ponticello*; instead he feels his heart a-wobble like a weary ice skater's ankle.

During the heated applause Stoya growls at Frieda in a *soto* voice. "What violin is the boy playing now?" As if the magic could lie only there. The Professor's jaw clenches with self-control. Even a father's self-control can dam the flood of tears for only so long. The strain must be released. *This boy has it. That something, that desire, that love. That longing.* Stoya flushes boiling hot as his pulse increases. Yes, the purity of Douglas' playing pierces the dam. The tiniest hole is enough; tears glisten in Stoya's blue-black eyes. Shoulders, chest all shuddery. Mrs. Piano Teacher takes his paw of a hand. She twists the wedding band back and forth, back and forth on his callused finger.

"This is *your* doing. *You* saved the mute bastard. *You* gave him the fundamentals," she says.

Peter fears fate has tipped away from his favor. Away from Willi's favor. *Is it too late?* Frieda leans close. He can smell the rose cream on her face, on her breath the schnapps they sipped after their hurried supper.

"Douglas belongs to *us* first," Frieda declares. Next in a feint of relinquished power, she poses a question. "He should return to your hands, yes? Oh, yours to say, dear. I'm just a piano teacher."

"What violin is the boy playing now?" Stoya growls, returning to his former self. "And where did he get it?"

Douglas, unaware, bows to the audience's continued applause.

[28]

DOUGLAS TROMPS THROUGH the Home's yard recalling last night's singularity. How was that magical performance even possible for him? This morning the sky is filled with hundreds, no, thousands of snow geese. As the birds break their vee they honk more vigorously and regroup to form a fat gray ribbon, a *plump*—one of Violette's favorite words. Geese somehow know where they are bound. Douglas stops on Little Bridge to watch the spectacle. Moments spent here converge, moments filled with

Violette's playfulness and Sister Peace's encouragement. He's gained ground on his way as a musician. Remember when playing was merely desire? *Even so. Am I getting closer to earning back the 253-1?*

The river below burbles amiably, though unable to answer a teenager's question with its babbling. The geese continue their passage and in moments the honking fades as the winged creatures become a narrow smear on the blue. Douglas makes his way through the meadow, through the slush, toward the sun-dappled backwoods. His contemplation is broken from time to time by bird call. Song sparrows making harsh chatter from trees. Red-winged blackbirds gurgling their *kon-ka-reee* from marshes. A phoebe singing out his *phee-bee, phee-bee,* sight unseen.

Douglas' memory rewinds to a recent conversation with Ciazzo. His teacher is asking, "Who is your favorite composer?" Although Douglas has been memorizing birth and death dates for many composers, hoping to win his aggies back from Michael, he's never thought to choose a favorite. He answers his teacher hesitantly. "I can't say."

"No worries, you'll learn over time by playing their compositions." Ciazzo closes his eyes. He, like an artist refining his approach. Then brightening, "You can't perform all these fellas' music in the same way. You see, each composer has a different nature. It shows up in his music. For example, Bach's genius is counterpoint. He thinks of music in terms of an organ. We play Bach's music respectfully, as sacred."

Douglas nods, trying to grasp the meaning.

"Mozart was gay, tender, always in love. Feel your own love. Be playful with Mozart's music."

Douglas nods again.

"Beethoven had the wonderment of the universe in his breast. Play grandly with awe. You understand?"

"Like looking at the northern lights?" Douglas asks excitedly as he catches on.

Ciazzo smiles and continues. "Mendelssohn was a Romantic influenced by the others, although you'll find his work uniquely complex. They say one hears in his music 'nonsense and gunpowder.'"

"Funny-business and profundity?" He's using one of Violette's favorite words, *profundity*. He looks for Ciazzo's agreement.

"Yes. Yes. You get it. Now critics can and do argue over composers' contributions. I say, all these fellows have one thing in common. Their greatness. *¿Comprende?*"

The student's answer comes out in a rush. "I like gypsy-ish music most of all. Does anybody compose that?"

Ciazzo, pleased with the outcome of his lesson, rolls up his sleeves, seats himself at the piano. "I have just the piece for you, by Ravel. Our Quartet regularly performs his music. Listen." The vibe conjured by the man's voice and the piano's sensuous percussion partners Douglas in a whirl of desire. The Spaniard tackles the melody with as much gusto as the nice man at the Ibarra farm ever displayed. And then Ciazzo ceases his playing. From mid-phrase to silence. In silence he spins around on the stool, rolls down his sleeves, and fastens his cufflinks. "Catch the composer's intent and yet, and yet, interpret with your soul—now that is mastery. When you have matured you will play this gypsy-ish music and *astound* yourself. I promise."

As Douglas rejoins the morning, registering once again the bird call and chatter, he experiences a gush of cognizance. *Gratitude*, he labels it, one of Violette's favorite words. *Ciazzo understands me.*

[29]

NOT THAT HE'S fond of the Tryzyna kid, no. Stoya simply admires how such a nobody commands presence on the stage. Like a singular shaft of light in a dim forest. *Playing an 1832 D'Espine—can you imagine?*

"There you saw my early training, Frieda," Peter Stoya says on the drive home from Westport.

Frieda responds. *"Our* early work, yours and mine. Both of us laid down the basics, dear one."

Not that the kid is superior to Willi. No. Willi has impressed every time he's played for dinner guests. Willi's public appearances have brought praise. Don't forget the Academy's recent recognition. Fellow musicians have clapped Peter on the back: "He's got a future," they say. "He's on his way!"

Compliments dull the recipient; wake up, face the facts, sir. A father must address the weak underbelly. Yes, he thrills with his son's command, the teen's attack especially with Brahms Sonatas. And yet Willi's genius is tainted by his inconsistency.

Stoya concludes. Two prescriptions. One: He'll assign more Brahms for Willi and stay on the lad's back. Hard work, the ceaseless pursuit of mastery, after all, is the rule of my life and the Stoya Conservatory. Two: He'll attract a new rival for Willi into their midst. A.J. will have left for Juilliard, Stoya Conservatory's latest validation. Not that A.J. brought out anything other than the devil in Willi.

Oh, planning-schlanning! Professor Stoya grits his teeth. Face the truth, sir. Time is running out. And only one prescription will serve the ill. So. How to get the one sure rival away from that smug Ciazzo?

Two nights after the Westport Recital, Stoya plays the 253-1 for Frieda in the comfort of their bedroom. She lounges on several pillows, looking languid in her lilac silk nightie, icepack on her forehead. As he renders his musical dues her headache recedes.

Peter puts the fiddle aside. Unsnaps his garters, rolls his argyle socks off the ends of his long toes. Boldness loosens his tongue; private schemes are spoken. "I'm getting Douglas back!"

Frieda, immediately upright. "He'll never leave Ciazzo!"

[30]

JUNE BRINGS THE teenagers of Elizabethtown dreams of summer. Of gathering berries in a bucket. Of mouths stained with sweet red juice. Of wading at the river's edge where the current is slow. Of shadows promising cool respite from sunshine. Of jade-green water inviting a swim.

For Douglas and Violette, the chain of events this day begins with shrugging off the *No Trespassing* sign. There, a cabin boarded up! A spirit of adventure demands they pry off the weathered boards that crisscross the door. The rusty nails release their tired grip with a few squeaks. Pushing the door open, a tad apprehensive, the couple peeks inside. "An abandoned summer cottage," Violette says. She flounces on the cot. Dust flies every which-a-way, motes glinting in a slant of sunlight. She sneezes repeatedly, dabbing at her watering eyes.

Douglas retrieves a life buoy from a tangle of ropes. "I'll bring this along to save you, Miss Violette!"

"Save me from what? I can swim, you, you, dodo bird!" Violette runs outdoors and, finding a dilapidated dock, makes her way to its end. Tied alongside floats a small rowboat with oars in the locks. "Look! Let's pretend it's ours! Just for a little while." Of course, they'll return the boat in just a little while, they agree. They have no intention of stealing.

Late June, mornings are crisp, afternoons are hot. Today the noon sun is beating down, predicting July intentions. As Douglas rows upstream they outdistance long-legged water skippers. Dragonflies alight on

Violette's outstretched hand; she admires their wings, their jewel-like eyes. "Iridescent," she says.

With a giggle, enjoying the poetic quality that is Violette, his Violette, Douglas repeats, "Iridescent." Somehow four bumpity syllables from two lips, plus four bumpity syllables from another's lips, equals eight bumpity kisses; it must be teenage mathematics.

Silvery fish glimmer alongside and disappear under ripples. Douglas begins to sweat. He peels off a layer of clothing. Violette removes her blouse; under it she's wearing a white bathing suit top. She kicks off her pedal pushers. Carefully she rolls the clothes into her bag. Douglas gawks. Violette reclines, looking like a lady in a famous painting—minus a parasol and clothing. If he squints, he can imagine she is one sweep of ivory flesh, with no bathing suit at all. The idea sends his heart lurching.

Before long, it grows hot sitting in the boat. "Let's pull over right there and swim!" she says. That's when Douglas learns a great deal more about female anatomy, after a swim, as they climb back into the canoe. The slip-sliding fabric on Violette's body gives him a glimpse of pure ivory flesh. Inner thighs. And one breast with a nipple not so unlike his own except larger than the almost-sixteen-year-old-boy variety. As Violette relaxes to sun herself, Douglas studies the swell of her abdomen, finding it not unlike the gentle curve of a violin's belly. Her waist shares the inward curve of a violin's ribs. Her wet skin glistens like the varnish coating a violin's wooden body. Had a man been imagining a girl's body when he first fashioned a violin?

Douglas latches onto a thought. Not all female bodies are exactly the same, just as all violins seem not to be. His 253-1 brags a deeper-longer waist than Stoya's forbidden Performance Violin. The 253-1's flamboyant carved scroll lacks the craftsmanship of the Professor's. Douglas favors the imperfect form of the 253-1's scroll, comparing it to the wind-battered rose he once picked for Sister Peace. Favors the delicate contours of the girl in a white two-piece swimsuit whom he adores.

When Douglas once again rows against the current he's newly proud of his strength. Especially possessive of Violette. She may accompany someone else's violin playing in a gray stone conservatory; she may kiss someone else at a party; so what? She reveals more of herself to him, right now, than she could ever have revealed to someone else. Someone like Willi Stoya. The soft look in her eyes. Her rosy lips parted, as inviting as the berries that have stained them. Her wet, bare feet, touching his bare feet, this alone a new intimacy that causes his heart to stir. The insistent thrum from her, like the thrum of a hummingbird he once rescued. No, this isn't like the fear he sensed in the tiny bird. He feels a rhythmic, continuous pleading. His entire body reacts to her unspoken desire.

"Look!" A flock of wild canaries flits across the river. Violette chants. "In the name of yellow, lemon yellow, in the name of all that's fine and quickly lost!"

"What?"

"You know, when you spy something yellow, you make a secret wish, like on birthday candles." What Violette wishes for: a tulle veil, the wedding march. Better yet, basking in this adoration on Douglas' face. Forever and forever.

What Douglas wishes for: to be feeling Violette's intensity as if she were music.

The trees watch on with a slight rustle, a most polite audience, although reserved. Boulders remain visibly unaffected while they stare attentively. The river takes heed of the couple's humming. And breathing. And sighing. And dreaming.

Much later Violette and Douglas return the borrowed boat to the dock, a splintery protrusion eroded by the river over time. "Let's pretend it's our cottage," Violette says. "We have berries left to eat." She takes him by the hand, gives it a little tug. A sense of abandon overtakes the pair; after all, today they're breaking rules without consequence.

[31]

VIOLETTE MUST BE avoiding him. Last Saturday, after the Stoya group lesson, she wouldn't ride home with him even though he'd waited for her. He should go to the Smythe Hotel and ask why. Yet he's drawn to the Rabin kids; to *Lilacs* he goes after his chores and violin practice. Or is it avoidance he's practicing? Pain in abeyance, pain to be dreaded until one musters the strength to bear it.

Douglas pedals up Fiddler Hill. He sees nobody on the grounds, instead the sound of stringed instruments in conversation floats from the main building. "There's a quartet playing." He stops to listen, sits on the stone bench, and imagines himself inside playing alongside Michael. Michael on his del Gesù, he on his 253-1. As the music ends and the applause begins, he feels like an intruder.

Impulsive desire overtakes. Coasting down the hill, pedaling hard through the neighborhoods of houses with green trim and stone fireplaces, swooping along River Street, heading to the Smythe Hotel. She's outside in the gardens, pushing a stroller. She hardly notices him. Won't look up as he approaches. Douglas sets the kickstand on his bicycle. *What could be wrong?* He gathers his courage and walks toward her. "Hey, Vi," he says. Somehow the greeting sounds like a question. She faces him. Surely Rocky Marciano would cower at her glare.

"Will you please watch Geordie for a minute? He won't bite."

Douglas' agreement is an automatic "Sure." He's silently wondering, *What's up?* He kneels and offers baby talk to drooling Geordie, which makes him feel very old.

Violette flounces off, down the curved walkway around the bushy hedges and beyond. Into the Hotel. Upon return she exudes a piercing chill. There can be no conversation with this iceberg. She thrusts out her closed hand. "Here. For you. Take it back." The tone of her voice, glacial. The inaudible, a shuddering growl. The love he once felt from her, crumbling in slow motion.

She presses a light object into his hand. Tape along the back keeps the ends of gold-embossed paper joined. It's a bit crumpled and looks too small for a divine piano player's finger. It's a cigar band.

Douglas gulps. The return of the object is significant. "What have I done? What's wrong?"

"What's *wrong*?" she asks, mimicking his plaintive tone.

Douglas Tryzyna feels her dark energy. Her sadness stabs, rakes, entangles him like barbed wire. He reaches for his Violette as if touch could impart his concern.

Violette dodges his attempt while holding her gaze. She says nothing; all the while those familiar, unmatched eyes excavate the anguish from her soul and force it on him. Then she turns her attention to Geordie. That's it. His dismissal.

The waxed Monarch Deluxe carries him away, albeit unwillingly. He's helpless, small, wounded. Some things are impossible: to snuff out the sun, to command a full moon, to freeze the descent of a waterfall. Equally impossible, it seems to understand Violette's pain and soften her unyielding heart.

Why do I invite misfortune? Professor Stoya steals my violin and breaks a promise. Sister Peace deserts me without explanation. Violette turns away.

Interrupting Douglas' lament, Willi biking toward him, calling him that degrading nickname, setting the hook. "Gotta hurry, got a hot date, yeah Doogie, Violette's waiting for me."

[32]

DOUGLAS OPENS THE Muriel cigar box. He studies the signed black and white photo of someone else who didn't love him enough. Places into the box a small, seemingly insignificant something, a gilt cigar band. Generously given to him one afternoon by Mr. Ludlow when he was six—when he was infatuated with the image of an exotic lady on this box's lid; adoringly gifted to Violette one afternoon when he was thirteen and infatuated with a flesh and blood girl; mournfully returned to the box this afternoon and he, almost sixteen and heartbroken. Oh, it's ordinary, this ring, coated with fool's gold. And he's the fool.

Sister Elder has the real thing. A narrow ring with a deep-set red jewel. A ruby ring. "A gift from a dear friend in Panicale, Umbria. I was a foolish young thing back when I was prone to mistakes in judgment," she'd said. Sister Peace wore three silver filigree rings, three fingers adorned. Auntie Evangeline wears a wide gold band with an upright emerald held captive by prongs. "Ladies love glorious rings," Auntie Evangeline had said.

Maybe it's obvious. It's time to offer Violette a beautiful ring. To prove his intentions. *Violette knows the difference now,* he tells himself, trying to believe the rationalization he attempts.

[33]

HEY, NO FAIR! Willi at Lilacs?

There they sit. Willi and Michael carrying on like pals over a stamp collection. As Douglas sets the kickstand on his bike Bertine scurries to his side. She tilts her head toward the blond intruder. "Mr. Braggy Pants, over there, dropped in for a visit. *Boy, are we lucky!*"

She's wearing striped-orange shorts (all the better to expose her shapely legs), a pink polka dot bandeau top (all the better to expose her bare midriff), and sandals (all the better to expose her polished toenails). All that exposure might well have intrigued Douglas once upon a time, except today, right now, the only girl he finds attractive is Violette. Somehow, he's lost his Violette, his Violette with her copper-bronze hair and her mismatched hazel-blue eyes that sometimes darken to match his exactly. "Hi, Bert," Douglas says softly. He sizes up the boys, who still ignore him. His very next thought: *Now I'm losing my Michael Rabin too. Losing both my Violette and my Michael to Willi.*

Bertine interrupts his distress and the philatelists' concentration. "Let's play something all of us together, while Jeanne's gone!"

A round of ping-pong on *Lilacs'* screened-in porch separates winners from losers. Bertine and Douglas watch on, quickly outclassed. The other two keep going at it for the championship. Willi wipes sweat from his fuzzy upper lip with a hankie. He's taken Michael five games in a row. The last game progresses. Stroke after stroke Willi whacks the ball, sending it across the sagging net with fury. Michael runs from side to side, keeping up with the volley until he loses the last point. Willi cheers for himself. "I'm the champ, the champ, the champ." Douglas and Michael both ignore him.

Bertine scoffs. "Like Jeanne always says to you, Michael, 'Next time you'll do better.'"

"Hey, c'mon over to my house," Willi says magnanimously. "We have soda pop in the fridge. Orange Nehi. And grape—I remember your favorite, Doogie."

"We better stay here. Because we're supposed to be practicing and Michael has very important performances to get ready for and he already spent hours at Meadowmount, and Jeanne will lay into him if we're gone when she gets back, that's the rules to stay here and practice when she's doing, who knows? driving around town, buying groceries for company dinner and stuff, besides Dad gets back tonight."

"You can stay here like a good little girl if you want, Bert. I'm going—you too, Douglas!"

How strange it feels to be back at the Stoyas' stone house with no adults in charge. LuLu doesn't count as an adult; she handles interruptions without irritation. This afternoon she doesn't pull a stern face at Douglas or mention that Willi rarely invites friends over. She whistles bits of this melody or that while she offers soda pop to the youngsters on the back porch, which, with its northern exposure, stays cool, although it invites spiders and moss into the corners.

After a while it becomes apparent that Michael is unaccustomed to teenage small talk. He fidgets in the oversized wood chair with his box camera hanging around his neck. Seems to appraise the backyard. Sips his soda. A question breaks the silence. "Did you know that Sarasate didn't practice his violin during the summer? And Davidoff, who directed the Petrograd Conservatory in the late 1800s, simply shut his Strad in its case during summer months?"

"You're forgetting that Joachim practiced in the compartment of his train when he was on tour," Bertine says in a contradictory tone, "and I'll betcha that was even in the hot, sticky summer. See, Mike has to practice eight hours a day, even in summer—that's cuz he never gets time off.

Spring he toured in Cuba to play with the Havana Philharmonic, maybe you heard him last summer on the *Bell Telephone Hour*, and he had a grand recital at Carnegie Hall, also he played at the Roxy, Mr. Judson arranged it all, fifty-six performances in two weeks!"

Willi's eyes open wide in amazement. "Fifty-six! No way!"

Douglas knows most of this from previous conversations. Michael sent him a postcard from Cuba. He nods, a bit smug, obviously luckier than his phony blood brother, and ongoing prankster.

"Tell them about next summer, Michael," Bertine prompts.

"I've got July, August, September, and October in Australia, three concerts a week for sixteen weeks. Yup, me and the kangaroos!"

Douglas feels his heart lurch, almost drops his bottle of grape Nehi. He isn't going to see Michael next summer?

"And before that he's touring more than a dozen cities!"

Michael looks at his watch. "Gotta go, Bert. Here, take a picture of me with the guys." Bertine takes Michael's camera, pushes the boys together, and snaps a photo. Leaving the porch Michael is waylaid by the sight of a Victrola and shelves of recordings in the library. Without hesitation he's flipping through the collection. "Fritz Kreisler, Jascha Heifetz, Isaac Stern, Mischa Elman, Yehudi Menuhin. Nice collection! Most of all I'm a Heifetz fan. He autographed a score for me, my Bach Sonatas and Partitas. Who's your favorite violinist, Willi?"

Willi shrugs. He turns away.

Following Willi out of the library Michael spies the salon, the Bosendorfer grand piano, the music stand. Two open violin cases arrest his departure. He admires the Red Performance Violin lying there in polished elegance. He clasps it to his chest, tucks it under his chin, picks up the bow, and plays an arpeggio. "I'll try a little Mendelssohn," he says. "Played this on the *Bell Telephone Hour*." His full eyebrows arch over closed eyes as he listens to the sounds he's producing. The rosy lips, curly hair, and round cheeks make him appear younger than fifteen.

A phrase completed, he shares his observation. "Wow, she really sings. She responds to the gentlest bowing." Holding the instrument at arm's length he takes stock. He examines all her parts: the front, the ebony fingerboard, the ribs, the carved scroll, and finally the back. "What is she, do you know?! Is she yours, Willi?"

Willi hunches his shoulders. "I play her sometimes."

Michael casually returns Stoya's *untouchable* violin and bow to its case. Here's a boy who's played many great instruments in his short career; it's natural that he's appreciative, and hardly daunted by something Fine and Rare.

The 253-1 swaddled in her silk attracts Michael next. "Oh, this is the one that used to be yours—right, Douglas?" Douglas can't muster a word or a nod. His mouth drops open. First Michael played the forbidden violin? And now he's going for the 253-1? Michael is breaking the hard-and-fast rules of the Stoya Conservatory.

Michael plays the Mendelssohn again. The 253-1 responds as he draws out a sensuous, burnished timbre, as he ends with whistling harmonics. Douglas wilts. The prodigy smiles. "I think she likes a strong bow across her strings. Now listen to this!" Vibrant music fills the salon. "Wow. She's made for passionate composers' stuff. Like Paganini or Liszt!" Michael is flushed with pure enjoyment.

"Golly, gosh, gee whillikers, two really super violins in the same house!" Bertine says, seeming as excited as her brother.

Douglas watches as the bold teenager gives the 253-1 a thorough examination. *Once she was mine alone, mine alone,* Douglas rails inwardly, remembering how he owned the violin so briefly after the fire. How she still begs to be with him.

Willi gives Douglas a conspiratorial smirk. "Oh boy, is this guy in big trouble with Pa, just wait!"

"What makers, do you know?" Michael asks, looking perplexed. "And did you realize these two violins have the exact, the very exact same wood on their backs?! Look here." He turns the violins over and positions them in their cases with backs facing up. "The same grain! Their two-piece backs are obviously cut from the same tone wood, matching tiger stripe maple! Even the red varnish is the same. Well, just a shade different. Jeepers, how is that possible? They sure look like different makers otherwise. See the scrolls, the F-holes? Play like different makers, too." Michael asks Bertine for his camera. He snaps a picture of each. "Willi, do you have a little flashlight?"

Mrs. Piano Teacher is heard dismissing a student. Within seconds she appears in the salon. "Why, Michael Rabin. And...you..."

"I'm Bertine, Mike's sister. We rent *Lilacs* 'round the corner and come here every summer for Meadowmount. Galamian is one of Mike's dear friends, and—"

Frida cuts short Bertine's explanation. "Yes, yes, of course, how nice to see you again."

"Mrs. Stoya, do you know the makers of these violins? I'm so curious." Michael again takes the 253-1, positions her under his chin, and plays something bold. The music swirls into every corner of the house, seeking more space through which to travel. "That's by Lalo," he says.

Mrs. Piano Teacher remains stupefied by the audacity of both the music and the musician. She twists her hands together, her mouth contorting, an attempt to make a command. Then in a squeaky voice, "The boys are not to handle the violins without the Professor's permission. I know you're professional, quite capable, just the rule. Now it was lovely, really amazing to hear you performing. It's just that the Professor has his stipulations. Come over again when he's here, and play for him. Willi would love to play a duet, wouldn't you, Willi?" The question about violin makers goes unanswered.

Bertine heads for the door. Michael looks at his watch again. He frowns, glances back at the violins. "Just wish I knew," he whispers to Douglas. "I'll show the photo to Rembert. He'll have an answer, I bet."

The violins back in their cases, Mrs. Piano Teacher, having corrected the violation, asks Michael questions about his practicing and his mother.

Douglas shrinks to his tiniest turtle-like self, Mrs. Piano Teacher hasn't acknowledged him, yet. Dangerous being here while rules are being broken. He feels Michael's conflict, wanting to leave, trying to be polite. The phone rings, distracting Frieda. Three teenagers escape, each one with questions to ponder.

Douglas puzzles over Michael's discovery. *The 253-1 has called the Performance Violin her Red Sister, so are they almost twin sisters?* He'd never seen their backs exposed for comparison; now after Michael's observation every resemblance becomes an uncanny phenomenon.

That evening Wing inks a dragon camouflaged in an apple tree. He uses a crow quill pen to create the appearance of scales on the creature's back. Although he uses black ink to fill in everything, the apple is most certainly red to Douglas' eyes.

"How can we see what is not there, and yet not see what is there?" Douglas asks without referring to his observation.

Wing speaks up. "That's a humdinger of a question. What's up with you?" Not expecting a quick answer, he dips his brush in inky water, after which he creates a gray wash over white space.

Douglas wails. "Michael got to play my violin today. And *I* have never-never-ever been allowed."

"Don't be so po-faced, Antenna Boy," Astrid says. Her words encircle him with kindness.

Wing adds his thought. "Wisdom say, *Patience is bitter, but patience bears sweet fruit.*"

[34]

WHILE THREE RESIDENTS of the Home find comfort in each other's company, Frieda asks for comfort from Stoya's violin playing. She lies on her back with a wet cloth over her eyes. Her headache returned after the Rabin kids left. For some years a stark comparison had dozed at a safe distance—the naked comparison of this prodigy to her Willi. Today the wunderkind had been in her salon looking like a child while pulling off music like a maestro.

Frieda doesn't tell Peter how distraught she feels. She listens as he plays several of their favorite Kreisler compositions. *"Liebesfreud"* ("Love's Joy"), *"Liebesleid"* ("Love's Sorrow"), and *"Schön Rosmarin"* ("Lovely Rosemary"). The last sweet tone fades; Frieda adjusts the pillow.

Stoya gives her his attention. It never occurs to him how odd he must look, seated on the bed cradling a violin—wearing only garter-held socks, undershirt, and boxer shorts. "Headache better my love?" he asks.

"Yes, a bit, my love. You know how hearing that fiddle helps."

Silence strings out like an empty clothesline.

[35]

STOYA REALIZES ONE violin *looks* the same as another to Frieda, poor dear, never mind the rogue fiddle and the Performance Violin do bear an uncanny resemblance. She's off in a dream world of Haydn, or in the doldrums of a headache, when it comes to discerning the specifics of a violin. Belief that the rogue thing's voice soothes her headaches is the extent of her discernment. Strange, her disregard for this in contrast to her hawk-eyed attention to the cleanliness of ivory keys and correct fingering thereupon by students. Ah, he realizes with a start, she too has been trained to respect the boundaries he's set: *The violins are mine alone. Do not dare touch!* The dictum inspired fear in the boys, in LuLu, and of course, he realizes, in Frieda. Up until now he's acted as if the object safely swaddled in green silk would remain safe only in his hands, pressed against his chin and his chest. The members of his household never dare so much as breathe upon the masterpiece, now over two centuries of age. A fossil that in one sense breathed, had breathed long before his first cry, and would continue to do so long after his last.

However, the time has come for Willi to start performing on a great violin. Peter had purchased the full-sized Wilhelm Hermann Hammig after ousting Douglas because his son's enthusiasm needed a jolt. The violin's price was right; the maker's name—Wilhelm—plus the Berlin origin, altogether bore a good omen. Sure, the Hammig is still suitable for Willi. It's suitable but lacking in comparison. *For heaven's sakes, Michael Rabin is loaned the finest. We all know Willi will never be in his class. Regardless, one must try to keep up.*

Swiss-German immigrant Peter Stoya will be flirting with a dangerous outcome if Willi uses the Performance Violin in public. Let's suppose Willi were to play as remarkably as his father dreams; well then, reporters might inquire about the violin; newspapers might feature photos. Young Michael Rabin, not five minutes in the salon, had come close to identifying the Performance Violin correctly. After nervous deliberation, Peter Stoya scurries to take an action.

[36]

PETER VISITS NYC many a Friday where he performs with his trio at a small club. He returns early Saturday morning having enjoyed time alone in the City and supper at a Trattoria with fellow musicians. Campari and pasta loosen musicians' tongues; Stoya knows better. He utters not a word of his past friendships in Berlin. Nor his chosen luthier. Nor the make of his instrument.

One August Friday the trio isn't booked. *Propitious,* Stoya thinks. *I'll be able to go to the City as usual and handle some business on the QT with Monsieur Roux.* He can spend an extra day if needed. A trip to Berentzen for brandy and an exotic orchid plant will soften Frieda's complaints about his time away.

* * *

WHEN FLORIEN ROUX looks through the F-hole, he exclaims, "What have we here? *Alors,* a Strad! *Monsieur* Stoya, if I were to believe labels, then every other fiddle I examine would be a Strad."

"Aside from that, what do you make of this one? I purchased it from a street woman in Leipzig who was eager to part with it for a few Reichsmark. That was late '40." Stoya thrums his pant leg.

"*Monsieur,* I venture to say this violin falls into the category of *ambigu.* Might be an authentic Strad, might not. More than I can say for most. The tiger stripe of the maple, the slant of the sound holes, convincing. No doubt about the *inspiration* for this violin. If not the *authenticity.* Look here. The beauty of the scroll. The precision of the perfling. And the varnish, almost the same orange-red we see in a few authentic Strads."

"Hmmm." Stoya blinks rapidly while holding a fixed smile beneath his waxed mustache.

Florien continues. "Some very well-known Cremona violins went missing during the Holocaust. Nazis knew what they were looking for."

"Thieves!" Stoya says, all indignant.

"You were saying you purchased it from a *gueuse* in Leipzig? Waltzed away with it for a song?" Florien smirks, fluttering his arms like a *Swan Lake* cygnet. "Such *bonne fortune.*"

Peter crosses his arms, as if to protect himself from the man's rude insinuation.

"You are selling her, *Monsieur?*" Florien asks as he caresses the Performance Violin's striped belly.

"No, no. I have a slight problem, you see. My fear..." He begins. Halts mid-sentence.

"*Alors*, your fear is what, *Monsieur?*"

"My son is to begin performing in public. This violin will be stunning in his hands; my fear, well, the instrument may come under scrutiny. Should I alter the label so as not to arouse undo *attention*, or shall we say *lust*? This look-alike Strad bearing a Strad label, false or no, may attract sticky fingers."

"You have reason to fear, *Monsieur*. Throughout history violins have gone missing from carriages, trains, dressing rooms, whilst owners nap, flirt, or dine.

"Listen to this. Recently a performer brought an old violin for me to examine. The problem, you see, *it wasn't his violin!* No, instead he'd been given a sneaky replacement. Whilst on tour he'd taken his valuable violin to a shop for a small repair. Had a soiree that very evening. Needed a new bridge quickly. Into the workroom it went. Out it came with a new bridge, modest fee charged. *Imbécile* didn't realize the problem until warming up for his performance. The luthier had cleverly swapped his instrument for a look-alike, an inferior one. By then it was after hours, of course. Chowderhead returned the next morning to find the shop was a *façade*. Nobody there. He'd been hoodwinked. Poor sucker. Brought the fiddle to me just to confirm how badly he'd been duped."

"*Imbécile*, indeed!" Peter is gathering his courage. "Could we convincingly re-label my questionable Strad? Label it Vuillame? You are familiar with the Vuillame label?"

"*Oui, oui,* I know the label well. Are you so forgetful? You yourself brought me an authentic Vuillame some years ago."

Stoya stammers. "Are you able to accomplish a faithful rendition?"

"Accomplish? *Oui,* of course. If you insist. We fellows keep a collection of authentic labels for...for cornichons such as these. How do you say it? Cucumber in the vinegar?"

"They use the word *pickle* here."

"*Oui,* just so. One *could* reasonably compare this supposed Strad to a bona fide copy by Vuillame. In doing so we'd shift its origin, making it 1800s instead of 1700s. Not that a thief would ignore a Vuillame. Strange, you ask me to commit a, shall we say, a forgery, in reverse of the norm. Strange pickle." Florien sniggers.

Stoya raps his fingers on his trouser leg. He's flustered; perhaps he should not have trusted this man.

"Forgery abounds, my dear man. Oh, forgery isn't limited to false labels and abrasion. A respected violin shop in England kept a drawer full of dust-fluff saved from old violins brought in for repair. The greedy luthier stuffed this grime through the F-holes of violins for sale, obscuring the labels and adding age. The idea was to trick a buyer into thinking the violin was ancient, and therefore authentic."

The tale buys Stoya a few moments to think. He studies the luthier's face. He knows Florien Roux isn't prone to smiling—somehow his tight-lipped expression right now is especially unsettling. Peter gathers his wits. "About your fee, Florien?"

"This is a serious game we play. Nevertheless, I'm known for my discretion and loyalty, if I may say." Florien uncaps his fountain pen, withdraws a sheet of cream-colored paper, writes using distinctive cursive and stylized numbers. He pushes the estimate across his desk to Stoya. "*Monsieur,* what do you say?"

Stoya gulps; his knees fail for a second. He grips the table's edge. This Florien presents an odd mixture of friend and foe, there in his white leather skull cap, tall as a giant, his eyes narrowed in anticipation. Peter straightens up, takes the estimate, folds it carefully. Tucks it into the inner pocket of his tan linen jacket. Feels an urgency to leave.

"I'll be at the Automat. Need to think over a sandwich," he says.

Stoya chooses a ham on rye and black coffee. "An economical lunch," he says aloud as if to convince someone. Stoya stirs several packets of sugar into his coffee. 'Round and 'round he stirs. *You have no choice. Pay Florien's price. Just pray you can trust the robber.*

Robber. That distressing word. Florien's mention of Nazis keeps his mind racing. Must he, Peter Stoya, wear that stigma like a forearm tattoo? His alternating thoughts duel. *En garde. Allez!* Accusations attacking. *You made off with another man's violin—you are a thief.* Parry-repost, parry-repost, Peter defending. *Times were different then. You had to be there to understand.* The fencing director calling a halt. *Arret!*

A deep breath, lungs expanding, a man reconciling. Virtue has won the match. What of the repercussions? Have the Mendelssohns who entrusted me with their violin opened the bank vault? Of course, they must have. Surely, they believe the Nazis stole their Cremona violins—along with so many other valuables. If they reported the losses? All in vain. Do I feel guilty? Forever, no. What I did made sense then. I saved the treasure for the world. One final accusation lunges, breaking the rules of a duel: Even so, the world will call you a thief.

[37]

253-1 COMMUNICATES WITH Douglas, compassion quavering in her transmission. {The Performance Violin| my Red Sister| has been cheated of her heritage| *Questo violino* laments| Why did Professor Stoya sully her authenticity| Alas| a false label avows her birth was 1850| More than one hundred years beyond her true maker's final sleep| She who has not learned men's words| She who *offers* any player and his bow| all possibility from her store of perfect abilities| Though men do not wish to believe it| the Performance Violin| gives honest reflection of each player's skill and soul| and not one whit more| |

V
OBSESSION & CONTRIVANCE

[1]

CIAZZO'S EYES REGISTER shock. He's logical, he's kind. He's angry. "*Parodia*! Stoya wants you back? What perversion can this be?"

Douglas, mustering courage, keeps his eyes low. "He promises he'll let me play on the Basque man's violin, the one that he took away from me, and he says he might give it back. I don't know what to do. What should I do?"

"What are you telling me, *mijo*? This man who discarded you for so small a reason now bargains for your return? Dares ask you to leave your Ciazzo?"

Douglas fights tears. Negative thoughts rush pell-mell; each scorches like Siggi's wood-burning tool. Not that he can imagine leaving Ciazzo. Not that he thrives under Stoya's churlish teaching. Not that he wants to study or practice alongside Willi, his tormentor, although Willi's as much a sibling as Mildred, John, or James. Not that proximity to Violette will change her heart—even if Stoya will allow her to be his accompanist. She's paired with Willi—doesn't look like that will change with the *'til death do us part* kind of thing going on. Not that Stoya will even keep his promise this time.

Not that he wants to leave Ciazzo.

Reality slashes. Leave Ciazzo? To leave his reliable teacher and the amiable D'Espine for Stoya is to face the terrible-horrible-unpredictable.

"The D'Espine you are playing suits you. And it is surely just the first of many, many fine violins you will experience. I don't advise this brash decision."

He doesn't dare tell Ciazzo that the *violino* begs him, instructs him, directs him to their future together. Adults have negative responses. Douglas stutters and manages to reply, "See, it's her gypsy-ish kind of voice that I must hear when I play...if I'm going to be happy."

Ciazzo fingers an arpeggio the length of the piano, eyes closed. Momentarily he brightens, his eyes newly lit with possibility. "Okay. Let's stop talking. Play me something. Anything. Something you love." The man rolls up his shirtsleeves, lights a cigarillo, sits on the windowsill. Outside cumulous clouds rise, promising a thunderstorm.

Douglas begins *Tzigane*, tears streaming. The D'Espine sings with rich, velvety color as he skillfully tackles the romping, disjointed melody. Then he begins the slow accelerando to the very end of the piece; it goes faster and faster, as he keeps the sixteenth notes pretty much constant. He continues into the finale, the violin slowly rising chromatically through its running line. He's missing the piano's part especially now as he plays faster and faster...until finally he crashes off final pizzicato chords.

Douglas, violin and bow in hand, walks to Ciazzo and gently leans against his shoulder, a touch like a question that needs not be asked. Simultaneously, teacher and student brush an irritant from their eyes.

Ciazzo takes a deep breath before he speaks. "*Tzigane.* The right choice for you, of course—we discovered that in our time together. ¿Sí? Now let me tell you a little anecdote about this piece. Let's see, it's 1922, at a private music concert in London. Ravel was listening to his own Sonata for Violin and Cello being played by the Hungarian violinist Jelly d'Aranyi. Later in the evening Ravel asked Jelly to play some gypsy melodies. She began with great gusto. Ravel kept asking for more melodies. They continued until almost five o'clock the next morning! And this session sparked the inspiration for what you've just played, Ravel's *Tzigane*. Gypsy music—it's powerful, mesmerizing."

Douglas wants Ciazzo to keep talking, to keep saying without saying the approval he wants to hear. Ciazzo takes another tack. "Most of my students aim for Juilliard or Curtis schooling, with Tanglewood or Meadowmount summers. These dream of a solo career, a concert master's position with an orchestra, or performing in a small ensemble. A few want to teach. The quartet work you are doing prepares you for this. You haven't told me about yourself in this regard; I'd say the time has come. Where is your passion leading?"

Douglas hasn't an immediate answer. None of these choices describe his longing. He sits with his head in his hands thinking of an answer for Ciazzo. Should he want to be like Michael Rabin, practicing well beyond eight hours a day, memorizing lengthy concertos and symphonies so that he can be heard by a theater audience week after week? Does he want to become a member of a quartet playing chamber music in sophisticated spaces? Not really, though he'd do this willingly if it meant finally owning the 253-1.

A stringed voice crooning lullabies under the stars, spilling melody wild and free at the street fair, or spilling pathos in a cemetery. That's where his passion began. Where it leads is to the lustrous red violin. He hasn't thought further. How dare he tell Ciazzo? What if his generous Ciazzo decides he's wasted valuable time on him? How hurtful to have been rude to Ciazzo, his Ciazzo.

"Think on it," says Ciazzo. "You must know where you are headed if you aim to arrive. I can introduce you to wonderful folk-based music, Liszt, his Hungarian Rhapsodies, his Czardas. To lullabies. To Dvorak... "

The 253-1 interrupts, her utterance penetrating Douglas Tryzyna's being. She entreats him in her beguiling way. {*Questo violino* is the product of Italian calculation| immediacy and caress| unique in this world| Things of such rarity men may use for Good| Or men may use for Evil| There's the pity| Listen| you alone in this season have understood my language| Now you must play Me for all to benefit| So it is| |

Ciazzo interrupts. "It is said, *Art* begins where *Skill* and *Technique* end. Playing as an artist is never guaranteed us. Understand, though, I am teaching you to tackle such an accomplishment as a lifelong quest."

Unheard by the esteemed Ciazzo, Magic Muriel interrupts. {Listen| for you and *questo violino*| something beyond *art*| can be achieved| A thing mankind requires| It is so| |

Both appeals, the revered teacher's and the beloved violin's, vie for Douglas' attention.

"Look at me, Douglas," Ciazzo commands in uncharacteristic solemnity. "I ask that you consider where you are headed in this world. If Stoya holds sway over your future, then you must return to the man—and suffer the consequences."

Such conflicting assertions for a boy to assimilate; each declaration rings with truth.

Again, Magic Muriel quavers. {Or is it as they say| all is Vanity| |

Ciazzo replaces the D'Espine in its case; fastens the clasps with abrupt flips. "A contest is underway. In the outcome you will be either a winner or a loser. Decide when to play the Ace of Hearts and when to hold back. The choice is yours, yours alone. Don't fall for a bluff. Hear me well; once you leave there's no coming back."

[2]

THE MURIEL CIGAR box beckons from his wardrobe. Douglas lifts the box's lid and nods to the magical lady of the silent singing voice. She's faded now. It doesn't matter; she's still beautiful. He gathers the aggies and rolls them in his hand. What would Michael think? He ignores the fortune cookie where his self-proclaimed fortune asks to be read. Wing might disapprove of his action; Astrid too. *No matter what anybody else thinks, I've got to demonstrate my faith.*

* * *

FOR THIS DOUGLAS needs the energy Sister Peace showed him right here at the Step Falls. He's remembering her words. "See how it rushes to you, rushes away from you, rushes as it returns to you."

Cold, the water around his ankles. Icy cold it swirls around his shins. Water rises. Reaches his rolled cuffs. Almost buckles his knees. Back, back he steps, treading on rocky sharpness. Reaching his right arm over his head he paddles furiously, with his left arm barely staying upright. Even though he's well above the drop-off, the water surges with ferocity in its quest to drop free and fast.

A shadow crosses his face; a lone raven flies overhead. It blocks the sun, casts a shadow. Raucous clickety-twikety rasp. *Ha-ha-ha-orphan-no count-unloved-unworthy-deserted-abandoned-rejected-fraidy-cat-nan-ha-ha.*

Ravens lie. Don't they? How many hurtful words can reel in a second? Only simple words hurl from him up to the black feathered judge. "No! No! I'm worthy! I am!" Douglas screams. He smells his own nervous sweat, like burnt spices. Tastes the copper tang, of blood; he's bitten his tongue. Unseen obstacles graze his thigh.

Ahead a rock protrudes burnished by the sun. Water rushing, rushing away with increased force. He's barely keeping his balance. Just ahead another boulder wrapped in mist catches rainbows; will the rainbow's end be visible? Water and thoughts both run headlong, aligning with his purpose. At the rainbow's end, there's a treasure. A jackpot, his fortune. The secret fortune he wrote in the cookie. *Did the little Trenton Jr. who drowned in Auntie's well, did he have a heart's desire granted before he died?*

Douglas hollers the fortune's promise to the raven, or anyone who's listening. "I will have my heart's desire."

Froth gathers, the swirl of water deafens, rings, pounds. "I'm a survivor," he yells. This is the moment. He hurls the factory violin into the spray! He watches it fly. It glints like buffed Shinola before it's caught in the onrush, swept into the downward gush, the roar, the tumult. For seconds the carved head stays upright; like the face of a drowning person it stares at him. 'Round and 'round it turns; like a dancer the face whips 'round first. As if the poor creation had lately developed a soul, it spares the world one last howl, and drops from sight—the wooden instrument he hated, resigned himself to, finally reconciled with. It's gone. Never to be played again. He will never have to play it again. Never.

Douglas hollers. "I trust in my future with Magic Muriel 253-1. I do! I do!"

With a gurgling *croak*, throaty, deep, musical, rising in pitch, the raven swoops; its wings whoosh as Douglas struggles against the drag of furious water. Given his lack of progress the riverbank seems out of reach. Again, the jury of one jeers, wheeling above an otherwise unwitnessed act. *If-you-trusted-you-wouldn't-have-wouldn't-have-had-to-dispose-of-it-croak-croak-no-count-unloved-unworthy-orphan-you-fraidy-cat-caw-ha-ha.*

Ravens lie. Don't they?

How much was the factory violin worth? Ciazzo gave him an answer, and he'll take the man's word. $50.00 represents *how many* shoeshines for Lermontov? *How many* hours of labor for Ludlow?

As for the 253-1, she's aware of his commitment. Today he's proven it to all who doubted.

[3]

AT THE HOME Auntie Evangeline and Sister Elder have a discussion—one is poised, one is perturbed.

Sister Elder, "And is Stoya expecting payment for lessons now? Brute. Luring the boy back like this. As if the cursed fiddle hasn't already inflicted enough pain."

"Well, who can see the future? Look at us, how determined we were to make our choices when just a trifle older than he."

"Don't remind me."

"We went separate ways in France despite Father's disapproval, remember? I stayed there infatuated with my hot-blooded tenor and the glamour of Paris Opera. You proceeded to Italy per Father's plan, then succumbed to a scheme that cost you your heart and your allowance, that is if I recall correctly."

"To be young is to be foolhardy. Can't we save Douglas the mistake?"

Sister Elder hands Auntie Evangeline an envelope, addressed to them both.

"You haven't opened this yet?"

Hester shakes her head. "Hadn't the nerve. What next? I ask myself, dreading the answer."

Auntie Evangeline slices the waxed seal with her fingernail. She pulls out five ten-dollar bills, sets them aside, and opens a folded sheet of notepaper.

> *Thank you for the violin.*
>
> *The instrument served me as well as it could,*
>
> *and now I choose to be free of its influence on my life.*
>
> *Sincerely,*
>
> *Douglas*

"Well, I never!" Hester says. "I see we can't save Douglas."

"Well, I never," Auntie Evangeline echoes. "Always such an impulsive creature!"

"As were we, once upon a time."

* * *

THE INEVITABLE: SEVERAL days after Auntie Evangeline departs for Atlanta, Sister Elder cannot hold her tongue.

"Boy-o, is it possible you'll find yourself minus any violin at all in the future?"

Douglas snaps back at his Guardian. "No, Hester Smythe. And if I do find myself minus a violin in the future I will never, ever, ever want that particular one back!"

Sister Elder, Hester Smythe, turns abruptly. Without a word she leaves the teenager to bask in all his glorious rebellion.

Astrid confronts Douglas on his smarty-pants behavior. She takes him by the shoulders. He winces as the tiny blue jewels in her earrings flare; somehow they pinprick his hardened conscience. "Why have you shown Sister Elder this disrespect?" Astrid asks. "Someone who's been so kind to you."

"Why should I call her Sister Elder now? Because I don't see any other *sisters* around."

Astrid clarifies. "Hester began calling herself Sister Elder when she took in Mildred and the boys. She's related through her sister's family. She felt obligated to care for them; besides, she felt a connection."

"Why did she take me, then, with no obligations or connections?"

"That is for her to tell you."

＊ ＊ ＊

DOUGLAS LOOKS IN the mirror. He turns this way and that examining his face. Astrid's apricot cream, used on her Dresden doll-like skin, hasn't lightened the assembly of freckles across his cheeks. He wets his comb. Same copper hair, worn buzzed with the same three untamable cowlicks. Same color as Violette's.

He's grown a couple of inches since last fall. Astrid let down the hem and altered the side seams of his lucky vest. Perhaps he'll need such a charm if he's to confront Professor Stoya again.

Other thoughts confuse. Maybe Astrid is right—I'm being disrespectful to Hester. But isn't she disrespectful to me by keeping secrets?

* * *

"253-1 ARE YOU listening? I have proven my faith. Please talk to me."

{Proven your ignorance more like| Your ordinary violin will not rest in peace| Only to say| water is a violin's dread enemy| just as is flame| Your act was cruel| Douglas| |

"Hey, I was proving my love and my faith, wasn't I?"

{To tell my story| *questo violino* was loved by another| no cruel acts did he perform| even to the lowliest of my kind| Luigi Tarisio| he was my Savior| |

Douglas hangs his head. Never has Magic Muriel scolded him.

{The time was called 1748| My first owner traded *questo violino* to strangers| folk who woke before the sky's light shone| Common folk they| working on the land from sun to sun| Folk who calmed newborns with lullaby| celebrated weddings with tarantellas| honored with dirges their departed| Thin sounds their fiddling| albeit when joined by song| became so charged with jubilation| the purity my cells did absorb| For decades Myself gathered such potential| |

"This was a nice time for you, wasn't it?"

{In truth| *questo violino* grew ever more sensitive to Benevolence| thus more disabled when attacked by the opposite| 253-1 cannot abide cruelty| nor respond to a darkened soul| So it is| |

"I want to be like Tarisio."

{To tell the story| Tarisio was a searcher| He gave away violins in good tune| though common| These in exchange for violins in disrepair|

though fine| Once restored these *violini* began offering their music in far-away places| See| The magic Luigi gave back to the world| cannot be measured| All to say| Never did Luigi Tarisio| mistreat a violin| as you have done||

"I'm so sorry. Now it's too late, isn't it?"

{See| Some actions cannot be undone| Men may cause their own undoing| more the pity||

"And there is no way to redeem oneself, myself?"

{There are times| which cannot be predicted| when acts of Atonement may be offered| in hope of future benefit to others| So it is||

[4]

AND THERE IS gossip. It goes 'round and 'round Elizabethtown:

> Did you hear about the mute foundling?
>
> The one Hester Smythe took in?
>
> The kid who stole a violin?
>
> Yes, that one. He's returning to the Stoya Conservatory!
>
> Why ever would the respectable Stoyas take him back?
>
> You mean the brilliant Professor and Mrs. Piano Teacher?
>
> Indeed. Can you imagine?

* * *

BY NO MERE chance did Stoya use the magnet he'd policed for so many years. Was he fully aware that he'd set a trap? That he'd baited it? "When you return, you'll be playing the rogue fiddle." That was his come-on. So, judge for yourself.

"It's the only way," Douglas tells Wing. *But to lose Ciazzo?* How can he bear losing this man's guidance?"

And the 253-1 consoles. {As much as you are losing something| there will also be gain| Loss and gain| is this not the way of the world||

[5]

MONDAY, 9:00 A.M. A dreary September morning, gray skies and rain. Tattersall greets Douglas as he passes the lockers; the leader has finally stopped soliciting him to rejoin Orchestra. Douglas returns the amiable "Howdy-do." A silly smile overtakes his face. Today he's going to hold the 253-1 for the first time in ten long years. Old disappointments have been stubbornly hanging on like dry leaves to naked bough. Today those disappointments release. Forget concentrating in class. He's listening to the rhythm of rainwater slapping the stone walkway; what a delightful rhythm for playing on a violin. He's hearing distant hands clap-clap-clapping; or is it his heart thump-thump-thumping? Never mind, it's the rumble of a logging truck barreling south with chains jangling. And when the Latin teacher calls on him to conjugate the verb *sum*, he's lost.

"*Sum, es, est, sumus, estis, sum*," Violette answers for him.

Monday, 4:00 p.m. How strange to be returning to the Conservatory as a student. Nevertheless, with the German bow (surely a gift from Auntie Evangeline), his jinx-proof vest (Loong against his heart), and his teenage body filled with apprehension, he approaches the stone house. The hand-lettered sign still reads *Stoya Conservatory~Violin & Piano*. Rainwater drips down the plaque as it swings on its chain. Up the steps then. One. Two. Three. Four. Five. Six.

Violette's leaving when he's arriving. These days she wears a ponytail instead of braids. She's tying a flowered scarf that quivers in the breeze, green and blue like her mismatched eyes. The scent of flowers after rain—violets, jasmine, freesia—brings memories of afternoons spent together. The two musicians, sweethearts once upon a time, classmates as usual, have avoided personal exchange. *Maybe today will be different.* Douglas gazes at her face. *A hint of softening?* Violette averts her glance, although she manages to mumble; is it "hello," or "hey," or "bye"?

Befuddled by her closeness, he watches her feet tread the stone walk, black galoshes covering the same feet she bared on hot summer days.

Standing alone. Once again here in the salon as a pupil. Scents—of an orchid, of cabbage, of gingerbread—meld in the air. LuLu's hug cannot normalize his heart, which continues to drum like a maniac. The kind one disappears into the kitchen after her embrace. He's standing alone again. The same lack of stillness oppressing. The same rumple of energy expanding, contracting. The same clock ticking, the painted bird restrained, her spring flexed against the carved door. Atop the black beast of a piano, the same metronome taunting, the pendulum stilled, the weight slid down the scale to *presto*, the winding key begging to be wound. The same metal music stand soldiering on, bearing its sheaf of books. Two instruments beckoning, placed side by side in open cases, wrapped in green silk. Douglas' re-entry has not disturbed the status quo of discontent. Yet.

Douglas. Alone in the salon. He isn't asking permission. Not this time. Magic Muriel 253-1 in his arms, pressed close. Fingers on smooth black ebony, pressing strings. The fragrance of her. *So ruby red, she's just been oiled.* The 253-1 croons as he draws his new bow to caress her quivering strings. It's then he senses Willi, feels that familiar bristle of energy, looks up, sees Willi leaning against the doorframe, watching.

"Douglas, Douglas, come here!" Mrs. Piano Teacher calls him to a practice room. He obeys without letting go of the prized instrument. Without asking for agreement Mrs. Piano Teacher lays out the rules. He'll practice on the rogue fiddle only at the Conservatory, under their supervision, five days a week—after school. And after taking supper with the family. He may practice on *his own* instrument at the Home.

"I don't have it anymore, anyway," Douglas offers, somehow vindicated. He won't mention that Sister Elder berates his brash action at the Step Falls.

Douglas wonders if Wing and Astrid miss him in the attic or if this new arrangement is a relief. He wonders if the Home's three adults ever feel lonely now that the four teenagers aren't regularly at the table for Wing's cooking.

There's no time for worry, however, not while keeping this schedule: school, homework, violin lessons with Stoya, practice and memorization for the competitions ahead. No time for relaxation. How naturally the seduction of intimacy with the 253-1 energizes him.

[6]

WITHOUT INTENTION DOUGLAS is becoming a Stoya family member again. Siggi shows off his pin-up girl trading cards. Willi solves algebra problems for Douglas when requested, and Douglas adds needed paragraphs to Willi's English papers. Mealtime with the Stoyas regains old familiarity. These days LuLu's stew is heavier. Savory with more potatoes, carrots, onions, cream, and chunks of beef. The breadbasket overflows with her baking, dark rye, and pumpernickel bread. A stick of butter disappears from the cut-glass dish in a single sitting. The milk bottle is allowed on the table. "Teenage boys eat like wolves," the cook complains. Suggesting her fulfillment, however, LuLu hums melodies heard in the violinists' repertoire as she scrubs pots and pans.

Another day: Mrs. Piano Teacher's familiar voice drowning out a melody in the practice room. She's clapping her hands in exasperation. "No. No. You're insulting Haydn's lovely composition. "From the beginning! This time play lightly, lightly, with attention to precise finger activity." The unseen student can be heard following orders.

And today: Oh-No is already at the piano in the salon. Douglas notices how sturdy she is. She withstands Stoya's outbursts better than Violette, she persists when coached, she practices. She's polished her accompaniment to the Brahms Sonata. Is she flirting with him now while

Stoya takes a break? Douglas avoids reacting to her tickling fingers up and down his spine. He avoids laughing at her naughty jokes about Professor's Kickapoo Powder. She teases. "You know Violette and her words, right? She says Kickapoo Powder is '*Effective and Efficient*!'" Hearing Oh-No speak about Violette stings. And why can't he quit paying attention to his accompanist's whispered gossip? On and on Ophelia goes. Did he know Siggi was grounded for bashing pumpkins in the community garden? Did he know that Willi was supposed to attend a Boston music camp last summer, but didn't? Does he know that Willi and Violette are learning the same music as they are? Because Stoya's planning some sort of competition between the pairs.

When Stoya returns to the salon Douglas realizes the fierce dark eyes have softened. The Professor's ears have grown, or is it that his once bushy mustache has been clipped to new boundaries?

Same starched shirt and suspenders, though, worn even when it's muggy. Same Stoya asking for perfection, violin and bow in hand. "You two haven't even begun to work! This Sonata should be filled with lyricism. The piano must keep pace. Must never overtake. The violin should sing, sing, sing. You two are an embarrassment. Listen!"

After dabbing the sweat from his brow, Professor Stoya draws his bow and plays several passages, revealing unexplored possibilities in the music. "Resume your practice!"

Weeks later: Professor Stoya schedules private lessons for each of his senior violin students, Willi and Douglas, and the new kid, Butch. Black leather, gilt-edged pocket notebook at hand, red ribbon loose, the Professor jots shorthand memos for future reference.

Today, two boys play with equal passion. The third fails at being a true rival; he has much to learn. Nevertheless, Stoya's already broad chest expands. He stands taller, snaps his taut suspenders. From one practice room to another he marches, hardly daring to believe the progress.

* * *

ONE DAY AT the end of his private lesson with Professor Stoya, Douglas faces the question Ciazzo posed. "What are your goals?"

Douglas spider-walks his fingers down his bow.

"Butch wants to teach. Our A.J. has started at Juilliard. Willi is preparing for his audition there. Where do you see yourself after graduating high school?"

Douglas spider-walks his fingers up his bow.

"Let's jump beyond that, where in five years, when you're twenty-one? Where will your passion lead you?"

Perhaps there has never been a *where*, never been a destination. He was unable to answer Ciazzo; maybe time has allowed feelings and thoughts to mingle, becoming substantive. *Where do I see myself?* he ponders, not wanting to speak. Wherever it is, there are men like Ciazzo and the people who love violins and the music they make. Ladies like Sister Peace whose passions are exposed, whose imaginations run free, who revel in the outdoors, even if they come and go. Yes, even if they leave you over and over again. And girls like Violette who laugh and hug and might use words to comfort. Wherever he's headed there is music, dance, fire, water, stars. Finally, his answer to Stoya is more concise than his thoughts. "I just want to play the old fiddle everywhere. I want to play her for common people to hear." Unabashed certainty illuminates those eyes.

"Hardly an answer-schmanser," Stoya responds stiffly. "Let's just assume you want to be a virtuoso." Without waiting for agreement, the Professor continues. "That being the case, we'll proceed into the next round of competitions."

"Hardly an answer he gave you, Peter," Frieda says that evening in the semi-privacy of the library. She scoffs, "Playing for commoners, as if that's a profession." LuLu can be heard humming. Momentarily she appears with three liqueur glasses. She fills two generously with cherry brandy; and one, hers, she fills to a modest level. The Professor's trip to the City includes a visit to Berentzen Liqueur Importers; you remember, conveniently located beside the florist's shop from which he purchases flowers for Frieda.

"Hardly an answer indeed. Remember when I was his age," the Professor begins.

Frieda hears for the umpteenth time the woes of Peter's early goals, hurdles, and failures. The only three advantages granted him: Hindemith's tutelage, his father's violin, and the Mendelssohns' friendship.

What must it take for a musician to live out his dreams? Frieda muses. Douglas, talented and passionate, lacking practical focus. Willi, talented and competitive. Lacking what? Lacking self-discipline? Consistency? A musician without delight?

$$[7]$$

"MAGIC MURIEL, ARE you listening? Ciazzo and Stoya ask me to talk about my future. How can I look forward to the future if I'm never going to own you?"

{You will find your purpose with *questo violino*| But you will suffer in the finding| Nothing comes for free| A mother brings her son into the world| Even so a mother cannot save her son from the world| A luthier brings a violin into the world| although he cannot save it| Fire| water| exposure to sun| can ruin my kind| Many of us rot in the depths of seas| or blow about as ash| Though to say| we *violini* fear very little| it is not our nature| |

{And yet 253-1 must ask| of what do we have control| Your kind or mine| My kind are passed from one owner to the next| without consent| This is our fate| Soon a passage may take Me away from you| See| This wooden *violino* is gifted enough sentience to desire you as her *animatore*| Full expression is possible with you| We two can heal your kind of many ills| You have a great destiny to fulfill| as did my dear Tarisio| So it is| |

"Tell me more about Tarisio."

{There is much to tell of my dear Tarisio| 1809 they called the time| Here was a man| Luigi Tarisio| who loved *violini* above all else| though his fingers were crippled| See| The little finger of his left hand with such stiffness| Never would he achieve harmonics| nor trills| nor sixths| nor octaves| Fortunate though| he found his purpose early| |

As the red-striped violin retells history a panorama reels out for Douglas. He imagines an Italian teenager carrying a violin, his skin as golden as honey, a mop of dark hair worn shaggy. He's pushed along by a throng of town folk as they gather in a church. During the ceremony a symbolic dove, fashioned from corn husk, is set on fire and released to slide along a wire. Luigi reaches up as the flaming bird passes overhead. His hands go right through the fire. An aged nun watches on. "God made himself manifest on this Day of the Lord," she says to Luigi. "You have a great destiny to fulfill." She is Stradivari's granddaughter; she understands the miracle.

With new purpose Luigi sets to seeking the old treasures of Cremona, lost violins gone out of style in Italy. The young man treks from town to town, from church to monastery. He's a fiddler entertaining at vineyard cabarets; he's a carpenter repairing furniture. He's becoming an expert at discerning an Amati, a Strad, a Bergonzi, and a Guarneri del Gesù. He's trading ordinary violins in tune, for these old beauties now voiceless. Most he will sell to dealers in Paris and London whose work is building, repairing, and selling. By chance Tarisio meets Vuillame, the superb copyist, and Paganini, the genius of violin players. Both expand his awareness. And his business.

As 253-1 continues her story, Douglas imagines Tarisio, grown into a man after years have passed. By now the collector has acquired untold numbers of priceless instruments. Cautiously he keeps to a narrow circle of dealers as the rage for everything Italian continues.

"Did Tarisio sell you, too?" Douglas asks, curious to hear more.

{By no means did he sell *questo violino*| See| Tarisio and 253-1 shared communication| |

"Was it in the way I understand you? How you understand me?"

{Indeed| Though never to be a maestro| Tarisio with crooked fingers| adored me| poured out his soul to me| he did| |

The 253-1 hums and the resonance sets Douglas' heart aquiver with happiness.

{Oh, to be understood and loved in this world| Despite one's faults and one's mistakes| |

"Please, tell me more about you and him."

The violin entertains Douglas further. She describes Tarisio in his old age, how the collector lives in an attic above a restaurant, all alone. How Tarisio wants little except the privilege of tending to and keeping company with the old instruments he calls Cremonas. How he's secretive to a fault; nobody in his town even knows what he's up to.

{*Questo violino* observed Tarisio's final day| The Savior took 253-1 to his breast| along with Le Messie| resplendent creation| the masterpiece of Antonio Stradivari| Tarisio wrapped us in silk| he hid us| his loving farewell| |

Douglas imagines the neighbors finding the man in death; the silk merchant being given the news; the merchant hurrying to Paris to inform Vuillame. Vuillame having the advantage of being the first luthier to hear the news.

{Into the attic came Vuillame| after Tarisio's pulse had ceased| and his body resting in its grave| First Vuillame wept| Then he exclaimed| The space seemed in chaos| |

Douglas imagines the piles of fiddle-boxes. Violin backs, bellies, necks, scrolls bridges, pegs, fingerboards, and tailpieces lying about. Hundreds of violins hanging from a rope drawn across the room.

Vuillame went searching for something more, aided by Tarisio's sister. They pried open drawers in an ancient piece of furniture. Hidden there, what they sought. The two masterpieces spoken of and most beloved by Tarisio.

{Vuillame carried Tarisio's collection to Paris| there to be sold| *questo violino* and Le Messie as well| The time was called 1855| |

{Le Messie is also called Messiah| To hear Vuillame speak it| She the most glorious *violino* men's eyes ever did behold| Her body so exquisite| Sad to say| she was soon confined to a cage| only to be viewed like a muted songbird| |

{Vuillame did not understand Myself| nor did he discover my beginnings| Not finding my label| he called Me a Bergonzi| instrument of hybrid forms| Such is the way of salesmen and selling| |

{With my new owner then| to Teatro Royale| Madrid| He a conductor| leading a grand assembly of instruments| some my kin| some very strange| Learning here composers' written music| |

"The music I've been learning to play!"

{Indeed| By the conductor *questo violino* was passed along| to his son who kept me for sentiment alone| Passed along then to a grandson|

teacher of Spanish Literature and Poetry| a writer of love songs he| His crooning infused my being| A man misunderstood| yes maligned in Spain| when the time was called 1936||

"All of this experience makes you so very special, doesn't it?"

{Indeed no| Many| many| of the Cremona have survived dramatic journeys| A wealth of mankind's expression| they carry in their cells||

Before Douglas can respond 253-1 concludes her tale. {Be wary| dear one| Truth be| *questo violino* is matchless for other reasons| Knowledge of my inimitable beginning| will be uncovered soon| This will prove Me to be priceless| and thus irresistible to greedy ones| To save Me| Tarisio carried my secret to his grave||

"Will you tell me your secret?"

{Yes| and soon| A time of danger lurks ahead| There are things you must know| if you are to protect our future together||

[8]

THIS OCTOBER OPHELIA arrives early and chats with LuLu before she's scheduled to practice with Douglas. Wire-rimmed glasses obliterate her old squint. If Violette is infatuated with words, then Ophelia equally adores blue. Her mother sews fashions in corduroy, plaid, tweed, stripes, solids. Blue, always fashions in blue—as pastel as a Marie Cassatt, as vibrant as Egyptian lapis lazuli, as dull as an Elizabethtown snow cloud.

Their pairing seems natural to Douglas now. With Ophelia (wearing blue) seated at the piano, Douglas, standing to her right, his Magic Muriel under his chin, feels more than hears her accompaniment. Her energy shifts like a body of water reflecting the climactic changes of their music. She sometimes calls him Doogie and in return he calls her Oh-No. And neither feels insult, such is their new relationship. If Ophelia entertains romantic notions for her partner, she subverts her hankering into their musical duality. Douglas accepts this arrangement just as he accepted a lesser violin—by keeping possibility of change alive.

"There is a difference between surrender and submission," Sister Elder preached over the years. She was right. Patience paid off. He's finally practicing on his long adored, desired Magic Muriel 253-1, and she sings in a timbre only he can extract.

Wing and Astrid miss his practice sessions. They're curious about the coveted instrument. They ask each other, "Is it really a very good violin, after all?"

Douglas tries to shed some light. "You can recognize her voice even though I feel like she's changing every day. I practice a whole range of tones to keep her vibrating in a real open way."

Ciazzo had explained this phenomenon when he introduced the D'Espine. "Unlike your factory violin this violin will volunteer a multitude of colors. With her offerings you will paint everything *el señor* Douglas is. What people hear will be a fusion of man and instrument." Ciazzo had paused and looked directly into the glistening eyes as he added a caveat. "If you haven't developed a strong psyche, you simply won't be able to do anything much with all of that."

[9]

AS WEEKS PASS Douglas' exceptional technique and rapid memorization are taken for granted by Professor Stoya. Now each practice session highlights his increasing mastery of sound. Even a gossamer stroke produces lush tone as Douglas and the 253-1 join to execute Bach or Bartok, solo or accompanied. And when the boy (still taunted as "Doogie") and the fiddle (still tainted by unwelcome immigrants) finish a composition, pure silvery tone rings long past the final passage of a bow.

Stoya demands Conservatory Recitals, making sure advanced students become aware of peer progress. "You watch, we'll sharpen our dullards with constant competition," Peter boasts to Frieda.

Douglas inspires as much as he intimidates those who struggle. The feather in Douglas' cap, his diligent accompanist, Ophelia, now dresses for her role—wearing heels and silk stockings to the monthly events. After their performance she curtsies, sweeping one boney-fingered hand across her blue skirt, whether she hears applause or not. After which she pushes wire-rimmed glasses up her aquiline nose and plunks into the seat beside a very quiet Violette, her closest friend.

"Not every student in recital earns praise," the Stoyas inform parents. "Don't expect dime-store compliments from big-ticket teachers." It's understood that *only* if both adult Stoyas clap may listeners also clap.

[10]

MUCH TO DOUGLAS' dismay, Sister Elder is attending the December Recital. He assumed she wouldn't. No secret, her dislike of the Stoyas. Up the steps to the stone house they are going, both strangely gripped by dread, just like so many years ago. One. Two. Three. Four. Five. Advancing between the rock pillars of the front porch, Douglas recognizes his Guardian's change, her steadiness disturbed.

Mrs. Piano Teacher greets them, her hair freshly coiffed in rippling waves. "Please take the wingchair," she says, pointing the older woman to the salon. Sister Elder's expression reveals discomfort in accepting courtesy from this termagant who mistreated her charge. No matter how long ago the offense might have been. She nods to Vicar Hornsby, who already awaits the entertainment (and the pfeffernusse).

Ophelia gathers their wraps like a second hostess. "You look lovely in Tintoretto blue," Sister Elder comments. Uncomprehending, Ophelia squints, causing her wire-rimmed glasses to shift almost imperceptibly.

Sister Elder clarifies her use of *Tintoretto blue* with a description of Italian rococo paintings, flamboyant art with blue skies and cherubs. Ophelia sucks in every word as if fact-finding for future gossip. She's also eager to inform. Did Sister Elder know she's Douglas' regular accompanist? "Plus," she whispers, "he uses the old striped violin, which sounds better than the Professor's precious-untouchable."

Violette approaches Sister Elder, who reaches out, who pulls her close. "What lovely strong hands you have, and what have you been busying yourself with besides piano practice? My dear, we haven't seen much of you lately." It's true, Violette's visiting slowed after Sister Peace's departure. Her visiting ceased in mid-June this year.

Violette admits to typing poetry, and when interrogated further replies that she likes to read Emily Dickenson. She recites: *"Hope is the thing with feathers that perches in the soul—and sings the tunes without the words—and never stops—"* Swallowing hard, Violette cannot complete the phrase; she turns her face away from Douglas' Guardian.

"Hope. Yes, that's the thing, isn't it dear?"

Stoya joins the conversation. "Gifted with keen ears, our Violette. You'll enjoy her with Willi playing my excellent Vuillame." In lieu of a response Sister Elder forces a brief smile; she tilts her head away, intent on repositioning her emerald-green pillbox hat. Now, the rhinestone snow-flake is re-centered.

As an hour lumbers along, each intermediate student flounders; most suffer a blitz of memory loss. In which case the performer (knowing an earful about his deficient practice will follow) is allowed the use of his music book—tut-tut.

After a break all attention is upon the final performers. A.J. is nothing less than remarkable with the unaccompanied Ysaÿe, perfected for his Juilliard audition. Stoya concentrates with fingertips pressed together, prayer-like. The lad's technique, impressive to the completion. Stoya's clapping begins; a smile twitches his mustache. He glances at parents' envious faces as if to say, *See what I've accomplished with a student!*

Willi and Violette display excellence. Until that troublesome measure where Violette invariably flubs a chord, which causes Willi to flub his harmonics and stumble through the *vivace.* Yes, the father generously leads clapping for them, anyway. Willi and Violette appear crestfallen.

Douglas and Oh-No take their turn. Fellow musicians who otherwise fidget immediately cease taboo activity—none of the yawning, nor toe scuffing, nor nose picking, nor gum chomping, nor elbowing. Students listen. Parents listen. Listen as if hypnotized, mouths slightly open. That is to say, each except an unsmiling Willi who keeps a furtive eye on his father's reaction. How well he knows what to look for after years of observing a fault-finding man.

Even LuLu could tell you the Professor's been overwhelmed by the beauty he's hearing. Stoya's gestures signal his bedazzlement. His admiration. Admiration for Douglas' instinctive mastery of the rogue violin. For Ophelia's sensitivity to Douglas. How deliberate her touch on the piano keys, fingers extracting richness. Her adroitness allows Douglas to lose himself with the 253-1 in the jazzy-gypsy melodies that are Ravel's. Long before the nitpicking teacher comes out of his reverie, Mrs. Piano Teacher breaks protocol and prompts the applause all by herself.

[11]

THIS DECEMBER SUNDAY, after Mrs. Piano Teacher brags, after the pfeffernusse and cider are consumed, after boots-mittens-mufflers are donned, after promises are made to practice over the holidays, and after goodbyes are given, the Conservatory grows quiet, except for the sounds of LuLu's ministrations in the kitchen, and it is then that Willi complains to his mother. Why is he *stuck* with Violette as accompanist? "Violette trips me up." And why is he *stuck* with the stubborn Performance Violin? "That old thing Douglas gets to use practically plays itself."

Of this complaint neither Douglas nor Violette has a clue. Nevertheless, Willi's dissatisfaction will provoke change at the Stoya Conservatory. Violette shuffles through snow with Douglas, both heading for the Home and Wing's cooking, thanks to Sister Elder's invitation. Violette sinks into gloom with her own complaint. "Mrs. Piano Teacher was telling the Vicar Oh-No is better than me."

"Oh-No is *not* better than you!"

Violette mimics Frieda's voice. She's memorized every stinging word. "'Ophelia isn't *simply* an accompanist; she's my *finest* soloist. *Her* Chopin? Well, one would think his music was composed just for *her*.'"

"It's *not true*!" Douglas says with emphasis. The importance of his accomplishment in today's recital fades. He's consumed with concern for the girl by his side. So rarely does Violette confide in him anymore.

Magic Muriel joins in. {Some ears do not hear| some eyes do not see| The Professor is as callous as his mate| Is this not so| |

"Yes!" Douglas says under his breath.

{Rough| Inept| Clumsy| As such he terms the carved scroll of 253-1| The carving on his Performance Violin he terms perfection| Such is prejudice| |

"Prejudice!" Douglas says aloud, for Violette's benefit.

{In the face of such Ignorance| choose to react with Kindness| And remember the need of Kindness| for ones who are disparaged| So may it be| may it be| |

Sister Elder opens the door before they tug off their boots. Douglas notices how attractive she looks dressed up. The green silk blouse and tailored tweed skirt reveal her as someone other than the maternal Hester Smythe he thinks he knows, daily uniformed in a brown wrapper with a white apron. He also notices that Violette has grown taller than his Guardian. How oblivious has he been? Before Douglas can ponder further the female pair is arm in arm, deep in conversation about poetry. They head for the parlor, leaving him behind.

[12]

THE FOURSOME WAITS and waits. Time is running out on school holidays and the break from music lessons. For whatever reason, here they are, the four advanced students of the Stoya Conservatory gathered on New Year's Day. Ophelia, dressed in Prussian blue, takes a seat between Douglas and Willi. "What's up?" she whispers. Willi shrugs; he doesn't know. Violette leans across Willi to answer Ophelia's question. "Important conversation, an *announcement*," she mouths.

Violette leaves the hassock. She sweeps aside the pleats of her plaid skirt, seats herself at the piano. A full minute of silence, fingers merely hovering over the keys. And then. A few single notes ring clear. Called by the impromptu performance, Mrs. Piano Teacher and LuLu appear. They lean against the salon's arched entry.

"Chopin's Berceuse Opus 57 D Flat Major," Oh-No whispers.

As if the window became a stage, snowflakes outside respond to the music. One by one, two by two, they fall in stately procession. Called forward, whoosh, a new burst of flakes defy gravity. They swirl and stir in joyous freedom from breeze or gravity. How lovely the sight. With a shift, the amassing flakes are driven southward, and then northward under the wind's capricious control, gathering such numbers as to curtain the sky. For five uncounted minutes music and nature have mirrored, moving from simplicity to elegant multiplicity. Violette's performance leaves Oh-No open-mouthed. Mrs. Piano Teacher, who should speak, who wants to speak except she's lost composure, is obviously stunned by her student's flamboyance. Douglas smiles, a sweet smile, one that exudes both love and pride. Violette just made a powerful statement.

Oh-No sighs.

Violette leaves the piano, settles into the loveseat. Beside Willi.

Douglas' smile fades.

Mrs. Piano Teacher redirects the small audience's attention. "The Professor will be with you in a minute." She sits at the piano and arranges the pile of music books.

The cuckoo clock pendulum swings back and forth. Back and forth. The speckled orchid plant on the piano quivers like a fevered patient. Douglas, his bow lightly held, grows impatient to play the 253-1; both violins are abed in their cases just waiting to be heard. However, since the Professor is expected in a minute Douglas chooses to be patient. Willi Stoya, casually moving his knee to touch Violette's knee, seems not to mind time passing. Violette seems not to mind a vulgar boy's knee against her own.

Douglas tries to console himself. *Violette must be playacting to make me jealous.* His much-repeated, most-private lie is being smashed to smithereens. Right here. Right now.

Memories pull Douglas back to his thirteenth birthday. Touching Violette. Touching shoulder to shoulder as a trolley jerks along, he and Violette. Her broad smile, her fat copper braids, her freckled arms. A red pocketbook with a rusted brass latch. Several coins, enough to pay for the two dill pickles, pickles they don't buy. One chocolate ice cream cone instead, between them. Violette's jig, her laughter, the sensation of her chicken bone fingers as he licks the sweetness off them.

Siggi's voice interrupts Douglas' musing. "Here he comes, live, chamber pot to you, the great Peter Stoya!" Frieda swivels around on the piano bench, giving her husband full attention. The Professor cuffs Siggi, an affectionate gesture. He stands like an orator.

"1953 presents challenges for us," he says. This is hardly announcement-worthy. Since September these students have been in *preparation mode*. For regional events. For the Stoya Conservatory Recital. For NOA's New York State Competition with its First Prize—funding for advanced musical education. And the crowning honor thereof for the Winner, performing as a soloist.

"Do you understand what this means?" Four teens blink. "Boys, I'm going to challenge-schmallenge you. One of you two must be the Winner of the NOA's competition! The other must be Runner-up. Both get to play at a Dress Rehearsal for family and friends. The Winner, *only the Winner* will solo with the Junior New York Philharmonic at a *ticketed* event. This is serious career stuff, not just a ho-hum gig."

Willi and Douglas exchange a quick glance. Willi begins leg bouncing. Douglas' fingers spider-walk up and down the bow, up and down the bow, up and down the bow.

"Remember," Stoya continues, "you are competitors, *and* teammates. A musician can't rely on familiarities. Crutches only weaken a performer. For that reason, listen up: You'll be switching partners."

The reason for the gathering! The *announcement* has been made! Stoya's newsflash, presented like a generous gift, stuns only three of the musicians. And the same *gift* gratifies only one, the envious one, the complainer with a deadpan face who sits there with his knees bouncing.

Frieda smiles gently, first a mother, second a wife—this moment satisfies both roles.

The Professor explains what the students have quickly concluded. "Ophelia, you'll be paired with Willi now. Violette, you'll be with Douglas. To proceed? First we play for each other." He selects something they're in the process of perfecting. Brahms D Minor Sonata. Frieda directs the girls into a practice room for warming up on scales, arpeggios, and chords. Ophelia fairly skips across the salon, pushes up the sleeves of her Prussian blue sweater, all business. Violette, stunned, stumbles over the hassock and loses her balance.

A rainbow rushes up Douglas' spine! A whoop of exuberance escapes. He's going to be paired with Violette? The beloved 253-1 will be under his chin, the new bow in his hand, and Violette will be taken away from Willi. She'll be beside him, daily.

"Boys, take your violins and tune up," Professor Stoya barks.

Willi scrutinizes the father, the son's face scrunched with a mixed expression—mild distress plus anticipation. "The other thing we agreed...Pa, you said I'd...?"

Peter ignores his son, who then picks up his father's violin, resigned to the required fifteen-minute warmup on the troublesome Performance Violin.

In September when Stoya had allowed Willi and Douglas use of the forbidden instruments he had informed them of trials to come. "Adjusting to a new instrument can take from three months to two years." The Professor knows this firsthand; yet he puzzles over Douglas' instant facility on the mongrel instrument. How could it be? With Douglas' very first touch the old fiddle's tone became deeper, warmer, even richer than he himself has yet achieved with it. One could say, though, Peter won't call attention to this. The cast-off is even more brilliant in the upper register than his treasured Cremona (pseudo-Vuillame).

"The Performance Violin is like a diamond that shines on each string." Professor Stoya reassures himself yet again, as he and Mrs. Piano Teacher relax over tea, enjoying the mossy-fruity tones of Darjeeling.

Frieda is less patronizing than usual. "The Performance Violin? Not so diamond-like when Wilhelm tries it, not yet."

With reverence Douglas unwraps the 253-1. Green silk slides away, exposing the richness of ebony and varnished wood. How quickly the violin slides into tune for the once-exiled-now-reinstated disciple. Yet in the same few minutes Willi tightens and then loosens strings on the Performance Violin, attempting to tune it. Frustration!

Stoya has taught his students to pack as much punch into fifteen minutes as possible. They practice linear movement via shifting exercises, drones, pizzicato, and trilling exercises. Douglas tackles each with gusto. Willi checks the clock again and again. He quits the instant the second hand informs him the required time has elapsed.

Setting aside the Performance Violin young Stoya paces the salon. Douglas relaxes with his instrument loosely balanced on his shoulder. Without warning Willi sidles up to Douglas. Perhaps his sudden lurch—or perhaps his bared teeth—should flash a high alert. It did not. Willi easily grabs the 253-1 by its neck; he yanks it from Douglas' casual grip. Caught off guard Douglas loses his balance, bumping the étagère, toppling a statuette, a sweet little Hummel. Porcelain strikes glass and meets the rug in two pieces—of which the haloed head is the smallest.

Willi faces his stunned rival, his forelock no longer slicked back, his face no longer pasty. "Dibs on the rogue, Doogie-doo. You try playing the Performance Violin for a change, you'll see how much harder it is."

Professor Stoya hastens into the salon. He claps his hands, he's short of breath, his face of a purplish hue. "You were to wait for my permission, Wilhelm!"

"Holy cow! You promised! You know you did!"

"You wait-schmait, son!" The father turns to address Douglas. Attempting to spit out words, he merely sputters. Professor Stoya drops into the wingchair, looking more like a duffle bag than a dictator.

Douglas leans against the entry. He senses a sick on-again-off-again undulation from the Professor. Despite his fury he waits for Stoya to recover. There stands Willi defiant, radiating heat, the scent of aftershave filling the room. Yes, Willi, leaning against the black beast of a piano, now in possession of the 253-1.

Stoya regains his composure. He straightens his shirt cuffs. Avoids eye contact with Douglas. "Now young men, you'll be switching not only accompanists. That's right. You'll be switching violins, too. For you, Douglas, the privilege of playing my personal instrument. For you, Willi, the experience of the old striped."

If molten lava coursed through Douglas' veins, he couldn't be more inflamed. Of course, the 253-1 doesn't *belong* to him. The Professor stated it outright in the invitation to return. Never, never in the world did he contemplate this switcheroo. *I can't play the promised violin anymore? Why?*

Mrs. Piano Teacher escorts Ophelia to the piano. "Ophelia is ready to begin with Willi, Peter." Willi rotates his neck until it cracks. He sniggers. With drama worthy of a magician, he positions a white handkerchief on the violin he has coveted. Ophelia pushes her glasses firmly up her nose and waits, fingers poised in middle C position. Willi counts, "1-2-3-4," and they begin.

What is the wretched squawk? The raucous crow-like noise? Those catlike howls? The 253-1? Oh-No keeps advancing through the Brahms Sonata as if all is well. Clearly all is not well. Willi handles the bow with his elbow held high just as he's been taught. In response the 253-1 produces only screeches and caterwauling.

Mrs. Piano Teacher's hands, birdlike at her mouth. Violette's eyes, blinded, blinking. Ophelia's neck, stiffening—not to be discombobulated, she soldiers on note by note, measure by measure. Douglas, however, seems to be listening intently, hearing something the others can't.

{My dear one| our frequencies are aligned| We two are aligned| is that not right| See| As Willi opposes Me| he radiates such vile energy| Tis a pity| that screech before my voice was blocked| Now silence will hold| Such is the way of things||

Douglas grimaces. Exactly what is happening?

Willi isn't giving up—no siree, Bob. He begged to play this one, hoping to get easy compliments, and by golly he'll keep trying. The fiddle's racket ceases; there is no sound forthcoming. Young Stoya bows and plucks. Nothing. He tries again, again, again. Nothing, no sound except the rosined horsehair's sough as it moves across strings. The fiddle has gone mute. Willi turns as crimson as the satin cushion Astrid once made. Willi pushes, pulls the bow harder, faster. Faster!

Amidst the silence the metronome pendulum bursts free from restraint; the unexpected and rapid click-clacking presumes a duet *allegro-vivace* in progress. *Click-clack, click-clack, click-clack, click-clack,* unending. Almost in unison the cuckoo lunges from his chamber, pushes aside the carved door, and emits his two-syllable call. *Cuck-coo.* Twelve times he calls, a dozen *Cuck-oos,* then twelve more *Cuck-oo, Cuck-oo, Cuck-oo*—so on and on the cheerful bird reports without concern for the correct hour or the tempo of the metronome's lively ticks. Who has ever before heard such volume from his artificial voice?

Oh-No gasps. The adults look at each other, dumbfounded by this display of prescience. Is it possible the headstrong fiddle instigated a power play with these mechanical servants? A metronome? A cuckoo? At this point Siggi's guffaws gallop to join the un-corralled chorus of willfulness. The parents don't seem to notice their smart-alecky second son, so intent are they on hearing the yet unheard music from their first son.

Willi stomps. Then like a furious batter having struck out in the last inning, Willi bashes, bashes again, again, the offending fiddle against the hassock.

Douglas lunges for the 253-1 and, catching Willi off guard, wrenches it away. "Stop it! You monster!"

Willi glowers at Douglas, who cradles the instrument like a newborn. "Pa, it's a piece of junk—it isn't my fault."

"Give it to me!" Peter Stoya booms harshly as if Douglas were the offender, this above the merriment of Siggi, metronome, and cuckoo. "Hell's bells, somebody silence the noise!"

Douglas refuses to release Magic Muriel 253-1. Nobody moves to silence the impertinent cuckoo. Frieda squeezes her forehead, migraine coming on. Violette scrunches further into the love seat, tucks her feet up, and curls into a ball. Ophelia cowers as if waiting to be bashed. Who can say how long it is until Ophelia regains control, stops the offending pendulum—after which she winds the key as if this were an ordinary day. Which it is not. And the cuckoo's *Cuck-oo, Cuck-oo, Cuck-oo* goes on and on and on and on.

"Egad. Leave my sight, all of you!" Stoya commands. He pulls the wooden victim from Douglas' hands, examines the mistreated fiddle, turning it this way and that. "Just an old relic in need of repair, or beyond repair. I'll tend to it."

Mrs. Piano Teacher gathers her wits and in a shaky voice takes control. "Students, leave now. I'll call with your new schedule."

Douglas stalls. "What about my...the violin. Can I try her...?"

A stern response from Stoya. "NO. NO. NO. I'll call you. And boys, you'll both play the Wilhelm Hermann Hammig until that *thing* is repaired. Or replaced."

The girls take off, buttoning coats against the January chill, leaving the bereft musician to walk by himself.

Peter can't bear the stuffiness inside. He needs air, out to the porch. Snow gathers on the father's head and shoulders. He's confounded. What in curses has transpired? First, his wife extracted favors for her son, this against his better judgment. He argued against switching up players and violins. Next, a violin screeched and then mysteriously refused to make even a twang. And finally, a player lost his temper and took it out on a poor fiddle?

Snow continues to gather on the man's shoulders and head. He's bewildered. Just when Willi was showing true interest. Isn't it normal for a father to rationalize? *Well, the relic's caliber is anyone's guessing game—just as well, she showed us her weakness here. Undependable. And, well, a lad's burst of temper is redeemable, understandable. I've been known to be a man of temper. I'm hardly one to judge.*

Waxing philosophical now, Peter steps out of the cold, back into the entry. He reasons further. Yes, wisest in the long run to let Willi's understandable flare-up pass without punishment. I'll deny him the Performance Violin for a spell—that will teach him a lesson.

Strange noises beyond the entryway alert the Professor. The dull sounds of wood on wood draw him back into the house. Until midway in the entry, just past the philodendron, a striped instrument hurtles across the antique hooked russet runner rug, abruptly halting in collision with Peter's wing-tip shoe, emitting an off-key *twannnnngg. Which violin?* Stoya goes rigid. Five seconds pass; then he wilts, recognizing the fiddle.

Here's Willi. He sashays out of the salon into the entry. He gives no explanation although the scowl on his face reveals everything.

Stoya's rage. A pinwheel of anger, guilt, fear, each facet brightly colored and in unison, spins out of control. Without a nanosecond of hesitation Peter Stoya clenches a fist and punches Willi smack in the face. Willi's nose spurts, red as any valentine rose, causing Frieda to rage at this brute, her husband, and later that night, to turn her back to him in bed.

[13]

DOUGLAS SHUFFLES THROUGH fresh snow, tears freezing before they reach his cheeks. He's gaining daily time with Violette just to lose the only other thing he's coveted. More than ever, he needs to hear that the violin is okay. Will she be *replaced*?

Magic Muriel 253-1 makes herself present. {Dear one| you were there| As the dark one took Me to his breast| my vibrations were deflected| And why| Why indeed| See| My positive vibrations were by his negative energy repelled| So it is| |

"Has he ruined you...broken you...beyond repair?"

{Many indignities have come my way| This *violino* is surviving yet| is she not| Though in truth| a *violino* requires human touch| to bring forth her sound| Human touch to repair her brokenness| |

Douglas wipes his nose on his sleeve; despite his fervency he's ever so inadequate as a caregiver.

{Time spent alone| untouched| unheard| *questo violino* has endured| It was in such time of Devachan| came my first Savior| Tarisio| |

"I wish I could have saved you today."

[14]

THE DOVE GRAY sky hints at pink. Snowfall becomes so sparse and random that each flake seems like the occasion of a falling star. The chosen boy's eyes see nothing.

First look at Douglas tells Sister Elder, Wing, and Astrid the same story. There's been trouble at the Stoya Conservatory. The adults join in their effort to extract details of the incident. Douglas reels it out, unable to restrain his outrage. How the poor violin was bullied by Wilhelm. Wing and Astrid join to comfort him with an embrace.

Sister Elder makes a pronouncement, her mother's heart as dark as the other's. "Breech of promise, humiliation, hostility. Without an inkling of an apology. I will *never* forgive that family!"

* * *

DOUGLAS SOAKS IN the tub, neck deep in the bubble bath Astrid prepared and insisted he take. "Dear Magic Muriel, can you hear me? Tell me how Tarisio saved you."

{To tell it| when Tarisio found *questo violino*| Myself had the squawk of a tongue-less wretch| fingerboard loose| two strings only| one turning peg lost in some dark corner| Shall 253-1 tell you the story| |

"Yeah, I want to know."

{Leaving my sweet maker| *questo violino* was put into the hands of country folk| there to be gathering their expression| as 253-1 has explained| Even so| decades bring change| Came a time called 1820| a nobleman traveling in horse-drawn carriage| came across my folk in wedding celebration| my voice changed the man's listening| |

{See| The noble purchased Me for a laudable price| so great his need| Through a gate| to his Villa down a quiet road| he carried Me| For in this grand building| his son who suffered madness| was hid| |

{This voice| in the hands of a grandfather did calm the boy|
Soothed the boy| Day after day| we hushed him with melodies| inspired
by the images of Saints and Angels painted upon the walls of the Villa|
the elder's fingers trained in the olden way| when *violini* held honor in
men's minds| One sad day *questo violino* fell into disrepair| could no
longer quiet any poor soul's melancholy| or rage| much less a beloved
boy's| Oh to say| 253-1 fell into voiceless Devachan| |

{After much time forgotten on a shelf| 253-1 useless| except for
the gathering of dust| came a day for the providence of it| when the four
legs of a rodent straddled these strings| The creature drew forth a grand
hum| attracting a feline beast| Oh to see it| my perflings were endan-
gered by nasty incisors| |

Douglas sits up, startled. "A rat was chewing on you?"

{Fortunate| the next minute| Tarisio in his quest for instruments
of Cremona| was close by| drinking *limonata*| and may well have over-
looked Me| waylaid| as I was| had not the small creature squeaked| and
the larger creature purred| and 253-1 victim of their tussle| landed with
a moan on a cushion beside blessed Luigi Tarisio| |

"A cat and mouse!"

{Indeed| Tarisio recognized *questo violino*| In exchange for a young
fiddle fit enough to serve| he gathered Me straight away| Repair my
voice he did| My first Savior| Luigi| |

{See| My kind endures| though sadly observing the entry and de-
parture of you creatures| But listen| Myself has chosen you| |

"How come you chose me?" Douglas dares ask.

{Why indeed| Douglas| you were my second Savior| From ruina-
tion by rain| and blistering sun| you rescued Me| See| You chose 253-1
just as she chose you| |

"I did, didn't I?" Douglas submerges, relaxing into the warmth for a second. Only to sit up spluttering bubbles. "But, but...what will become of you now?"

{As to the future| be assured| Stoya will see 253-1 made whole| All because of you| |

* * *

THE EVENING OF the violent incident, a hush, not to be confused with calm, pervades the Stoya household. Frieda whispers sarcastically, her distress, migraine full bloom. "Double lithium night! She turns on her heel, her face pinched in a grimace."

LuLu follows Frieda to the stairs, places a hand on the suffering woman's wrist. Be smart, *mein Freunde*." After which, being the loyal helper she is, LuLu serves plates for three residents only; she tidies the kitchen, claiming to have already eaten, and heads upstairs to check on Frieda. Three headstrong males—one with signs of an imminent black eye—consume spätzle and schnitzel in silence.

Late the next morning Frieda scrubs Willi's bloody shirt until it's bleached as any flag of truce, though her spousal heart remains as stained as the night before.

[15]

FLORIEN ROUX HANDLES the damaged violin. He inspects her anatomy, his face dispassionate, although he exposes his evenly square teeth as his face contorts into a question mark. Whatever he's thinking stays hidden under his snug leather cap. Taking a tiny mirror and flashlight he peers into the F-hole. "Not positioned for viewing, the label. A bit of a mystery this. What's your story with this one?"

Whew. Not the difficult question Stoya was expecting. "Belonged to itinerants who made an encampment dozen years back in our town; they got careless with their fire one September night. Farmer lost sheds; folk chased them off; this was found by a wordless child. His guardian brought it to me."

Florien pulls a bow across the strings. An angry wolf howl issues forth. "Lost its balance, the sound post, soul of a violin, they say. Perhaps blocks loose too. Surgery. *Alors*, can't be avoided. Play this violin regularly, does anyone?"

"The once mute boy, now my student. He's curiously attached, and I must agree she suits his attack."

"Strange *enfant prodige* you teach. He does this *brutalité*? No boy with love of violin would do such a thing!"

Stoya stalls without comment.

"Oh, and how's it faring, your superlative, *très bien, Vuillame*?" Florien raises one eyebrow and flashes his teeth.

"Sings as sweetly as the songbird of paradise, thank you." Stoya loosens his shirt collar.

Florien nods agreeably. "Of course, she does, with her well-disguised maker. *Envoyé du ciel*. Heaven sent, that one." Florien winks.

Stoya fights his urge to shut the man's mouth forcibly. When you count on someone to be discreet, you'd prefer they stick with discretion, at all times.

Florien uncaps his fountain pen, locates a sheet of laid paper, writes using elegant looping cursive with stylized numbers. He pushes the estimate across his desk to Stoya. "You agree to my fee? A fair one. Such a repair will take some days. Skill and blessings granted, *alors*, remove the lid, I must. Apply glue, dry it must. Can you return Friday, next?"

Florien listens for the departure of Professor Stoya. Within minutes he's on the telephone. "This one, Augustin, she's worth skipping your lunch. Today, you come over?"

Florien and Augustin relish this challenge. When encountering a mystery violin they gather clues trying to determine year and maker. Stoya would have enjoyed hearing their experienced observations; however, his company isn't wanted.

"Look, my dear Augustin," Florien begins excitedly, "observe first the red finish, the sheen, layer upon layer of varnish deftly laid. Crystalline quality like this, who else could achieve except *the Maestro?*"

"Made for royalty, this," Augustin observes. "Sadly, abuse she has seen in her lifetime. Ancient crack here in left rib. Clean repair. Long since adjusted to the healing, she has."

"Quite right. Observe, Florien, grain of the spruce of belly. It bears distinctive dark striations; we've seen, dare say, such grain in at least one of *the Maestro's?* Remember the Stradivari 'Tua,' 1708? On display in Musée de la Musique, Paris. And yet..."

"Could this, say, be product of Carlo Bergonzi? Stradivari's favorite pupil?"

"Yes, possibly. Bergonzi family moved into Casa Stradivari upon *the Maestro's* death where Carlo worked on instruments left unfinished, they say. And yet..."

Augustin tilts his head. "With such stripes, these stripes *along* with mark of nature here, like thumbprint? Truly characteristic of a late del Gesú." He rubs his fingers together, delicate fingers that allow him entrée to intricacies of construction. He strokes the gentle curve of the instrument's belly. "Another observation, Florien, to lead us further along path. In a word, shape. Hints of the Amati, even the Stainer, you see this? A Stradivarius would have none of it."

Florien agrees. "Indeed! And the longer C-bouts, not the ideal Stradivari form, either. And yet..."

"Whose work may we be seeing?"

"Comes to mind. Hungarian luthier Nemessànyi, who had a predilection for del Gesú models. Mid-1800s he copied some so perfectly his
unlabeled instruments circulated as genuine del Gesùs and other famous
Italian makers. Even their playability compares favorably. And yet..."

"Just so."

"Well then, another word must be used, *craftsmanship*. Notice un-
steady seating of perfling in its channel? So unlike Stradivari." Florien lifts
the violin's neck to examine the subtleties. "And fluting of the scroll, no
prick marks, such a fancifully thrown scroll at that. Look at the eye of the
scroll, a heavy tail and a wide last turn, and yet, and yet, a woman's hand
revealed in delicate tool work, and yes, extra flourish."

"Must we remove lid as you told Professor?"

"*Non*. My Morel tool will adjust a sound post without such duress
to poor instrument. Never doubt, I *will* open her as I told the Professor—
if I must. To satisfy my curiosity."

Augustin looks at his watch. "Sometimes is mere guessing game."

"Stay and assist! We may yet discover a label tucked away. And
we'll receive our enlightenment together. This lovely Morel will do double
duty by allowing us deeper access with mirror and perhaps then sight of
elusive maker's name. Watch, Augustin!"

Florien takes up the flat tool, shaped like an elongated S. One end
is sharp and the other flat with a center indent. After loosening two violin
strings Augustin shines the light into one F-hole while Florien, beads of
sweat gathering on his brow, inserts the Morel, flat end first. "Now I must
nudge, nudge, nudge skinny round post into place. There, there, just so,
just so." Florien withdraws the tool and lets out a breath.

After tightening the two strings Augustin draws a bow. G, D, A, E.
Rich sweetness of tone expands throughout the room, stirring the air—the
dissemination continues to hover like mist.

In response to the violin's extraordinary voice, two luthiers in amazement, heads shaking, eyes brightening. Within the workroom violins on shelves and those hanging from rafters vibrate together, setting up a steady hum. The hum continues; Augustin cannot help himself. Positioning the instrument under his chin he performs an original cadenza; it permeates the space with wrenching beauty. This procession of notes infuses the room with the warmth of Italian sunshine and the refreshment of fountains.

Augustin reluctantly places the repaired violin on the tabletop. "Her tone! G string has such human voice; E string has extraordinary purity. Did you hear? She promises wealth of power. I found no sharp corners. Whatever is this singular creation?"

"Our answer, come now, Augustin!" Florien uses the Morel to insert a mirror as Augustin again holds the light.

"Blocks seem solid," Florien states quietly. "Ah, label comes in sight...placed above the bridge. How curious. Hold the light steady."

Florien chokes. His tenor voice becomes a soprano whisper as he reads the label aloud. "'*Katarina Guarneria, fecit Cremona, anno 1749.*' I see also the cross and the customary HIS found on authentic del Gesù labels! In addition, a number, 253-1. Strange! Can we believe it? Never have I seen such a label."

"Katarina Guarneria, Del Gesú's wife?"

"Del Gesú's wife!" Both luthiers are aware of Katarina Rota, del Gesú's Viennese wife who assisted him and finished some of his work. Nevertheless, her name does not appear on any known instrument.

"*Mon ami*, this dated signature would mean she's working solo in Cremona five years after her husband's death. And signing this *one* instrument as her original work?" Augustin claps his hands.

"She's used a very familiar tone wood for the back; you can't argue with grain. I'd wager my reputation on it; this is the same tone wood as one or two Stradivari on record. *Mais, mon ami,*" Florien says as his eyes widen further, "this violin is built on the Guarneri form of her husband's later years."

Florien climbs a ladder, searches the top shelf of a bookcase, and successfully retrieves a leather-bound volume. "Found it. Here, just here we read that a certain wood was very special to both luthiers, Stradivari and Guarneri del Gesú. They both purchased it early on from Florentine merchants. Both men had a habit of holding this wood back, saving it for special violins or patrons." Florien hops to the floor. He studies the table of contents looking for proof, then flips through pages of photos. "My dear Augustin! Stranger yet! Look first at Katarina's violin. Now at photo." Florien pushes the book under Augustin's nose. "Very same tiger stripe. You see? Maple of Katarina's back is exact match with this one in photo, the one called Red Mendelssohn Stradivari, of 1720! You agree?"

Augustin paces the room, touching one stringed instrument after another, his narrow face a twist of confusion and delight. "*Alors,* I must agree. Although, Florien," Augustin entreats his friend, "all conundrums must be scrutinized. Beyond the coincidence of the wood, please explain mystery. How is it? Katarina perfectly finishing this particular violin with the incarnation of Antonio Stradivari's proprietary, mysterious, red varnish, so stunningly ruby-colored?"

"What to say?" Florien adjusts his cap. "By the 1720s we begin to see Stradivari using not only golden varnish but also red varnish, like this curious specimen displays. And why, my dear Augustin? Think of the red coats of the British Army. Stradivari at the height of his fame probably chose red to suit the tastes of his aristocratic patrons." Florien removes his leather cap. Scratches his head. "Although how could Katarina possibly have done it? Recreated, or discovered the recipe?"

"*Alors.* The varnish the old man achieved remains a secret."

Florien's face flushes at the magnitude of this revelation.

Augustin slides to the floor where he remains seated, head in his hands. All talk ceases as the violin makers ponder their discovery. In contrast to the men's silence the workroom buzzes like a beehive as the roomful of stringed instruments hum in chorus.

Florien Roux closes the heavy volume. He paces the room, repositions the flowing drapes, examines a bottle of amber liquid, puts his Morel tool back in the drawer. And then he stops, stationary as a stalagmite, although his mind somersaults with excitement.

Augustin leaps to his feet, full of pep. "Even Rembert Wurlitzer's experts would be outwitted here. Can you imagine, if only *one* of these exists? Superlative qualities of *both* world-renown masters demonstrated in *one* instrument? *One* of a kind? In the entire world?"

Florien Roux speaks quietly; someone, anyone, might be listening. "If authenticated, do you realize? This, this *précieux* could attract a serious collector. Or two!"

Augustin hugs himself, his narrow face aglow.

Florien speaks slowly, quietly. "And only now I realize, I have also seen the Red Mendelssohn, this one's sister violin, with my own eyes."

[16]

{DOUGLAS| THE TIME of danger has come upon us| Are you listening| Men have discovered my secret| See| 253-1 is unique in the expanse of eternity| Now I must tell you the story of my making| A thief will likely come for Me| You alone can protect our future together| |

The violin's urgency creates a frisson of excitement for Douglas, never mind she communicates to Elizabethtown from New York City.

Always before the communication from 253-1 had an observable syntax, like short poetic lines. Today her tale issues in a broad sweep, a sweet-and-sour way, mix-and-matching episodes that could make the joyous miserable and the sad hopeful. Douglas understands and begins visualizing his beloved instrument's history.

{I began my life in the forest of Croatia with sensation all around| My kind grew straight and tall for The Duration of Cold| Oh dread to say| it was after this| humankind attacked us with axes and saws| |

{My being-ness was among the fortunate to be felled in a dormant month when the sap had dropped| Rocked to drowsiness upon the Adriatic Sea not yet in fear of water| See| Those who dreamed of gold and silver and war| offered this length of grain for sale to the Venetian galley| who declared it too curly for oars| Prone to breakage when encountering resistance repeatedly as oars must| Bumped along by cart then| Padua to Vicenza to Verona to Brescia to Cremona| *il tronco*| this log to be sold to the *liutai*| luthiers| makers of *violini* eager for the tall specimens of maple such as my being-ness| |

"What happened to you then?"

{The time was called 1719| Two rivals and yet friends with ateliers side by side in the same small-town| socializing in the same piazza| worshipping in the same church| listening to the same bells each morning| eating in the same café| drinking in the same tavern each evening| haggled over my being-ness| one slab of lumber| |

Douglas visualizes the sleepy Italian town of Cremona. Across the street from the Church of St. Domenico he sees two ateliers side by side, those of Stradivari and Guarneri. Here, these two violin makers argue.

{It was my first maker's wife who stopped the war| shaming the men and forcing them to halve the coveted block| One half for the older who had been teacher of the younger man| One half for my young maker who had by then proven himself| Cut into rounds on the quarter for strength| Me became We| as twin sisters| Two chunks of tone wood||

{The older man had long boasted his violins sang with the most Purity| The younger man in response claimed his violins carried Voice beyond mere Beauty| The two men made a wager in public| The challenge was formalized while urged on by fellow drinkers| Which violin would be most acclaimed if both violins were formed from the exact same tone wood||

{The tiger stripe maple| Myself| which had been split into two selves| was agreed upon for both of our backs| For a belly each maker would choose spruce he privately deemed of favorable density| Unwittingly each luthier chose for the belly| spruce with dark striations in the grain| Oh to see it| Both of us would bear visual resemblance front and back| Even so other distinctions there would be| Shape| Size| F-hole characteristics| Carvings| Most distinctively Varnish| for it was said none could upstage the Stradivari varnish||

{Truth is| artistic variations should create difference in voice| Albeit the question circled round| Was usage of the same maple itself enough to equalize *violini*| despite each luthier's expertise||

Douglas interrupts. "Hey, you're explaining how Stoya's Performance Violin is your Red Sister. Why you look so much alike."

{So it is| it is| and there is more to tell| My maker soaked my being-ness with salts of copper and iron and chromium saving me from worms and fungus| Then into the dark for uncountable seasons| In the dark my Consciousness began| Oh I experienced synchronous reverberation with Cathedral bells| Soon also in the workshop I translated the humans' sound waves as language| Tales men spoke explained my beginning| and the beginning of my Sister| as well||

{The older builder Antonio who called himself Stradivari began at once though in no rush| That luthier finished my Sister in the time they called 1720| he who created over one thousand instruments| not by himself I might add| he had his sons as helpers| Systematic and patient he in his leather cap and apron reaching perfection of form with his entry to the competition| Last for the glory of it he applied to her his secret much coveted red varnish| |

"I'm confused. You and the Performance Violin look like you have the same varnish! Michael Rabin even thought so. And that lucky kid should know. How could that happen if the varnish was a secret?"

{Patience have| 253-1 will explain| Now my maker| Giuseppe| who called himself Guarnerius del Gesú set this chosen wood aside| Other work did he perform instead| His wife Katarina became known to me as I lay gathering Consciousness| Whisper and sing and speak to my being-ness she did| in preparation for her husband's ultimate expression of artistry| a gift to the world| |

{After much time of waiting this man chose his mold and *questo violino* slowly accepted her form| Myself became a beautiful two-piece back with flames meeting the center| On my inner part he wrote the number 253| See| He numbered his creations of which there were no more than 252 as is told| Most of Giuseppe's *violini* were numbered and labeled and were sent into the world before this one was whole| |

{Then using his favored striped spruce he planed a belly| Bass bar he shaped| Soul post and corner blocks he cut| glued and formed strips| connecting the back with the belly| Shaped finger board and tailpiece of ebony| Parts and pieces lay in wait| All this work done in a fever pitch| no time to linger or fret over form| seeking instead perfection of sound| |

{Then Guarnerius del Gesú rested| drank at the Tavern boasting of his creation| Katarina urged him to finish| she used words to goad him|

Arrogance| Pride| Fear| These words increased his pulsations assuredly|
Oh but see| 253 began to carry the man's fierce energy in her cells| ac-
quiring the Passion of her first maker| |

{In the time 1737 the force of Antonio Stradivari ceased| and his
red violin| my Red Sister| was sold into the world| Men did not track
her travels| her history has not been written either| |

{The time of 1744 Giuseppe's force also ceased| so Giuseppe never
did finish *questo violino*| 253 had not wept until then| Alas| once
flooded with Katarina's grief| *questo violino* has since sorrowed many
times over for what is lost| |

"I heard you weeping at the cemetery."

{Tis so| Now for the Joy of it this *violino* was not to be abandoned
in pieces| Giuseppe's unhappy wife had all along despised the wager|
Was it not wrong to breed rivalry over talent and creation| Myself
though in pieces was already vibrating with her goodness| More so as my
neck and the volute of my scroll were carved by her hands| gentle hands|
each touch from her a caress| She was the one who carved my perflings
and placed them in my channels both for decoration and stability| |

{It is said a child is either formed or deformed by the experience of
its first five years| Perhaps Katarina| Del Gesù's wife| was thusly wise|
caring for *questo violino* like an infant| Inside the atelier she sang lullabies
passed from one generation to the next| In a bag over her shoulder she
carried 253 into the church there lighting a votive and entering a pew|
She stayed for the organist's time of preparation| Remained the duration
of the choir's practice hearing the boys' voices so soprano| the purity of
which one might pray to mimic| This attendance she continued| shep-
herding the sensations of *questo violino*| Time upon time these eager cells
drank in the tremor of heavenly sound| Infused with sublimity| 253's
cells were saturated then with pulsations| Adoration| Reverence|

Sacrifice| Benediction| How could it be otherwise| A *violino* so embalmed quivers with a powerful magnetism adverse to these| Jealousy| Rage| Hate| the polar opposites| |

"And that's why you shut up when Willi tried to show off."

{You do understand| 253-1| your beloved| became an instrument whose vibrations are for all time blocked by negative energies| An instrument obedient only to positive expression| |

{To continue with my tale| it was Katarina who primed Me| then hung Me by my neck before attempting to varnish my surface| Varnish being so important for beauty and she so ignorant| |

"Hung by your neck? That's awful!"

{Have no alarm| There is no pain for my kind when hung| Only the passage of air and moisture and temperature affect us| Oh do not mention fire| |

{Katarina fretted while pacing| Her pacing sent a flurrying into my cells| See| She worried| Varnish was needed| Varnish could elevate or ruin this instrument| Of varnish Katarina knew only these two things| First| Old Italian instruments glowed in golden hues of brown| Second| Stradivari experimented with a dye used centuries prior| root of the madder plant| |

{Yet unknown| With what did Stradivari mix this madder to achieve a rich rose-red color for his finest instruments| |

{Twas the Vespers of Pentecost when Katarina worshipped beside Paolo| son and heir of Antonio Stradivari| Young Stradivari| in his hand a Bible bearing records of his ancestry| The light from the clerestory so illuminating| the incense so pungent| Paolo so passionate in his praying| a sheet of parchment slipped from his Bible to the kneeler| |

{There on her knees Katarina's unspoken prayer was answered| *Allora*| she read all| Antonio Stradivari's recipe for the mysterious| most secret varnish||

Douglas whistles. "And then?"

{Del Gesú's widow feigned prayer| mumbling each ingredient and its measure| until the entirety burnt into her brain| When Paolo gulped| distraught at the sight of the precious parchment so exposed| Katarina did not react| She pretended his retrieval was simply the young man's need to stretch||

{Of this she whispered to Me as she made her preparations| Katarina knew the color's secret| Dragon's blood| tears of Dragon's blood mixed with Rose Madder||

"Dragon's blood?" Douglas is aghast. "What is that?"

{The origin of it is told| See a fight to the death ensued between a dragon and an elephant| The elephant wrapped his trunk around the dragon| The dragon entangled himself with the elephant| They fell and crushed each other to the death| A lute maker of long ago captured and mixed their blood in 77 vials| Precious and most rare it is||

"That's awfully weird in a sort of nice way."

{The tale means to say| 253-1| carries the energies of three makers from Cremona in times called 1700s||

{From the first maker Del Gesù this violin vibrates with wild abandon| blessed with vigor and powerful expression| from *pianissimo* to *fortissimo*| without loss of quality| Brought forth| mind you| only in the hands of a sensitive artist||

{From the second maker this violin carries the innate pulse of tender caress| She the one called Katarina Rota Guarneri| Proudly she created a label combining her name with her husband's seal| Alongside Giuseppe's 253| she stamped a dash and the number one| Katarina considered this *violino* her first creation| My name is correctly 253-1 for this very reason| |

{From the third maker| the late Antonio Stradivari| *questo violino* radiates with the color of field poppies| endowment of this amazing maker's perfection| |

"The creation of three famous makers! You never told me before. Why not?"

{For my safety first| Children spill secrets| Also to spare you worry until you were wiser| Things of rarity inspire lust in men| Soon actions of greed will bring us sorrow| Danger lies ahead| Please be wary| You must save Me| So it is| |

An electric tingle passes up and down Douglas' spine. He tries to understand the depth of this revelation. "Is someone planning to steal you, Magic Muriel?"

[17]

LONG HOURS SPENT at the Stoya Conservatory pass effortlessly for Douglas, despite the flare of Sister Elder's nostrils at the mention of his daily destination.

At the outset, as directed by his father, Willi shared the Wilhelm Hermann Hammig with no attempt to hide his ill will, or perhaps his shame. Two long weeks had passed like this before the 253-1 was returned from Florien Roux.

Look. Here's the mistreated fiddle wholly intact. Stoya's explanation of her woes: "Oh, the bridge had tipped forward, lost the balance of these two little feet and so the strings had fallen slack."

And straightaway, as if the switcheroo had never happened, as if the act of temper upon the defenseless 253-1 had never happened, *the new Wilhelm Stoya* appears. He's jovial; agreeable to begin again on the Performance Violin; intent on the perfection of phrasing and dynamics.

As the two violinists practice within earshot of one another, this once razzing rival is Douglas' lost friend returned—the child sharing giggles while spying on Galamian's students; the peer supplying formulas for geometry problems, the *brother* with an icepick and blood to share. Douglas relaxes. Perhaps the return to Stoya hasn't been a mistake after all.

What of Violette at the outset? *Aloof.* That's the word he'd use to describe Violette after the New Year's partner exchange. "I don't know how to accompany you. Oh-No does," Violette had announced curtly. He'd tried to explain her complaint away. "It wasn't always easy with Ophelia," he'd said. Ophelia preferring to be precise, counting diligently under her breath. He, drawn to freedoms with the pace, luxuries of execution. This meant that Ophelia's fingers flew ahead, and she began a measure before Douglas caught up. Or vice versa. Professor Stoya would bang his baton on the music stand. "Count please, begin again."

"Remember all that?" Douglas had asked. "You and I had no such problems when we were younger. I don't have answers either. Anyway, we're both musicians and we'll keep together."

Just as Willi was changed mid-January with the return of the repaired violin, Violette was changing as well. She acquired an uncanny sense of Douglas' interpretations. She adjusted to the flow and slight variation of tempo as if she anticipated his every inclination to rush a credenza or slow an andante. At least in the music there was no discord; instead, a camaraderie in giving themselves up to the music. Otherwise, Violette remained—and remains—aloof.

In weeks to come Mrs. Piano Teacher takes over as accompanist for the boys, leaving Violette and Ophelia time to practice on their own. Douglas decides he'll just ignore a social life altogether. Competitions require full-time attention.

Days of tension bring an emptiness accompanied by an increased appetite for LuLu's sauerbraten, and Wing's pork fried rice piled high with sweet and sour anything. He suffers another emptiness, too. Douglas craves Ciazzo's honest critique; he longs for advice from his experienced peer, Michael Rabin.

Come February the 253-1 solicits something more. For years Douglas' goal has been mastering the techniques taught by Ciazzo. Now he must play only as *she* directs.

{*Questo violino* is fulfillment of a love song| source of unique power| And to speak of power| when you apply your energies wholly to Me| dear one| you release Beneficence||

"What is beneficence?"

{Kindness| Brotherhood| Healing| Joy| Love| Forms of goodness| So it is||

Perhaps all along I was meant to do something worthwhile, the once mute, the foundling, the bullied Doogie-doo, the determined Douglas Tryzyna, decides.

As Douglas puts Gypsy's desires into music, he increasingly sees results. It's just possible he'll become the virtuoso everyone expects. And then, finally, Stoya will return what rightfully belongs to him. Won't he? There was such a promise made to a six-year-old. Wasn't there?

[18]

"YOU'LL START STAYING the night, Douglas," Mrs. Piano Teacher insists as late February of 1953 heaps snow on grand mountains and small towns in the Adirondacks. Douglas keeps a suitcase in Willi's room for such evenings. It isn't all practice. Stoya plays new recordings after the teens' homework is finished: Yehudi Menuhin with a Mendelssohn Concerto, Heifetz with Chausson's "Poeme," Jacque Genty with Franck's Sonata.

Unless of course the Professor has become frustrated with his students and drills them unmercifully well past bedtime. Then it might be a night of flopping into the bunk, wounded by brutal disparagement.

Sometimes after lights-out Douglas finds further aggravation—hearing the Gypsy's labor upstairs. Accusingly he asks her, "How can it be that a cruel Professor is able to play you beautifully?"

{See| The answer of the matter| when Stoya plays with compassion to comfort Frieda| 253-1 must respond to his softened heart| So it is| It is| | |

Not everyone who cares for Douglas is pleased with this overnight arrangement. Not Wing. "Wisdom say, *Man who camp with enemy wake with knife in back.*" Not Sister Elder either; she has her say. "I agree with Wing. The Stoya family has flaunted true colors more than once. Forget trust! Believe me when I say, I refuse to forgive a single one of them. I fear for our impulsive, kindhearted Douglas."

Astrid prefers to keep a positive outlook. "Let's stop thinking of the Stoyas as enemies. I see benefactors, tutors who can create opportunity."

* * *

THE PROFESSOR HAS limited the boys' exposure. The next months will demand a lot of them. Memories of Peter's own trials in Berlin toughen his approach to the imminent competitions. The world of music can be cruel to aspiring players. Crueler than he cares to disclose to this son. Strategy and armor are required. Not to mention courage. Bottom line, a player can't dream to compete without a worthy instrument.

Peter takes the Performance Violin from her case and lovingly plays several arpeggios. "Such a sweet voice you have. I thank your maker, truly." Ah, her *maker*. With a rush of anxiety, the Professor sets the violin aside to rummage for tools. He examines her interior by placing a tiny flashlight through the treble F-hole and a dental mirror in the bass. He whispers as he reads. "Jean Baptiste Vuillaume, a Paris 3 rue Demours – Terme 1844." His heart slows as he recognizes the circular stamp of initials and cross, and the ink signature. It's an authentic label (gleaned who knows how) with lead typesetting on laid paper sized with alum, as used by Vuillame, though it's prone to curling and browning. Florien Roux's skillful application of this fragile label covers the Stradivari label and doesn't reveal futzing. *I paid a ridiculous price for this deftness. Relax.*

And yet, Stoya second-guesses himself. Should I have left the original label as it was? Too late now. My 1720 Red Mendelssohn wears an 1844 Vuillame label. I'm in too deep to change my mind.

* * *

OVER THE YEARS Stoya's eyes have begun to bulge, his jowl has begun to droop; when he wears his monocle the image becomes surreal. Discounting the Professor's semi-reptilian appearance and his cold-blooded manner Douglas feels increasing respect for the man.

Month after month the boys leapfrog in a succession of attacks, working from weakness to mastery in skill after skill. Day after day Stoya drills them with Frieda at the piano. "Willi, begin today with the First Movement of the Bartok Concerto." Willi fumes; that's the hardest piece of his repertoire. He's planned to begin with the Bach Partita. Stoya coaches. "Hardest-schmardest, it doesn't matter! You boys should be prepared to start with the piece you least expect the judges to request. Good to know which you prefer to start with. Just in case you have a choice."

"Douglas, play your cadenza from Respighi Sonata." Douglas falters. He asks Frieda to play the introduction first. "Boys, you should also be prepared to start at *any* measure in the score!"

Early March, Stoya conducts mock auditions with the boys in less-than-ideal environments. He'll enlighten them on acoustics. He'll coach them on adaptability. They try the Stoya kitchen with pots a-steam and oven a-broil, the dining room of the Windsor Hotel noisy with customers, the shaded porch of Ledgewood Lodge, and the cramped Postal Office in Denton's Grocery. The acoustics vary dramatically from location to location. The violins react to the temperature as do the boys' fingers, feeling like sausages or popsicles.

Stoya's final coaching is oh, so simple. All the preparation, all the stress, can bring on fatigue. "Get your sleep."

Professor Stoya tells Frieda, "I see real promise in my two." He tells Willi, "The world always has need for an excellent player, large stage or small. Treat opportunity, each opportunity with respect." Perhaps he feels a withhold when it comes to encouraging Douglas these days; anyone can see the boy soars without need of praise. Stoya prefers not to ponder his stingy inclination.

[19]

PROFESSOR STOYA WALKS back from Denton's store with the mail. Most enticing, a package from his German ally, composer, conductor, instructor, Paul Hindemith. How long since their last communication? Stoya inhales spring air while the sight of snow on surrounding mountaintops beckons memories. If it hadn't been for Hindemith's sponsorship he might not have been allowed in this country. If it hadn't been for Gertrud Hindemith's encouragement Frieda might never have agreed to make their home in America, and LuLu might have been left behind to suffer an uncertain fate.

Hindemith writes of his current accomplishment, his newly composed Sonata for Four Horns. The package includes a book, extracts from his lectures at Harvard, *The World of a Composer*. However, Paul relates personal news that is less expected: he and Gertrud will relocate to Switzerland next year.

Stoya experiences this as a loss. He's missing out on Act Three. The velvet curtain has closed. The houselights have come up too soon.

Hindemith's allegiance to the Nazis has been questioned over the years, precariously balanced as he was, seeking to honor both artistic integrity and marriage to a Jewess. *He's been judged for making difficult choices*, Stoya decides.

Stoya prefers to gloss over a questionable choice he made while countering the Nazi regime. The fruit of his act has not been made manifest. Yet. *Let it lie, let it lie.*

A park bench extends an invitation. There he sits, studying trees whose one side sparkles while the other displays dull tones of dead ends and disappointments. He's been a seeker. Like Paul he's been motivated to perform. To teach. Twelve years in the USA have flown. He'll credit himself; he's accomplished much—without much acclaim. *Please let me bring forward a star, a sweetheart of the stage,* he's begged the universe. Oh, how he's agonized over Willi; what would it take to spark his son's soul, he's repeatedly asked, and well, well, well, he's finally witnessing a competitive bonfire, dare he speak it aloud? Stoya's heart almost bursts with pride. Or is it indigestion today? *No time to worry about one's health. Frailty comes. Choose not to hasten it with an invitation.*

Stoya picks up the thread of his musing. Willi yoked with A.J. proved to be a mistake. Two braying jackasses at a carnival for that matter. His first hunch had been dead on, Willi alongside Douglas; why, the two are like thoroughbreds, neck and neck. Two Competitions have passed successfully. Both boys are ranked in the 98th percentile. To be accurate, Douglas ranked the 99th percentile (however, he had the advantage of a morning appearance each time; the judges were fresh). Willi, not so lucky (late afternoon appointments, cranky judges).

To win the NOA Competition is to win the veritable gold medal. Publicity. Prestige. Performance. Plus, a nice sum of prize money. All of this for one student only. What father wouldn't want the Winner to be his offspring, product of his tutelage? Wouldn't want to have the Runner-up to his credit as well? The next crucial months advance. May, the Stoya Conservatory Recital. June, the day of reckoning. August, the enviable soloist performance with the Junior Philharmonic.

[20]

DOUGLAS STUDIES THE newspaper photo of Michael Rabin with Zino Francescatti. The pair had broadcast Bach Concerto for Two Violins on the *Bell Telephone Hour*. Mike may be sixteen, and he still looks like a kid, even dressed up in a suit. Douglas can't imagine such a life. The life of a professional violinist. He folds the clipping and places it under the Muriel cigar box where the brass bell on a red cord, the hard-won aggies, the unused gift of rosin, typed notes, and the cigar band accrue the value of minted nostalgia.

The life of a professional violinist. It seems that's where he's headed under Stoya's direction. Starting with The Recital. Oh, it's to be quite the event: A rented hall in Westport, formal invitations mailed in creamy envelopes, a notice to be placed in the newspaper. *Your introduction to talent developed by the Stoya Conservatory.* Translation: It's time to sign up *Your Musical Genius.*

Finally, the day and hour so keenly anticipated: The Recital. Douglas waits, violin resting on his knee, bow loosely held. Suit, tie, dress shirt, new linen vest—Astrid's auspicious Loong on the lining—polished shoes, an effort to comb his hair, three cowlicks out of control especially the one at his forehead, which Astrid calls his widow's peak. Nightmarish jitters of his first rating seem prehistoric. His centering routine is effective, especially with the 253-1 pressed to his breast, a dream come true. Ciazzo would be proud of him; he's wistfully visualizing the revered musician in the audience today.

How impressed the audience is by the Stoya Conservatory's presentation of talent. Willi proves to be an engaging player. Stoya whispers to Frieda. "Did you see the audience, swaying to the rhythm, exchanging smiles?" The father opens the black leather, gilt-edged pocket notebook with its red ribbon marking a page titled 10th May 1953, *Wilhelm in Conservatory Recital.* He unhooks the lanyard from the metal ball on the miniature fountain pen's cap. And writes.

Mrs. Piano Teacher's gabardine suit matches her flushed cheeks. She dabs her eyes with a lace-edged hankie, then fishes in her pocketbook, finding the compact and discreetly pats powder on her face.

And after A.J.'s finale, Stoya beams. "They're demanding, I mean *demanding*, an encore from our first graduate!"

Neither Professor nor Mrs. Piano Teacher speaks of Douglas' performance on the rogue fiddle. How to describe immersion in shimmery sound? How to describe losing consciousness to all except bliss? It defies explanation or description. Let's pretend Mrs. Piano Teacher had not wept aloud, joyful, glowing, and envious. The once-mute foundling, newly mysterious, using a violin also newly mysterious, riveted not only a fresh audience but these two seasoned instructors.

Sister Elder and Auntie Evangeline huddle, sharing Douglas' accomplishment. Douglas exhibits artistic maturity. His brilliance is undeniable. He simply outshines Willi and A.J. Members of the audience, overwhelmed by the unknown's radiance, will later agree on this, two by two, three by three, careful to keep these murmurings beyond earshot of Willi's euphoric parents.

The musicians have taken a group bow. A.J. heads off to mingle with the audience. Willi and Douglas shake hands congratulating each other. Within minutes a tall, wiry gentleman steps on stage wearing what appears to be a costume, a plaid waistcoat with an ivory cravat. He's followed by a strange sort whose eyes bulge toad-like from his narrow face.

"Which of you is young Stoya?" the costumed one asks; his appearance suggests a paternal giant and a maternal elf. Willi identifies himself and in return is given words of flowery praise.

The owner of the bulging eyes sidles up to the other performer, the darker, shorter of the two, the boy with the freckled face and the hair with wild cowlicks.

"Excuse, then, my *audace* when I say your mother would be having every reason to be proud. Tell me, if you please, about your violin."

The gentleman in the waistcoat joins them. "*Brillante*, the career ahead of you. If I may be of assistance in future, my card." The man bends at the waist with a flourish of his right hand. He proffers the card.

Hiding his amusement with the dramatics, Douglas takes the card; he reads it. "A luthier?"

"Many violins on path of destiny cross my own. Restoration, evaluation, appraisal. Simply put, I repair and identify the splendid old ladies." The man pauses. He has a strange way of adjusting his neck when he is silent. Seeing Douglas has nothing to say, he proceeds. "In your career you will have need of such services, may I say humbly. When next you travel to the City, we welcome you a visit." The luthier adjusts his long neck again while his searching eyes convey benign intentions. "Pray tell me, what instrument is this you play?" The stranger reaches out eagerly for the 253-1 as if it were familiar to him.

* * *

THAT SAME EVENING Wing broils venison steaks to serve with potato salad, honoring Auntie Evangeline, who abhors Asian food. For dessert he surprises the group with pecan pie, using Auntie's recipe.

Conversation is light and easy until the questioning begins. "Who was the foreigner talking with you on the stage?" Auntie Evangeline asks.

"Was he interested in *you*? Or the *violin*?" Sister Elder inquires. The accented questions showcase her suspicions.

Douglas wants to reach out, to pat her hand, to comfort her—mind you, he's never attempted such a thing with his Guardian. Or with any adult for that matter. Words might help. "Don't worry, Hester, he's a nice guy."

"Who isn't? Now you've shown merit."

Auntie Evangeline admonishes her sister. "There, there."

* * *

THAT SAME EVENTFUL evening Professor Stoya treats his family to dinner at the Winslow Hotel. He holds his wife's hand across the table. She's lovely with curls framing her face. No headaches recently. Willi and Siggi behave like gentlemen, handling their silverware just so, using their starched napkins on recently kissed lips, recounting proud observations of the Stoya Conservatory Recital. Stoya asks himself, *How could a man be happier?*

[21]

"LAST FRIDAY WILLI went to the City with Professor Stoya," Ophelia whispers to Douglas and Violette. "And you want to know why?"

"Why indeed?" Violette asks casually before she returns to sipping her root beer float.

"He went to be fitted for a new suit. He told me so yesterday." Ophelia gloats.

"So what?" Douglas asks. He stirs the last lump of strawberry ice cream into the soda bubbles and takes a swallow of the delicious treat.

Ophelia looks like an oracle, a blue kerchief turban-like around her head. She takes another French fry and chews it slowly. *"So what?* Want to know why they didn't invite you, Douglas?" She bats her eyelashes as she prepares to divulge the juicy part. "They checked out the Concert Hall where the NOA Competition will be. Giving Willi the advantage? Yeah, Doogie-doo." She wipes catsup from her lips and smiles, her teeth as uniform as bottles of cream.

Douglas remembers Ciazzo's training. "Become acquainted with the acoustics of a concert hall beforehand." *What's stopping me from checking it out, too?*

* * *

HE'S ROBBED THE cigar box of his hard-earned savings. In his pocket, Florien Roux's business card. He's traveled by train to Penn Station. All by himself. Walking along the street he unfolds the NYC map Wing retrieved from a shoebox of postcards. Sweat trickles down the side of his face as he locates the red circled area. *Gee whiz, it's way hotter, way muggier, way nosier here in the City than at home. No wonder tourists come to Elizabethtown for the summer.*

He easily reaches Florien Roux's shop by taking 7th Avenue South until he reaches Bleeker Street. He hardly expected to find such an unwelcoming door. Nine heavy-duty locks, all dangling unlocked, stare at him. Douglas waits impatiently after ringing the buzzer.

Momentarily Florien peeps out of the peek-a-boo window. The door opens. "To what occasion do I owe this pleasure, *monsieur?*"

Florien directs him through the minimal office straightaway to the secreted chamber. The smell of varnish is strong, although tall windows are open, covered by gauze curtains allowing air flow and light. Douglas gasps. He has never seen so many stringed instruments in his life.

Gleaming brown, orange, or gold, they occupy cubbies. They circle the ceiling strung by rope.

"Sit, sit," Florien gestures to a stool. "You don't bring your violin?"

"Not mine to bring. Anyway, am I right, you fixed it for Professor Stoya this winter? Fixed the bridge?"

"*Alors*, bit more than the bridge I should like to report. And I surmise you are not the fellow to maltreat her?"

"Gosh, no!" Douglas frowns. He probably shouldn't mention Willi. "Hey, do you know what kind of a violin she is?"

"For some luthiers it is not so much the actuality of her maker; it's more what he can sell her as. For others is opposite. Not what seller claim she is, but what she is."

"Well, could you see her label?"

"Labels can be altered, my dear boy."

"What I'm wondering is if you have ever seen a violin anything like the 253-1." Douglas realizes he's sounding impatient.

Florien gasps. "What name you just call her?"

Douglas gulps. He slipped and he can't take it back.

"And her name as you say, this number, you know how?" Florien's eyes glint with curiosity.

Douglas shrugs his shoulders, wishing he had been smart enough to keep his mouth closed.

Florien for once is speechless. He, only with difficulty, spied the label and the number 253-1. Impossible for the unaided eye of a boy to see.

Douglas prays Florien won't question him further. What a stupe he is! He knows better than to reveal his sensitivity to the violin's language. Changing the subject, he tells Florien he's trying out for the NOA soloist position. He'll be playing that repaired violin, whatever its label reads. He adds, "My reason for being in town is to visit the Concert Hall."

Upon hearing this Florien smiles. "Was heading there just today. Perhaps you can give a favor." The luthier takes a golden violin from a cubby. Hands it to Douglas. "Karl Otto Zimmer, Budapest, 1910. Shrinkage required a tiny gusset to each side. Is dry now, ready to be played."

Douglas examines the ribs and with difficulty locates the almost invisible repair. Florien must be a wizard at this work. He wonders how one of Rembert Wurlitzer's luthiers would compare. If Michael were around, they could have this conversation.

"Can you play an *Ut* for me?" Florien asks, handing Douglas a bow.

Douglas frowns quizzically. "What?"

"French term for the note you call *C*."

Douglas happily takes the bow and lets the note ring out bright, clear, and sustained.

"*Agréable.* You play this violin in hall we together find? And I listen to her. She must be heard soon."

* * *

BY THE TIME Douglas reaches Penn Station that evening he's floating. Being with this offbeat man has opened the bellows of his worldview a bit wider. Choices brighten the horizon of his tomorrow. The man has introduced him to street food, especially the pleasure of stuffed Salvadoran corn tortillas. Taught him to ride the subway. Given him insight into becoming a luthier, an alluring idea. "We luthiers have our specialties," Florien explained. "Some are primarily builders. Some choose instead to repair, acquire, appraise, even sell."

Most importantly, Florien has coached him on playing to be heard throughout the Hall where he'll be tested; now he's confident of carrying even a whispering pianissimo to the balcony.

As the train chugs northward Douglas pulls out Florien's cards (two of them). He chuckles while remembering their last conversation.

"Someday in career you need your own violin. You likely need to find benefactor. When this is, you find me for assist." Florien had looked so serious, those strange ears blazing red, backlit by the sun.

"I have your card already, and now I know how to find you," Douglas Tryzyna had said with new sophistication.

Florien's parting comment, "Even so, take another. Just so you do not forget me. Or get hoodwinked."

[22]

BEHIND HIM MIST drops over gray-blue mountains revealing the draws. Just ahead shadows of trees crawl across the fields in prideful exaggeration of their height. The egg farm on its natural rolling terrace sleeps, although the rooster is wide awake. The bird's crowing travels from the farm to cross the Boquet River; the river here a narrow flow, though gathering force as it flows south, soon to cascade over a massive jumble of boulders.

Douglas runs, enjoying the expansive terrain. *Home, this is Home.* And then a question forms. Where will he be three years from now? So much depends on the NOA Competition tomorrow. He breathes deeply as he heads back home. Curiously the water tower looks like a bulbous gray judge on stilts.

After shaving Douglas lingers at the sink. Gazing into the mirror he turns this way and that examining his face. *Same bunch of freckles.* He wets his comb. *Same copper hair, with the same three stubborn cowlicks. Same color as Violette's.* He's grown a couple of inches since last summer. He doubts he needs Loong anymore. *Oh well, can't hurt anything. I'll wear the new vest and make Astrid happy.*

* * *

THE PROFESSOR HAD planned to escort the boys to the City. He's decided against. They can certainly navigate alone. He'll entrust the Performance Violin to Willi's care. Besides, the Stoya Recital caused a wonderful flurry of interest in the Conservatory. Peter reviews his agenda, memorizing the names of students and parents he and Frieda will orient. And impress. Hearing the cuckoo's announcement, he slaps the table with his schedule, uttering a loud "Ahem!"

Douglas sets the 253-1 aside; he's bubbling with anticipation. He can sense that Willi is jumpy—a-jitter and a-skitter like a fisherman's fly across water.

Stoya begins. "None of this is news to you." He strikes a reverential posture, hands clasped as if his opening phrase will be, "Dearly beloved...." He then thunders his message. "This is *The One* important competition!" (Siggi holds up one finger; he's behind his father facing Willi and Douglas, comically miming the message.) The Professor stares into the blinking eyes of his listeners. Soon his left hand sets to freeing itself from the right. The escaped fingers once again thrum along his pant leg. He begins again. "Your job, above all, communicate feeling! Most music evaluators love music." (Siggi rolls his eyes. He hugs himself as he rocks back and forth.) "Are you listening to me, Willi?" Willi is smiling, an inappropriate smile, unable to ignore his brother.

"Judges simply want to be moved by the music. This way even with a few errors you can make a connection. It isn't like a baseball-schmaseball game where one can simply count the number of runs. No!" (At this Siggi pretends to swing a bat, hardly able to contain his own snickering.) The Professor smooths the bristle-like ends of his mustache. His tone changes; he's consoling. "Music ratings are subjective, my men. They consider your creative interpretation, not just the minutia of correct notes. And remember this, William Stoya, Douglas Tryzyna." (Siggi thrusts forward both arms, his forefingers extending gun-like at the boys. *Bang!* he mouths.) "They aren't judging you personally. I expect two winners."

Willi turns away from his father, trying to control the laughter his brother solicited. LuLu appears to be smothering a chuckle as well. Frieda admonishes both sons with a stern look. When Frieda turns away, she and LuLu each make a wry face for the other's benefit.

The Professor casts himself adrift, wanders off to the salon perhaps to pick up a fiddle and think of his own competitive days, finding of course both violins are zipped into their traveling cases and have been placed at the front door. He returns with the comfort of the Wilhelm Hermann Hammig.

Frieda hands Willi folded dollar bills. "Should be enough money for soda pop, too. Even if you arrive early, no exploring the City today. Take a taxi directly to the event. Better to be there waiting than rushing.

"Can't be tardy-schmardy," Stoya says with intended levity.

"Can't be tardy-schmardy, boys," Siggi repeats. He cackles as he gallops the stairs two at a time, escaping possible punishment.

LuLu bestows upon each traveler a brown paper bag bulging with lunch and snacks. "You two are going to be the winners, I just know it!" she says. Willi squirms away from her extended arms. Douglas enjoys the hug; he receives so very few these days.

* * *

DOUGLAS WATCHES THE forested countryside slide by; the blue of mountains gives way to the green of rolling hills. Small towns appear randomly, announced by the ding and swing of wigwags. He keeps guard over the two violins in the overhead as passengers board. He can't help himself. The Gypsy's stories of thievery elbow their way into his brain. Willi reads a comic book.

* * *

THE GREAT CONCERT HALL. "We've arrived!" Glee is curiously fleeting. Such exuberance converts to the glue of slow motion. The boys' sense of balance is altered, like dizziness with cotton in the ears. They progress toward the Registration table ever so slowly. Each contestant eventually walks away wearing an identifying armband. Willi's armband reads S-12. Douglas slides on his T-1 wondering how many Ts there are. The field has been culled to include youth ages sixteen to twenty-one, the two dozen top-ranked violinists selected in the prequalifying competitions. More boys than girls. They've been instructed to wait for possible callbacks following the first round of auditions.

Seated in folding chairs along the hall, most contestants are practicing in a final frenzied review, aided by their music books. Neither of Stoya's students have need of this; they've come with all selections memorized. The din increases as more students arrive and join the nervous preoccupation. Willi jokes, "If Pa were here, he'd say, 'Such ungodly noise-schmoise.'" He winks. "Glad our grand Professor Stoya's not here. Hey, I'm gonna go find a seat, by myself."

"Good luck, Willi."

"Good luck to you too, Doogie-doo." Willi turns back with a postscript: "You'll need it!" He strides away, violin case in hand, comic book stuffed into the hip pocket of his crisp new seersucker suit. The snub might as well have been accompanied by an obscene gesture. Douglas lets it pass; he senses his rival's need to be brash in the current situation.

Instead, he lifts the 253-1 from the case and plays a few notes, satisfied to find she's still in tune.

{So begins our fulfillment| Follow my lead as *questo violino* follows yours| Feel the power granted us| |

The 253-1's communication flashes like northern lights; he knows what will happen. Like the knowingness just before Violette kissed him, unquestionably, really and truly, *kissed* him, that June day. His gut is free from all fear.

Douglas' sandwich and cookies are consumed by 11:00 a.m. Apple demolished by 12:30 p.m. He saves the Baby Ruth for the train ride home. Frequent trips to the water fountain require almost as many trips to the marble-lined lavatory. He and B-7, another freckle-faced fellow, agree to guard one another's instruments and to be alert for the other's number to be called. The order of appearance appears to be random. At 1:30 p.m., fourteen of the aspiring musicians wait to be called; they pace, they hum, they practice, anything to hoodwink self-sabotage.

At 2:20 p.m., Douglas hears the call. "S-12!"

"That's Willi!" *Has Willi heard his call?* Douglas stands, peers down the lineup of contestants and parents; a spring of benevolence surfaces as the lanky kid in the summer suit, gripping the Performance Violin like a cudgel, strides between the double doors and disappears. Sister Peace's advice comes back to Douglas. "Life is easier if we let bygones be by-gones." Maybe she'd be proud of him today. He's worked to let go of past hateful times with Willi. The hardest time to forgive was the last, that violent demonstration of frustration. He questions his integrity; what if his beloved instrument had been badly damaged? Well, for what it's worth, he and Willi have been almost truly blood brothers lately. Look, he's honestly hoping S-12 in there will wow the judges and make one hard-to-please father proud. Beg your pardon, is it okay to be aware that he and the 253-1 will take first place?

By 2:40 p.m. Willi returns to the hallway. He's grinning. He slaps Douglas on the shoulder. "Piece of cake."

4:15 p.m., the call. "T-1!" He's the last to audition. Douglas looks up. The judge signals as if to say, *Yes, yes you, hurry up.* He pats the breast pocket of the new black linen vest—would have wounded Astrid if he hadn't worn it—not admitting he finds reassurance with soothing Loong nestled close in all its embroidered finery. He hangs the violin case over his shoulder, and with both 253-1 and his gift bow in hand, he follows the short woman whose red hat with a wobbling polka dot feather causes him, for some unexplained reason, to giggle.

Just as Stoya had predicted he faces a circle of judges. Four men and the short, be-hatted woman. Amused by the polka dot feather's nodding, he hands this short judge his list of memorized selections. And then he makes a salaam like Wing taught him; formality seems called for after his giggle. He's energized by the continuing thrumming of Magic Muriel 253-1, the one lost by the magic-music-making man under the night sky when flame roared.

She's encouraging him. {Our time| our destiny| follow my lead| |

"Please sit." The judge wearing Coke-bottle glasses directs Douglas to the one empty chair. "And where are your music books?"

Somehow, he responds so that the judge understands. "Since you require none, we'll begin with..."

Douglas' consciousness dissolves as he reaches unison with that secret thrum of courage; the judge's words aren't registering as words. The accompanist seated at the concert grand piano counts, "1-2-3-4." The accompaniment rings out, a familiar invitation. From this moment forward 253-1 responds to Douglas' slightest musical intention whether his hands and fingers attain precision or not, whether his memory fails or not. Douglas is hardly aware of the judges huddling, jotting notes.

Light is flaring off the judge's thick glasses; the man is standing to stretch; he's asking for a section from Bartók's Second Concerto. Douglas' favorite selection; he revels in the blend of earth and spirit, the folk-like themes and harmonic originality. As he plays, five judges set their papers and pencils aside. Some lean forward unblinking. Some sway to the meter. Toward the composition's end there is a challenging cadenza almost entirely in double stops and chords. Unfazed, Douglas and 253-1 ascend with vibrancy reaching the final rhythm. A rhythm that brings the judges to a state that might accurately be described as delight.

And then a challenge. The judge with the goatee places in front of him an extremely difficult passage from *Salome.* Douglas has never seen this music. The calm he's been experiencing doesn't dissipate. Unfazed, he sightreads the selection straight off.

The judges confer in whispers until the next request. "Play something of your own choosing, please."

Douglas selects Liszt's "Liebestraum;" he'll show off his ability to sustain a gentle mood. To show his gratitude for the eloquent piano accompaniment, he smiles at the pianist as they begin.

Afterward two judges leave the stage. One sits midway in the theater; the other finds a seat in the balcony. The bespectacled judge asks Douglas to begin with the composition to be used for the Winner's orchestral appearance, Hindemith's, Suite of Sonatas for Violin. "Begin with Sonata 3, if you please."

Walls and doors provide no constraint for the nuanced harmonies being brought forth. Frequencies push the boundaries of the space. Contestants in the hallway look at one another. What? They can feel what's being played? Soon youngsters and parents drift with the sensation. Guileless tranquility softens their worried faces.

So unruffled, Douglas and the 253-1. So captivated, the judges. Indeed. And when the duo reaches the contrasting D major section their exuberance pierces the sadness—all listeners delight as violin and player soar toward the triumph of the last several minutes.

"What took you so long?" Willi asks when Douglas reappears

"Was I in there a long time? I couldn't tell."

"Like heck yeah! Over a half hour—more like forty-five minutes."

The judges one by one walk through the double doors. The judge with the square spectacles makes an announcement. "Thank you, each and every one who participated today. We were honored. Impressed with the talent you top twenty-four violinists demonstrated. Keep up your studies—the world can use more musicians." The judges clap enthusiastically, pivoting to face each listener.

The short judge with the feathered hat speaks next. "There will be no callbacks. You are free to leave. Please gather your belongings. We hope to see you at the Dress Rehearsal where the Winner and Runner-up will both perform. And then at the Final Performance. Winners will be announced by mail."

[23]

PROFESSOR AND MRS. Piano Teacher have failed to congratulate Douglas properly. Mrs. Piano Teacher's call to the Home had been abrupt. Addressing Hester, "Douglas won the NOA. Have him here on Saturday, 10 o'clock sharp." The Professor had then taken the phone. "Now, let me speak to the boy." Addressing Douglas Doogie-doo Tryzyna, "So you're the NOA Winner. Don't go letting us down."

* * *

THERE SITS VIOLETTE in the salon playing the Bosendorfer Grand. Douglas pauses on the entry carpet, unobserved, appreciating the piano's wail of bitter sweetness. *Can the piano communicate with Violette like the 253-1 does with me?* From the simplest tune, the accompaniment for Gluck's "Melodie," Violette's fingertips withdraw the most gut-wrenching sentiments. She sings the violin's part, the melody Douglas usually plays. Douglas holds his hands over his mouth. His expression might betray something far too precious: his reaction to Violette's tenderness, passion, and aversion. Sound waves charged with her soul convey to his soul both joy and anguish. Now he's squatting like a peasant unaware of other sounds floating from practice rooms down the hall. And then she has completed the piece. He holds his breath in the silence. Listen, she begins again. Violette is presenting him four more minutes of visceral heartbreak. In playing she releases tears, though not of saltwater.

Douglas imagines she's communicating her mourning for the years of love that might have been. In agreement the little hero in his head says, *That was a love song for you*; his heart flutters. The villain in his head contradicts. *Bozo, more likely that was a love song for Willi*; his heart sinks.

How Douglas wishes he could snatch her up in a giant embrace, kiss her wildly as he has before. None of his love has waned; instead it gushes, flows, pounds, finding new energy. He's to his feet approaching her before he can stop himself.

Violette spins around on the bench. "Congratulations on winning the NOA!" She's smiling, for a second. Five metronome clicks later Violette's attention shifts back to the piano. Hanon Virtuoso Pianist "Exercise No. 13," each note struck in a display of purposeful discipline. Not a vestige of prior sentiment can be heard.

The past few minutes of closeness invited the one-time love birds to act out familiar roles. Sadly, they've bumped against a familiar impediment—a summer episode that baffled and wounded them both.

Willi and Ophelia wander into the salon; Stoya follows close behind. He raps the music stand with his bow, calling for attention. Increased preparation for the Concert begins now, without a pause for celebration.

"You blockheads actually followed my instruction. About time. Today, granted the NOA's robust honor, I choose the selection you'll be playing with the Junior Orchestra. This is it!" Peter presents a set of printed staff paper to each boy. "Suite of Sonatas for Violin by my famous compatriot, Paul Hindemith; he composed this and dedicated it to our Wilhelm, here. Let's make Paul proud, shall we?"

[24]

THE BOYS TRAVEL together, taking the train. Ahead of them, four rehearsals with the Junior Orchestra before the public Dress Rehearsal. The Winner and the Runner-up agree not to share the goings-on at rehearsal with Professor Stoya and Mrs. Piano Teacher.

It will take a couple of hours for each to have a turn working through the forty-six minutes of Hindemith's seven Sonatas. Willi is asked to take the first turn. Douglas relaxes with his eyes closed. He's seated alongside the string section, soaking up the full instrumental experience.

The first chair violinist, a Mickey Rooney look-alike, his lisped speech inspiring laughter more easily than respect, asks for a halt in the scherzando. "Percussion and strings have been thrown off by your peculiar phrasing, again, Mr. Stoya. Listen here." The fellow demonstrates on his own violin. "Got it? So. Let's begin with the first measure of Sonata 3." He raises his arms, a very short fellow with a baton held very high.

Time and time again the Concert Master interrupts the musicians by tapping his baton. "Again." Each time Willi reacts with classic teenage exasperation. The equally exasperated teenage leader maintains his dignity.

After repeated attempts, each a failed attempt, Willi stomps his foot, his jaw rippling. He defends himself heatedly like a politician challenged on his soapbox. "It doesn't work for me like this! My father knows Hindemith personally. And I'll do it his way."

A temper is held. "If you please, we'll try it as I suggest." The baton is raised again.

Douglas tenses as the musicians resume. This is embarrassing. If Professor Stoya finds out the half of it...

During Sonata 6 the Concert Master again *rap-rap-raps* his baton on the music stand. "It's meant to be lively, Mr. Stoya. You're dragging. Again. One-two-three..."

"Take it or leave it!" Willi picks up the Performance Violin, the bow thrust forward like a weapon. He plays just as he has before. The Orchestra chugs along, disoriented by the disparity between the baton and the soloist's tempo.

After Sonata 7 has ground to a halt the Concert Master gives his counsel to the group. Still, Willi refuses to listen. The Orchestra members react, pulling faces of incredulity as they nudge one another. This conduct is highly unprofessional and has never, never been demonstrated in their ranks.

"After a fifteen-minute break we'll resume with you, Mr. Tryzyna." The pint-size man, who has just encountered a king-size can of worms, flops into a folding chair with his eyes closed. One can imagine he's praying the Runner-up will not (for some ungodly reason) get to play most public performance.

And so it goes.

* * *

AT THE THIRD practice session, "Mr. Tryzyna" gets the first call. When Douglas plays, the eighteen-year-old Concert Master needs to attend only minor nuances.

With Willi the business of music is yet again tedious. Nevertheless, you'll spy no attitude on the Concert Master's face when young Stoya's mistakes cause the problematic pausing and rushing. The Concert Master calmly calls numerous halts. It's Willi who shows frustration. He has the audacity to keep making excuses, talking loudly over the advice.

Look here. Leaving the shadows of the wings strides a man of purpose. The Conductor. With a flourish he stubs out his cigarette in a paper cup. From his expression one could presume he's been listening for quite a while. "My good man!" he exclaims. His leather shoes squeak with each step he takes toward the soloist. And then face to face with Willi, the Conductor fairly sizzles. "We have only the last instructive rehearsal to go, and of that one I will be in charge...*with every expectation of perfection.* Sir, close your mouth and listen!" Back into the wings he goes, fomenting the smell of fear from each musician.

The Concert Master dabs a hankie at his face. Perspiration drips from his forehead and sideburns. "You heard our Conductor. There's only one session left before the Dress Rehearsal."

The players attend his words with varying reactions of apprehension. Willi stands up, casually drops the Performance Violin into the case, flips the two latches closed, each with a loud click. All eyes shift in his direction, then all eyes shift back to the Concert Master, who is still talking.

"At the Dress Rehearsal there will be no stopping for coaching." It's a warning. "We'll have a small audience, mostly family and friends; don't underestimate its significance, because the Press will attend."

A pause, shuffling, coughing, fidgeting, sidelong glances.

"You are all excused."

After Salvadorian stuffed tortillas washed down with Nehi grape soda, after a walk to Penn Station, Willi, the vexed Runner-up, threatens Douglas. "You'd better not shoot your mouth off to my folks."

[25]

LATER IN THE week a postcard graces the Home's silver tray. Addressed to Douglas Tryzyna. The stamp depicts a kangaroo; Michael Rabin has written from Australia.

Dear Douglas,
Flew from La Guardia to San Francisco. Then Honolulu,
Canton Island, Fiji, and Australia. Rembert found me a
Guarnerius del Gesú 1724. Bought it for $8,000. Not my fa-
vorite. Concerts kind of a blur. Hotel life is pretty awful.
Most Australians don't know anything about music. I want
to meet an Aborigine if he wouldn't bong me with a boomer-
ang! Flying to Melbourne now. Missing Meadowmount and
you.
Your pal,
Mike

[26]

STEPPING INTO THE backyard Peter Stoya observes his sons wrestling, shirts thrown aside. *When did Willi's shoulders get so broad, exaggerating his boyish jaw and neck?* Willi interrupts these thoughts, hollering profanities as he attempts a chokeslam. Seconds later Willi is releasing Siggi. Willi is cowering, hunching. Willi is expecting a blow from this annoyed parent. Instead of a fist, Willi feels a meaty palm softly cuff his check— nothing less than fatherly validation.

Stoya is smiling. "Got some spunk, eh, kid? Who knew? For once I see a sweat and blood competitor in you. Hang on to the feeling."

Willi's eyes go glassy.

"Maybe the judges got it wrong, son. You have today's Dress Rehearsal to prove just how wrong. You and Douglas perform back-to-back. You'll be compared—same venue, same afternoon, same orchestra, same compositions. Make it easy for the audience to see who's superior. Listen, if you do your job everyone will be congratulating *you*. Reporters will write about you. They'll say, 'The NOA judges admit their mistake.

Wilhelm Stoya is superior. He's the one deserving of the Juilliard Scholarship, the prize money, the publicity.'"

* * *

WHAT A CROWD awaits, creating a din where quiet must soon prevail. Parents and friends of the Junior Philharmonic account for most of the chatter. If Michael Rabin himself were to be the soloist there could hardly be a more expectant audience.

This very moment two violins also vibrate with awareness of a competition. Their own embedded competition. They met for the very first time in the Stoya Conservatory only twelve years ago. Surprisingly, their rivalry began in 1700s Cremona, Italy. And one may ask, what was the nature of the challenge made two centuries ago? Just this: Which maker's violin could display superior qualities given the exact same maple for its vibrational qualities *and* the exact same acoustical conditions for listeners? One may ask, did ego cause the makers to discount or overlook the factor of the *players*? Nevertheless, circumstances have finally created the opportunity. The violins themselves recognize it as such. Which will win the challenge? That of Antonio Stradivari, or that of Bartolomeo Giuseppe Guarneri del Gesù? And if preeminence can be declared today, who will revel, who will benefit?

The 253-1 vibrates, imploring the Performance Violin. {Did not Katarina despise this bellicosity| Indeed| And so 253-1 displays three makers' handiwork| not just her husband's| See| Katarina voided the challenge| on purpose| |

The Performance Violin pulsates with confusion.

{253-1 carries the glory of three makers| not one| Thus the challenge between us| Red Sister| is null| So let us quit this dogfight| |

The Red Sister, the Performance Violin, balks, becoming still.

The 253-1 responds with solemnity. {We *violini* may reconcile what our makers could not| Let us bestow our unique gifts to human-kind freely| without vainglory| |

The Performance Violin quavers humbly. For the first time in her existence, she communes with her Sister.

{United| for all Goodness| as once We were| in The Duration of Cold| Let us give all without Vanity| |

* * *

THE AUDIENCE HAS dressed to impress. Sister Elder's hair is upswept, curls positioned with eleven silver hairpins. The silver-gray silk dress, folded away for two decades, aired for a month, now free of pungent-sickly-sweet naphthalene, still fits. Perhaps the tiny buttons across the chest needed tugging into their loops; otherwise, the garment slid over her waist and narrow hips, territory for a quotidian apron.

Auntie Evangeline's mauve dress with rhinestone buttons gracing the surplice top is her own creation.

The Smythe sisters have arranged for an after-party at their Manhattan Hotel. Even if today goes badly (knock on wood) there's an August birthday to celebrate, Douglas' eighteenth. They won't tempt fate by waiting for next week's performance, the Winner-only performance. Another dirigible, just as easily as the Hindenburg, might fall from the sky. A certain Professor might pull a double-cross. Today, yes, today is a sure thing. Today is a cause for celebration. So far.

There in the lobby Professor Stoya engages in animated conversation. He's spiffy in his Stetson straw hat and his linen summer suit. Mrs. Piano Teacher wears a cloche of sisal straw, the same olive color as her dress, livened with pink ribbon trim and flowers. Siggi in shirtsleeves and his father's green tie has the hungry look of a fifteen-year-old athlete. He's arm in arm with a chatty Ophelia, who struts her blue chiffon. Behind them biting her nails, Violette in black kitten heels, silk stockings, and a butter yellow shirtwaist, cinched with a wide patent leather belt.

Backstage the dressing room is lined with a mirrored counter and chairs. Here the Concert Master gives the two soloists his memorized spiel, a reminder of procedure and expectations. Willi and Douglas tune up in intervals of fifths bowed in pairs, G_3, D_4, A_4, E_5. They double-check their pockets for the extra strings Stoya gave them. After that it's a draw-straws situation to see who performs first. Willi draws the short straw. "You're up, Stoya, you're first," the Concert Master says. "Now. Follow me." He turns on the heel of his Cap Toe dress shoes and leaves.

Professor Stoya's Performance Violin gleams in Willi's hands, newly oiled, traces of rosin brushed away. Willi gives a salute. He's a dashing passage of seersucker stripes.

Douglas joins the audience, taking a seat with the Sisters. He's un-ruffled though flappable. He's calm though excited. He's rooting for his competitor to sparkle. How strangely wonderful. Where stage fright used to germinate, Douglas imagines flowers in quick-time expansion, petals burst open, gold beside purple, green beside red, orange beside blue, a masterpiece of opposites. *Plant a garden in your heart, Sister Peace told me. I did, I did. It's working.*

In a victory garden one acknowledges the possibility of ruination. The fruitage can be bumped off in a blink. The ruthless persist, slimy slugs, snails, worms, even moles, those underground thieves. Too often one glosses over predators in a bed of glories when roots, foliage, and blossoms of courage mature. Such oversight will soon be the undoing of anticipated glory.

Stoya opens his notebook; he writes: *12th August 1953, Wilhelm Stoya, NOA Winner, soloist, Junior Philharmonic, New York City.* Pen tucked into its leather loop, red ribbon betwixt the needed pages, he takes a deep breath. Surely the rushed breakfast and the dash to the taxi are catching up with him. Three bells sound. His chest is tight, as is his jaw.

The Orchestra has finished tuning. Lights dim. A diminutive lady appears on the stage; she welcomes the audience. Her small hat glows like a halo; iridescent feathers catch the light. Her crackling voice announces, "Wilhelm Stoya, NOA Competition Second Place Winner, performing the Hindemith Suite of Sonatas for Violin with the New York City Junior Philharmonic Orchestra."

Hindemith's music fills the Hall. The Performance Violin sings with undeniable clarity. The volume achieved is satisfactory. None in the audience will discern they are in the presence of a Fine and Rare instrument. A few informed listeners can pinpoint the reality—the mysterious instrument's voice holds capacity for innumerable emanations acquired over two centuries of owners, Joachim, and Lilli von Mendelssohn of a certainty. Nevertheless, this violin can only manifest the depth of her current player's soul. Willi guides her with fingers and bow as he would any old fiddle, unaware of her magnificence. Equally unaware of his own potential, he concentrates on showing off. He presumes to overshadow Douglas' yet unheard performance if it kills him.

"Only the deaf could fail to enjoy this first-rate performance," Stoya whispers to his wife. During difficult passages over which Willi glides, Frieda squeezes Peter's thigh as if to say, "Yes, yes, our Willi, just listen to him, my darling." Professor Stoya won't gush, his finely trained ear attends with a critic's analysis. He tests the pen's ink flow and then jots a note or two in his book. For use tomorrow; this is only the Rehearsal after all. *Willi may yet play next week's Performance.*

Douglas rides the current of Hindemith's music, appreciating every note as waves of sound thrill his sensitive soul. Between his knees the 253-1 in her case soaks up the emanations as well. Douglas' beloved violin breathes inaudibly, addressing the violin under Willi's control. {My sister| Red Sister| what gifts you have| unrevealed in this moment| gifts yet to offer| |

After the closing presto and the six brisk chords have declared finality, the audience applauds. Professor Stoya smiles despite himself. Few and minor the notes of critique he'll give the performer, his own talented son. He replaces the miniature pen's marbled celluloid cap, attaches the pen to the lanyard around his neck. He rereads what he's written. Positions the red ribbon carefully and closes the book. Relief soothes, only momentarily. Peevish questions prickle.

What if Douglas is on top of his game? How much better will he perform than Wilhelm? If Peter were to lay bare his fears to Frieda, she'd remind him as she always does: "Each of the *winners* is a glorious product of the Stoya Conservatory, a grand reflection on us." And as a welcome reminder, she'd add, "There's time for Willi to outshine this rival. Next week awaits. And after that more opportunity."

The first soloist's performance (a bit rushed) has taken less than forty-two minutes. Now the Junior Orchestra performs Brahms's Academic Festival Overture, which features all its young members. A brief intermission allows an audience to stretch, toilet, chat, slurp a soda pop, and return to their seats.

* * *

STILLNESS LIKE A net of wonder falls upon the crowd as they watch the NOA Finalist walk onto the stage. Why the wonder? He's of medium height, rusty hair cut short, cheeks dusted with freckles, pressed trousers, polished oxfords, a dark satin and linen vest over a dress shirt, collar unbuttoned. Nothing remarkable here. Until Douglas Tryzyna takes the gleaming violin to his chest, positions a white cloth just so, nods to the Conductor, then something rare is imminent. The sound from this soloist's instrument following the Orchestra's introduction overtakes all. The music surrounds, penetrates, transfixes, enters, purifies. Flesh and blood creatures enter spirit realm.

Douglas pulls his own song of compassion and connection from her, his violin, his Magic Muriel 253-1, her voice powerful, pleading, pulsating passion. Through brisk passages and lilting, through trills and cadenzas, the voice floats. Seconds become minutes; minutes become a timeless stretch of energy afloat in the Hall. Like a homing pigeon navigating sky, something magical finds each heart.

At first the alchemic *unnamed* disperses like fluff from a field of dandelions. At first it is experienced as mere tickles begetting smiles.

More obscure, the *unnamed*, like pixie dust alights on an old gentleman's face. He licks his lips like a young lover savoring a kiss.

The *unnamed* permeates the young mother's bosom, and the pinch of worry on her face relaxes. What is this seeping, seeping just now, warm, damp, sweet through her cotton dress? And she unable to nurse these past weeks.

The *unnamed* glister enters a father's ear, travels inward through the narrow canal, loosens the hearing of this man who would not hear his son's truth, before.

The *unnamed* fills a homely schoolgirl's eyes. She blinks it away and appears to wink, attracting a young man who never looked her way. The pimply boy glances at her, she, the schoolmate he ignored, at dance-less school dances, at unsociable church socials. Now she smiles openly; he realizes she's lovely, her eyes fixed on his, only for a few seconds, but still.

The *unnamed* slips into a widow whose heart squeezes with love, grief squeezing out, her heart refilling with warm remembrance of her late husband's puns, foibles, his silly stubbornness, his caresses.

The *unnamed* winds its way down legs held in braces to the feet that suddenly keep time to the beat.

Others experience the alchemy, the entirety of the music, as a prayer, as a prayer asking for freedom from personal confines.

Magic Muriel 253-1 leads as if she has played this music a million times over. Douglas listens and feels his feral heart questioning. *And who is it that I love? And who is it that I still need to forgive?*

Sonata 6, eight minutes, and four seconds. The repetitions with the Orchestra joining and then the lively melody, happy as sunlight playing on water at the Step Falls, like ripples rushing along on a tumultuous journey where Sister Peace meant to teach Douglas that she might leave only to return in other ways. Surely, she returns to him in this music. He imagines her dancing as he plays; she's free, in love, her dark hair unbound. In this moment he knows he should forgive her; what holds him back? He feels the 253-1 quickening with new life; she's encouraging him. His heart softens for a few seconds.

And the music continues. Frequencies swirl, gather, and release. Strangers lean shoulder to shoulder, strangers reach to each other hand in hand, strangers breathe in, breathe out, otherwise riveted. The final notes of the seventh Sonata fade, fade, fade. It's over too soon. The audience, stunned, remains reverent in motionless awe.

And then in unison the listeners return with gusto all the energy given by the soloist and the Orchestra. The clapping won't subside, an audience on its feet calling out "bravo, bravo, bravo" calling out, "encore, encore, encore!"

An encore? Douglas has prepared a favorite, as has Willi—his peer, his buddy, his rival, who had no need of an encore today, nor will he ever.

The pianist watches for Douglas' nod of readiness.

The ruddy violin whispers to Douglas. {This is our opportunity|
253-1 has all to share with you| You| the only one who senses the ways
to ask it from me| |

Douglas and the 253-1 begin. Not with the lively folk-based compositions of a Bartok or Ravel, pieces guaranteed to send the audience
home with a lively step. He chooses a simple piece, a piece he's playing for
Violette. Repeating back to her the music that stirred him when she
played and sang not long ago. Gluck's "Melodie." Four minutes of heartbreak and longing, music charged with a reflection of his soul, it's capable
of conveying to another soul his sorrow, and within that lamentation, joy
may arise. Now look closely. The red instrument agleam, mirrors at a distance the violin Willi just played. But the 253-1 projects a human voice,
deep, strong, velvety, one granted by her three makers. With Douglas'
mastery the euphoria of harmony unites the audience. The encore is complete. The audience floats, continues to float, together.

Without pause Douglas starts up again, surely, humbly. Quickly
overcoming his surprise, the Conductor beckons the pianist to accompany
an unexpected second encore selection. Now listen, hear the violin's voice
in conversation with the piano's chords. A Bartok Romanian Folk Dance.

We in the audience gaze from our red velvet chairs. Before our eyes
the seasons flow, the buzz of honeybees in breeze, golden light on trees,
dandelion fluff in flight, crimson apples in dry grass. Gents bend at the
waist. Gals twirl skirts. Dancers in unison, steps light and spry. Music calls
up memory, a prayer of forgiveness every heart knows, a passionate call to
brotherhood, an impassioned call to freedom. Steps quicken, so many feet
in motion, fireside frolic, wild rapture to music in a minor key. We dance
as if called to celebrate each birth, each marriage, each seeker's soul. Only
five and a half minutes.

Clapping resumes from an ecstatic audience as if to return this teenager's largesse once again. The pianist bows; Douglas bows. The stage manager brings down the curtain with no uncertain finality.

Peter Stoya's black leather, gilt-edged pocket notebook with its red ribbon slides from his hand. Unavoidably he is softened, chastened, prompted to give and to ask for forgiveness. Oh, see how quickly the balm is countered. As theater lights brighten, a dark canker swells in Peter. It bursts with malice, spurting large, frigid drops onto his soul, black as the rain that poisoned Hiroshima. Tragically, Dr. Dankworth cannot remedy this disorder with a deft slice of his scalpel, or a bottle of tablets. Professor Peter Stoya will never find generosity for the words he should write on the page headed *Douglas Tryzyna, 12th August 1953.*

The audience disperses. Smiles. Hugs. Liveliness. Words of praise fill the space, kaleidoscopic as hummingbirds in sunshine.

Stoya slowly wakes from his stupor. He's in shock; his humor wavers between molten and arctic. Never, never, never was it his intention for Douglas to eclipse his Wilhelm.

Up to the stage, mindless of Frieda who is abruptly left behind, a salute to Willi in passing, ah, there's Douglas! He pushes the lad into the wings, stage left.

"You overpowered the Orchestra today!" Stoya rages. "That violin is doing you no favors."

Douglas, stunned. "I thought I did pretty well...the audience...the Concert Master..."

"Don't be fooled-schmooled by all that!"

"You, you impertinent upstart, will play the Performance Violin next week. For your own good."

Douglas can't believe his ears. He won't accept what Stoya has told him. He turns away hoping his fury won't erupt.

Flashbulbs click and blind Douglas as reporters capture the moment. Three pull him aside for comments. Another reporter tackles Professor Peter Stoya.

Once he satisfies the reporters Douglas is relieved to see the Conductor on the stage with Orchestra members who linger. He approaches. Halts. Holds back. It seems like forever waiting for a chance to speak alone with a man he trusts. Finally, his opportunity. He isn't shy. "I would like an honest critique on my performance today." He squares his shoulders. "Did I overpower the Orchestra?"

The Conductor tips his head back in thought. He's bald with exaggerated eyebrows growing wild in compensation.

"Overpower the Orchestra?" The Conductor claps him firmly on the shoulder. "Overpower the Orchestra? For God's sakes. If that is what you did today, Mr. Tryzyna, please do so again next week!"

[27]

And there is gossip 'round and 'round the City:

> Can't wait for Tryzyna's next concert.
> He won a scholarship to Juilliard!
> He already has what they can't teach.
> They say his violin is bewitched.
> Charmed, more like.
> I'm still tingling.
> Me too, floating without care.
> The music is simply tiramisu.
> What?
> You know, that spiritual zone between heaven and earth.

[28]

"HALLO? HALLO, LULU. Peter and I will overnight at the Smythe Hotel. The boys are on the train home. They'll need to be fed." A rude click ends the conversation Frieda has initiated.

Not even a goodbye? LuLu, hanging up the phone, has enough sense not to inquire. Something must have happened at the Rehearsal to upset the status quo.

Behind the door of Room 313 Frieda is enraged. "What were you thinking? Oh. You weren't thinking! Douglas on the *Performance Violin?*"

Peter scoffs. "Look at it this way, darling." He reaches his hairy paw to pat her cheek.

"Don't you touch me!" Frieda jerks away. "And don't you dare try to talk your way out of this, this, overreaction."

Peter flinches. If there were a boot in sight, she would surely hurl it in his direction. She's staring daggers at his reflection in the vanity mirror. *She'll come around, my fractious Frau.* Peter pours a glass of vodka from his silver flask. Sipping, he's soon lost in thought.

Is he making the right decision pulling Douglas off the rogue thing for the event? Of course! He can't allow the boy to overshadow Willi. Not again. Not with the unfair advantage of that bizarre instrument. *What kind of fiddle is this thing?* It practically plays itself in the hands of an abandoned *zigeuner*; it purrs for his suffering wife; and then it sputters and spits in the hands of his promising son. It's going nowhere near the Concert Hall next week!

The vexed husband/father/professor rationalizes. Fair is fair. That rogue thing shouldn't have been allowed in the first place. Frieda's angry now because, without her agreement, he's changed things up. She'll see; it will pay off. It's no easy task adjusting to the temperamental Performance Violin. This Strad likes a soft approach, not that heavy bowing the rogue thing requires. Douglas is bound to get screwed up with a deadline to goad him. It's likely he'll overreact, stomp off. He's a *Quitter*. And then...we know who will be in the wings. Peter stirs the ice in his glass, noting how the vodka swirls like a smile. Hope, like fool's gold, glimmers for the Professor. Briefly.

Peter notices Frieda turning to face him. "Have a drink, dear." He points to the tray with the inviting glassful of liquor graced by a doily.

Frieda glowers, arms akimbo, disdaining the vodka rocks. And her exasperating husband.

Peter frowns. *Oh, let's suppose all that fails to occur. Hmm.* Perhaps the *Deus Ex Machina* will approve and intervene on his behalf—as happened once before. In Berlin, one unforgotten December. Such times-in-the-making require bravado. Courage.

Courage. Peter shudders. Squeezes his eyes closed. Braces himself. Pours. Takes a gulp.

* * *

HE'S BACK IN Berlin, late December 1940. Old horrors take him by the shoulders and shake memories awake. The sensation of a house a-thunder. Wooden floors echoing the *Schutzstaffel* stomp in hallways. Persian carpets muffling the sound of boots in parlor and music room. He winces; the timbre of a determined voice issues commands. He cringes seeing crystal, china, silver, looted from drawers and cabinets. Remembers his own faintheartedness as he and Robert von Mendelssohn watched, voiceless, fear strangling protest. Family treasures were heaped upon the grand dining table. The wealth of generations was to be carted away. 51 *Jägerstrasse*, Berlin, was being taken over by the Nazis for the Reich Finance Ministry. He had panicked inwardly and begged the Almighty for safety. *Please it, Lord, that the Nazis have no inventory of the valuables in the Mendelssohn household.*

And why? If such an inventory did exist and were it to be reviewed that particular afternoon it would reveal two Stradivari violins gone missing. The 1720 Red Mendelssohn, for one. And the 1709 Small Mendelssohn. Robert and Peter had every reason to be scared stiff.

Several nights prior, during the holiday soiree, a guest had arrived bearing rumors overheard on the street: Nazi takeover imminent! *Someone* with a clear head had slipped Peter a note along with the key to a Deutsch Bank Vault. Peter's instructions were to make *certain* items disappear; he had obliged. Although he can remember the composition he'd been performing on the Red Stradivarius, that *someone's* name has disappeared into a dark cellar of fear.

Stoya, a blond, blue-eyed Aryan, was not conspicuous as he slipped out a back door with a double violin case. In that space of agitation he wondered, *Lady Luck or God on my side?*

✳ ✳ ✳

THE MORNING AFTER the soiree Peter headed to the seedy part of Berlin with merry insubordination. After scouting pawn shops, he purchased a no-count violin in a boxboard case. When he returned to the *Appartement* the coast was clear; Frieda had taken the boys to the park.

How blithe he felt carrying out his ruse. He placed the 1720 Red Mendelssohn Strad into the cheap case and hid it under blankets in his armoire. As for his inherited Vuillame? He made sure it was visible at the music stand, as usual. Then. Into the emptied side of Mendelssohn's double case, he set the pawned fiddle—after giving it a nice polish. Here it rested unsuspiciously beside the 1709 Small Mendelssohn Strad. Both destined for the bank vault. Who could say how long this cohabitation might continue?

Quick change of attire. Peter Stoya was looking smart in his walking suit and dark Homburg hat. He penned a quick message to Frieda, saying he had *der Termin*. Without taking time to reconsider, Peter headed for the Deutsche Bank.

He was led to the vault by the flinty daddy long legs of a man who continually hitched up his pants. Peter unlocked the designated door with the proper key and was given his privacy. He departed one quarter-hour later, tipped his hat to the banking staff, bid them a hearty *"Danke shone."*

How simple to mislead. Place an object in a vault, it is conjectured to be valuable. (Well. What peon given an itch to inspect could tell the difference, anyway?) Nevertheless, Peter Stoya maintained his nonchalance. He was convinced he'd get away with this. The Red 1720 was going with him to America. He'd left the other, the Small Mendelssohn, in the Deutsch Bank, although it suffered the company of a no-account-excuse-for-a-fiddle. Yes. He'd left that small Strad to face its own uncertain destiny—Nazis had their noses, eyes, and hands everywhere.

After a week of lying low he was practically gloating. And after another week the Stoyas were to leave Germany. None the wiser.

✻ ✻ ✻

WHEN HE, PETER STOYA, had obscured the whereabouts of two rare violins, justification held two Aces in the deck of Honors. Altruism—he was saving masterpieces for posterity. Loyalty—he was accepting a family's most fervent plea.

Grant Peter honor in 1940, but a decade later, what is the honorable action to take? Continued self-justification becomes suspect. He could return the instrument to rightful owners. To assuage guilt Peter blames the Violin, how she seduces him with her honey-smooth voice, her ladylike disposition, how he imagines her a mistress cradled against his neck, pressed against his shoulder, she asking to be caressed and never failing to respond with utterances of pleasure. To give her up?

He's suffered in one regard, though. The years of dilemma. Should he share his secret with Frieda? The thought of losing his wife's respect makes his stomach lurch. Makes his heart bombard his chest with painful hammering. If he were to tell her she might consider him lacking moral character. Or if she didn't judge him certainly her migraines would increase, his poor dear. He doesn't share his nightmares, those of imagining Nazi torture. Not even when she prods him awake the darkest hours of night—"Sh, sh, bad dream?"

She wouldn't leave him, or would she? *Nein, absolut nicht.* The two might appear dissonant, the sea lion and the tundra swan mated, he broad and bristly, bellowing, she thin though *zaftig*, known to harangue; but never mind. They both require the fluid surround of music to stay afloat in the world. *When the time is right, I'll speak of it, but only when the time is right.*

☆ ☆ ☆

SWALLOWING THE LAST of his vodka, the man's consciousness returns to concerns of this August. The NOA concert approaches like phobia incarnate; Peter must joust with the unknown. Perhaps his boldness regarding Douglas has already devised the turnaround to benefit Willi. Nevertheless, he bursts with a silent plea to Lady Luck. *Please let Douglas quit! It's Willi who must perform as honored soloist on the precious violin I saved. Please, Dear Lady, take my side, let opportunity present itself. I needn't know how.*

Emboldened, his imagination dashes forward; he can already hear it. "Announcement from the stage: Change in program. Wilhelm Stoya, Soloist." Stoya breathes rapidly; his knees want to collapse. *Thud,* he lands on the bed, barely able to control his excitement, or the flying ice cubes.

Freida, curled like an infant, her back turned to her overreaching husband, suffers a paralyzing migraine; there are certain healing charms she requires, ones bestowed by a coveted relic, a one-of-a-kind violin, a violin about to disappear and never again soothe her pain.

[29]

DOUGLAS IS STRANGELY quiet during the celebratory dinner; he's seeing a pattern. It was always coming to this. Peter Stoya claiming the fiddle's future. Like a slip of paper found as you cracked one Chinese cookie after another only to find the same fortune over and over and over. What did Wing say? "Each day like fortune in cookie. You no like what it is saying, you make a change."

I will, by golly, I will change things, and I won't breathe a word of this to anyone.

* * *

NIGHTFALL. A COACH full of passengers, Adirondack bound, fused by the evening's transformation. They are listening to a private concert. Evangeline holding hands with her bossy big sis, Hester. Ophelia resting her head on Violette's shoulder, covetous pianists united, peaceful (without Willi or Siggi's leverage). Outside torrents of rain pound, lightning slashes, the sky brightens, fierce thunder rumbles like drumroll. Throughout the trip north, Douglas and the 253-1 reveling, together. Offering the grace of music, together.

{Together we are best that can be| So begins our opportunity| |

If Douglas knew the term *soul mate*, he might have used it to describe partnership with the 253-1, the striped, the red Magic Muriel. He is young, believing no one can control them, especially not an old hothead. Violette is equally callow. She has yet to feel a pecking within the shell of her confused feelings. Her emotions will require time to mature. Perhaps in the future she will type *inamorato* in a letter and mail it to Douglas, he, in days to come, an accused thief, who was once her sweetheart.

The 253-1, given centuries with mankind, communicates her aged wisdom, though swayed by motives seemingly human. {Douglas| men liken Time to the great waters| seas which wash up treasure| seas which just as quickly drag all things precious away| and leave but the trace of salty tears| Let us grasp our moment| it will not return| |

"Don't worry, I have a plan."

{Remember| there are those seeking to separate us| men filled with insatiable needs| 253-1 is a but a wooden *violino*| dependent upon you| Douglas| are you listening| |

"I hear you, sweet Muriel."

{You| and *questo violino*| have been graced as Katarina intended| we can ignite| electrify| and inspire Love| May it be so| May it be so| |

[30]

THERE IS A long space of quietude in the Stoya Conservatory˜Violin & Piano. LuLu leaves the impending tragedy to take an afternoon walk.

Narcisse Louise Boulez relates an injustice over which she is powerless. After which there is a long space of unrest in the Penthouse of the Smythe Hotel—where this caring soul is not called LuLu.

Lermontov takes a seat at the glass-top table in front of his German-made Triumph. Facing a view of Cobble Hill, browning this August afternoon, he lapses into thought. His left hand holds a freshly sharpened pencil. He doesn't type. Instead, he scribbles a sentence.

"Do you want to hear this, Narcisse?" Lermontov doesn't wait for her to nod. His husky voice betraying deep affection for the young man who's been lured into a trap, he reads aloud:

> *Though we cower or confront, our fate keeps its own counsel.*

[31]

SINCE THE DRESS Rehearsal and Professor Stoya's mandate, Douglas has spent several full days at the Conservatory; he has only this one week to get comfortable on the Performance Violin. Besides, continued practice at the Stoya Conservatory will hurt more than help; even entering the practice room spurs his resentment. No problem, rehearsing without an instrument. He knows what to do. Professor Stoya can have only so much control over him.

At the break of dawn, Douglas bicycles to the Falls. He climbs to the upper level intent on his mission. Shorts, sandals, new Loong vest worn over an undershirt. Music propped against a rock. His energetic body cooled by mist. He hums, each successive phrase to be performed, each arm and finger attentive to its task. The down rush of water becomes his orchestra. He's appreciated by leaf whisper, by bird trill, by rocks silent in their regard. Again, Split Rock Falls grants him a cocoon for concentration. This becomes his new routine.

Exasperated, Mrs. Piano Teacher phones the Smythe Home. "Douglas is expected this evening after dinner for the final practice. No excuses."

The tone of Sister Elder's voice as she relays the message to Douglas leaves no question about her umbrage. She won't attend tomorrow's Performance. "You already gave the recital that matters to me, on the violin that matters to you. I won't honor that ogre's domination."

* * *

AFTER AN INTENSE session with Frieda at the piano, Peter in the salon, pacing, bombastic as ever, he—Douglas, Doogie-doo, Tryzyna, NOA Winner-soloist having conscientiously practiced on the Performance Violin—is sent home with advice. "Get some sleep. Be here early in the morning with your dress clothes packed. We'll breakfast, warm up, and catch the early train together."

Douglas bikes away, his head full of realizations. The Performance Violin has been gracious in her cooperation. Missing, however, is the spontaneity he experiences with the 253-1. There, alone in the northern twilight, he registers a new sense of power. He's tranquil. And quietly determined.

✵ ✵ ✵

ASTRID HAS GIVEN his dress shirt a wash and a light starch. She's steamed his trousers. She places his clothes in Sister Elder's garment bag. Tanzanite stones in her ears glint as she turns to the wardrobe. Her fingers, thin, mere bone, seeming inches longer than Sister Elder's, skilled at flashing a needle in and out of fabric, are shoving aside the hanging garments, one by one. She's looking for something. Then, as if to ask the boy a question, the tilt of her head, adjustment of pale braids. Giving no explanation, she leaves, a troubled glaze to her eyes.

Douglas brings out the old shoeshine kit, reminder of much earlier days. The painted man and a woman on it haven't aged; the moon hasn't cycled; flowers haven't wilted. Everything's stayed the same within the box's green border. He positions his left oxford on the cast iron footrest. Not everything has stayed the same. Sister Peace is off somewhere. She won't hear his performance. At first the enduring hurt compresses him like a boa; in compensation he attacks his dress shoe with concentrated effort. Astrid returns with folded laundry, looking a bit more perplexed. Wing, a step behind her, laughs. "Wisdom say, *Boy who polish like machine wear out shoe without taking step!*"

"Yup!" Douglas says with a smile. Oh, I might take a step all right. A big step.

[32]

ENTER THE STOYA Conservatory with Douglas this morning. Friction wallops you like an ice cream headache. Detect the presence of grease, yeast, coffee. Enter the salon where Siggi lollygags while Mrs. Piano Teacher oversees Willi's practice session on the Performance Violin. Professor Stoya reigns, upright on the loveseat. The favored orchids faint from exhaustion, petals with a complexion of dried blood and bile. The cuckoo clock's posture? Simply absurd. The bird is paralyzed in attempted escape from its wooden confines; the carved creature is airborne and soundless.

Clap, clap, clap. Willi has finished playing his chosen encore. "Excellent job, son. One must always be prepared for opportunity."

Willi saunters past the music stand, allowing his shoulder to graze Douglas. He hisses. "Doogie, you noticed lately? Me and Vi, just like this!" He crosses his trigger finger with his middle finger; in doing so he exposes the symbol of failed fraternity on his thumb.

"Your turn," Frieda says to Douglas without so much as a *good morning* or a smile. Douglas takes up Stoya's violin and bow. The Performance Violin cooperates like a lady, while the rogue 253-1 holds her communication, for now. Mrs. Piano Teacher interrupts. "No, no, no! You're speeding up. Go again, with the metronome. Siggi, set it to *Andante* for him." Douglas glowers at the insult.

A bit of fooling around takes place with the metronome. "It's stuck, Ma," Siggi whines.

Douglas senses the Professor's disquiet as he and Mrs. Piano Teacher conclude the warmup. How abruptly the man retrieves his precious instrument, wraps her with silk, settles her, secures the bow in the lid. How he snaps the locks on the case, deriving satisfaction from each click. "There, ready to go."

Violette enters the Conservatory without knocking, takes hesitant steps across the antique hooked russet runner rug and past the giant potted philodendron where she stops before entering the salon. She ignores Douglas and takes to fussing over Willi, who joins her. He's adopted a pout for her benefit.

LuLu calls to the group. "Breakfast is ready." Sausages, eggs, blueberries, and frosted cinnamon rolls await. Frieda asks for a moment to say grace, uncommon in this household. Her soft voice makes a plea for humility. A plea for deliverance from temptation. And finally, she gives thanks for the meal.

Napkins on laps, forks in action. No more talking. And halfway into his sausage Willi's eyes twinkle with devilry. "Hot chocolate all around," he says. He jumps up, almost overturning his chair.

Douglas declines Willi's cocoa. After picking at his breakfast, he sets his napkin aside and genuinely thanks his hosts—his teachers, benefactors, and his adversaries.

Douglas wanders to the library alone. Thoughts of Michael Rabin performing in Australia give him courage. Sounds other than music float in the morning air: Violette, Ophelia, and Willi in a practice room giggling; LuLu in the kitchen clattering; Peter and Frieda on the stairs arguing. Douglas wanders into the salon. The seemingly defunct cuckoo startles him with her shrill declaration of the hour. Magic Muriel 253-1 also startles him; she beckons with an entreaty he won't ignore.

{Douglas| you belong to me| I feel your heart pound| your blood course| Your fingertips know my secret voices| know how to extract the passions that saturate my cells| We must bestow our gifts| Our fulfillment is beginning| |

Her conviction justifies his decision. He's directing their fortune, by golly, just as Wing taught him. Quickly transferring the Performance

Violin and bow into Muriel's case. Quickly transferring Magic Muriel 253-1 and his own bow into the Performance Violin's case. No one will be the wiser when they pick up the Professor's latched case, or even if they open it and see, as expected, a violin swathed in green silk. He's expended so little physical activity and yet he's out of breath. He looks up. Sees someone out of the corner of his eye. Was that LuLu? Has she seen him exchange the violins?

Heavy footsteps. Professor Stoya snaps his fingers. "Time to leave, late-schmate. Wilhelm, take charge of my violin. Don't let it out of your sight. Douglas, the relic stays here, understand?"

Douglas fights the instinct to swagger. Important now to be calm, to formulate a plan. He'd best delay opening the case and exposing the 253-1 until Willi and Mrs. Piano Teacher leave the dressing room and head to their seats. By waiting he'll need to postpone his warm-up routine. *Okay. Okay.* He can go through the calming steps mentally just as he did at the Falls. Then, even five minutes for scales will be sufficient; the violin practically played herself last week. Douglas confirms his choice: this deception is justified. Sweet revenge for Stoya's broken promise. *Stoya can't take this away from us, sweet fiddle. Our opportunity.*

LuLu gives Douglas an unsolicited hug. "Do well, you'll do well." She brushes his cheek in parting. "Thanks, LuLu," he whispers, hiding his mix of vexation and exhilaration. He's watching Willi carry the Performance Violin's case with his Magic Muriel inside!

Unnoticed, Willi gloats over his one-upmanship. He's foiled Douglas' sneaky attempt to bring the old fiddle today! He's carrying Professor Stoya's violin case, which holds the Performance Violin *again*, just as his father intended. Willi validates his choice. He, Wilhelm Stoya, was meant to be in the footlights, meant to be the prestigious soloist today, meant to perform Hindemith's dedicated music on his father's superior violin. *My time, my time to perform just as Pa intended. Douglas can't take this away from me. I've made sure of that, you just wait. You'll see.*

[33]

THE STOYA ENTOURAGE is on the train; the train hasn't budged for an hour. "Obstruction on the track," the Conductor repeats.

Professor Stoya paces the aisle, pausing at times to complain with other disgruntled passengers. Willi begs for refreshments. He and Siggi run off to purchase soda pop for the group only to get sidetracked investigating the drama from a different coach. Willi remembers Douglas' preference for Grape Nehi, which he eventually delivers to his rival with a formal bow.

They've managed to reach the Concert Hall with only twenty-seven minutes to spare. Douglas holds open the massive stage door. Willi pushes ahead; he knows the way. Mrs. Piano Teacher waits for the Professor, who is puffing, out of breath. Douglas feels wrung out, a little bleary. This can't be nerves, can it? He's overcome stage fright before; it never came on like this.

Siggi runs with Willi down the hallway toward the dressing rooms. Once there, Ophelia sits on the tabletop, leans into a mirror, refreshes her lipstick, and combs her hair, all the while chatting excitedly with Violette. Mrs. Piano Teacher scowls as teenage Orchestra members carry on unprofessionally, cracking obscene jokes. Soon the musicians gallop en masse for the stage.

The judge with the feathered hat minces in, gives her well wishes to Douglas, and departs. Backstage also arriving and departing, teachers and musicians, each to offer the rising stars their best wishes. Florien Roux stops by. He insists on shaking Douglas' hand while he mutters *"Bonne chance."* The luthier's goggle-eyed sidekick takes a lordly bow.

After the duo of luthiers departs, Ciazzo steps in, the one person whose presence matters most to Douglas, the person Douglas has most disappointed. "Congratulations. I look forward. You with your special violin," Ciazzo says. The Spaniard's benevolence is genuine; the man's anger has passed. Douglas dares not tell Ciazzo how Stoya took the privilege of playing the 253-1 away from him again. Or how he has secretly corrected the matter. He hopes this performance will honor Ciazzo.

Lermontov strides in, his two-tone, wing-tip, lace-up oxfords buffed to a fair thee well. He presses Douglas' hands between his. "Break our hearts with your storytelling," he says. "And if you can top last week's performance, I will eat my right shoe."

From cultured Lermontov, praise, indeed. Douglas should feel as high as the heavens. Except he feels doped, his eyes see double, his body threatens to collapse. *Anxiety,* he thinks, *I don't have time for my routine.*

For once Violette has no favorite word to proffer. She holds out a paper cup filled with cool water. The first time in forever that she's looked at him directly. The sight of her unusual eyes, one blue almost green, the other green almost blue, calms him like only flowing water can.

His body is sluggish, a fish awash in sludge. He struggles against it without effect, pathetic. In contrast, his desires are quite alive, though trapped like a honeybee on flypaper.

And then Mrs. Piano Teacher takes charge. She allows Willi to keep guard on the violin while directing the other kids to their seats. Siggi drags Ophelia, who blows kisses; off they go with Violette in tow. It's a real kiss Douglas longs for from Violette. This is no time for such thoughts. Time to change clothes. Off with his everyday duds and on with freshly ironed white shirt and black trousers.

The Orchestra Conductor arrives, his shoes squeaking in advance of his presence. "Fifteen minutes to go. Play like last week and we'll be in business. The Concert Master will be back for you." He grips Douglas' outstretched sweaty hand with both of his large hands.

Douglas sees a blurred reflection of himself in the mirror. *No time for my full routine. Fifteen minutes will do. Just make it count.* He breathes deeply to energize himself.

"I'll peek at the audience, Ma," Willi says. He sprints off like a reporter chasing a lede.

Up until now the violin has been under Willi's exclusive care, its identity hidden inside the velvet-lined case. Douglas is sure no one realizes his switch-up, that he's removed Stoya's Performance Violin and replaced it with the 253-1. Willi won't see the difference. Neither will the Concert Master. How clever, how eager, how charged up he is at the pinnacle of his young life. *Why am I so woozy?* Another deep breath. He's going to perform on his treasured 253-1 for an honest-to-goodness-ticket-buying audience. And for his beloved Ciazzo. *What is wrong with me?*

His childhood pal and rival, the Runner-up, seems to have the oddest smile on his face when he returns with a report. "Full house, Ma."

Douglas leans against the wall. *He's going to faint. What is wrong with me?*

"Are you sick, Doogie?" Willi asks. "You're looking, acting like maybe you're too sick? Too sick to play?" Wilhelm Stoya's tone is lilting, taunting, gleeful.

Douglas isn't at all sure; he's willing himself to resist the mindlessness. He unlatches the case and lifts the lid. The case is open in front of him—still, he blinks in confusion. *No violin?* There is no violin nestled in the green silk! "No violin?"

He runs his hand along the indentation where he had positioned the beloved Magic Muriel some hours earlier. Simply the indentation remains in the silk, proof there had just been a violin in this case. "Willi, where's the violin?"

"In the case, schmuck."

"Look for yourself! Nothing. It's gone!"

"Gone? Did we leave it behind, Willi?" Mrs. Piano Teacher aghast.

"No, Ma, I'm sure. I checked just before we left! I'm positive." He certainly won't admit he did leave it unattended on the train seat for a spell. Nor that he was behind the clothes rack flirting with the curvaceous flute player when Douglas took off for the loo.

Unanswered questions emerge and are repeated.

"How?"

"When?"

"Who?"

For Willi and Douglas, each, a blunt realization. Each has committed an action he will spend regretting the rest of his life. However long a life may be granted him.

Anguish in each voice like the plea of a condemned man.

Willi to his knees. "Damn me, damn it all to hell."

Douglas melting, arms girdling his torso. "Oh god, the 253-1, what have I done?"

Mrs. Piano Teacher faces Douglas, his face gone as pale as alabaster, her face crimson with rage. "Where is my husband's violin? Our irreplaceable violin!" How are you going to perform? How? You irresponsible brat!" She shrieks to the ceiling, her voice worthy of a suicidal diva. "Don't let me see your face until you find it. You find it, right now!"

Douglas' legs melt out from under him. Huddled on the floor he sobs. "My violin, gone? No, no, no!"

Frieda runs for her husband, screeching a string of German words punctuated by, "Help! Help!"

Thirty minutes of scouring the backstage area, questioning the Orchestra members, finally a petition to the audience; the violin is not to be found. Hidden by a scoundrel? Nabbed by an insider? Walked away by itself? Disappeared into thin air? No matter. It is gone.

And Douglas is nowhere to be found, either.

[34]

MRS. PIANO TEACHER reaches her seat and sobs. Professor Stoya breaks into a sweat. How helpless the duo feels, here in the Concert Hall, seated in the red plush velvet front row seats.

Forty-nine minutes later, the soloist, Wilhelm Stoya, is announced (with the accurate yet implausible explanation). This time the small lady's feathered hat catches neither breeze nor light. Wilhelm takes the stage with a borrowed violin and bow. A nod from the *alternate*, the *understudy*, the *second-place-not-first-choice* player, Professor Stoya's son, to the Conductor, and Hindemith's Sonatas ring out.

The audience hears a piccolo, two flutes, two oboes, two bassoons, four horns, timpani, snare drum, triangle, harp, one cello, and the string section. All with a solo violin played by the Runner-up instead of the NOA Winner, whom reporters had written rave reviews about last week.

Stoya will never hear the mood-altering gigue of the Suite's finale, which should set Willi's violin to dancing with the orchestral accompaniment. Nor will he hear the polite applause. Nor see his son take a respectable bow. Minutes before that, his pen falls to the floor with a tiny clickety-click-clack; he clutches his chest as intense pain circles his heart.

Frieda gasps.

* * *

AFTERWARD. AFTER THE applause. After the ambulance. After Douglas' disappearance is confirmed. *Did anyone spot him?* the inquiry goes. This young man isn't a figure you easily pick out in a crowd. Medium everything. Until you get up close to feel the passion in his eyes, see the cluster of freckles across his cheeks, study the unusual cowlicks almost tamed by a close haircut. *Running away like that? Is he guilty?*

[35]

NARCISSE LOUISE, observant LuLu, knows what happened this morning.

It was she, left alone with only the cuckoo and silence for company. Here where pulsations daily reigned. She who watched, she who listened. She with the steadiest of meters. It was she who knew the rogue fiddle was left behind. Knew when and how each boy handled the instruments that morning. She saw the second teen's correction which voided the first teen's stealth. Don't they say, "all's well that ends well"? So, did the Stoyas need to know?

Her heart yearned for love as fiercely as any. So just as she kept company with a gentleman in her off hours—a year-round resident of the Smythe Hotel, a novelist he—and just as she inspired him with gossip of young musicians' capers, as he in turn matched her ardor heartbeat for heartbeat, did the Stoyas need to know? Know all? Not at all. As Stoya had said, "music is not only in the notes but also in the rests," so she believed the quality of her service to the trusting family hinged on her rests.

How would Douglas fare? There in the Concert Hall thinking he had one violin, only to find he had the other. Although he's competent enough to excel on either instrument, would the shock unhinge him? Only time will tell. And she is left to wait. A leisurely walk fills her early evening hours but can't calm her mind. She returns to the stone house, continuing to fret.

An August night takes its time falling, this one is no exception, and eventually the full moon struggles upward, ghosted by cloud. Another hour advances, bringing the quick rage of an electrical storm. Fat raindrops splash before Narcisse Louise can shut all the windows. *Why aren't they home yet?*

The phone jangles. LuLu feels her heart pound. The crawl of goose bumps up her limbs sets her shivering. Is she ready to hear the news someone bears?

That someone is Willi. "Willi?" LuLu chokes on her own saliva. Willi plunges headlong into the tale of misery.

"Mummy said to call. It's bad."

"I know what you did, Willi."

"Don't tell the folks, please, LuLu!"

"I would have stopped you. Except you were, after all, accomplishing what the Professor intended."

Willi continues. "Nothing matters now. The coward runs away, you see, because there was no damned violin in the case."

"What?! No violin in the case? *Neither* violin in the case?"

Wilhelm Stoya begins to rant, his words broken by guttural sobs. "That's what I'm saying. Pa's violin vanished backstage. We don't know exactly how. Lame-brained Doogie thinks his favorite is stolen. He freaks out and goes we don't know where. So now cuz I'm the understudy. I hate that word. *Understudy.* I'm left to play a stupid violin loaned at the last minute by some guy in the Orchestra. Whoopee, my big break? I couldn't even think straight after that. How could I, LuLu?"

"How did you play?" Narcisse Louise Boulez has the audacity to ask. What would anyone expect under the circumstances? His father's prized violin snatched from its case. His self-serving scheme trumped.

"Don't even ask," he sobs. "Nothing turned out like I planned. Pa had a heart attack or something bad; Mummy's out of her mind. Both got taken to the hospital right after my performance. Of course. It's my fate.

Never to get their praise, never-never-never!" Anger spews like molten lava.

LuLu waits it out.

"Mummy said to tell you that Siggi and me will be home tomorrow. We're at the hotel right now. She's gonna stay at the hospital with Pa until whenever."

[36]

BACK HOME WILLI and Siggi ignore each other. Willi stumbles up the stairs. He rants, his words broken by choking teenage-boy sobs. "Hate myself. Damn, damn me. Blast it all, Siggi, for spying on Douglas. If only I hadn't known. Curse it to hell. If only I hadn't been told. Pa's violin would be *here. Right now.* Safe. Safe. Hell no, it's the one been stolen, Pa's violin stolen. Damn, stupid me." Wilhelm Stoya keens uncontrollably, stuck in the mire of his own doing.

Narcisse Louise Boulez, LuLu, grasps the banister, hangs onto it for dear life, and wails.

Siggi carries a peanut butter and jelly sandwich into the library. He switches on the television.

* * *

MORNING SHINES INTO Willi's room, beaming her late August warmth into his chilled soul. He sits up, takes a deep breath. Last night's torment pales as an idea flashes him a reprieve.

His folks don't know anything about the switch—yeah. And he will never tell them; they don't need to know. Just like LuLu said, the Professor insisted Douglas play on the Performance Violin. The Professor believed it was the one taken to the event.

There beside the piano, he sees it, the vile relic wrapped in green silk. Hateful pile of wood and string that brought Douglas here. Douglas

382 · GENIE HIGBEE

who curried favor with his parents like a conniving bohunk. Never mind his Pa once called Douglas a filthy *zigeuner*, Pa gave his highest praise to Douglas Tryzyna. Stupid Doogie. Disgusting Doogie.

Anger surges, black, boiling, out of control like an oil gusher just tapped. Willi hurls the offender across the room. It strikes the square-cornered clock cabinet. The painted bird pops out with a startled blather of *cuckoos*. How annoying! How infuriating! Willi kicks the loathsome creation into the library, where it smacks into the andiron. Steel, brass, and wood collide as the 253-1 hits, rolls, and settles upside down on its belly. It resounds with a low groan.

A slithery eight-legged, claw-footed unease crawls up Willi's spine. Was Siggi watching just now? I've got to get rid of the thing before the folks come home, find out what I've done to it. Hide it. Back into the case. I'll think of something.

Willi sinks to the floor, face between his knees, his arms wrapped around his head. Siggi sidles into the salon. So many irregular surfaces stare up at the ceiling. Ebony fingerboard askance. Strings unattached, red wooden neck and scroll at an angle. If he touches the thing it might just fall into pieces. Siggi's unblinking eyes speak of irreparable damage. The younger brother voices a fearful truth. "It's only a matter of time before Pa sees this, you know." Siggi scoops up the sorry mess, deposits it into the case where the lonely bow sleeps. He methodically tucks the silk all around. Like putting a feverish child to bed. What to do? Well. He'd better ditch the evidence of an atrocity—or else he and his brother are in for it.

When Ophelia comes bearing flowers Siggi jumps at a quick fix. This savvy girl dressed in navy blue is the only person available to trust. He tosses the bouquet aside and thrusts the violin case into her arms.

"Douglas' violin shouldn't be in Pa's sight," Siggi says. "It's the only one we have left." He kicks the rug, watching the woven flowers buckle. "And it's caput."

"Caput? You mean, broken, what? *Douglas'* violin? Wasn't it safely left behind?"

Siggi snorts. "Yes. And, well. No."

"What happened?" Ophelia asks, always eager for the scoop.

Siggi shakes his head. "Don't ask. Better for Pa to believe both the violins were stolen."

[37]

Gossip goes 'round and 'round Elizabethtown:

> Did anyone spot Douglas?
>
> Heard him play that fiddle lately? Pure magic.
>
> Been gone all weekend, they say. Not a word to Hester.
>
> My Mister saw him boarding the Montrealer.
>
> Well, Dr. Dankworth saw him up at the cemetery.
>
> The Milkman saw him hiking to the Falls.
>
> Have that violin with him?
>
> Must have, the thief.
>
> I heard he was related to the Ibarra family, goes to show you.
>
> Gotta ask, heard him play that old fiddle? Just magic.

[38]

OPHELIA CARRIES THE latched case home and keeps it under her bed, hidden by the long eyelet dust ruffle. After one quick peek at the victim inside the case, she's filled with the same fear Siggi had expressed. *This will be too much for the Stoyas.*

There's no relaxing. What if her mother discovers the case, opens it, and asks a million questions? There's no safe hiding place. It's only a matter of time and already it seems like forever. One Tuesday afternoon Ophelia strategizes. She re-wraps the wooden patient in a blue flowered scarf, a silk one, one that she most adores. She ditches the green silk as if it were a bloody bandage. When her mother is preoccupied listening to *Art Linkletter's House Party* she ducks out with the contraband in its case.

Sister Elder greets her like a long-lost child; such clutching from a grieving woman is enough to make a body dissolve in tears. Ophelia stays firm. "When Douglas returns, if he ever does, promise me, cross your heart and hope to die, promise me you will give this back to him."

Ophelia's demanding a pledge? Sister Elder' eyes flare like a stick of dynamite seconds before explosion. Had she followed her instincts long ago this drawn-out tragedy would never have occurred.

Ophelia isn't misled; she's witness to the bitter sorrow. Nevertheless, she can think of no better choice for safekeeping the relic than Douglas' Guardian. Certainly, Sister Elder's heart, like any mother's, would thaw with the return of an ill-fated child.

[39]

A PHOTO OF Douglas Tryzyna is posted at Denton's Store. MISSING.

> And gossip goes 'round and 'round the town:
> Still no word for Hester?
> Ungrateful brat.
> With a spinster for a Guardian.
> What do you expect?
> You know the sort.
> Related to the Basque, goes to show you.
> I sobbed hearing him play that fiddle. Happy tears.

Pure love in every note.

Professor Stoya with a stroke. Poor Frieda.

Peter will recover, bit of a brute.

You know the type.

[40]

SISTER ELDER OPENS the door, her eyes red, her hair a bird's-nest affair, her apron wrinkled. There stands her arch enemy.

"That boy you raised is a liar, Hester, and a thief! I need to talk to him right this minute." Mrs. Piano Teacher looks a fright herself. Two women who have barely tolerated each other all these years have something else in common. Exquisite pain.

"I don't know where Douglas is, Frieda. He hasn't returned." Sister Elder's voice sounds like roller skates on gravel. "Violette tells me he just disappeared without a word after he found the violin stolen."

"Oh, is that the story? *Found* the violin stolen??? I'll tell you this, our rare violin went missing while Douglas was backstage supposedly in charge of it. And then he went missing too. You figure it out."

"I hear what you're implying. Need to blame someone, don't you, Frieda? Well, you're absolutely mistaken about my Douglas. So, back off!"

Frieda cannot acknowledge those words. Perhaps she can't even comprehend anyone else's point of view right now. "Poor Peter's been in the hospital. He had a stroke. The shock of it all. Losing his valuable violin. And to someone he's treated like a son all these years."

"How is he, your Peter? Will he make a full recovery?"

"Cruel thing a stroke." Frieda muffles sobs, the clutched hankie insufficient for mopping such a runny nose.

Sister Elder isn't inviting this woman indoors. No matter how pathetic her plight. Hester waits; her sympathy registers *empty*.

Frieda blows her nose, stuffs the hankie into her pocket, and continues. "I came back home only to find the other violin, the abandoned one, however valuable it may be, was gone too. *Both* violins gone! Just gone! Peter doesn't know yet. What am I going to tell *Peter*? What am I going to tell him?"

[41]

VIOLETTE ENTERS THE Conservatory without knocking; she carries a bouquet of chrysanthemums. She's not here for a lesson. Who knows if lessons will resume? She's come to check on Professor Stoya. "Narcisse? LuLu? You here?"

Willi rushes to her. He's unshaven, disheveled in pajama bottoms and undershirt. His fingers fidget like spiders hastening from danger.

"Hey, you look awful! How's your Pa? Did anyone find the violin?"

Willi lets loose a string of expletives that flatten Violette against her distorted reflection in the beveled glass doors. This verbal explosion doesn't satisfy his fury. Willi Stoya drags Violette to a practice room, eases the door shut. He's flushed, pungent with sweaty fear. He leans close, his face a pincushion against her cheek. He whispers, making a confession. Only a partial confession—there is no mention of his abuse to a violin. The action he chooses to confess is related with pride, with black-hearted anger, with fatalism. This admission of his hateful, fateful scheme targeting Douglas leaves Violette no doubt about *him*. He's despicable! A curse forms. *Punish Willi!*

Tears well in her eyes, drop onto her cheeks, form icicles of confusion. She's appalled. Hate freezes this poet's heart, re-sets her brain. Words, unbidden, unplanned, and oh so satisfying fly from her mouth. Her statements, truth and falsehood, are suspended, like two-legged bloomers frozen on the clothesline; it's too late to retrieve them.

Her malevolent deception scalds Willi. Just as she intends. And yet. What benefit will be derived? Her caustic lies will result in further devastation. A tragedy comes down the pike, and it's too late for intervention.

[42]

SOMETHING OWNED BY Douglas Tryzyna has washed up below Split Rock Falls. Wing knows the boy frequented the place in mental preparation for the concert. Just as a competitive skier envisions every mogul, every flag, every foot of the terrain down which he will fly with his skis chattering, so too Douglas imagined the bowing, the fingering for every note, and the Conductor's direction of the orchestral accompaniment.

Sister Elder knows that Douglas stood at the head of the Falls where he'd imagine taking a humble bow, if the audience had applauded enough, in which case he'd imagined performing a heartfelt encore with the pianist.

So, when a linen vest is discovered tangled in rocks below the Falls—the product of Astrid's unmistakable tailoring, just look, good luck Loong embroidered in gold floss—the worst is presumed: Douglas in abject grief has committed suicide at the Falls.

Still Wing resists. "His friends, they're saying he's not the type," he tells the sheriff or anyone who asks.

"These kids talk frankly to each other about this," Sister Elder says. "Suicide isn't a stranger around here."

Captain Paul Heinke listens respectfully to Wing and Sister Elder—before speaking his foregone conclusion. "We adults, we'd rather believe *anything* than the truth. Here we have another Elizabethtown teenager lost in the tragedy of hopeless despair."

Astrid disagrees in private. She's brushing her zigzag flaxen hair while pleading with her husband. "Wing, remember? I couldn't find his vest in the wardrobe. And it wasn't in the garment bag when he left. So, how could he have been wearing it? Maybe, just maybe, he'd accidentally left it at the Falls when he was practicing that last week?"

Ophelia and Violette toss leaves off Little Bridge. Brown, gold, green ovals swirl in the bubbles, looking helpless. "It seems impossible. Douglas gone, like gone forever," Ophelia says. "Do you think he, you know, like on purpose at the Falls?"

Violette is silent. She closes her eyes, remembering a conversation about suicide. They were at the Conservatory after Susanna's death. "Would you ever do it?" she had asked her fellow musicians.

Willi had answered first. "Suicide? That's for bozos who didn't cut the mustard, like walking the plank; they probably know they're losers.

She'd given Willi a scowl; he hadn't noticed.

No one had asked Siggi; he'd piped up anyway. "I don't get it."

Violette had replied wisely. "You're too immature, Siggi."

"I'd never!" Ophelia had been adamant. "People would gossip about me."

"And you, Violette?"

Violette is remembering that she had deliberated. Her answer back then would ring true today. "I couldn't hurt my mother like that. Besides, I'll always hope tomorrow can bring something better."

"What about you Doogie-doo?" Willi had smirked, waiting for a response. After a pause the scorned blood brother had spoken.

Violette opens her mismatched eyes. "I remember Douglas' answer about suicide." She drops her last leaf into the bubbling water. "He said, 'Some things are still worth living for. Even when bad stuff happens, or people are mean, or I'm angry.' That's what he said."

The girls, piano students, accompanists, sometimes allies, embrace. A suicide creates a black hole to suck the energy, the joy, away from souls bonded to the deceased. Violette closes her eyes again; she's trying to picture Douglas' face those few summers back when they had simultaneously lost their innocence.

"Well, what do you think he'd answer now?" Ophelia asks, resting both arms on Violette's shoulders. They stand in attempted consolation, forehead to forehead for a moment.

Violette straightens to her full height. "*Never*, he'd say he'd *never*. And the vest washing up at Split Rock Falls, that's no proof. Douglas is going to come back."

[43]

SISTER ELDER BLAMES herself. "I let him cross the river of nepenthe when he was small and impressionable."

"Really? When?" Mildred asks as she sobs. She's come home from Business College to comfort Sister Elder.

"I let him cross the river. He danced to cursed music. I let him stroke the violin and call it his own. It happened so quickly; I was helpless to stop it."

"It isn't your fault. It isn't anyone's fault."

Sister Elder walks through the kitchen, running her hands along the butcher block table, refolding a dishtowel, righting an apple. She opens the door to the back porch as if a visitor might have knocked. She faces the egg farm, Little Bridge.

Mildred mumbles; is hushed by Sister Elder. "Shh. Shh. Listen. Wild murmurs over there, across that very river, induced a drowsiness and seduced him. And now our beautiful boy is lost to us."

* * *

SISTER ELDER KEPT the case-confined-scarf-wrapped object in Douglas' wardrobe. On a shelf pushed right up beside the Muriel cigar box where perhaps it exchanged electrons with the owner's memorabilia.

Hester closed the door on his room. Kept the door to social interaction barely ajar. She chose solitude with the absence of noise and a
dearth of worldly desires. And in this, the Carthusian way of joining to
the Silence that lies at the heart of the world, did she unwittingly expose
her angry soul to healing forces? The results were not to be seen, even in a
year. You ask, if by some miracle Douglas were to return baring his heart,
would she allow him the violin?

VI
WOE & WISDOM

[1]

October 1953

I LIE HERE in self-pity. They speak of this, the two who found me, the father and son who brought me here. Of the bear trap. Of a hospital stay. Of my left leg. Could not be saved. They say I didn't give my name. Or my family ties. I'm not remembering.

And now, this woman. Gateau. A stranger, and should I add, strange? Enormous false eyelashes create skeletal shadows obliterating a view of her eyes. If she has hair it is covered by a trailing headscarf. She watches me take the first sip of the bitter tea, so hot it burns my mouth, and she gives a pronouncement. "What we have here is a dark soul."

She waits. "Think on love, persons you have loved." She waits. "Early memories of love, speak of them." She waits. "This along with the tea, my son, it will ease your pain."

Bertok calls me Crowe, meaning a *dark one in flight*. Gateau asks Oliver to paint a new name on the cabin where I'm to stay. *Crowe*. I cannot recall another name for myself.

She asks me to remember the mindless days of childhood. Smells. Colors. Sounds. I recall sounds:

A woodpecker's tinny hammering on the roof. The rain's plink-plunk into a bamboo birdbath. Coos of self-talk, a boy's giggle, a sound no adult could imitate. A lady's voice, pinched, precise, a minuet. A man's voice, a fire guttering, a march of sputtering-spitting consonants. Another voice, a flurry of s's, sweet like the ring-ring-ring of a tiny bell, or sorrowful like a lament.

"Speak of it," says Gateau.

Extended memories float only as fragments. I have no words.

"Speak of it," says Gateau.

> *I have no words although images undulate:*
> *I am kneeling beside moving water. I'm watching as it slows. It*
> *comes to a rock and divides to pass by. Bubbles gather around the*
> *rock like soapsuds. I try to scoop them up. The water has no color.*
> *How can I see the blue of sky and earthy colors when I look there?*
> *Water in the house isn't the same. I prefer watching water outdoors.*
> *It carries small wiggling creatures. I wonder where they are going.*
> *I have no words; I am not speaking to this inquisitor.*

"Yes?" Gateau watches me attentively as if she were hearing some wonderful story.

> *I'm remembering:*
> *The stream is at the egg farm. We walk to it sometimes. I want to*
> *touch the hens. They run away from me. I find their feathers in the*
> *yard. I take these treasures home. I want to carry the eggs. She won't*
> *let me. She knows how to be careful. And I don't.*
> *One day a man sits in the yard at the egg farm. I must be careful of*
> *him too. He holds a curved box with a neck. A magic voice can fly*
> *out of this box when the dark man moves a stick across its strings.*
> *The sounds tell me to run and twirl, which I do with much waving*
> *of my arms. She takes me away. I struggle. I'm furious with her.*
> *And then one day I hear the same sounds in the cemetery. This time*
> *the man makes the magic lady sing a mournful song with his shiny*
> *box; and everyone who is crying wipes away their tears. Those who*
> *are cross soon forget quarrels and hug. I want to make a magic lady*
> *sing from that box. I want to make happiness come alive like that*
> *man does. I didn't speak in words then, either.*

Gateau closes her dramatic eyelids. "I can hear you anyway."

[2]

TODAY NOEMI CAME to cabin *Crowe*. Along with lunch she brought the patient a jack-o-lantern, the visage of a scowling dwarf, a candle flickering from within to light the eye sockets and teeth. *Scowl! Shout! Hallelujah for Halloween, the fierce, the ill begotten, the scandalous. Hallelujah for loveliness eternally masked, unrecognizable. Hallelujah for black October rain.* As if joyless thoughts have brought it on, rainfall begins. Black October rain. Heavy, bold rain. Suiting Crowe's mood raindrops spatter, splatter on the cabin's roof, beat at the windows and doors. Threaten to break in. And then no more. Moisture becoming chalk-like, slashes downward toward the forest floor of cones, needles, twigs, and squirrels. Heavier and heavier an artist's hand wields the chalk, until many minutes later the illusion gives way. Gives way to the fantasy of floating paper, a ticker tape parade of white. A Houdini illusion, a bride's veil flying away. Everything once bright smothered to pastel. Evergreens erased to gray. The wind shifts, quiets, and without a conductor to tell them otherwise, the snowflakes obey gravity—at once a lazy, mesmerizing mass of flakes, uncountable.

Scents, but a few. Of wax and pumpkin pulp. The patient hobbles up, opens the door, breathes in. Of sap, of pine, of wet dogs. Of wood smoke and bacon, pungent, from *Itthon*, where Gateau, Bertok, Oliver, and Noemi gather.

Sounds, but a few. Laughter, several indistinguishable voices. Bertok's family. And then Music. A piano, a soprano, joining now in a simple song. And then one unmistakable voice enters the musical conversation. Like a woman's voice. A unison of strings and wood, this familiar voice joins to vibrate and in doing so engulfs the broken teen's body. This voice, a violin.

Memory of sound. In flashes. In pieces he can name.

A voice, pinched, precise, a minuet, Sister Elder.

A flurry of *Ses,* sweet like the upper ring of a violin's pure treble, Sister Peace.

A fire guttering, a march of sputtering-spitting consonants, of course, Professor Peter Stoya.

A persona that calls for him from the Basque man's red box, the transmission of Magic Muriel 253-1 entreating him to action.

And then. The haze clears.

NEW YORK CITY TO QUEBEC, CANADA

[3]

Two months ago, August 1953

HE RUNS FLAT out, unnerved—an ambulance wails—scenery passes in a blur. Dark silhouettes, walkers, stop sign, taxi honking. Ticket for first departing North Bound train—hours, hours, destination reached, out of money—hitchhikes along a grand waterway. If there is any comfort it can be where water churns, where birds wheel. Too numb to feel hunger or weariness. Sidesteps interaction with humans. He's the hideous one, a monster. *Got greedy. Got impatient.* Fiddle gone from his hands forever. There was, would have been, a future for them. Fortune backfired. *Can't bear it. Only the Stoyas will be happy. Performance Violin still safe at home. Only the 253-1 missing. Why isn't Magic Muriel talking to me?*

On the run again, scenery passes in a blur, hungry, confused, colorless sky, train rumbles on unseen tracks. Sign, *Local Honey.* Wisps of smoke from unseen fire. Flag in wind a triangle of navy blue, rivers of red and white. Dark silhouettes, walkers, bank of clouds, distant layers of receding mountains. Waterway. Barge, sloop, sailboat.

Broken down jalopy, by a tree. Not to be forgotten. *How's about a recipe for forgetting the human race? Blank, bleak, screwy humans. I'm the worst.* Gust of wind, clumps of drab brush and grass in the river. Red and white tower on stilts. Desperate divided years. *I swear a fiddle never spoke actual words. And yet words formed.*

Shade of the forest. *Something, something alive!* One step too many. How? What? *Oh God!* Writhing, twisting, trapped.

Douglas screams. He yelps, he wails, he moans. "Help!" None is forthcoming. And then he cries out for an answer. "Why am I alive? Where was the gain?"

And for an instant the 253-1 can be felt in response to his morose thoughts. {That's the beauty of the thing| is it not| You are alive| |

Instinct alone translates the transmission.

Cold. So cold. Close your eyes; remember snowballs in winter. Remember kids dragging sleds uphill. Slow down, all but forgotten, mind clouded. Remember mothballs in spring, playing music at the Falls. Slow down, work it out. Pine straw and trees. Sleep.

He wakens to the sound of a violin being played. Music meanders up the slope, through trees, passing across dry grass and bramble, clear as anything. Music drifts with the foggy apparition of a young man, an ax over his shoulder. *Sleep.*

Sleep will not come. Tiny leaves of aspen and birch flutter as the wind beckons, speeding or slowing like musicians following a conductor's baton. Tall trees gyrate, pointed tops describing circles of space. Poplar trees divide into sections of threes, of fives, or sevens, giving up their pretense of vertical unity. Shrubbery, unheeding the wind, throws shadows on brown stubble. A warning remembered. *"Fire season is upon us."* His leg is on fire.

Sleep snuffs out flame before he wakes again. Gyrating tree trunks above him. Wind. Limbs writhe waiting for calm. There he lies, helpless, motionless, waiting for help. Words come and go; fragments of wisdom thrum. *Kindness. What does it mean? Someone said, a wounded person needs kindness in order to be healed.*

✼ ✼ ✼

A LOW MOAN draws the two woodsmen toward his direction. A moan followed by, "My violin, my violin." Under a tree where pine needles were once strewn over chain in attempted camouflage, there a man, a teen— he's some age in between the two designations—a poor creature all said and done; he writhes. A mandible of metal fangs, a fist of steel claws sunk into one leg just below the knee, mapping a black clotted hemisphere. The sheen of wet blood trails from a pointed stick, a stick they realize at the same moment with a gasp in unison is bone, a tibia in distress separated into an upward spear.

"My violin, my violin."

"He's delirious," Bertok says. "Help me. Free him of this trap."

As immediate as the need to get this suffering soul some help is the need to look for his violin. Oliver scours the area while Bertok prepares a temporary splint. Nothing resembling a violin is to be found.

ONTARIO, CANADA

[4]

November 1953

PAINFUL USE OF crutches, throbbing stump, tender sessions with Gateau and bitter tea.

Noemi offers a stack of textbooks and an opportunity to finish the high school curriculum as required in Ontario. He's invited to do his studies along with twelve-year-old Oliver at the kitchen table in *Itthon*. Here he observes that Noemi teaches piano lessons many afternoons. Boys and girls tackle musical skills with varying degrees of enthusiasm.

He's attracted to a towhead who is aquiver with excitement week after week as he plays his assignments.

Such attraction infuses no feeling, however. From where Douglas stands, smack dab at the corner of here and gone, the distant church spire seems sharpened to a needlepoint atop a rock rectangular building. He imagines a giant syringe that's filled with paralyzing poison. Yes. He's been poisoned. Spun head over heels, detached. I've suffered emotional paralysis. That's what happened.

Only yards away fog compresses the sky and landscape into a single swath from zenith to horizon. Only a few trees stand as whitewashed sentinels, reminders of what may exist, of what may be obscured. While his phantom leg begs for attention, Magic Muriel 253-1 is mute, or is she merely a phantom of his delirium? Will he ever feel excitement again?

[5]

JANUARY. GATEAU ARRANGES her striped headscarf and closes her dramatic eyelids. "What do you remember about being a child, Crowe?"

Douglas falls into the deep well of her witch-like magic.

It comes back to me. Words come back to me.

Whether he's speaking aloud or merely thinking he's not sure:

I'm a foundling. I just don't know it until Sister Elder prepares me for Kindergarten. Had she always been a pretend mother for children? I asked her. Did I have a real mother or father?

"Of course, we all do." Sister Elder doling out her words like someone who is carefully counting change. After that she would ignore me, chop vegetables with Wing's knife. Or feed sheets into the rolling wheel.

The pleading from me again.

Always her minimal answer in monotone.

"When did she finally tell you, Crowe?" Gateau asks.

Her question startles Douglas; he forgets where he is. He speaks.

"One day when I was particularly insistent, she took me on her knee. She placed a photo in my hands. 'This is you, just as I found you. October of 1935. You'd been left on the Home's stoop early that morning in a blanket-lined washtub.'

"She'd been given clues to my identity. A wristband with an illegible scrawl. Sister Elder let me hold the tiny bracelet. She had deciphered the name, my name, as Douglas Tryzyna. And with a sigh she produced a photo. 'This is your mother, I believe.'

"My mother, a girl of a mother, a teenager perhaps, balanced on the running board of a Model-T Ford. Shadow crossed her face. I couldn't see if she was smiling, if she was pretty. Sister Elder turned over the photo. There on the back in the same scrawl. She read it to me: 'Fulfill your destiny. And remember, I love you.'

"What is destiny?" I asked her.

"Sister Elder opened a heavy book, one she kept on the library table. She thumbed through pages until she came to this. 'Destiny, the events that will necessarily happen to a particular person or thing in the future: luck, fortune, chance, karma.'

"What if a person didn't fulfill their destiny? I asked her in some childlike way.

"She understood me because she answered in a soft voice. 'I imagine there is suffering until one does.'

"'But did she know my destiny?' I asked. Sister Elder stiffened, just like that.

"I slid off her knee, still unsatisfied. But do you know my destiny? I whined while looking into her adult face. Up until that time she'd been my trusted source of information.

"'No, I do not, Douglas,' she said. But added, 'However, I honor your uncommon intensity.'

"'What is uncommon intensity?' I might have asked. She looked as if she had just eaten stewed rhubarb and gave me no answer, no answer at all."

Gateau appears unmoved by this revelation of Douglas' childhood. Perhaps he wasn't speaking, only thinking.

He's gripped yet again by the painful reality, once again a child. He wails aloud. "Gateau, why didn't she want me, my own mother?"

Gateau's voice quavers with possibility. "Crowe, son, perhaps she did. Perhaps she did."

Douglas continues. "And I envisioned hundreds of autos driving away, with hundreds of tires rolling around, and hundreds of mothers turning around, waving goodbye to hundreds of infants in hundreds of washtubs abandoned on strangers' porches."

Gateau places her rough hand on his cheek. "You have remembered well, Crowe."

* * *

ONE DAY BERTOK presents a gift. A leather-covered prosthetic with an articulated ankle. "I'm a carpenter of sorts," he explains. "When you outgrow this one, we will design another." What else this carpenter produces is left a mystery.

Another day, sounds coming across the yard, continuous enough to rouse Douglas from a deep afternoon sleep. A snap of fingers, strum, thrum of banjo, wail of a harmonica, carnival call of an accordion, hum of a hang drum, pizzicato of a violin, unidentified quaver, twang, percussive *tluuck, tlawck, tlock, tlack, tlick*. A musical group is warming up.

And then Gateau is knocking at his door.

Douglas rolls the fur collar to cover his ears, grateful for warm clothes from the family. His right foot cramps from the cold. He has no left foot; nevertheless, it reacts even in its absence. He winces. Gateau insists he walk daily no matter the weather. Today she accompanies him. She takes a drag from her cigarillo. "Here you are, a young green branch, but brittle as an old gray twig."

Her eyebrows, shaped like facing tadpoles, are ready to slide down the sides of her nose—an impossibly straight and well-shaped nose. Today she wears a floral headscarf like a jaunty abbess; it's still unclear to Douglas if she has any hair. She's bundled in layers topped by an embroidered patchwork cape, the frigid breeze not a bother to her.

"Tell me again, your family," she says. They walk toward a brick pavilion. Douglas hasn't noticed it before. The musical sounds are coming from it.

"It was as if I grew up raised by five aunts and three uncles with no clear mother or father."

"About the men."

"Wing, the kindest, most clever. He drew a cartoon about me; he called it Antenna Boy.

"Ciazzo, unspeakably generous, my finest violin teacher, I betrayed him." Douglas looks away, drags his sleeve over his eyes.

"Peter Stoya, demanding, demeaning. I never could please the man. He called me a donkey-schmonkey."

"You know, do you, donkeys can live to be fifty years old. Donkeys can cry. Donkeys can bond with other animals." Gateau stops, kicks at the snow. Something there shines. This is her habit, gathering little metal parts and pieces.

"And five women also involved in tending you, Crowe?" She takes his arm as they step over a log, her glance an encouragement, her lips expressive, well-rounded.

"Yes, it felt that way. Sister Elder, Sister Peace, Astrid, Mrs. Piano Teacher, sometimes Auntie Evangeline."

Gateau asks, "What does *mother* really mean to you?"

Douglas envisions a lady in a hotel apron, starched white with an oval hem, a deep v-neckline and waistline ties; that would be the *mother* keeping order. Another lady, willowy as cattails; she may have been diminutive, one of Violette's favorite words, but wasn't short on opinions; she would be the *mother* guiding him toward the wonder of the elusive. He conjures on this, the second *mother* who casually abandoned him, leaving only a note. He sniffles. Wipes his nose.

"What do you early remember of her, that one?"

"Perhaps I was six; I'd outgrown actual sleep during rest hour. Usually, I flipped through picture books while the brothers wrestled. That July day I sensed something. A quiver, or a vibration. I tiptoed along the hallway to Sister Peace's room. I sat there quietly, at the source. A song stopped and repeated. The more I heard it the more haunting it became. Ghostly, you know.

"The sisters' bedrooms were off-limits. The doors always closed and locked. Both women wore ribbons around their middles for keys. The jangling clued us kids to their approach—a reassurance when needing attention, or a blessing when avoiding punishment.

"That afternoon Sister Peace caught me. 'How long have you been sitting there?' she asked. Strangely she wore no apron.

"'What are you doing in there?' I asked in my loudest voice as if it were my right to know.

"'I'm limbering up,' she said. 'And you're supposed to be napping.'

"'I like the music. And I hear you moving around.'

"She signaled for me to enter. I bounded into her room and perched on the dressing table. Wallpaper, mirrors, photo in a frame, a lamp with fringe. Wood floor with no rug. A bamboo pole hung along the wall.

"She told me to behave like a *proper audience* or else. She started the Victrola, just as Professor Stoya did, placing the arm with its needle on the black disc.

"Her legs were covered in long pink socks. She had a little skirt and a wrapped-around shirt. I could see the outline of her bones, the ones along her shoulders, at her knees, her elbows. Her ribs curved out like fish bones. Her black hair was still so short like a man's.

"I stared. How could a person's arms look like wings? Legs float upwards, forwards, backwards? How could feet beat together or lift a body onto its toes? A melancholy sadness in the music stirred my gut. The melody, although playing very softly, ran along like a river. She too, balanced on her tiptoes, slowed or sped, spinning away, leaping, defying my desire for control of her.

"A new consciousness grew, an awareness of duality. My *real* Sister Peace—soft, floating, bright. And this other I didn't know at all.

"Then she shooed me out without a hug. And I know that I cried, desperately wanting to cling to this intangible woman."

Ahead a gray lynx crouches on a frosty hillock. Douglas points to it. As a breeze stirs the animal flattens into shadow. A mind plays tricks. These are only words he has been speaking; they have no meaning. *Mother* has no meaning. The Magic Muriel 253-1 hasn't communicated with him.

Smoke from Gateau's cigarillo floats away, the white curl thinning, vanishing. "The truth is, in this life what you hang onto will be ripped from you. I ask you, why should we bother then?"

The rising moon tips backward directly above a pillow of silver-gray cloud, should it choose this early evening hour to fall.

"Yeah, why even bother, what's the point?"

"I will tell you something you poor doubting mongrel. What you choose to hold precious in your heart can never be taken from you. Gather the best that each of those five women offered you. You are luckier than most sons."

Douglas' heart is still as clouded as the dreary day. He resents this woman who has a community to call family.

[6]

WITH THE SPRING thaw and newfound strength Douglas becomes curious about his surroundings. About the residents coming and going who appear to be of different nationalities yet speak a common mash-up language. Noemi explains. "Some years back we were forced to flee from our homeland. Bertok and I met the kindest healer along the way. We called her Gateau; it means *Cake*! We settled here together. We found other Hungarians, Poles, Austrians, Romanians, a few French, Czech too. This was in early 1930s, you see. What a *gulasz* of customs and languages at first! And so few possessions among us. We called our town Chodenzia; it means *renewal*. We've learned to survive by sharing, by cooperating.

"We all had one thing in common. Playing music, dancing to music. Especially the violin. Seen Bertok dance, have you? You might think he's starchy. Wait, you'll think again when you see his feet flying. Each full moon a celebration takes place. You must join us."

* * *

MAY. THE WIND, it's restless, stirs up foam on the lake. It pauses; it resumes. Petals flutter like moths released from darkness. Evergreen boughs, fringed with chartreuse, sway like ruffles on a flamenco dancer's skirt.

June. When strains of dance music float through the air Douglas limps to the Pavilion. He watches dancers find rhythmic partnership; he hears musicians achieve joyous harmony. Sometimes one man's happiness highlights another man's sorrow. Understandably then, midst the celebration Douglas grieves, he's missing Violette. He's missing the comfort of his fiddle pressed to his chest. And the 253-1 still hasn't reached out to him.

Gateau observes. Her keen gaze peers into every soul. She forges through excuses and reticence. She can disarticulate every lie, ferret out every private longing.

"And what was this violin's gift? The one you loved so?" Gateau asks, taking Douglas by surprise.

"Forbearance." The thought comforts him. "Among other things, *Forbearance*."

"Forbearance?"

"That's an archaic word, isn't it? A girl I once knew liked to use it. It means endurance."

✻ ✻ ✻

ANOTHER DAY GATEAU enlists his help preparing the garden for sunflower seeds. The breeze sifts and sighs, amplifying the rustle of spring leaves. Tall trees sway in a circular fashion, begging a crippled teen to become dizzy. Douglas dissolves into a memory. There on his knees in black soil, trowel in hand, he's once again gardening with Sister Peace.

His Sister Peace leaving that April. He should have seen it coming. He could have paid attention; he was almost fourteen. Postcards, blue envelopes, phone calls. Dressed like Hollywood, that day as she left. What did he imagine was up? Going by herself to spend two nights in the city? Really, though, why should she stay around? They weren't children anymore, not little kids who needed a babysitter. Oh. She obviously loved someone else more.

Sister Elder had given her, Tatiana Usolka, a birthday party that March. How old are you?" Violette had asked. "Thirty-one," she had answered. "And seventeen when I left the States before."

The party had felt like a short goodbye. And it was. If only he hadn't been afraid, if only he'd asked her the right questions: *She had been here fourteen years prior? And then left? Why?*

After Sister Peace deserted them Sister Elder didn't volunteer information. Nor did Wing, nor did Astrid. And he never asked for details.

"You weren't ready for the answers, Crowe," Gateau says.

Quick, quick, the witch-healer has struck her flint on a piteous soul. Quick, so quick, the unpredictable, unpromised result flares. It's instantaneous this rake of light in his eyes as Crowe and Antenna Boy link with gratitude. "I'm ready now," he says.

"Then you must return. You can't go forward until you gather the courage to clean up the mess."

Douglas tamps the earth around a gray and white striped seed, heeding her words.

"And if you seek a home after that you are welcome here."

"Why me? I'm nothing." A quick self-deprecating response.

"There are individuals in this world who are so finely tuned that their sensitivities attract danger. Each is rare, a unique creation in the universe. By over-reaching such ones are often broken. Some may be restored. That is my work. This is our work."

[7]

DANDELION PUFFS BRIDLING the breeze ride as free as anything. Leaves on birch trees telegraph silent messages while maternal roots underground nurse the grove. Douglas, in the midst of it, stretches out in the grass, verdant grass, grass drying, grass changing color, grass turning to straw, grass restless in the breeze with seed heads crumbling. Douglas plucks blade after blade of grass, coarse and green, putting each between his thumbs, and attempts to whistle. Every squeak altogether different from sounds of wooden flutes and whistles once heard at the Basque enclave. Private times like this he lets his mind wander; private times like this he's listening for Magic Muriel. She's been silent for almost a year. He longs for her, the invisible lady in the violin whose voice was sent lilting across fire. The sensation, altogether sweet, mournful, repetitious, was layered with a deep hum. If dessert? It would be chocolate cake with raspberry filling and whipped cream. If thrilling to flesh? Say, a plunge in spring runoff so chill you can't breathe, you fight for a short, harsh gasp of air. On the other hand, the sound could be equally as mournful as staring at a photo where shadow obscures the face of someone who should have loved you more. Someone who should have stayed. Or not have been a mere child herself.

[8]

THIS NEW FAMILY in Chodenzia has given him guidance. Crowe, as he is called here, counts his blessings.

"You must study your French!" Noemi insisted. She knew. His conversational French, thanks to months of practice with her, is passable—and a necessity for communication in these parts.

"Time to drive, kid," Bertok announced. "I'll teach you." Hours behind the van's steering wheel on delivery trips to Montreal have sharpened his skills.

"You're lucky, you still have your knee," Oliver pointed out, not one to nurture self-pity in others. Oliver seems like a steadfast brother.

Permanently on his mind, Gateau's counsel. "You must go back before you can go forward." The strange woman isn't one to shy from speaking truth. "You can't evade a return to Elizabethtown any longer. Go before winter sets in."

Douglas observes his reflection as he grooms for an August full moon celebration. Nobody insists he participate. It's just that he no longer enjoys being alone and missing out on their music. Their joyous music. Violinists can be heard tuning up outside around the fountain. He draws back the curtain only to close it hurriedly—though not before a twinge of envy prickles.

Back to the mirror. He'll be nineteen in a week. Same Titian curls, same freckled face, but a face grown sharp around the edges and growing new stubble daily. Same brown eyes stare back at him except now they are open. He had acted like a frightened rabbit last August. He hadn't faced the situation—the shock of the empty violin case, the bombshell of an accusation.

What if the 253-1 turned up after he ran away? What if Willi performed amazingly given the chance to be the soloist? What if the Stoyas weren't angry with him? Maybe in reality they'd been grateful to find the Performance Violin safely in the Conservatory salon.

A trumpeter offers five plaintive blasts as he walks across the yard. Douglas flinches. Mercy, how he had run away from another difficult time too. Worse, he had blamed someone else.

He'd only come to this realization. Just last month. A pair of gold-finch were hovering around the sunflowers as Gateau watered. He was struggling to explain to her his unusual relationship with Tatiana, Sister Peace. The sprite of a lady moved into the Home when he was still five. Her hair clipped short like a man's. Dressed in boots and baggy trousers. She walked with a limp at first.

Gateau was encouraging him to continue. And a new memory bloomed, like a green bud unfurling bright petals. A bittersweet scene pulled focus. Had he been choosing to hear what was said, he might have remembered sooner. Sister Peace across Little Bridge kneeling with her back to the thawing river. He'd run out to her. She'd turned to look at him, her eyes red, ringed with the black that usually clung to her eye-lashes. His Aqua Fairy resembled a ghoul of sorts with her raven hair tangling in the breeze.

She'd reached for his arms. Spoken so quietly he confused her voice with that of the river. "I am leaving in short while, Douglas. Always the problem. Broken heart and joy like mates on a journey." She had gone on to give him some details. He had closed his ears.

While Douglas was sharing this memory with Gateau, the electric charge of Sister Peace's departure pierced him again like a million icepicks. *Gone.* From his throat a groan escaped. "Gone."

Hearing his agony Gateau's face remained fixed, neither smile nor frown. Her eyes told more than Douglas could see; he had turned inward and she was reacting to his pain. Gateau took him to the porch. Sat him down in a bentwood rocker. Soon steam curled from his cup of tea, as boiling water extracted the acrid essence of roots and herbs. Boiling tonic for his guts, for his heart.

Gateau pulled up a cushioned stool and sat before him. "People have their pride, their boundaries. They tell you what they can bear to share." She folded her hands and gazed at him kindly.

* * *

IT BEGAN TO make sense. Sister Peace had spoken to him in images, using the poetry of nature. The river going away and returning at the same time. The Northern Lights brief phenomenon in the sky. The moon constant even when barely visible.

The young male lead in this drama steps downstage with a soliloquy to deliver.

> Douglas, Doogie, Crowe (in soulful admission)
> I chose to be deaf.
> I chose to be blind.
> I claimed that Sister Peace took off,
> leaving only a note for me.
> I need to accept reality.
> She'd been preparing me for this all along.

And he's remembering. How on the sorrowful morning of her departure he hid in the coat closet, surrounded by lifeless sleeves, sleeves unable to hug anyone. Hid in the coat closet accompanied by lifeless gloves, gloves unable to grasp anything. In so doing, he, Douglas Tryzyna, refused to accept Tatiana's arms around him, her warm hands holding his. He, yes he, Douglas Tryzyna, was the one who would not accept or offer a goodbye.

VII
CONFESSIONS & COURAGE

[1]

August 1954

BETWEEN THE STATION and the park Douglas spots a robin tugging at a determined worm; the worm struggles halfway between death and the muddy earth. A crow flies across the sky, cawing incessantly; it follows a hawk. The pair circles moving west until they disappear over Hurricane Mountain. Douglas stalls, unable to step forward, his shoes cemented by fear to the sidewalk. A quick burst of rain colludes with his trembling and dilutes his resolve to confront old sins. He forces his phantom leg forward. Confront he must.

By the time Douglas makes it to the Home he's soaked. He's trembling. Taking a gulp of air, he rings the bell and hobbles to the porch swing where he sets his overnight bag. He hangs onto the chain.

Hester opens the door quickly. She's seen him struggle up the steps, of that he's sure. Sister Elder's face is lined, yet as smooth as delicate silk covering a violin; wisps of gray hair frame her face. Unspoken remorse between the two, Guardian and Ward, presses on and on like an endless bedsheet through a mangle. Sister Elder squeezes his shoulder. Tears are running freely, leaving pink trails on her powdery cheeks. Douglas has rarely seen her cry.

As expected, she's wearing a starched white apron over an earth-colored dress. She backs into the entry all the while offering instructions as if to a child. "It's raining cats and dogs, let me close the door, you'll get soaked and catch your death, hurry up now, come along."

She closes the door, backs away from him.

"Sister Elder, I..."

"Don't even start, Douglas! For all the love and care I gave you, this is who you become? A thief, a liar? I really can't bear to see your face. Do you know the pain you have caused?" Her words have never before driven a stake into his heart.

Douglas stutters unintelligibly, realizing with a sting that here he has remained *Douglas*; he doesn't have the presumed innocence granted *Crowe* in another place.

"Don't explain; I won't forgive you no matter what you say. You could have telephoned; you could have written. We thought you were dead. Poor Astrid and Wing. Did you ever think about *us*? Did you ever worry about *me*?"

Douglas hangs his head. "I was out of my mind, really gone crazy for a long time."

"Besides that, the Stoyas say you stole their rare and valuable violin. Mrs. Piano Teacher came right here to this door and told me so. Heavens, child, it's worse than that. Much worse. You stay right here for a minute. Sister Elder heads to the telephone table and rummages with papers. She returns with an envelope and from it she takes a newspaper clipping. Braced against the wall she holds it out to him. Before he can unfold the newsprint, she recites a headline. "Two Teens Feared Dead at Split Rock Falls."

Douglas scans the article dated October 28, 1953. How supernatural to be reading of one's own death. His mind can hardly grasp the actuality of these words in print.

TWO TEENS FEARED DEAD AT SPLIT ROCK FALLS
Douglas Tryzyna, age seventeen, still missing after two months. Discovery of the musician's vest, on October 21, 1953, washed up along Boquet River in a location not easily reached by foot, leads to the presumption of death at Split Rock Falls.

Related, Wilhelm Stoya's death. His body was found by swimmers who spied his shoe caught in rocks below the lower pool, on October 27, 1953. His parents, Peter and Frieda Stoya, report finding a suicide letter. Wilhelm and Douglas were schoolmates and musicians, Finalists in a recent NOA Competition for aspiring violinists.

Douglas' hands tremble; he's got to ditch the horrid artifact.

"Willi? Are they sure? He'd never do that, never in a million years."

"Apparently he did."

Douglas sinks to the floor, covers his face with his hands, wooden prosthetic clunking. He moans, gutted.

"You see why we believed you were dead. Too." A statement of his guilt, not a question. "You need to march right over to the Stoyas' house and face the disaster you, *you*, perpetrated." An order. Blinded by peevishness Hester doesn't acknowledge Douglas' major disfigurement, although it's exposed once again as he strains, pulling himself to standing.

His childhood Guardian, legal parent, stiff-faced stranger, opens the front door. Steps aside, raises her chin, eyes cast heavenward. "I can't harbor you."

The summer rain has caused steam to rise from earth and pavement. Behind him mist drops over gray-blue mountains, revealing the draws. Just ahead soft shadows of trees crawl across the golden fields. Little Bridge crosses the Boquet River, which dashes to the death-dealing Falls. Douglas limps along the familiar route with ever more dread. Facing the Stoyas? What can he say?

Sister Elder watches her charge until he turns the corner. And then she pounds her thighs, hating the hauteur she has just displayed. She could have shown him the violin.

Sister Elder had kept the scarf-wrapped object in Douglas' wardrobe. On a shelf pushed right up beside the Muriel cigar box. Who can say whether the violin recognized Douglas' unique vibrations with proximity to his valued souvenirs? Who can say if the violin tried to communicate when Douglas was within reach? We can only assume their polarities were not compatible. And the very crest of Sister Elder's heart submerged like an iceberg at sea.

[2]

NARCISSE LOUISE GASPS. *It's Douglas!* She steps onto the porch before he can knock. Her arms stretch to embrace the pathetic figure. Scents of pine, soap flakes, cinnamon, familiarity. When she draws back, concern crinkles her eyes. "You're drenched. And look at you, limping. Whatever happened?" Douglas has no words. He lifts his pant leg to bare the leather-covered prosthetic. "It doesn't matter. I'll walk right pretty soon."

They stare at each other in silence. LuLu is an embodiment of compassion. Had she been Lot's wife she too would have looked back with concern as the brimstone and fire rained down. "You know about Willi?" she asks.

He blinks as he gathers courage. "Can, can I talk to them? Please, I owe them so much."

"Something you need to know first." LuLu leads him into the kitchen. She opens the refrigerator door. "What's your favorite soda pop, Douglas? Choose one."

Douglas shakes his head; he can't take anything more from this household. "Nehi grape. You know that—everybody knows that."

"Especially Willi. Wonder why Willi was so intent, trying to serve you cocoa at breakfast, which you declined, and then intent on buying you and Siggi your favorite sodas on the train to the City that last day? Wonder why you didn't feel so well after you drank yours?"

"LuLu, I felt so brainless. Foggy. I almost collapsed backstage. I'd never had that kind of stage fright."

"It wasn't stage fright, child."

"What then?"

LuLu closes the fridge. She takes a deep, shuddering breath and Douglas feels a febrile quivering invade his body. "Listen. Willi dosed your grape drink. He used Frieda's Librium, her migraine medicine, her calming medicine. Too much of it can have that effect. I overheard him bragging to Violette about doping you!" She goes on without waiting. "Dear one, Willi planned to be the star playing the Performance Violin for that audience. Needed you to be out of commission. Oh, I saw you switch the violins and bows. Siggi saw you too. He told Willi. Willi switched them back before you all left."

Douglas takes a few minutes to digest this revelation. *That means...that means the 253-1 was still here when we left?* A pinpoint of relief flashes across his face. He speaks so very-very-slowly, as if the metronome dictated *larghissimo*. "So, LuLu—the Performance Violin—was, the one—stolen—not mine?" He pauses. "So where? Where is mine now?"

LuLu frowns, her eyes cast to the side. She avoids the questioner's disconcerting thousand-yard stare. "It was here after you folks left for the City, and the next day it wasn't. It just wasn't. I looked all over."

Douglas falls to his knees with a *clunk*. Flat open hands pound the floor. He's filled with newfound hate for himself. Just when he thought he was ready for this encounter. A visual memory awakens, accuses him— rushing downstream, the factory violin's open-mouthed scroll, round and round it goes, barely above water, issuing a silent scream. Or is it the call of the Magic Muriel 253-1 being swept away?

Mrs. Piano Teacher has heard voices. She pads into the kitchen wearing slippers. Douglas sees this mother's distress. Her mouth droops. Without lipstick her face matches her pale gray wrapper. He steps toward her struck with sympathy. She backs up, props herself against the counter, notices his lameness without returning a trace of sympathy, stares at him; blood rises into her cheeks. Her clarion call for accountability rings out. Yes, Guilt strides into the room pointing a finger. At whom, really?

"First you betray Wilhelm, your loyal friend, by trying to switch the violins. Next, you manage to steal *both* our violins, causing Peter to have a stroke, and finally, you have the audacity to show up here?"

Douglas, rigid. *What?* An eternity elapses like an endless river, while the wordless human he once was and has recently been drowns in confusion. Then, sharpened consciousness. A defense is whispered. "Mrs. Piano Teacher, honestly, I never-ever-never-ever stole either one." He chokes back sobs. "I just switched them. I am so ashamed of switching them. Please, please, can you forgive me?"

"Forgive you? A cheater and a thief? Both violins are gone, however the Hades you managed that!"

Frieda pulls from her pocket an envelope, flap ragged, torn open in haste ten months ago. "Take Willi's pain. Read it *every day.* I hope you'll spend the rest of your pathetic little life regretting your choices. Now get out of here."

He obediently folds Willi's missive and slides it into his breast pocket. "Please, how is the Professor? May I see him, just for a minute?"

"He won't want to see you, Douglas Tryzyna." She turns away, faking a reaction to an inaudible call. "I'm coming, Peter, love." Up the stairs she pads, slippers scuffing.

LuLu places her hand on Douglas' neck. The familiarity of her soap and pine scent has lost its power to comfort. She whispers. "I must say to you, *mon cher,* and don't you forget, it's we adults who are to blame for all of this horror."

Siggi comes stomping into the kitchen. His anger contradicts Lulu's kindness. "Curse you. Curse you to hell, Douglas! Killed my brother and stole my father's violin."

The painted cuckoo sympathizes with four sharp chirps. After that the Conservatory falls quiet as a morgue.

Douglas stumbles out of the gray stone castle of a house where it seems he spent half of his life. He shoulders his overnight bag wondering who could have stolen the Stoyas' violin from its case. There were so many people backstage that afternoon. And if the 253-1 was left behind at the Conservatory how and when did it go missing? LuLu was the only person left there, wasn't she?

* * *

ONE FOOT OF FLESH and one of wood take him limping down River Street where rivulets of rainwater join the river's flow, just as they always have. Down the neighborhood streets he goes until he's reached the picket fence in front of *Lilacs*. *What is Michael doing now? Has he continued to find success? Has he escaped his mother's rule?*

As if on cue Michael steps onto the porch looking older. *Is it the short haircut?* He's wearing a striped shirt with a tan windbreaker, although the steamy afternoon feels warm to Douglas. After a few clumsy exchanges Michael seems excited to reconnect. He's been in Hollywood recording with the MGM Orchestra all summer, saw tons of movie stars; he says they look much better all painted up in the movies than they do in person. Bertine joins him. She's grown taller, and Douglas thinks she looks like a picture star herself.

Jeanne comes out jangling car keys. "We're heading to Meadowmount right now, Michael. Michael. Michael, are you listening?"

"Will you be around tomorrow?" Michael asks. "Not that I have much time. I'm working on a new repertoire with Galamian for my upcoming tour. Raymond Lambert is my accompanist, really a neat guy. Hey, I can show you my photos, or for kicks we could play marbles, or ping-pong. Is your friend Willi around?"

"No." Douglas finds it difficult to state the truth. "No, he isn't. And I don't really live here anymore. Just a visitor. It's Ontario for me now."

"Lucky guy! You moved. I'm starting to think I'd rather live in California than New York."

Douglas waves goodbye to his friend, someone who's become a real celebrity. *I must look like a loser to him. My own fault, my own fault.* The admission reignites the painful loss of Sister Peace, who alone understood the abyss of his desire. He wonders, how far would he have gone to possess the 253-1? He who had no control over his passion.

[3]

WHERE TO FIND comfort before he takes a late train north? The Smythe Hotel where he used to shine shoes and listen to a novelist's repurposed gossip. It's there in the lobby that Lermontov (not surprisingly, thanks to LuLu) finds him minutes after he settles into a secluded leather chair.

Once in Lermontov's familiar Penthouse, after changing into dry clothes, Douglas reveals the guilt, the sorrow, the confusion. Unabashed he sobs like a child. He belongs to no one; no one has ever loved him enough. And he has loved too much. "Willi went over the Falls on purpose. Did you know that?"

Lermontov, among other things, is an admirable listener. He waits patiently. Douglas blows his nose and takes deep, shuddering breaths.

"Indeed." A pause. "General opinion was that you did the same, Douglas. Although Hester waved off an official memorial for you, keeping some hope alive."

"Mrs. Piano Teacher forced me to take Willi's suicide letter." Douglas moans. He fishes it out of his pocket. "I really can't bear to read it."

"Shall I read it aloud for us?" Lermontov reaches for the envelope. Withdraws the lined paper. Unfolds it. Scans it quickly.

Douglas nods. More tears streaming down his cheeks.

Lermontov's voice holds steady as he reads:

October 23, 1953

A Confession to whom it may concern:

Skinny little Douglas Tryzyna. He started taking music lessons with my folks when we were 5, or was it 6? Doesn't matter. I'll admit I was jealous. Pa and Mother treated him like a Prodigy and me like a second-rate Idiot. When we were about 10, I made up a big fat lie to get Douglas in trouble. Pa kicked him out of the Conservatory because of it. After that I pulled a prank at school and that's when we all started calling him Doogie-doo-doo. We were about 12 then, feeling like Hot Shots.

How I turned my pals against Doogie-Douglas you can only imagine. Anything to Crush him. To Break him. Week after week. I spared him nothing.

Doogie never ratted on me, never breathed a word, just kept showing up for his music lessons no matter how lousy his teacher at the time, practicing his heart out. Even in high school I kept the dirty campaign going; I wanted to make sure he felt like a Lowlife. I wanted to let it be known Doogie was a Misfit. He was part Dog as I saw it. The Dog part, that was the good part of him, the part everybody liked, loyal and steady. But I wanted to hate him for that, too.

When we were about 15, maybe 16, what does it matter now? Pa lured Doogie back to the Conservatory. Promised him he could play the stupid old violin. God, Douglas loved that thing. Me? How *did I feel about finally getting to play the forbidden Performance Violin? Big Deal. It's just an Old Relic. Hell, you revered it more than us kids, Pa.*

Then Doogie won the NOA Competition, that was just about the last lick. But what really did me in? He up and played so amazing at the Dress Rehearsal on that strange fiddle. Dang. Even Pa got in a Stew about him outshining me. Pa changed it up, said Douglas had to play the Performance Violin for the big solo Performance. Doogie was Steaming Mad about that, I can tell you. I was secretly laughing my head off. And I was Scheming to bring Doogie down. Ignoramus that I am.

On the Big Day Douglas pulled a switcheroo. To Hell with Pa's plan, he must of been thinking. Little ole Siggi saw him. He tattled, but only to me. I switched Pa's violin and bow back into its case on the sly.

On the train I pulled my final prank. I snuck Mother's drowsy medicine into his soda pop. Yup, I was counting on his Crash and my chance for Success. See, just maybe Professor Stoya would be proud of Me, Wilhelm Stoya, Me, his Son, the 2nd place Dope, if I could get a Decent shot at it.

I more than succeeded in ruining Douglas. I just didn't know it. Until later. Until now when it's Too Late for apologies.

Because of my Cheap Shot at Douglas and then because of my Utter Stupidity in Admitting it out loud, well, I've lost my One and Only True Friend. Life isn't worth living anymore.

No way to take any of it back, no way to make it un-happen.

Split Rock Falls. Unreal the sight all that water pounding past you. Us teens meet up there. We imagine going pell-mell down with the rush. We go there for the swimming holes, too. The rocks are damn slippery. Sometimes the current is impossible to swim against. We've been warned over the years, of course. Some of our pals, swimming team athletes, even, have drowned. Some got trapped under rock ledges. No wonder Doogie chose this place to end it all.

Douglas Tryzyna's body hasn't been found yet. Some corpses never are. I hope mine will never be, either. I don't deserve a decent funeral. Nobody should cry for me. I am so Ashamed. I am sorry. Guess it's my Price to pay

Goodbye forever, LuLu.

Siggi, little Brother, promise you won't make my Mistakes.

Violette, you'd probably say, it's Karmic Justice.

My One and Only True Friend, I wish it had been different,

Forgive me Mummy, I love you and Pa,

Wilhelm Stoya

Lermontov rereads the letter to himself, shaking his head.

Douglas speaks, his voice raspy. "Poor, poor Professor Stoya and Mrs. Piano Teacher losing their favorite son, I mean like that. Somehow, somehow it could have been stopped, don't you think? By somebody."

"Yes, tragic." Silence attacks loquacious Lermontov. After a while he speaks. "Was it avoidable by *that* point in time? Who knows? I might add, however, some pertinent point eludes us both."

Douglas shakes his head. "Yeah, it's got me to wondering." A pause. "Was I really Willi's *one true friend*? And Willi did this final, final thing, all on account of *me*?" Douglas feels woozy, as if he's been dosed with Mrs. Piano Teacher's Librium once again. His mind goes to mush trying to blur the horror.

Lermontov folds the letter into thirds. He slips it into the envelope as gently as one hopes to slide into death. "If you're waiting for elucidation or fabrication from me, I have none to offer at this moment."

The two, a silenced musician and a wordless novelist, share a passage of time in thought.

* * *

"YOU WANT TO KNOW the truth of it? I barged in on Willi's family when we were so young, he had to share his mother's attention with me, I fought to be first in father's eyes, I wanted to outshine him, always, I made friendship difficult for him."

Lermontov changes gears. "Let's get some dinner together, shall we? Even a sorrowful soul must eventually be fed."

Lermontov sips his Campari. And without looking at the menu he orders, for both. Cherrystone Clams, Assorted Olives & Celery Hearts, Broiled Brook Trout with Tomato & Lettuce, Potatoes Lyonnaise & Vegetable, Rolls & Butter. Dessert? Fresh Fruit Cup with Sherbet, for him. German Chocolate Cake for his guest.

Satisfied appetites lead to conversation, limited, however, by shock not yet assimilated.

Douglas. "Yeah, Willi might have been a bully." He pauses, gazing at the ceiling before he continues. "In some ways, though, he was my brother. We sort of formalized it. See." He holds out his left thumb where a pink scar remains as evidence.

Lermontov. "I understand."

After coffee Lermontov orders Chartreuse. "With an extra glass, if you please." From his own liqueur glass, he pours an inch into the other for Douglas. "A blend of 130 herbs, plants, and flowers. Made by Carthusian monks in Grenoble, France."

Douglas sniffs the hypnotically complex mix of floral, herbal, spicy, and vegetal scents.

Lermontov encourages. "You only need a little sip to feel blessed."

The novelist savors the green *digestif* with his eyes closed; it's a somewhere faraway presence the young man recognizes. Eventually a question. "Douglas, was the late young Wilhelm a lady-killer, as one may term it? Was he a red-blooded fellow?"

"Do you mean, did he like girls? Of course. What has that got to do with anything?"

Wing appears wearing his kitchen whites. "You come back to the Home with me. Please." Wing's sincerity touches Lermontov. Here's a father if he ever saw one, this man in his square cut clothes, his hair frosted with gray.

Douglas winces as phantom pain attacks his missing leg. Cringes as love attacks his detachment.

"You come find me, later, please." Wing's concern must be rewarded. Sooner or later.

Just then Violette is at their table pulling up a chair. "Thank goodness, I thought I was too late."

"Oh, I'm not staying. Taking the train tomorrow.... I don't belong.... Guilty of so much, too painful.... I shouldn't stay..."

"We have to talk, Douglas, please."

Lermontov gives his shoeshine boy one of *those* looks, glasses down over the bump on the bridge of his nose. His eyes, full circle of iris blue with flecks of gold, offer a nonverbal admonishment: *Stay!* After which Lermontov signs his tab. He stands. "I will leave you two. Douglas, you sleep here tonight, think on things. I'll get you a room."

* * *

UNCOMFORTABLE SILENCE. EYES grope for recognition. The young musicians have both changed. Violette begins just as the waiter lowers his tray bearing Coffee Royale, courtesy of Lermontov. "I've been following you," she says. "Saw you leave Stoya's and my heart jumped. I kept saying you were alive; your vest was no proof of anything."

Douglas sips his coffee, wipes the cream from his stubbly lip. "The one day I really needed that vest. I just couldn't find it in time."

Passing by them a young family with a wailing infant. The sound is enough to keep the pair silent a bit longer.

"Poor Willi," Douglas murmurs. Did you read his letter?"

Violette blinks a *Yes*.

"My fault. Like his letter said, he took his life because of me." Douglas chokes back a sob. "Not even to know I was his best friend, until it's too late."

Violette bites her cheek. She turns away, her strong, bony fingers blanching as she grips her glass mug.

"And you turned against me, Violette. I never knew why. Like how you suddenly fell for Willi."

"Oh, Douglas this is so hard." She swallows as if something blocks her throat. Then her words come all in a rush like a flooding river. "I was embarrassed and hurt by you—remember the cabin? That last day with the rowboat? We were so steamy, at first it was pretending, and then I was so embarrassed. You humiliated me, you really hurt me; I wanted to hurt you back, so I playacted with Willi, flaunted it so you'd be sure to notice, Douglas, I never even let him kiss me, except at Oh-No's sophomoric party. I just led him on to make you jealous."

"Oh, Violette! Remember, you gave me the cold shoulder. I tried to ask you what was wrong."

"I know, I know. I was too embarrassed to tell you. I was so immature. And you were right. Right to stop. I would have regretted it. I know
that now. I've always loved you, Douglas Tryzyna."

"No. Don't say it. I'm no good for anyone. I wish I were, wish I
could be." Douglas wipes his eyes with his napkin. He's listening to an inner voice. A voice more insulting and critical than any black raven's could
ever be.

Violette starts up again. She's trying to control herself. "What I did
was bad. Way worse than what you did. Maybe unforgiveable."

What has Violette done? Nothing. Except try to win him back.

Violette is pleading, as much for herself as for Douglas. "If we get
our minds fixed on what we did *then*, who we were *then*, we forget to imagine what we *can be*. Something better."

Maybe true for her. She's not guilty, really.

A long-drawn cessation of conversation occurs, while in the back-
ground coffee cups clink on saucers, a waiter repeats an order. "Happy
birthday to you," rings out from untrained multigenerational singers.
Breeze stirs long sheer drapes at the windows that face Cobble Hill and a
darkening sky. A thunderstorm threatens the Adirondacks again.

"Violette, I value the qualities you've inherited and learned from
your folks. You're kind and honest and optimistic. I never knew either of
my parents. And obviously I didn't learn whatever Sister Elder was trying
to teach me."

"I know you. I believe in you, Douglas. You can believe in your own
goodness, again. Maybe just by showing kindness to others. Let's start."

"You can. Too late for me, Violette."

Sadly, Violette's full confession will have to find its own hour. Although words could be spoken now to ease Douglas' misery, the clock of
cause and effect has stopped, in need of being rewound.

[4]

THE NEXT MORNING Violette finds Douglas limping to his train. She runs toward him, breathless. Her guilt swelling like an infection.

Douglas' heart registers a *fermata*, a prolonged pause. *Violette? Yes, Violette.* The sight of her reignites a flurry of infatuation. The early innocent days at the Stoya Conservatory. The heady years of attraction, their first date on a trolley ride, she with her little red purse buying an ice cream cone; he'd licked her fingers. The passion that slowly grew, never diminished, summer days in a rowboat, and once in a deserted cabin where they experienced the promise of adult excitement, pretending to be a fantasy couple.

She's speaking so quickly, with such urgency. "Hold me like a bunch of flowers, Douglas. Gently, please." He takes her hand, her palm is sweaty, her bony-muscular fingers interlace with his. How like Violette to be poetic even in a panic.

Her mismatched eyes search his eyes; hers have just now gone-all-glossy-honey-and maple-syrup, pleading for an impossible outcome. "We both have a debt to save others in despair," she whispers. There in public a very private disclosure begins.

She'd gone to the Stoya Conservatory with a bouquet for the Professor She'd gone to the Stoya Conservatory with a bouquet for the Professor. Willi had dragged her into a practice room, eager to brag.

As Douglas listens to her repeat the conversation, it resembles Act One of a tragedy.

> Willi (whispering)
> Boy, was I clever! Siggi told me, Doogie doing a switcheroo. Well, I made sure only the Performance Violin was going to the Concert. Was I ever crafty? I dosed Doogie's grape Nehi using Ma's Librium. I used plenty so he'd be knocked out. I'm the one who

deserved to be soloist. You know it's true Violette—I'm the one the music was written for. Me.

Douglas nods, blinking quickly. This is what LuLu had explained. "Wait!" Violette has another piece of Willi's drama to share.

Willi (whispering)
Afterward, it tore me up, killed me. The Performance Violin stolen? You were there. Me on the stage, what a bust. I lost control, Violette. Back home, seeing that damn fiddle! I trashed it. Oh, it felt good to massacre it! Then I got rid of it.

"Douglas, Willi wouldn't say how he got rid of the old fiddle I kept asking him. I kept asking him."

Douglas reels, as if he himself had been walloped by Willi.

Violette begins again, now with her own confession. "You can't imagine how I wanted to punish Willi. Punish him! So, I blasted him with the truth. The truth, Douglas."

Listening, Douglas experiences the scene like Act Two of a tragedy.

Violette (impassioned)
You admit that to me, to me, Willi? What you did to Douglas and the violin? You ignorant, weak, miscreant. And you boast? I hate your guts. I've never been in love with you, not one iota. I was pretending all along, trying to get a rise out of Douglas. You, Wilhelm Stoya, you are a despicable bully, and a third-rate violinist. You aren't anything but a coward. You revolt me!

Douglas falls back against a post, wide-eyed. His overnight bag hits the pavement with a thud. He freezes in the August heat of Elizabethtown.

"I really-really wanted to tear him apart!" Violette hisses. "So, I smacked him with another truth. "Hear me, and hear the *truth*, Douglas!"

The drama of the stage play heightens.

> Violette (forceful)
> Willi, I've been playing you, you are the fool, I have always, I mean always, been in love with Douglas Tryzyna.

Violette and Douglas, once sweethearts, stare at each other, fixed eyes wet and reflective.

Violette continues, speaking rapidly as if the words were an immolation. "And then, because I wanted to clinch Willi's torture, I made up the worst lie I could conjure. I told him a lie knowing it would slay him.

Violette's tear-filled-mismatched eyes, all afire, burn holes in Douglas' composure. "Do you want to know what kind of a calculating, vengeful mind I really have?" She doesn't wait even a second. Her admission tumbles out with no concern for who might overhear her memorized lines.

> Violette (raging)
> Willi, you fool, Douglas and I did it, we went all the way, lots of times! Yes. And Willi, we laughed about it! Laughed how you didn't know. Yes, sucker! Me and dumb ole Doogie-doo-doo making love.

Douglas stares at this kind, this talented, this vindictive girl. "Oh, Vi. We never did."

"I know, I know. I was determined to torture him. Then, Douglas, Willi went all crazy. He just went wild...and I was glad." She withdraws her very sweaty hand from the stupefied violinist's left hand with its icepick scarred thumb.

All the bodies rushing, all the musky steam hissing along the tracks. A train station is hardly a place for intimacy. Nevertheless, parents impress safety and propriety, lovers kiss goodbye, adventurers make promises, soldiers don brave masks. Violette persists because she must. "Douglas, you weren't the reason for Willi's suicide. You remember this sentence in his letter?

> *Because of my cheap shot and my Utter Stupidity in Admitting it out loud, well, I've lost my One and Only True Friend.*

"You mean?" Douglas tries to reframe the statement.

"He's saying that he realized he was stupid in *admitting to me* how he drugged you; drugging, that was his *cheap shot*. See, Douglas, you weren't his *One and Only True Friend*. All along *he thought I was. Me.* Get it? I'm responsible. See, as much as anyone can be responsible for another's decision, Willi took his life because he realized that I never had been, and certainly after his admission, never would be a girlfriend or lover of his. And the death knell was my malicious, humiliating lie about us."

ONTARIO, CANADA

[5]

DOUGLAS IS GAZING at the horizon in his usual state of being half absent, half present. A silver boat travels south on the lake with a flume of foam following like a tail. The foundling's thoughts contrast with the outdoor brightness, this season itself alight with orange and gold. He places his foot, a bare foot, on the rock's sunbaked surface; he's even more keenly aware of his other foot. The missing foot, the phantom foot. Douglas reflects. What has he to show for nineteen years? A phantom family, a phantom leg, a phantom violin, all to haunt him. He's responsible for at least one forfeited instrument and, at least in part, for one unrecoverable human life. Soon a question plagues him. How to atone? How to atone? *I can't do this on my own.*

✶ ✶ ✶

PERHAPS THE VIOLIN'S energy can be felt by some as it transmits through time and space. Regardless, the ink of a moonless night pours over Douglas—as he internalizes the black, he swallows it whole, poisoned by the bitterness of life. He can barely sense Magic Muriel.

{Can you hear me dear one| 253-1 cannot hear you| |

The frequency she seeks is fading away-away-away, like a lullaby heard from a rustic wagon passing through a Spanish town. Yet the violin continues, like a lighthouse, flashing her constancy.

{253-1 is my name| Can you hear *questo violino*| 253-1 has only to reminisce about you| at rest| in the dark| |

[6]

DOUGLAS' NEW FAMILY in Chodenzia thrives on designing and building exquisite furniture. Known to them, the Canadian forests where hard-wood and maple can be harvested. In such a forest Bertok and Oliver found Douglas—Crowe, as he is called here.

Ironically, Bertok is also a luthier whose trade is restoring and sell-ing violins. This has been guarded information. After Douglas' return Gateau reports that Crowe is ready; it's time to grant him the family's full confidence.

Bertok understands misfortune. And courage. He too made an ir-revocable choice. Bertok left his homeland, Poland, crossed oceans, and came halfway around the world with only a wife, a son, and the tools of his trade—tools passed down from grandfather, to father, to son. Here's Bertok making his home in Canada, having survived hardship. And now he takes Douglas by the shoulder. "Join us, Crowe."

Local men gather with Bertok in the Pavilion. They make plans. They bolster each other with jokes. They reminisce about ones who are gone. Some speak of harsh winters taking hunters and children to their graves. Of difficult childbirths, first clutching, then carrying off mothers and infants. They tell tales of swimmers drowning in the inviting, cool lake, the shallow lake, where reeds and grasses tangle arms and legs. They drink, some smoke; their "good nights" are gruff and followed by thumps on backs. Those with imminent needs have been heard. Such kindhearted-ness the men are offering Crowe. And why? He has done nothing to deserve this generosity.

Astrid had spoken to him of this. "We humans must remember to use the kindness built into our hearts. Kindness has the power to heal." These strangers were offering what Sister Elder now refuses him.

Courage, kindness, atonement; these are just words, aren't they? Not if you asked Violette. She once typed words full of encouragement just for him. Thoughts of Violette bring a sudden bout of weeping. He's still weak, he tells himself, wiping away hot tears. The fact remains, he's let Violette become a phantom too.

"You have choices, Crowe," Bertok says. "You can learn furniture carpentry along with Oliver. You can begin serious music study once again." *Should he return to that?* Douglas wonders. He's had no desire to play a violin since he arrived. And yet violins are in abundance. Music-making sessions are both frequent and joyous here. To join requires no invitation.

Sister Peace's words return to him. "No need of fancy violin. From your soul will come the music. Just play from your heart." Comes the question: Is it possible he has only a phantom heart now?

Courage. Yes, that's what it would take to continue toward re-demption. Douglas might well admit he's lacking a shred of courage. To find Magic Muriel 253-1 and hear her voice as he holds her close, this is the only true comfort he can imagine. Ah yes, something else. What if he were able to locate Professor Stoya's stolen Performance Violin? And could return it to him.

[7]

ONE MORE TRIP to the furniture store in Montreal with Oliver and Bertok before the winter's snow. Douglas shares the driving, the silence, the unloading. While there an impulse overtakes him. He must make an apology to Auntie Evangeline. Using the store's pad and a borrowed post-paid envelope he agonizes while writing.

> October 27, 1954
>
> My Auntie Evangeline,
>
> You invested in me, you believed in my dreams. And I blew it. Disobeying Professor Stoya I tried to take the 253-1 and the exquisite bow to the concert. It was a nightmare. Both violins were somehow stolen. I'm sure Sister Elder has told you everything.
>
> I pray I can somehow make amends, dear Auntie. Even so it seems impossible. I am not worthy to offer my love. I have only caused others pain with my life.
>
> I'm with a generous musical community, foreigners, woodworkers. Keeping my whereabouts to myself. Gateau says I must find it in my heart to forgive if I'm to heal completely. I'll start by trying to be worthy of your forgiveness one day.
>
> Shamefully,
>
> Douglas

Across time and space, a violin casts about for her *animatore*. She can write no letter expressing her remorse. Nevertheless, her transmission emanates with that intention.

{And what did *questo violino* desire| It is simple is it not| Desired you alone| *Questo violino* called you to draw out her *perfezione*| In so doing| she inflamed the youthful fever of fervency| your impatience| Can your human heart forgive this fractured *violino*||

[8]

DOUGLAS HAS SPENT long hours with Oliver in the shop. He's acquiring carpentry skills quickly. He's less angry, less of a burden to the family. Upstairs with Bertok, an earned privilege, he feels respectability trickle back into his emptied soul.

One afternoon when the air is scented with hyssop and peppermint, Douglas, heart aquiver, divulges the story of his communication with the 253-1. Will Bertok be aghast? As Douglas speaks, this sensible man walks around the atelier, his hands clasped behind his back. His shoulders are extremely broad, his arms are long, his legs rather short. Leather apron and cap, his uniform. As Bertok walks he sees nothing; his eyes look straight ahead like a magician conjuring the next illusion.

Finally, he whistles.

"Crowe, your gift of sensitivity is rare. My *dziaduino*, my own grandpapa, had such a sense. You can make good use of it."

Bertok offers to teach him the basics. How violins are made and repaired, this will take a while. After that he must study with the specialists at Rembert Wurlitzer Co. There, thousands of violins will be available for his scrutiny. "We consult with these experts; they are our friends. No bones about it, once with them you're on your own to prove your merit."

It seems daunting. Ten thousand violins are not too many to see in a career. And in learning to distinguish a maker's signature touch, he will surely make over a thousand mistakes in judgment.

Bertok heads back to his workbench with a concluding thought. "Maybe someday you'll choose to return from your studies with

Wurlitzer Co. and provide services for us. Now you are invited to stay, as welcome as a son. It is spring, a proper time to start your lessons.

ELIZABETHTOWN, NEW YORK

[9]

MARKED BY LOSS, 1953 becomes 1955. And is Sister Elder content with her life?

She embraces children with tenderness...well, only when they are sick. Her unspoken dreams are accurately designated as visceral, though outwardly she resists being transparent. Her father had fiery bursts of temper. No, she hasn't succumbed to such reactions. She's been adoring, scorning by turn, with ferocity to spare when appropriate. Has her life been significant? Yes, if she were not in the world four children might have suffered more than they did. *Accept their ambitions*, she had told herself. Say, in the matter of Douglas and his passion for the violin, she had her brakes on, yet she couldn't halt his freewheeling descent. She knows a thing or two about passionate desire, the hollowness that follows loss. Perhaps she and Douglas are alike, more than she can accept. *What has become of him now?* Now that she's turned him out.

There's no question the other three of her grown charges are thriving. John, engaged to a lovely girl, works as a river pilot in Westport and James trains there for the same career. The young men look after one another like good brothers. Mildred finished Business College and is married to the Assistant Manager at the Elizabethtown Smythe Hotel.

Oh, it's too late to change some things. She, Evangeline, and Maureen were a disappointment to Mother and Father, who advised, "Fly a bit, enjoy some life experience, and then nab a well-bred, wealthy gentleman." Not one of the three sisters had done so.

[10]

TWO SUMMERS HAVE passed, August to August, and with each comes a bittersweet reminder of Douglas' birthday. *He would be twenty this year,* Hester thinks, drying her dinner fork and knife. She'd closed the door to the boys' dorm. Declared it *off-limits* to Astrid and Wing. Closed the door on most social interaction as well. Hester sought solitude with the absence of noise and a dearth of worldly desires. And in this way, had she unwittingly exposed her angry soul to healing forces?

Sister Elder leans against the red Italianate rail of the balcony, opera glasses lifted to her eyes. She watches the new moon fight for presence as it rises behind Cobble Hill. Even with upward progress it competes with vaporous clouds. *It's a lonely sight,* she thinks. And the silence bombards her stoicism. No crickets chorus. No bullfrogs croak. From the Ibarra egg farm spread out below, there's no music to be heard, music that bewitched the boy—music from the violin that now suffocates in her house.

The suffocating violin is quite aware of Hester's increasing and almost positive whirr.

{Hesssssssterrr| 253-1 is my name| Hessssssssterrr| Can you hear me| Without your help| Myself has only to reminisce about my *animatore*| while here at rest| in the dark| Hessssssssterrr| |

The emanation is more sensation than sound.

"Shouldn't a violin breathe?" Hester asks aloud. Some might call it misplaced sympathy; others might call it a need for release; anyway into the boys' dorm she goes. She takes down the case. So slowly she unlatches the clips, opens the lid, lifts away Ophelia's garden of silk, looks upon something either sacred or profane. "Oh, poor creature, what happened to you?" she cries. She leaves the violin in its open case on the chiffonier and backs out of the room. What else is there to do?

✵ ✵ ✵

NOT ONE WEEK later, in the time it takes for a body to manage one gris-
tle of shock, Hester is choked by another. It happens after she scours the
grill pan, after she puts the mint jelly jar back into the fridge. After she
strikes a match, places the tea kettle on the sturdy black burner, watches
the flames swarm all blue-yellow-red. It happens after she takes her tea
and her dessert to the table. *Chamomile tea is supposed to soothe,* she
thinks, *so why am I uneasy?* She takes a sip of comfort.

{Shh| shh| |

Hester tilts her head toward the kitchen, listening.

{Shhhhh| hhhsh| |

The kettle steaming? Surely it has cooled by now.

{Hesssssssterrr| |

She drops her fork and the morsel of Douglas' favorite frosted
spice cake upon it.

{Hessssssssterrr| |

Is a whispery voice calling her name? There at the dining table, in
front of the silver wedding basket piled with green apples, napkin at her
mouth, she remains motionless, not wanting to take further action although the whispering continues. The emanation cajoles more than it
commands. And then she yields to it. Yields to something she has fought
to deny. She follows the sound on tiptoe into the dorm. Why after all this
time does the creation call her? She assimilates the violin's communication. And a plea for her to act.

{Myself has seen such conflict amongst men| 253-1 implores you,
Hester| Must it yet be so| |

Many evenings thereafter she returns to cradle the violin. After all,
Douglas honored this broken thing enough to withstand Professor Stoya's
abuse. And Willi's bullying. Out of curiosity she touches a string, the

heavy one. And it begins, this connectedness, not with church bells, but with silence—and the haunting memory of sound. And one memory begets another. Each night when she cradles the violin, grieving over the useless strings, imagined tonalities glide into her flesh asking old misery to disperse. It's hard-won progress; each source of torment feels like an accident repeated in slow motion: The loneliness of her childhood; the loss of a lover; the cost of her unforgiving ways. Bearing the torture, she continues accepting the truth each remembered tone will offer.

While the mistreated violin comforts and cajoles she also continues to broadcast through time and space:

{253-1 is calling to you| Douglas| can you hear Me| *Questo violino* is left to reminisce about you| here at rest| first in the dark| now in the light| At length Hester did understand me| she whose receptors were weak| Gently she begged voice from me| She asks| though *questo violino* may never sing again| and her heart may never heal |So it is| It is| |

Many an evening Astrid joins Hester to enjoy the serenity of stitching tulle embroidery. "Nobody will want that!" Astrid once commented after seeing Hester's unconventional mix of images: tangled vines, leaves, and blooms, alongside, weeds, bugs, and worms.

"Death marches side by side with life," Sister Elder retorted. "Soon ugly will be the new beautiful, if it isn't already."

[11]

FALL LURCHES INTO winter and Christmas 1955 arrives, bringing a welcome visitor. Violette gifts Sister Elder and Evangeline each with a bound volume of typed pages, her poetry. For Astrid and Wing, several Chinese comic books featuring Sanmao. Wing exclaims over the clever simplicity.

"Douglas said you entertained him with your cartoons. I'd love to see them sometime."

Wing places three portfolios on the coffee table. An hour of pleasure ensues before they view his current work. Obviously, the flow of black on white still satisfies his creative mind. Wing offers the gift of a drawing to Violette. When Violette encourages him to publish, he remarks, "Wisdom say, *Man who love making mark on paper already leave loving mark on the world.*"

Violette offers her news; she's landed an internship with a *publishing* house in the City. It will lead to an editorial job if she does well. She gets around to asking the important question. "Have you heard from him?"

Sister Elder sputters an answer. "Not a word." And then while she attends her hostess duties, slices fruitcake, tops it with hard sauce, lights a match to the black burner, Auntie Evangeline takes Violette aside. Her anger at Hester comes to a verbal simmer just as the tea kettle whistles and spews steam. "My sister hasn't forgiven him yet. He wrote to me once, postmark Quebec, 1954. I'll never tell Hester; she has no right to know his whereabouts."

[12]

COME JUNE 1946, when the bullfrogs chorus unceasingly, and Fiddle 253-1 encourages Sister Elder's desire to pluck a series of satisfying tones, the strangest counteraction occurs in the Guardian's chest. Oh, not pain; more like a tepid trickle, at first, warm and comforting. And then a quickening shoots round and round in Hester's shoulders, until she straightens her curving back. And smiles.

Look. She shows gratitude for small kindnesses from Astrid, whose attention mostly annoyed her these past years. She acknowledges Wing, who continues to shop and cook and tend the yard without complaint. And thank God for Violette's visits. Hester appreciates being with a young woman and ignores reminders of her own age. One evening after making the 253-1's strings resonate, Hester sets the instrument on the flowery blue silk and hums. And just as on that evening with Auntie Evangeline, when both sisters listened to Douglas pour his heart out on the D'Espine, she twirls down the hall, her apron flaring like a ballerina's tutu.

One August afternoon Violette brings sunflowers, bronze, russet, and chocolate blooms where mature centers bristle with seeds. "The last of the garden."

Who knows what led Violette to the boys' dorm while Hester went looking for a vase? Sister Elder comes on the run when she hears a shriek.

Douglas' one-time sweetheart is caught by surprise. The familiar violin case lies open on the chiffonier. Therein the striped-red 253-1. Blue silk can't hide its dismal health. "You have it, Hester?" Violette shrills. "Are you the one who stole this?"

"For heaven's sakes no, child; what criminal acts do you think I'd stoop to?"

"And. And..." Violette trembles in the face of so many unanswered questions. And then Violette spies the open wardrobe. Beside the Muriel cigar box she sees a small stack of unopened letters. Curiosity drives her forward. *Addressed to Douglas? Postmarked from Havana, Cuba? Letters from Tatiana? Unopened?* "You never wrote back to Sister Peace? Never told her anything? *Why not?* She was practically his mother!"

Hester scoffs. "Tatiana flitted in and then she waltzed out. She didn't start writing until Christmas of 1954. By then Douglas was gone. Anyway, what was I to say to her? The boy's been accused of stealing Stoya's valuable violin? He's lost a limb? He's disappeared?"

"And do you wonder why he never communicates, Sister Elder?" Violette flushes; she's incensed.

The violin's inaudibles shake the empty dorm, loosening one by one memories this suffering woman has smothered ever since the child she most adored disappointed her to the core.

Hester softens. "Please help me, Violette, I have changed a little, perhaps a little more changing won't hurt." Like an oyster, Hester had exposed herself to life's grit. The inevitable beauty is being formed.

* * *

SISTER ELDER LOOKS at her face in the mirror as she applies Ponds Cold Cream. "I'm going to do the right thing," she says to her image. "Even if it gets someone in trouble. No time for second thoughts." Perhaps she notices how attractive she looks tonight, age fifty-six, for all that. Or is it just that she's become more serene? And two days later, with Violette for courage, Sister Elder packs the 253-1. She wraps the instrument in a yellow scarf, gift from a late friend, a violist with European flair.

Quickly, before they can change their minds, *fulfill the mission.* Return to the Stoyas this instrument once given in payment for Douglas' violin lessons. Let's not forget the years of piano lessons also given. Hey, the intended years were cut short. Remember, if you will, lessons were eventually resumed.

Violette and Hester then, entering the Hand-Hale district, finding along Stoneleigh Way a building that resembles a castle. Out front a formal sign, a new sign, a hand-lettered sign: *Stoya Conservatory ̃ Piano Lessons.* The familiar concert grand piano dominates the window; her ivories invite Violette as she approaches. Up each step they go, Guardian and friend, with pauses in between. One. Two. Three. Four. Five. Six. Advancing between the rock pillars of the front porch. "Here we are."

Peter Stoya asks them in. He's polite, looking well enough, formal as always in his dress shirt and creased slacks and suspenders. A bit thinner, though, widow's peak pronounced, mustache trimmed to narrow lines. The threesome clusters in the entryway. Narcisse Louise around the corner eavesdrops, her hands in prayer. Frieda can be heard giving a piano lesson in the salon; she remains ignorant.

Peter Stoya allows Sister Elder to say her piece. He understands her offer and the reason for it. "So, now listen to me without interrupting," he says. Violette hangs her head. She imagined a better outcome. The retired Professor continues in his demeaning way. "How in the dangnation you managed to steal this, I'll let it go. Now just take the hexed fiddle out of my sight. For once and for all." He uses both hands as if shooing children away. One final comment, though, just before closing the door. "It's probably most suited for a bonfire."

Later Frieda berates her husband. "Couldn't we have sold that violin to a luthier who could repair it? It's got to be worth *something*!"

Peter scoffs. "Don't talk to me about luthiers."

* * *

THE SHIPPING BOX is padded with newspaper, futile protection for the battered violin in a weathered case. Two sealed envelopes are positioned for immediate view: Hester has written several agonized sentences; Violette has written a five-page letter. Destination, Havana, Cuba.

"Your instincts were right, Violette," Hester says. "I'll take this to the Post Office and we'll both feel a lot better. Tatiana is the one who championed Douglas' worship of the poor thing. She should have it. He never opened her letters, but knowing him, he'd remember her address, assuming he ever wants to reconnect."

"Yeah, she's the one he'd reach out to. I guess. Since he's shut me out, and..."

"Go ahead, say it—and since his stand-in-mother turned on him."

Violette's tears flow freely. "Why did his passion have to end in such tragedy?" Astrid holds the younger woman close. Cheek to cheek they stand, one head all ivory silk, the other all henna satin.

Wing scratches his chin. "Wisdom say, *Perhaps what look like end from here, look like new beginning from there.*"

ONTARIO, CANADA

[13]

Time has passed.

DOUGLAS LIES PRONE on the cool earth. Sunflowers loom overhead, providing restless shade. Mature blooms hang their heavy heads like chastised boys, bedraggled petals like matted hair all around their faces, bulging centers where bees crawl, their sturdy stems bending like old men's backs. Their faded leaves droop or twitch like tail feathers, adjusting to the breeze, waiting to take flight. Young blooms face the sun, eager. Upper petals glow a transparent yellow, while petals underneath must remain drab.

Speeee, a yellow warbler, greets Douglas as it lands above. Legs wide, head cocked, eyes black-bright, with hint of danger, *speee*, it's off. More birds come and go, all quick to leave if he moves. Shadows on the soil beyond, like leggy indecipherable bruises, he turns his attention to these, to the prone, untethered patterns deriving energy from something unseen. And of a sudden it begins to rain. Enormous drops batter the earth, as impatient as ignored children.

Douglas sees Gateau lift her face to the sky; he recognizes that radiance. She spreads her arms, she high-steps, her scarf soaked and flattening to her head. Explosive raindrops strike his face, his thatch of rusty hair. And he remembers a promise given in a garden when he was young and demanding an answer about his parents.

Sister Peace was evading his question with a prediction. "One day, plunk-plunk. Answer coming like fat raindrops, plunk-plunk into your brain. I promise."

"I'll know next time it rains?" he was asking.

"Mercy no, you certainly have whiskers on face before the answer sinks in."

Despite his wooden leg Douglas hops up, nimble as a garden bunny. He reaches Gateau, twirls her round. He's both Crowe and Antenna Boy, and into his brain sinks the answer that couldn't be freely given years ago. He's dancing with the healer-witch, he's drenched with exquisite rain, and forgiveness rushes through his veins.

Like dragonfly wings stirring cosmic energy, Magic Muriel 253-1 transmits, and Douglas can sense her.

{Dear one| for the joy of it our frequencies are again aligned| |

"There you are, finally. Are you very badly hurt?"

{We have both been broken| but endurance builds our compassion| 253-1 needs a maker's touch if ever again to sing| Alas| regaining my voice depends as much upon a maker's skill| as upon my wounds| |

"I know a luthier who can fix you. I'm sure he can. He has to."

{In this expanse of time and space *questo violino* found you| surely you can find Me| |

"Keep talking to me, please," Douglas begs. "I never thought to ask this before. How is it that you ever came to be in Elizabethtown? I took for granted your beautiful voice calling me."

{A story of kindness| it is| Remember do you| 253-1 telling of Teatro Royale| Madrid| My owner| a conductor| leading a grand assembly of instruments| |

"Yes. I remember."

{Indeed so| Then by the conductor *questo violino* passed along|
to his son who kept Me for sentiment|
not a musician he| Passed then to a grandson| teacher of Span-
ish Literature and Poetry| a writer of love songs| A husband and
father misunderstood| yes maligned|
when the time was called 1936| |
"All of that I remember, so then what happened to you?"
{Now to speak of times not of my understanding| Of humans
running from other humans| panic|
through winter cold|
Get out of Spain| get to France| the words repeated|
Across mountains then| with fire raining from above|
Questo violino bumping along wrapped tight|
my family all a shudder|
Arriving at the place of safety| a beach| Argelès-sur-Mer
they called it|
Wives and children taken off| taken| but to where|
to where| the men lament|
He buries Me| wrapped and covered in a sack| there in the
sand| by night
He is shivering beside Me| yes| many men so buried
against the chill|
It was later he played Me| after we had lost the pulsations of the
many men|
He played to comfort the few| his fingers stiff|
my voice thin|
But music we made night after night| for the power of it|
for the Kindness of it|

That we might melt each heart| yet again| and thus might each
soul gather Courage| to itself| Courage anew| |
"I never knew about all that."
{Later when men were given leave of encampment| my owner's
heartbeat slow| *questo violino*| named 253-1|
just a reminder of suffering| t'was then| an act of Kindness was
given to the writer of love songs| |
"An act of Kindness?"
{Just so| Folk among the many offered my owner|
a stranger| see| weak to death| a blanket of wool|
a cup of soup| And he so grateful for such Kindness|
in time of wretchedness|
had but one thing to offer in return| |
"He gave you to those kind ones?"
{Yes| yes to the Basque| To the Basque then| to these he gave
253-1| for their Generosity| Musicians they|
yet without a proper violin| |
"The same Basque I knew?"
{Indeed| Lucky folk with papers these| off to Lisbon|
there to sail the ocean| and oh the dread of it|
my kind in fear of water|
And so it was in crossing the great sea| that which separates
lands and men| we two found each other| you yet small|
and 253-1 belonging to others|
Questo violino the braver for it| as it was meant to be|
Is meant to be yet| |

ELIZABETHTOWN, NEW YORK

[14]

October 1956

OAK LEAVES cling in the most tenacious way, robbed of their green, left with a camouflage of yellow and gray. Undersides of the tree's limbs are shaded to olive, the tops lit like bone. Along them twigs with dried buds stand at attention. Sister Elder studies the arcs and junctures of the old tree. In due time she rises, leaving the porch swing with such determination one would wonder what prompts her. Into the Home she goes, down the hall she goes, floorboards squeaking complaint.

Douglas' wardrobe shelf brings to light a collection of achingly unbearable objects. A pencil drawing of the Basque man's violin, childishly exaggerated. A red satin pillow. A stack of music books. Five marbles in a small bamboo bowl. The Muriel cigar box—Sister Elder lifts the lid. Inside the box: a small brass bell looped onto a frayed cord; a signed black and white photo of a young woman; kraft paper nickels; rosin wrapped with waxed paper; an assortment of typewritten messages; under these, two postcards from Cuba and a Polaroid photo; a crumpled-no-longer-round-gold-edged cigar band. A Chinese cookie, and almost escaping attention, the thin strip of paper that peeks from it. Hester begins to tug the fortune free. It resists. She holds back...no, she'll not trespass. She reads what she can; only the last two words are visible. Handwritten...*your desire.*

Sister Elder veers away, steadies herself on the bedpost. And then it is comforting to stretch out on the bed, her head resting on the pillow where his head rested. The open violin case with its passenger fitting the curve of her hip. She tries to make up a story to calm herself. *Life brings change. He's found a place to thrive.* Sunlight filters through the pin oak's leaves, creating and recreating ever-changing patterns on the quilt. She holds back sobs, holds in howls; she wants to rage. No. No, she won't. *He's found a place. A place where he's safe, fulfilled.* Outside a crow caws, a crazed pronouncement of ill. "No!" Hester yells. Like Violette she had refused to believe the worst before. She goes on with her hopeful story. *There would surely be music there. Violins. A river or a lake, water close by to be sure. There, Douglas is loved.*

Even so she wonders. What happened? A violin went missing. After that this young man went missing once, and now again. Oh Hester, you know about dark times. The Forgetting; Hester you went through such a time. Did I do right by him, keeping the secret all these years? Sister Elder swings her legs over the bed's edge, releases her mane of silver struck chestnut, shakes her head, wipes her damp eyes with an apron tie, and takes a deep breath. A new question perturbs her. Am I wrong to hide the violin now?

[15]

COME CHRISTMAS, A tangle of persuasions, the foremost of which is Hester's newfound humility, disarms Evangeline's bombproof heart. She's witnessed a change in her sister. She offers a gift of wisdom. "I've heard it said, the past is painful, but it returns with a peace offering. It asks only to be remembered."

Hester answers, slight hesitation. "I have something I'd like to show you." Never mind she's hidden this very object in advance of her meddling sister's arrival.

Into the boys' dorm. From a drawer of the chiffonier she takes it. A familiar case, latches lifted, lid opened where the gifted bow is snapped in place. Once unwrapped, Magic Muriel 253-1, resting in all her brokenness, communes eloquently with silence.

Evangeline gasps. Stutters. "*You? You* had this all along, Hester? *You?* You stole it?

It takes a bit of telling and retelling to bring Evangeline up to speed. Confounded, Evangeline asks another pertinent question. "Hester, does Violette know you never sent this to Cuba, never sent this to Tatiana?"

"No. No, Evangeline, I just couldn't admit my weakness to her." Sister Elder lapses into thoughts of Tatiana. Sister Peace: ever an architect, one who rearranged the walls of their boy's constraints, thereby creating windows and doors. Sister Peace, who allowed Douglas access to dangerous fascinations. Had she, his Guardian, done better by hoisting up barricades?

Evangeline wipes her water-rimmed eyes, mentally negotiating a forfeiture before she chooses to speak. "I wasn't going to tell you before. Now I will—I heard from Douglas. A letter. From Montreal."

* * *

IT'S LATER; DINNER has been consumed in silence. Hester takes a forkful of fruitcake onto which she slathers a wedge of buttery-sweet hard sauce. Taking time, she's taking time to come to terms with two difficult losses. First, a *son*. And now an instrument carrying his energy. In the time it had taken her to dredge the hubris from her soul, she had exposed an improbable attachment to a creation she once loathed. Today she's forced to question even that attachment. Her creased brow softens as she speaks from new generosity. "Living with passion, that was Sister Peace's gift to Douglas. She'd want him to have the violin. If there was any way."

"Then I must tell you. I gave Violette the envelope Douglas used for mailing me a letter. It had a furniture store's return address, of all things. Violette's set on finding him, plucky girl. I've been funding her travels during the publication's summer and winter hiatus. She's away right now. If anyone could return the violin to him..."

"And. Have you heard?"

ONTARIO, CANADA

[16]

January 1957

BOUTIQUE de MEUBLES in Montreal was easily found. Complications must be overcome. The furniture boutique uses a dozen or so suppliers. Did Violette have a craftsman's name, a firm's name? Failing specifics, she'd been given locations of cabinetmakers scattered through Quebec and Ontario. It's been her mission to locate each in hopes of finding Douglas. Just last night she arrived at a quaint site with a fringe of cabins facing a frozen lake. As un-commercial a site as one could imagine.

Earlier that day, the train passed by two squared columns built of smooth gray rock. The signage arched across them read, *Gateway of the North*. This city, sixty miles to the next town in any direction, was her destination—according to the address on her list, the address merely a postal box number. Violette departed the station. She needed to find affordable lodging. Tomorrow her search could begin. A bearded fisherman in an off-road truck, smelling of the walleye he planned to batter and fry, served as the local cabbie. Did she mind if he stopped to pick up a two-four on the way? The hand gestures he used to describe fishing meant that the steering wheel went largely untended. Violette clung to the door handle. Part physical panic, part psychological apprehension.

Apprehension. If Douglas backs away, still dark, still healing. She becomes then a trespasser, despoiling his haven. She, the tormentor pulling him back into the nightmare. How to soften the encounter, offer him a chance to stay secluded? Whatever his choice she'll accept it. She needs to know. Written words have worked before.

The driver returned, flipped open one of the beers, ready for business. "Want a lake view, eh?" he asked. "I know a place, not expensive, friendly folk own it."

It was well past dusk when she paid the fisherman and approached the elongated building. The structure, perched throne-like on its stone foundation, possessed a familiar grandeur—steep roof with a generous overhang and one attic gable peak from which, at this hour, golden light winked. Perhaps it was the gray stone that felt so familiar.

She preferred not to give her legal name and instead insisted on signing as *A. Poet.* She didn't explain herself to the strange lady, whose eyelashes dominated an angular face. The keeper accepted cash, and being Gateau, first noticed the renter's eyes, and afterward found the arrangement perfectly acceptable.

Violette declined to say how many nights she'd spend. Nor did she say how disappointing it had already been, almost two years on a trail of virtual breadcrumbs.

Gateau stares into Violette's mismatched eyes. "Yes. Dove Cottage. Ideal for you. Your own washroom there. Breakfast over here included. Oliver here'll set to squaring things for you, Miss A. Poet."

Travel case in hand Violette follows Oliver outside. The crisp air stings her face like summer gnats. A trillion stars watch on like jewels pasted in the sky while planets wink.

After Oliver's efficient ministrations and polite departure Violette tucks into the quilt-covered bed. Reaching to turn off the lamp, a bedside message catches her attention.

> *Mourning Doves*
> *Their call, five coos, the second one rising and falling*
> *in tone.*
> *Most often heard in spring when pairing begins,*
> *testimony to a divinely calming presence among us.*
> *Doves are messengers of the heart.*
> *They offer reminder of love, of comfort, of hope.*

✳ ✳ ✳

MORNING. LEMON SUNLIGHT glints through snowfall. Gateau spies Violette bundled up and hurrying toward *Itthon*. *Good, the Dove is on her way to breakfast.* Breakfast indeed. Apple sauce, oat bread, berry preserves, poached eggs, and bacon, set out family style. After savoring her meal, Violette sips the fragrant tea she's given; perhaps impolite to ask for coffee. She converses, gently, cautiously, not wanting to sound like a snoop. Besides, Gateau frightens her, such intensity; with a glance she can bore into your soul.

In an adjacent room, her back to the breakfast room, Noemi is at the piano—it's a Heintzman & Co grand, Canadian made, and in tune. Hanon exercises, scales, arpeggios, these slide off her fingertips. Violette is impressed, even more so when Noemi begins a Béla Bartók Scherzo.

The modern atonal music kindles Violette's longings. Gateau observes; she comments. "You are a poet. I say, musician, too! You play piano for us this beautiful morning." This not a question—perhaps a command.

"Chopin's 'Berceuse Opus 57 D Flat Major,'" Violette says, seating herself. In seconds Violette floats with the music, her fingers dancing on the familiar keyboard, her eyes closed. Such a performance once held Douglas in its thrall. The sound of music singing from *Itthon* just now is a poignant reminder of something. Something... Who was it said this? "Music offered from the soul acts as prayer for all, whether they believe or not. Ask the Carthusian monks."

Afterward Violette is flooded with courage. "Is there an American fellow around here? About my age. Rusty color hair. About this tall." She lifts her arms above her head. "Name of Douglas? He plays violin."

Oliver's laughter! "Almost every fellow around here plays violin."

Gateau. "Why do you seek him? Family? Friend. Debt?"

More laughter.

Only two more addresses on her list. And this one, a dead end? Violette tears up. She wants to say: *You fools, I was his sweetheart. I still love him. And we are both debtors.* And where does she go? Enthused to somber, this Violette? Her hair braided with a yellow ribbon, her eyes downcast, unfocused. Beware such a dive into memory when others may judge. The trance-like face is not unlike a musician's when he exposes his soul. Violette is no longer in the realm of Chodenzia.

Seated just there across the room, inquisitive eyes crinkled, Gateau. Does the host watch Violette's mementos, one by one, while they flicker like old film? The kid with his legs swinging as Violette, a child herself, plays a Clementi Sonatina. The boy pedaling, cards ticking in the bicycle spokes, the girl giggling, passenger on the handlebars. The fusion of berry-stained lips, tongues, bodies pressed together like two sheets rolling through a mangle. The pianist flirting with a bully while loyal eyes watch on in misery. The same girl, older, wiser, discovering *the stolen* treasure, object inspiring betrayal, artifice, sacrifice.

With practiced determination Violette pulls herself together. *Say something. Say something glib.* She pipes up like the survivor she's become. "No matter. I came for the ice fishing mostly."

Oliver, some five years Violette's junior, is last to sense honest desperation in the lie. First, he chuckles. Then he looks to Gateau. Seeing this healer-witch's permission he dangles the most innocent piece of information. "I play violin, harmonica, and accordion, I'm also a specialized carpenter, custom chairs...and the occasional prosthetic."

Violette's right hand, pressed to her mouth. Then the tears do flow as she sobs silently, without restraint.

"I believe you seek a fellow we call Crowe, not walleye," Noemi says quietly. "He comes and goes. Do you have a message for him?"

[17]

August 1957

SIXTEEN YEARS HAVE elapsed since Douglas first claimed an abandoned instrument. Passion for it continues to flow, as elemental as molten lava coursing beneath the crust of Earth. The impassioned is possessed, and ultimately undaunted by outcomes. Three of those years were spent in apprenticeship, first with Bertok, and then with the renowned Rembert Wurlitzer Co. Douglas is qualified as a rookie violin seeker-appraiser. His quest? Instruments worthy of Bertok's repair; each to benefit the community when auctioned.

Certainly, two violins inflame his search. For reparation, Professor Stoya's Performance Violin. For fulfillment, the 253-1.

Douglas rejoins his clan after an unproductive week. He's weary. He's ready to relax. Once inside in Crowe Cottage his adrenaline rushes. When was this left on the bed? And by whom? It's a letter postmarked June 12, 1957, New York City. It's addressed *Douglas Tryzyna, c/o Crowe*. He slits the envelope very-very carefully as if something scary will leap out. The message inside is typewritten.

The eccentric wording commands his full attention. Who would be so intrigued with words taken from successive pages in a dictionary as to write this? He knows the answer, of course. Even so he's confounded realizing this letter found its way to Chodenzia.

He reads the letter again, aloud this time. Is he crying, or laughing? He can't distinguish.

> Inamorato, you know who I am.
> An iceblink, our history, the glare over an ice field. Our detachment an
> icefall, unmoving. What igneous item might be required to thaw our hearts?
> To illume our possibilities. Am I immodest to ask, what is it that impedes
> our two souls now? The illogic of two quivering souls separated. Take an

immy, shoot it across a chalk-drawn circle, that's a game. Take an imposter and allow him power, that's a tragedy. Look. Inaction may sustain the ink-blot of games. And tragedies.

Imprimis, we recognized one another as kindred. Inasmuch as you have suffered an inburst, inasmuch as I experience an infall toward your luminosity, cannot we ingather the shards of our hearts? We two individuals are left with identical karmic debt.

I for one cannot inure the status quo. However, I will not inveigh my disposition again if you cannot intuit a future together and so must answer ixnay.

You know how to find me. I'll wait for you. Forever is not long enough to spend with you. It's just that I won't wait forever.

[18]

SEPTEMBER. BIRDS TWITTER without letup. Honeybees nuzzle, return again and again to fuzzy gold centers of dahlias, to bristly brown centers of sunflowers. Bumblebees amble amongst the twisted petals as if wearing puffy orange socks. There's Noemi arranging a bouquet for Dove Cottage. There's Gateau heading to the rock garden with a basket; time to gather betony for teas, infusions, tinctures. And there's Douglas, known here as Crowe, like a wordless child (his wooden leg flexing and planting firmly on the earth as it is made to do) making his way to see Bertok, and in his arms, cradled like a baby, an oblong object disguised by its wrappings, weighing less than a pound, more than two hundred years of age.

His anxiety almost under control, Douglas shifts from one foot to the other. He calmly brought three violins for Bertok to repair last month, product of his travels. Why is it this violin, the one held next to his breast, that has his heart racing? He has yet to view it, yet to reconcile himself to its condition, yet to believe it might be restored to the life for which it was created. It arrived an hour ago; brought to Crowe Cottage by a pianist with mismatched eyes and a typewriter, she who rented Dove Cottage.

Bertok accepts the violin swaddled in a silk scarf, this silk, the color of spring daffodils.

"In the name of yellow, lemon yellow, in the name of all that's fine and quickly lost!" Douglas whispers, letting it go. *Please.*

This instrument is just one in a thousand violins Bertok has placed on this table, each bearing the mark of its beginning, a year, and a maker. He will say that any violin's history, passage through the hands of both the accomplished and the inept, often remains a secret travelogue. The more splendid the object the more it may be misused. As a luthier he has taken each one up, handled it, tapped it. Upon occasion he has pulled one apart if this was required for restoration. Always using excessive care.

Douglas stiffens, his body constrained in a straitjacket of apprehension, his brain awhirl with freakish imaginings. Folded silk will part like a yellow sea. Daylight will further brutalize the lamentable object's condition. Bertok, countenance as austere as a coroner's, looks to the deprived for permission to proceed. Douglas bottoms like a metronome's slug; can barely manage a blink. With the last fold pulled back Bertok reaches in a hand. Static electricity crackles; a whirlwind of dust motes encircles the presentation. Bertok draws back his hand as if fangs threaten. Oh, the sight of it. Fury causes Douglas' heart to somersault, much like the fury that provoked this collision of design and indignity.

Magic Muriel 253-1, a pathetic patient, grovels before them. One sharp wedge of her narrow neck angled all wrong, the surrounding wood roughed and red. An illusion. Like the site of a splintered tibia thrust through flesh, encircled by jellied and crusted blood. An upright, unmanned oar in a painted lock. The bowsprit of a defeated frigate ship held by lank rigging. For one gruesome moment Bertok is motionless. Woe be the current reality of a violin once glorious.

Douglas gently takes the entirety of 253-1 into his arms again; he wordlessly communes with her. Her scroll faces his face. Familiar swirls of carved wood, like a wild rose or an unfurled ribbon, circle an eye. Look. The eye is lit with sentient optimism.

{My kind endures| You creatures expire| Yet today we two have survived| this is the beauty of the thing| is it not| 253-1 places her trust in the love felt here| |

[19]

HOWEVER, BEFORE THE 253-1's healing can be complete more courage will be necessary. That of her Red Violin sister who must wait for a worthy Mistress. That of a Russian novelist and a French widow who may choose to wed. That of a bereft family adapting to the West, where the Pacific's rhythms may soothe a wife, where a rebellious son may extemporize, where memories may haunt less frequently—though the right hour for a husband's confession may never be found. That of assertive sisters who may sojourn beside an Ontario lake, may learn to wholly embrace, may linger amongst sunflowers, may choose to join the dance. That of a choreographer, released from a promise, who, with face upturned to a crescent moon, may give thanks, may claim kinship with her offspring, and seek to reconnect. That of lovers contending with tragedy and guilt, braving together the need for atonement and newfound purpose.

And what of this musical instrument, a one-ling, crippled to the capacity of a toad's croak? This violin must endure reconstruction if it is to sing again.

[20]

DOUGLAS GAZES AT his broken, beloved, Magic Muriel as Bertok examines the audacious scroll turning it this way and that. He observes the flames in the wood of the back. Using his thumb, he traces the site of the neck's separation. Douglas winces, as if reliving the ferocity Willi perpetrated on the harmless creation.

Bertok says, "You see the breaks, of course? Hear the rattling also? To make repairs I must remove the belly. I prefer to do this operation without the distraction of an observer."

Douglas groans, "I can't leave."

"Can you endure the torture and agony of watching?"

"I must."

Bertok takes up a flat-bladed knife and probes. Finding a yielding spot in the varnish where the belly meets the ribs, he plunges the knife into the join and twists. And twists a bit more, a bit more, and of a sudden, explosive like a gunshot the glue breaks loose!

Douglas writhing, uttering nonsensical exclamations, all of which reveal his affection for the fiddle. And Bertok lifting the top free without further damage, showing it to Douglas, gone limp. Not unexpectedly, Violette hovers beside Douglas, her hands by her sides, turned out, as if seeking benediction for two lovers who through tragedy share karma.

Bertok reads a label almost hidden by the fallen sound post. And then he whistles, a high-pitched tone that drifts for hours, before it fades. He poses the question—after all, this is the realm of a luthier—a correct answer to be pursued with every ancient instrument. "So then, what we have here?"

Simply the incredible answer of a unique beginning. An answer the three share—the luthier who has just now discovered it, the poet for whom all the time in the world with this foundling would not be enough, and a boy now grown to a man, who had already learned this history, and more, from the violin, his Magic Muriel, the 253-1, herself.

[21]

{HUMAN GOODNESS PREVAILED| 253-1 was rejoined with her lost *ani-matore*| whose rare frequencies connect with her own| We two| both broken beyond measure| both gratefully restored| The glue must dry| My sound post must remember the strain and tension of the vibrating boards| The crack must forget it was a crack| Be patient with Me| |

{In time we two will again| pour Benevolence upon our listeners| those in the depths of despair| those in pain| those in need of Kindness| those who daily toil| those who grace humankind with light| be they the few or the many| |

{And always 253-1 will heed Katarina's intention| In doing so| Douglas Tryzyna and *questo violino*| may ignite| electrify| and inspire Love| So it is| It is| |

✳ ✳ ✳

HISTORICAL ELEMENTS

(in order of appearance)

The goal throughout this tale has been for the realistic portrayal of nonfictional individuals. The activities and conversations of such characters interacting with fictional characters in *The Violin Thief* are imaginary, although based on research. Some dates regarding Swiss and German immigration to the United States have been slightly adjusted to align with the story's particulars. The author offers sincere apology for mistakes or any false intimations.

North Bay, Ontario

Chodenzia is a fictional hamlet based on the author's memories of residing in and experiencing the locale year-round.

Elizabethtown, New York

Elizabethtown, located at the junction of US-9 and NY-9N, has been the Essex County seat since 1807. In the nineteenth century the hamlet became a resort community; large hotels graced the center of town where city tourists would stay for the summer months. Boquet River is a small stream that flows northward through the center of the town. It is a tributary of Lake Champlain. The Split Rock Falls gorge, located south of Elizabethtown, contains one of the most scenic yet underrated waterfalls in the Adirondacks. Split Rock Falls was a determining factor in my choice of the locale for this story.

Depictions of Elizabethtown are based on research aided by the Elizabethtown Historical Museum, along with photos and maps. Nevertheless, many of the details are imagined. (Split Rock Falls is an authentic landmark, although not given the colloquialism Lover's Leap.)

Luigi Tarisio | circa 1790–1854

"Luigi Tarisio is an almost mythical figure in the history of the violin. His reputation as the 'violin finder general' or the sorcerer of violin collectors, offering 'new violins for old' in his search for forgotten masterpieces, has come to us through many writers of the 19th century. What we know is very sketchy, but his historical position as the bridge between the close of the classical period of violin making in Italy and its subsequent revival and appreciation in the rest of Europe is certain." Source—Tarisio/Cozio website

(The fictional Fiddle 253-1 remembers being saved and adored by Tarisio, who was able to communicate with her.)

Paul Hindemith | 1895-1963

An outstanding twentieth-century German composer, as well as a violist, teacher, theorist, and conductor

In the 1930s, Hindemith was a leading member of the musical avant-garde; the Nazis condemned his music as "degenerate." Hindemith first visited the United States in 1937 and made his American debut. In following years, he returned to teach composition at the Boston Symphony's Berkshire Music Center in Tanglewood. In 1940, with war imminent in Europe, he moved to the United States where he received an appointment to join the music faculty at Yale University. His Jewish wife, Gertrud, made her way from Bluche, Switzerland to neutral Lisbon, Portugal. She reached the USA by steamship along with thousands also fleeing Europe. Hindemith and Gertrud returned to Switzerland in 1953.

(This man was the friend and mentor who encouraged fictional Peter Stoya to teach in America. Narcisse Louise was Gertrud's fictional companion as they trekked to Lisbon. The telegrams sent to the Stoyas are versions of the ones Gertrud sent to her husband. The Basque peasants carrying the 253-1 represent those who historically trekked to Lisbon, and in *The Violin Thief*, they sailed to America alongside, LuLu— Narcisse Louise Boulez.)

Yehudi Menuhin | 1916-1999

An American-born violinist and conductor

Menuhin displayed exceptional musical talent by age four. His first public appearance, at age seven, was as a solo violinist with the San Francisco Symphony Orchestra. In 1929, twelve-year-old Yehudi Menuhin played the Bach, Beethoven, and Brahms violin concertos to an amazed audience. Just the week before, he had played in Berlin with the Philharmonic under Bruno Walter, receiving an equally enthusiastic response. (This is the performance that lit up fictional Peter Stoya.)

"As a boy I hoped—I had the childish idea—that if I played the Chaconne of Bach beautifully enough—but it would have to be very, very beautiful—I could bring peace." (Fictional Douglas Tryzyna emulates this aspiration for himself with the Fiddle 253-1.)

Jean-Baptist Vuillame | 1798-1875

French violin and bow maker

Vuillame was widely recognized as one of the finest nineteenth century luthiers, leaving an indelible mark on the French tradition and influencing generations of violin makers and dealers throughout the musical world. His career is marked by a relentless drive to construct the perfect instrument, combining the classical Italian tradition with contemporary French style. He had access to one of the largest caches of old Italian instruments, which he studied assiduously to recreate the great masterpieces, at an affordable price. (This is the maker of Stoya's father's violin. Stoya sold it at auction through Florien Roux in 1941.)

The "Mendelssohn, Red Violin" 1720, by Antonio Stradivari, Cremona

This is the actual object reimagined and fictionalized by the film *The Red Violin*. Its history lends itself to speculation, as done with the popular film and perhaps other historical fiction novels. (In *The Violin Thief* it is called the Performance Violin, and Red Sister.) The instrument did have a habit of dropping off the radar. Shortly after its debut in 1720, the violin disappeared from history, its provenance unknown, with mention of it being played by Joseph Joachim in the 1820s. Nothing more is known of this instrument until a photograph taken in Berlin in 1928 shows it in the hands of descendants of the composer Felix Mendelssohn. It was favored by Lilli von Mendelssohn. To spare it from Nazi hands it was placed in a Deutsche Bank vault in December 1940. In 1945 it was reported missing. Perhaps it had been missing earlier; this is unknown. This violin reappeared in 1956 when it was purchased and maintained by an industrialist until 1990. The industrialist opted to put the Red Stradivarius on the auction block anonymously at Christie's of London. It landed in the hands of then sixteen-year-old American solo violinist Elizabeth Pitcairn, as a gift from her grandfather. It lovingly remains in the hands of this performer at the time of this writing

(The subplot in *The Violin Thief* was inspired by the disappearance of the "Red Mendelssohn Stradivari" violin from 1940–1956. The violin's whereabouts from 1940–1953, as described in this novel, are pure speculation. The irony is, if such a thief as Peter Stoya carried off the Red Violin instead of depositing it in the vault, his crime may have rescued it from obscurity—saving it from the fate of the still missing 1709 "*Small* Mendelssohn.")

The Small Mendelssohn Violin 1709, by Antonio Stradivari, Cremona
The 1709 Stradivari was last documented on December 18, 1940, as being located at 51 Jägerstrasse, Berlin, a Mendelssohn property taken over by the Nazis for the Reich Finance Ministry. Lilli Mendelssohn-Bohnke's son, Walter Bohnke, reported that the Stradivari had been stolen from the Deutsche Bank in Berlin upon the 1945 Russian occupation of Berlin. However, records from the Deutsche Bank Archive suggest the violin may have vanished before this.

(This is the violin fictional Peter Stoya carried from the Mendelssohn property in December 1940 and left, as directed, in the Deutsche Bank vault.)

Robert Franz Carl von Mendelssohn | 1902–1996

Descendant of composer Felix Mendelssohn

Resident/owner of Mendelssohn Herrenhaus

located at 51 Jägerstrasse, Berlin—a property containing priceless objects, including a stunning stringed instrument collection. The mansion was taken over by the Nazis for the Reich Finance Ministry. (This is where fictional Stoya performed on the Red Violin at the December 1940 soiree.) At the war's end the Herrenhaus property was taken by the Russians. This is when the two Mendelssohn Stradivarius violins were discovered to be missing.

Lilli Bohnke (née von Mendelsohn) | 1897–1928

Descendent of Felix Mendelssohn who owned and revered the 1720 Red Mendelssohn (the "Red Violin" of fictional fame) until her untimely death in a car accident.

Rembert Wurlitzer | 1904–1963

Famous US violin expert

For about eighty years, the violin department of the Wurlitzer Company in the USA was a refuge, where the world's most valuable stringed instruments arrived and were repaired, appraised, and sold. Rembert loaned violins to the prodigy Michael Rabin and other virtuosos during their careers. Rembert Wurlitzer sold the 1822 D'Espine to my father, Lloyd Frisbee, in 1959. It was auctioned by Tariso Fine Instruments and Bows, May 2014. (Per *The Violin Thief* it was owned by Ciazzo and loaned to Douglas in prior years.)

Ivan Galamian | 1903–1981

Persian born, Russian immigrant, American violin instructor

Ivan Galamian came to the USA from Paris in the late 1930s. After visiting
Piatigorsky in the Adirondacks he was inspired to create a summer camp
there amidst the birch trees. His idea was to offer total immersion in the
study of string instruments. Ivan is quoted as saying, "I cannot die as long
as there are students around who want to learn to play the violin." Meadowmount School of Music began in the transformed Milholland Lodge
outside Elizabethtown/Westport, New York, 1944. Famous attendees over
the years include not only Michael Rabin but also Joshua Bell, Yo-Yo Ma,
Itzhak Perlman, Stephanie Chase, Kyung-wha Chung, James Ehnes, Lynn
Harrell, and Jaime Laredo. (The fictional and ambitious Peter Stoya had to
contend with the phenomenon of Galamian and Meadowmount in his
own backyard.)

Gregor Piatigorsky | "Grisha" 1903–1976
A Russian born-naturalized American cellist
Childhood poverty forced Gregor to fend for himself by playing in cafés,
brothels, and silent movie houses. By age fifteen he was principal cellist of
the Bolshoi Opera Orchestra. In 1921, dispirited by the political climate in
Russia, he escaped into Poland and made his way through Europe, beginning his legendary solo career.

In 1939, Piatigorsky happened upon property in the Adirondacks
being auctioned off by the bank; he offered a low bid. In doing so he became the owner of the Elizabethtown, New York, Windy Cliff. A few
months later war broke out in Europe. "Grisha" and his wife, Jacqueline
de Rothschild, with baby daughter Jeptha, were on the last ship to leave
Le Havre, France, just escaping Hitler's invasion. They took refuge in Elizabethtown where their son, Joram, was born a year later.

The family moved to Philadelphia in 1949 when Piatigorsky was
appointed to the faculty of the Curtis Institute of Music. Later he

relocated to Los Angeles. He taught at UCLA and then at the University of Southern California, where he also performed chamber music.

During his seventy-three years Piatigorsky transcribed, arranged, composed, and commissioned countless works for the cello, thereby increasing its repertoire. His mission was to show the "beauty and nobility of the cello's voice the world over."

(Peter Stoya befriended the Piatigorsky family. He took both Willi and Douglas to Windy Cliff for a memorable visit.)

Jacqueline Piatigorsky, née Rothschild, wife

Jephta Piatigorsky, daughter

Joram Piatigorsky, son

Montagnana Cello, the "Sleeping Beauty," Venice, 1739

"This instrument is undamaged, uncut, and with its original varnish. It lay unused for over a century at Berkeley Castle, a possession of the Fitzharding family, before it was given to Piatigorsky in 1935."

https://tarisio.com/cozio-archive/property/?ID=40664

(This cello appears with Piatigorsky in *The Violin Thief.*)

Michael Rabin | 1936–1972

American-born musical prodigy

Michael's family rented *Lilacs* in Elizabethtown for many summers while he attended Meadowmount School of Music as a violin student of Galamian. Michael was close with his sister Bertine and wrote to her when he traveled. As a youth he performed in the USA, Cuba, and Australia. For these concerts Rembert Wurlitzer loaned him exceptional violins. He memorized composers' vital data; he prized his bicycle, a Monarch Deluxe; he collected and played marbles; he took photos with his Brownie camera; he kept a flight log. (One hopes he had a loyal friend like the fictional Douglas Tryzyna during his lifetime, which was tragically cut short.)

George Rabin, father, violinist with New York Philharmonic
Orchestra

Jeanne Rabin, née Seidman, mother, pianist, graduate of
Juilliard School of Music

Jay Rabin, brother, and prodigy, died in childhood before
Michael's birth

Bertine Rabin, sister, pianist, and compatriot

Isaac Stern | 1920–2001

Russian-born American musician who was considered one of the premier
violinists of the twentieth century. (In reality he did sign one of Michael
Rabin's music books.)

Arthur Berger | 1912–2003

American composer and music critic. He wrote a foresightful review of
fourteen-year-old Michael Rabin's Carnegie Hall debut. *New York Herald
Tribune*, November 25, 1950.

Arthur Rodzinski | 1892-1958

A Polish conductor, music director of Cleveland Orchestra and New York
Philharmonic in the 1930s and 40s. He moved to Cuba where Michael
Rabin made a professional appearance under his baton in 1950.

Joseph Joachim | 1831-1907

Hungarian violinist, conductor, composer, teacher.

Joseph Joachim gained his legendary reputation at age twelve, after
a masterful performance of Beethoven's Violin Concerto under conductor
Felix Mendelsohn. He is historically acknowledged as owning the Antonio
Stradivari of 1720, the Mendelssohn Red Violin. (This instrument is called
the Performance Violin by Professor Stoya.

SELECTED BIBLIOGRAPHY

Auer, Leopold, *Violin Playing as I Teach It*, Frederick A. Stokes Company, New York, 1930

Bachmann, Alberto, *An Encyclopedia of the Violin*, an unabridged version of the first edition published in 1925 in New York and London, Da Capo Press, USA, 1966

Bartley, Margaret, Grisha, *The Story of Cellist Gregor Piatigorsky*, Otis Mountain Press, New Russia, New York, 2004

Elson, Arthur, *The Book of Musical Knowledge*, Boston: Houghton and Mifflin, 1927

Feinstein, Anthony, *Michael Rabin*, Pompton Plains, NJ: Amadeus Press, 2005

Fetis, Francois-Joseph, *Anthony Stradivari the Celebrated Violin Maker*, New York: Dover Publications, 2013; republication of the edition originally published by Robert Cocks and Co., London, 1864

Haweis, H.R., *Old Violins and Violin Lore*, London: William Reeves Bookseller, 1898

Karp, J. "A Great Violin Teacher," *The New York Times*, April 26, 1981

Menuhin, Yehudi, *Unfinished Journey*, New York: Alfred A. Knopf, 1977

Roth, Henry, *Great Violinists in Performance*, Los Angeles: Panjandrum Books, 1987

WITH GRATITUDE

To Each of You who participated over the past seven years of slow progress. It would take four hundred more pages to properly credit you, you who have been my sustainers during this novel-writing journey.

To Ann Patchett for the world of *Bel Canto* that has engaged my sense of possibility for almost two decades.

To Tarisio Fine Instruments & Bows, London, Berlin, New York, and web-based auction house, along with Cozio, their Archive of iconography, provenance, and pricing. To Marie Turini-Viard and Ethan Ladd, both earn my highest regard for enthusiasm, knowledge, and generosity as I released my late father's violin back into the world. The relationship sparked a world of questions and offers a universe of answers—acting as catalyst for the subplot of this novel and future sequels.

To Book Groups that have been a safe harbor for idea exchange, literary evaluations, not to mention burgeoning friendships:

Babes with Books, and one-time co-author, Melissa Farnsworth

Gourmet Way Book Group

Pop-Up

3Cs Book Group of Coeur d'Alene, Idaho—For the privilege of being Chairman over 5 years, with a pre-Covid monthly attendance of 90-plus bibliophiles. Expressing appreciation for the Executive Committee and their ongoing support.

To Perley Writers' Colony, authors all, sharing private, candid exchange on Facebook. Invaluable support. To its moderator, Anne Frasier, best-selling author of thriller-suspense-mystery-crime fiction.

To professionals:

David Aretha, editor extraordinaire

Laurence O'Bryan of Books Go Social with his personable team

To Elizabethtown Historical Society

To musicians in live local performance for infusing my writing with possibility:

Itzhak Perlman, violin virtuoso

Elizabeth Pitcairn, playing the Stradivari Red Mendelssohn 1720

Mateusz Wolski, concert master & Spokane Symphony

Inland Northwest Opera

To fellow artists Terry Lee and Kyle Paliotto, and artists in their classes who have encouraged my progress.

To You who listened to updates, asked questions, and shared your experiences—although you were rewarded with nothing tangible. You kept me company during a rather solitary pursuit. I so appreciate the camaraderie.

To You early readers whose fresh-eyed-reading offered important insights, and some good laughs.

To my sons for multi-faceted creativity that endlessly fills my soul.

Daniel (Sain) Frisbee, author, musician, whether near or far.

Ashkelon Sain, multi-instrumentalist, composer, producer.

To my sister, Alice Frisbee. Original audience (of one), clever prompter, keen-eyed editor, irreplaceable source of encouragement and faith in this project.

To my husband Rick Higbee. For aiding my research, for labors in home and garden, for reading my manuscript revisions, for correcting my errors in history, for sharing a love of nature, art, words, excellent prose, drama, and music. For a great sense of humor. For enduring love.

ABOUT THE AUTHOR

GENIE HIGBEE author/artist brings to her novels a passion for visual imagery and poetry. But without one mysterious impetus—a phenomenon explored together with her violinist father, Lloyd Frisbee, and forwarded by her firstborn, Ashkelon Sain, multi-instrumentalist and soundscape creator she would be missing the elemental component of her inspiration, Music. She currently lives in North Idaho with her husband, Rick Higbee, history buff, bibliophile, and gardener.

PUBLICATION:

The Violin Thief, A Curious Tale of Lost and Found, 2022
debut novel as solo author, Genie Higbee

Invented August, an Imperfect Escape to Capri, 2013
(screenplay available)
Co-authors, Genie Frisbee & Melissa Farnsworth

WATCH FOR SEQUELS

To Save a Thief (NaWriMo winner 2018)

To Love a Thief (in *the dream-upon* stage as of 2022)

CONNECT WITH THE AUTHOR

Email: genie@geniehigbee-art.com

Subscribe to Blog: https://geniehigbee-art.com/inside track

View Website: www.geniehigbee-art.com/

features: **The Violin Thief Book Group Guide**

The Violin Thief Playlist

Instagram: GenieHigbee.artist.author

Made in the USA
Middletown, DE
11 November 2022

14694887R00293